RALPH ARNOTE

"If you crave original, pulsating suspense, put Arnote on your menu!"   —E.J. Gorman, author of *The Marilyn Tapes*

"In Willy Hanson, Arnote's created one of fictions's most enduring heroes."   —Ken Goddard, author of *Wildfire*

"A rowdy, rollicking roller coaster ride through the entertainment underworld with hitmen, movie stars and avenging agents. Great fun."   —Warren Murphy, two-time Edgar winner and creator of the *Destroyer* series, on *Fallen Idols*

"Arnote is a godsend to thriller fans."
                    —Molly Cochran, co-author of *The Forever King*

LUCK OF THE DRAW

"Your friend was very lucky." The swarthy bartender jerked his head in the direction of the empty blackjack table. "After winning the jackpot on the poker machine, he beat me for a thousand at the blackjack table."

Willy grimaced, thinking grimly about Lefty's "lucky" night. "Was Lefty alone that night?"

The bartender broke into a broad smile. "Oh yes, he was alone, but he didn't want to be. You see, there was this babe. I tell you, she was like no other woman I've seen in a long time. Tall, long reddish hair and moved like a jaguar. A real classic."

Willy finished his beer and tossed a few singles on the bar. The bartender looked up and said, "If I see your friend again, I'll tell him you stopped by."

"He won't be coming back." Willy paused. "They found him a short while ago in a ditch north of town with a bullet hole in his head."

EVIL'S FANCY

RALPH ARNOTE

A TOM DOHERTY ASSOCIATES BOOK
NEW YORK

EVIL'S FANCY

Cover art by Beavers

A Forge Book
Published by Tom Doherty Associates, Inc.
175 Fifth Avenue
New York, N.Y. 10010

Forge® is a registered trademark of Tom Doherty Associates, Inc.

ISBN: 0-812-53880-3

First edition: January 1996

Printed in the United States of America

0 9 8 7 6 5 4 3 2 1

To Ed Gabrielli, for stability in rough terrain and for favors too many to count.

Lovers shouldn't kiss and tell, but it's okay when readers read and tell me just what they think. Like Barbara, Delores, Kathleen, Rosemary, Linda, Bobby, Jolee, Mildred, Deena, and of course, Angelique. Thanks!

Purple-robed and pauper-clad,
Raving, rotting, money-mad;
A squirming herd in Mammon's mesh,
A wilderness of human flesh . . .

—Byron Rufus Newton

1

Lefty Grogan was out in the cold. A few of the employees at his level in the company had been retained when they agreed to relocate. Some who cooperated in the merger had even received a golden parachute. But Lefty refused to relocate and fought the merger to the bitter end, burning all his bridges.

His severance might take care of necessities for a few years, but ultimately he knew he would have to re-enter the job market. In the meantime, he was determined to spend his life doing something he really wanted to do.

He drove his aging Toronado into a truck stop and pulled a map down from the visor. The blistering heat still hung around 118 degrees, though the sun now hung low in the western sky. He opened the map and studied the thin red line that climbed north from Baker, California, into the Mojave desert and across the Nevada line. His eyes then fell back to his present location and followed a narrow blue line that trailed off the main road and emerged north of the Mojave near Furnace Creek. With a grunt of satisfaction, he folded the map and stepped out into the oppressive heat.

The truck stop was now empty except for the cashier. Lefty quickly collected the provisions he would need—a bottle of water, a six-pack of Coors, a large bottle of diet Pepsi, a package of twelve chocolate-covered donuts, a jumbo package of Twinkies, and a five-pack of Swisher Sweets split-end cigars.

"That will be thirteen ninety-five," the cashier said, smiling from behind her register.

"Thanks," Lefty answered. He knew it was all junk food, but he didn't care. He reasoned that he was in a lot better shape than were most men his age, thanks to his rigid exercise program. "How's the road north of here that's marked one seventy-six?"

"Oh, I wouldn't go that way mister. This time of year they get washouts in the creek beds. There's nothing much up there anyway, just sand and rock and a few rattlesnakes."

"Sounds interesting," Lefty mumbled, picking up his sack of provisions. Waving, he turned around and walked back to his dusty Toronado.

Lefty started the engine, popped the top off an ice cold Coors, and tore open the pack of Twinkies with his teeth. He pulled out of the truck stop, driving with one hand. As soon as he reached Route 176, he turned off onto it.

Lefty Grogan, six foot two, was a dark complexioned man with thick black hair that showed not a single strand of gray despite his fifty years. His recent divorce settlement, coinciding with the loss of his job, had left him looking tired, with dark circles under his eyes. But he was looking forward to spending several relaxing days fishing on the American River, south of Lake Tahoe. He was to meet a group of old school friends for their twentieth annual fishing expedition, though only five of the original twelve would show up this year.

The first sixty miles of Route 176 slipped by as if he were traveling on a super highway. But when the road headed into Death Valley, it rapidly deteriorated. Soon it was little more than crushed rock, and the Toronado slowed to a crawl. The road finally ended at a washout. A flat, dry, creek bed of smooth sand stretched out ahead a quarter of a mile before the road emerged again on higher ground.

Lefty got out of his car and popped the top off another can of Coors. The desert air in the waning sunlight was still blazing hot and dry. He absorbed the beer like a sponge, popped the top off another Coors, and walked out a hundred yards or so over the sand. He decided it would handle the weight of the car.

Behind the wheel again, he began picking his way over boulder-strewn washouts that would have been a challenge to any four-wheel drive. An hour of driving brought him only twenty miles, and it became obvious that he would never make the rendezvous with the others in Carson City by midnight.

The old Toronado began to overheat, and he was forced to turn off the air conditioner. Studying the map, he determined that he was probably half the distance to the junction across the Nevada state line. By the time he reached Furnace Creek it was already dark.

Finally crossing the Nevada line, he found Route 95. It was still over ninety miles to Tonopah, the first town of any size at all. He decided to stop there for the night and continue on to Carson City in the morning. He would call Willy and say to expect him in the late morning.

The driving was easy now. Lefty's thoughts turned to Willy Hanson, his closest friend among those who would be at the annual get-together. Willy had just completed a transpacific voyage on a large ketch, and he would no doubt have some fascinating stories to tell.

When he reached Tonopah it was after eleven o'clock. It was midweek and the old mining town was very quiet. He stopped at one of the small brightly lit gambling casinos, hoping to find a phone and a place to stay.

The Old Silvermine Club was virtually empty. Two men sat at a blackjack table, across from the dealer, quietly absorbed in their game. A tall young woman sat at the bar, her long auburn hair reflecting the blinking neon overhead. Lefty walked toward the bar, but saw no bartender.

The woman turned to face him. Striking hazel eyes over high creek bones—she was a knockout, dressed in a silk sheath like she was ready to go out on the town. She might be a hooker, Lefty thought, but for a softness about her that said otherwise.

Lefty sat down near the woman. He had long ago killed his six-pack and was ready for another cold beer. "Howdy, miss. My name is Lefty Grogan."

"The dealer over there is also the bartender. I think he sees you now."

"Forgive me for asking, but are you alone in this one-horse town?" Lefty couldn't resist the question.

"Well, not exactly." She hesitated. "My business associate is the one over there trying to break the bank."

Lefty looked at the man. He wore a well-tailored dark suit. A necktie hung loosely around his neck, the

4

white silk shirt unbuttoned. "You and your associate certainly bring some class to Tonopah after midnight."

The woman smiled. "Hacker's sister got married in Reno this afternoon, and we didn't bring a change of clothing with us." She glanced toward the end of the bar. "Here comes your savior."

The bartender walked behind the bar toward Lefty. He was tall, dark, and well muscled. "What'll it be, mister?"

"Make it a cold Coors, and can you tell me where I can find a telephone? Another drink for the lady, too, if she'd like one."

"Thank you. My name is Ellie-Jo, by the way. What are we celebrating?"

"I guess I'm celebrating just getting here. I took the scenic route across the desert and it took me all day and half the night." He continued to appraise Ellie-Jo as he spoke. If she had any flaws, he couldn't find them in the dim light. She was certainly a surprising sight in this dusty, old mining town.

The bartender interrupted. "The phone is down there at the end of the hall, past the last slot machines."

Lefty pushed a ten across the bar, nodded to Ellie-Jo, and walked off to find the phone. He dialed the number of the Nugget in Carson City. They connected him to Willy's room but the line was busy. He hung up and glanced over at an elderly couple seated against the far wall playing the nickel machines. A half-dozen video poker games lined the wall near him.

Lefty fished around in his pocket and came up with five quarters. He stuffed them into the slot of the nearest poker machine. Ace, king, queen, jack, and ten of clubs turned up one by one on the monitor in front of him. There were no bells, no whistles, no nothing, just the royal flush. The progressive monitor over the row of machines told him that he had won $1,910.20.

Incredible! Things like this never happened to him. He had played such machines for hours, even days, and never had collected the big payoff. Keeping his eyes on the machine in the empty casino, he once again called Willy Hanson. This time his friend answered.

"Willy Hanson here."

"Lefty Grogan here, you old son of a bitch. You're always the early bird. I got hung up on some bad roads in the desert. I'm in Tonopah and I'm shot, so I'll see you sometime tomorrow."

"Relax and get a good night's sleep, Lefty. There's no one else here either. Where's Tonopah?"

"It's about two hundred miles south of where you are. Hey, I just won nineteen hundred dollars waiting for you to answer the phone."

"Lucky Lefty! I deserve a cut then."

"The first dinner we all have in Carson City is on me." Lefty looked back toward the bar and could see Ellie-Jo sipping her beer. Then he turned to make sure the royal flush still stared at him from the poker machine.

"Look, Lefty, go to bed, get some rest, and stay out of trouble."

"I don't know, Willy. There's a gorgeous girl at the bar here named Ellie-Jo."

"Aha! Now the truth comes out; you'd rather chase some honky-tonk bimbo than see your old friends."

"Don't worry, Willy, my luck isn't that good. Her friend is all tied up at the blackjack table, some guy she calls Hacker. His sister got married in Reno today."

"Lefty, you're in Nevada. She's probably a hooker drooling over the nineteen hundred you just won."

"Hell, she don't even know about it yet. Don't worry about me. I've been from here to East St. Louis, you know."

"See you tomorrow. Stash the money in your socks, and get a good night's sleep."

Lefty hung up and saw the bartender-dealer walking toward him. "Hey, pal, I just hit the progressive royal flush."

The man looked disbelievingly at the five high clubs. "Congratulations. That hasn't been hit in a long time. I'll take care of it in a few minutes." The bartender continued on to the men's room.

Lefty sat on a stool in front of the royal flush. He wasn't about to move until he got his payoff. He glanced to his left and saw Ellie-Jo walking his way with a bottle of beer in each hand. The lights behind her were filtering though her skimpy silk skirt with devastating effect. He decided that she must be a hooker, after all.

"I brought you your beer, Lefty. Didn't want it to get warm." The royal flush on the poker machine caught her attention. The big hazel eyes widened as she read the figure.

"Nineteen hundred and ten dollars! I can't believe it! I've never hit one of those things. So quick! You haven't been gone ten minutes."

"Ellie-Jo, it cost me all of five quarters." He couldn't help but gape at Ellie-Jo's long legs. A delicate scent of perfume wafted his way as she brushed her hand through heavy auburn hair. "Ellie-Jo, you are a work of art."

"Well, thank you, Mr. Grogan! I betcha it's rare that a woman gets a compliment like that here in the Old Silvermine Club." Her lips puckered as she brought the beer bottle to her lips for a long drink. Lefty was delighted by the whole ritual.

"After the wedding in Reno this afternoon, Hacker got this great idea that we could rent a car and drive back to Vegas. He wanted to show me some wide open country. The fact that I didn't bring clothes for such an expedition didn't bother him a bit."

"Ellie-Jo, it sure doesn't bother me either. You've brought cheer to the end of my day."

She grasped his hand in both of hers. "Oh, come on now Lefty! I think the cheer comes from winning that jackpot." She dropped her hands from his and looked up at the progressive sign.

"How's your friend doing in the blackjack game?"

Ellie-Jo shrugged. "He's an addict. You never know whether it's going to be ten minutes or ten hours."

"Well, that's lucky for me." Lefty looked up to see a man he hadn't noticed before coming toward them.

"Hello, sir. I'm the night cashier. I'm really sorry about this, but you're going to have to take all of this in tens and twenties. That okay?"

"Sure, that's fine with me." The slightly built man wore a green eyeshade and seemed a bit nervous as he started to count out the money. Lefty watched him. When it was handed over, Lefty did not recount it but stuffed it into his two side pockets.

"This machine hasn't been hit in weeks. You're a lucky man, sir." The cashier handed him five quarters and told him to play off the winner. The play brought nothing.

Lefty walked back to the bar with Ellie-Jo. They say down next to each other. "Are you staying in Tonopah tonight?" he asked.

"No, Hacker will probably want to drive on through to Vegas, even though we won't get there til daylight."

"Too bad. I'm going in the opposite direction. I was going to stay here overnight, but now I feel completely invigorated. I guess I'll drive on to Carson City tonight."

Ellie-Jo brightened with a thought. "About thirty miles back, we passed a motel that looked pretty decent. You might check that out."

"Thanks, I'll take a look."

"Since you are leaving," Ellie-Jo said quietly, leaning toward Lefty slightly, "there is one thing you could do for me."

"You name it, Ellie-Jo," Lefty replied, looking down at her beautiful crossed legs.

"Hacker is playing against the dealer. The other man is just watching. That's the way he likes to play. If you were to sit down and play for a few hands, he'd get up and we'd be off to Vegas."

Lefty frowned. He had really never won much at blackjack. In fact, he disliked the game. He looked at Ellie-Jo. She scribbled something on a cocktail napkin and then passed it to him. It was a phone number.

"Lefty, whenever you are in Vegas, please call. Okay?"

"Hell, Ellie-Jo, I'll make a special trip." He watched with great pleasure as she uncrossed her legs. "Ellie-Jo, I'd be happy to help you out."

Lefty sauntered over to the blackjack table and took a seat. Hacker scowled. Lefty shoved two hundred dollars at the dealer and asked for change in twenty-five dollar chips.

He played a hundred on the first hand and doubled down on an eight and a three. The next card was a ten. He let the four hundred ride on the next hand, was dealt a blackjack, and was now looking at a thousand. Lefty decided it was indeed his day. Bravely, he made a motion to let the thousand ride.

The dealer reached for a sign at the corner of the table and tapped on it. It read Five Hundred Dollar

Limit. Lefty withdrew the thousand and pushed out a twenty-five dollar chip for his bet.

His fast good fortune completely unnerved Hacker. Grimacing at Lefty, he rose from the table and made his way toward the cage to cash out.

Ellie-Jo was watching from the bar. She looked right at Lefty and gave him a big thumbs-up sign and said a silent thank you with those beautiful lips. Lefty felt like a big-time operator.

2

Outside, once again in his old Toronado, Lefty decided that he had enough gas left to reach Hawthorne, about a hundred miles to the northwest. Once out of Tonopah, a sliver of new moon and a million stars cast an eerie light on the road. There were no other vehicles in front of him or behind him for as far as he could see. He relaxed, reaching into the paper bag next to him for a chocolate-covered donut.

Lefty glanced back in the rearview mirror a moment later and did a double take. About a quarter of a mile behind him, he thought he saw another vehicle driving with its lights out. Lefty eased up on the gas pedal until the car slowed from seventy to about forty-five miles per hour. The vehicle behind him kept its distance. Lefty floored the accelerator until the needle pushed over ninety. The vehicle behind him sped up too, and even seemed to be gaining on him.

For the first time since leaving Tonopah, Lefty became conscious of the money stuffed in his pockets. He started to sweat. The vehicle behind him, still running without lights, was only about a hundred yards away now. He could tell it was a large vehicle, perhaps a pickup truck.

Lefty was pushing the old Toronado as hard as he could, yet the truck edged closer. He scanned the highway ahead hoping to see lights beyond the hills—but there was nothing.

All at once the truck's lights began flashing wildly on and off. Lefty kept the accelerator to the floor, but the pickup truck closed in and was within inches of his rear bumper. Then the truck smashed against him. The Toronado fishtailed crazily and the truck backed off about a hundred feet or so as Lefty fought to regain control of the car.

Lefty thought of the .38 revolver packed away with his fishing gear in the trunk and cursed aloud. The one time in his life he might need the damn thing, and he couldn't get at it. Driving with one hand, he fished in his pocket for his wallet and the rolls of bills, and tossed them onto the seat beside him. Maybe, he thought, he would have a chance if he told them to take the money and be gone.

Suddenly, the pickup pulled out and accelerated as if it was going to pass. It pulled up beside him, running parallel with him. The lights in the cab went on. He glanced over and saw Ellie-Jo laughing and waving, the window rolled down. For a moment his spirits surged. If this was a game they were playing, it was a cruel one. But he could forgive them.

He waved back, trying to grin, hoping they would pass. But Ellie-Jo pointed to the shoulder ahead.

"Pull over, Lefty!"

He had no trouble reading her lips. Against all better judgment, he pulled over onto the shoulder and stopped.

He watched in the rearview mirror as Ellie-Jo climbed out of the pickup and approached his passenger side door. She opened it and leaned in. "Lefty, you drive like a demon! We decided to spend the night in Tahoe, and Hacker says it's okay if I ride with you."

Glancing down, she saw the money and the billfold on the seat. Then her smile vanished. "Is that all of it, Lefty? I must say, you are very accommodating."

She raised a small automatic to full view and waved it at him. "You have to get out of the car, lover. You're a nice guy, so I'm going to give you a break."

"Please! You've got everything I—"

"Shut up, jerk! Get out of the car, walk across the road, and go down the embankment. Then run as far as you can as fast as you can. Stay out there til you can't see our taillights anymore. Now!"

Lefty stared at the automatic, toying with the idea of lunging for it. Then he opened his door, ran across the roadway, and scrambled down the embankment.

Ellie-Jo circled the car and climbed into the driver's seat of the Toronado. She started the engine and waited for a few moments in the dark silence.

A single shot rang out from somewhere down the embankment and echoed loudly against the foothills beyond. Soon Hacker appeared and crossed the road to the Toronado.

"Did you clean him out?"

"Yeah, Hacker. He was a pussycat."

"Follow me back towards Tonopah and we'll dump this junker. If we're lucky, they won't find the stiff for a few days."

Hacker turned and took a couple of steps toward the pickup, but then returned. "Ellie-Jo, this was stupid. I know you like to practice, but it's plain stupid to do this kind of thing for peanuts."

"You want out, Hacker?" Ellie-Jo leveled the automatic at him.

The man backed up a step and shook his head. "Sorry, baby. I'm thinking of you. You know that." Hacker turned and walked back to the pickup.

About ten miles down the road, Ellie-Jo pulled the Toronado over on the shoulder, got out, and climbed into the pickup. She put her arms around Hacker and nestled close to him as he drove.

Ellie-Jo pulled herself closer and whispered, "Stuff like this excites me, Hacker. You've got to take good care of me tonight."

3

For Willy Hanson, the fishing was the least important part of this annual get-together in the Sierras. What he enjoyed most was the drinking, the eating, and the storytelling that brought the friends up-to-date on each other's lives.

Willy Hanson, fast approaching fifty, was the senior member of the group by a year or so. His once blond hair was now dominated by steel gray. Well over six feet, he looked physically fit and moved with a quick athleticism that eluded many men his age. His skin was bronzed from having just spent six months crossing the Pacific with the love of his life, Ginny. Ginny was off now, seeing old friends in Seattle while Willy made his annual pilgrimage to the Sierras. Now retired, he wrote books and sailed with Ginny, an idyllic existence for both of them.

Willy missed Lefty Grogan. Staring into the campfire while the others rambled on and on about the fine points of flycasting, his thoughts turned to his conversation four days ago with Lefty. It was hard to figure why Lefty would take the trouble to call and then never show up. He had talked of some flashy woman he had met in Tonopah. He tried to imagine Lefty sidetracked on a wild exotic binge with a strange woman. Somehow, the picture didn't fit.

Willy rose to his feet and selected another piece of the now crispy trout frying on the campfire. "Guys, I'm heading out of here in the morning," he said suddenly.

When he closed his sleeping bag against the cold night air, his thought turned again to Lefty. He was worried; the bastard would hear about it, because it was costing him sleep.

After a pleasant morning drive to Reno Cannon Airport, Willy returned the rental car and made his way to the ticket counter. He was in luck. Reno Air had a flight leaving for John Wayne Airport near Newport Beach within the hour. At a newsstand along the concourse, he picked up copies of all the daily papers, then sat in the departure lounge. He paged through the Reno paper first. A headline over a small article several pages in caught his eye.

BODY FOUND OFF ROUTE 95

The body of an unidentified man was found by a road repair crew at the bottom of an embankment off Highway 95 about forty miles north of Tonopah. State troopers reported that the victim, who had apparently died of a gunshot wound to the head, had been there several days.

Several miles south of where the body was recovered, the police found an abandoned 1984 beige Toronado with keys in the ignition and the door locked. So far no connection has been established between the automobile and the body.

Willy groaned. Lefty had loved his '84 Toronado. Willy stood, grabbed his duffle bag, and walked quickly back down the concourse toward the terminal. He took the escalator back down to the Avis counter.

"Back already, sir?"

"How far is Tonopah?"

"Well, not too many people ask that question. Let me see." The young woman looked down at a map on the counter. "It must be over two hundred miles, sir."

"I'll need a car. The one I just checked in would be fine."

"It would be quicker just to get you another one, sir."

"Okay. That would be fine." Willy watched the young woman complete the paperwork.

He couldn't get Lefty Grogan off his mind. There was a chance that the dead man wasn't Lefty; maybe a slim chance, but Willy had to find out.

4

Ziggy Lemon was a skinny, forgettable man with eagle eyes and a memory like a steel trap. He also had the rare quality of being totally devoid of personality, which allowed him to blend easily into any crowd.

When Ziggy first met Florence Dupre, she was not looking at him. The raven-haired beauty was gaping at the handful of hundred dollar bills being thrust at Ziggy by a pari-mutuel clerk at Louisiana Downs. Ziggy turned away from the window, still counting and folding his winnings, and bumped squarely into her.

"Golly! I wish I could get that lucky just once," she remarked, staring at the wad of bills now pressing into her bosom. "What's your pick on the next race?"

Ziggy looked up into the face of the exotic woman who towered above him. He reddened. "Sorry, miss." He couldn't help but be distracted by the ample cleavage in front of him. Women, like everyone else, usu-

18

ally didn't even notice him, much less ask him questions.

"Picking a winner is easy," he said, then quickly added, "sometimes." Flustered, he tried to step around her.

Florence persisted. "Please, teach me. Here, look at the program with me."

"I never look at the programs. My father used to tell me that the program was for suckers. It's for all the people who don't know any better."

Florence studied the slender young man in front of her. She pressed closer to him and opened her program to the next race. "If you don't look at the program, how do you ever pick a winner?"

He could smell her perfume, heavy like lilacs from his mother's yard. He noticed men who passed them turned to look at her, even paused and pretended to look at their program as they savored the movements of her body as it pushed against the short skirt that she wore. Ziggy wondered what it must be like to be so noticed. In all his thirty years, he couldn't remember anyone making a special attempt to look at him.

As bashful as he was, he forced himself to speak. "You go with the smart money, lady. The smart money usually knows who is going to win."

Florence smiled, wondering how this odd little man would know anything about smart money. "By the way, my name is Flo. What's yours?"

"Most people call me Ziggy." He met her eyes. God! They were green. Flushing again, he looked away.

"Ziggy, I have never known a Ziggy. Are you going to give me a tip on the next race?"

"I'll try. Sometimes it's impossible. We have to go over there." Ziggy nodded toward the fifty-dollar pari-mutuel betting window. "Are you with someone?"

"Not any more, Ziggy. I had a little spat with the man who brought me. Some guys think they own you when they give you a little money to bet on a horse."

Ziggy shrugged. He had no idea what she was talking about. He stopped at a point about ten feet from the fifty-dollar window and took a position next to a post. He opened his program and pretended to study it, but Flo could see that he was scrutinizing the lines of bettors at the window.

To his consternation he noticed that the men in the line were casting side-glances at Flo. By attracting so much attention to herself he, too, was getting noticed. His success depended on his blending in with the crowd. He wondered if he could make it work. He would like to. Just once, for the sake of the beautiful woman.

His eyes were now riveted on a man now counting out a wager. The man pushed a stack of bills toward the pari-mutuel clerk.

"Number seven," Ziggy said, in a whisper to Flo. "Number seven. Quick! Come with me. We've only got a couple of minutes."

Flo followed Ziggy down the line of betting windows. He stopped at one where only several people were in line. When he reached the window he placed the bet. "Five to win on number seven," he instructed the clerk.

Flo, in line behind him, bet the same and then followed him out through a tunnel beneath the grandstand. They stood with the crowd near the finish line.

"Why did we bet on number seven?" she asked.

"Because the smart money is on him," Ziggy answered.

"How do you know that?" Flo looked questioningly at the strange little man.

"The man at the fifty-dollar window just bet fifteen hundred dollars on number seven. It's stable money. He's friends with successful, stable people." Flo clung tightly to his arm now.

"How do you know all of this?"

Ziggy cringed at the thought of having revealed his precious secret to this woman. "Because I follow him around. I know who he is."

"You follow him around! Does he know that?"

"Oh no, I am very good at it," he boasted.

Flo stepped back and looked at Ziggy from head to toe. She decided the man was right—no one would notice him if he weren't pointed out.

The race started. It was a six furlong race starting almost directly across the oval from them. When the horses thundered across the finish line in front of them, number seven was five lengths ahead.

"Ziggy! We won!" Florence squealed, hugging him to her bosom.

"I told you I win most of the time." Ziggy was beaming at his success, all the sweeter for being witnessed by the beautiful woman.

"Tell me, Ziggy, why did we only bet five dollars?"

"We won almost twenty-five," Ziggy said proudly. "Sometimes I bet only two dollars. Once in a while, when everything is certain, I might bet lots more."

Flo hugged Ziggy again. "I would like to know more about your system, Ziggy. I have to go now, but maybe we could meet sometime, and we could talk about it. I think you could make a lot more money at it than you do."

Ziggy nodded. "I would like to meet you sometime."

"Why don't you come by where I work. We could talk there."

Ziggy could barely respond. "Where do you work?"

"At Threes Are Wild, down on Bourbon Street."

"What do you do there?" The smell of lilacs was now intoxicating.

"Ziggy, I take off my clothes." She bent slightly to kiss his cheek. "If you come, I'll dance especially for you."

5

Willy's stomach still felt queasy. Lefty Grogan's body had deteriorated badly in the desert heat. But it was Lefty, no doubt about that.

Willy was told that one small-caliber slug had entered the skull through the middle of his friend's forehead and exited through the rear. No bullet had been found, and police told him there was little hope that it would ever be. It could be almost anywhere amid acres of sand, rock, and sage brush. His death was now classified as a homicide committed by an unknown assailant.

Willy could offer little help in naming the next of kin for the authorities. Lefty's divorce had been a messy affair, and Willy had long since lost track of Magda. Lefty's aging parents were probably still living in the Phoenix area, and Willy thought that Lefty's father was named John.

He told the police about the telephone call he had

23

received from Lefty. The officer's eyes lit up when Willy said that Lefty had won a nineteen hundred dollar jackpot that night.

"Well, I'll be damned. Now we may be getting someplace. I heard a story over coffee down at Lacy's Cafe a few mornings ago. Jeff, the night cashier down at the Silvermine, said that some stranger came in after midnight and hit a machine for nineteen hundred. He said the place was about empty at the time." The officer paused, trying to remember the story. "You know, you hear so much bullshit about gambling in this town that you tend not to pay much attention to what people say. I do remember that he said this stranger and some real fancy woman were buying each other drinks after he won the jackpot."

The Old Silvermine Club was only a few blocks away. As Willy drove, he tried to jog his memory for the details of Lefty's phone call. "Ellie-May . . . Ellie-Lou . . . Ellie-Jo!" He spoke the names aloud. "Ellie-Jo, that's it." Lefty had called the dish Ellie-Jo.

It was late afternoon when Willy pushed through the swinging doors of the Old Silvermine Club. Business didn't look too good. Perhaps a dozen people were feeding coins into a variety of slot machines throughout the small casino. He made his way to a massive oak bar that lined one wall. Two customers, dressed in work clothes, sipped draft beer. Some taxidermist had done a fine job on a massive stag's head that hung above the bar. The bartender was tall, dark, and muscular. He looked like he might be Mexican.

"What'll it be?"

"I'll have a draft." Willy decided that he might as well start with the bartender.

"A friend of mine told me he won a big jackpot in

24

here a few days ago," Willy ventured. The bartender slid the beer stein across the bar.

"Then your friend is luckier than most people." The bartender smiled, then started tidying up the back bar.

"It was last Saturday night, probably after midnight."

The bartender looked up. "A man called Lefty?"

Willy's pulse quickened. "That's him all right, Lefty Grogan. He talked to me on the phone from here. Told me about his good luck."

"Your friend was very lucky." The swarthy bartender jerked his head in the direction of the empty blackjack table. "After winning the jackpot on the poker machine, he beat me for a thousand at the blackjack table. He did it in only a few hands, and then he walked away. Not many gamblers do what he did."

"Yeah, he told me about it." Willy stared at the big stag over the bar. "Good old Lefty. By the way, was Lefty alone that night?"

The bartender broke into a broad smile. "Oh yes, he was alone, but he didn't want to be."

Willy pushed further. "He didn't want to be alone?"

"He sure didn't. You see, there was this babe. I tell you she was like no other babe I've seen in a long time. She sat at the bar, while her boyfriend played cards. She and your friend, Lefty, kept buying each other drinks."

"Ellie-Jo?"

"Hey! That's right. Ellie-Jo was her name. You know her?"

"No. Lefty just mentioned it."

"She was some classy woman. Tall, long reddish hair, moved like a jaguar." The bartender paused, continuing to smile as he recalled that night. "I think her boyfriend got pissed off at her for talking so much to your friend."

"What was her boyfriend like?"

"He was a mean looking guy. Well dressed, though. Just came from his sister's wedding in Reno. The woman called him Hacker. I remember that because it seemed to fit, if you know what I mean. He seemed to order her around. I always wonder how good-looking woman get tangled up with guys like that."

Willy finished the cold beer and tossed a few singles on the bar. "I guess I'll be heading on."

"Thank you, sir. If I see your friend again, I'll tell him you stopped by."

"That's impossible."

"Oh?"

"Yep. They found him in a ditch north of town with a bullet hole in his head."

Willy turned on his heels and left.

The drive back to Reno seemed to take forever. His planned visit to the county clerk's office would have to wait until morning. The visit was a long shot—Hacker could easily be a nickname.

Willy spent a sleepless night in a motel near Cannon Airport. He tossed and turned, his mind recalling the good times he had spent with Lefty over the years. Lefty had been a good and ethical man. It wasn't in his make-up to be devious, and that had cost him his job. One thing was for certain, Lefty didn't deserve the fate that had befallen him. Willy ground his teeth and groaned aloud when he thought of the bloated remains he had identified.

He gave up trying to sleep and went to a coffee shop for an early breakfast. Restlessly, he turned the pages of the *Reno Gazette Journal*, hoping to lose himself in the sports pages. But on page seven of the main news section, a headline caught his attention.

HOMICIDE VICTIM'S BODY IDENTIFIED

Police report the remains of a man found off Route 95 near Tonopah have been identified as John "Lefty" Grogan of Phoenix, Arizona. The body was discovered by a road repair crew six days ago. No suspects have been named yet. Investigators stated the matter will be pursued with authorities in Phoenix.

Willy looked at his watch. It was still several hours before the Washoe County clerk's office would be open. It was a long shot, but if Hacker's sister was recorded among the marriages of last Saturday, and he could locate her, she might know where to find her brother and Ellie-Jo.

Three hours later, Willy sat in the clerk's office. He found no record of a bride named Hacker, but Doris Hackley of Laguna Beach, California, had married a William Merton of Santa Barbara. Willy scribbled down the names and addresses of both Hackley and Merton, then booked a flight for Los Angeles.

6

It was ten o'clock Saturday night when Ziggy Lemon entered Bourbon Street from Esplanade. Even on Saturday night, this part of the French Quarter was quiet. Mostly residential, at night it held little interest for the tourists who jammed the Quarter at the other end for a half-dozen blocks just inside Canal Street. In fact, this end of the Quarter was always a little spooky to him. Until he passed Lafitte's old blacksmith shop, the only sound he heard was that of his own footsteps. Once in a while, music filtered through to the street from some residential courtyard or from one of the apartments refurbished to conform to the old Quarter, most of them very expensive digs these days.

Ziggy carried a lot of money this night. He had selected a horse for his biggest client that day, and the horse came in paying nine to one. Against his clients instructions, he had bet a hundred on the horse himself and realized nearly a thousand dollars. Added to that was a three hundred dollar tip from Manuel Lapara, his happy client. His pockets were fuller now than at any other time he could remember.

He crossed St. Peter Street and the noise level began to pick up. Bourbon Street was blocked for pedestrians, mostly tourists clutching paper cups filled with their last drink as they moved from one watering hole to another. Barkers blatantly described the intimate pleasures to be found inside each of the strip clubs, now occupying almost every building that Ziggy passed.

Even the barkers seemed to ignore him. Other people were taunted, badgered and coerced, but he was mostly ignored.

Once, the sidewalk cleared for a moment. The shill blocked his path bellowing, "The little lady takes it all off. We can't stop her. We've tried, but we can't. She's just crazy nuts about taking it all off. Hey pal! Take a peek in the door. She's getting ready to bare it all."

Ziggy sidestepped the man who was now shouting in his face. The man broke into gales of laughter as Ziggy was forced into the street. "Don't bother going in buddy. You haven't got the balls to handle it."

Ziggy turned and scowled at the barker. Peals of laughter erupted from a group of tourists who had watched the exchange.

In the middle of the block ahead, he spotted the sign identifying the Threes Are Wild Club. Mercifully, there appeared to be no barker to contend with as he neared.

Inside, the club was dimly lit. The bar ran the length of the narrow building. A row of tables ran along the wall opposite the bar, and far in the rear were a number of booths around a small dance floor. A drummer, a keyboard man, and a sax man were in the process of setting up on an elevated stage behind the bar. The sax man evidently did triple duty; a trombone and a cornet hung nearby. Ziggy took a stool at the bar.

Beyond a curtain in the rear, a shouting match was going on. He could hear a gravel-voiced man and at least two women exchanging profanities. It seemed to go on and on until finally it was overpowered by a roll from the drummer as the trio started to play.

He glanced toward the door where a barker was beginning to work the passing crowd. A few people began to straggle in. Almost invariably, the men made their way to the bar. Several couples sat at tables along the wall. Every now and then Ziggy could still hear the argument going on in the rear. He ordered a beer. He slid a five across the bar. There was no change.

The drummer grew louder with an intense grinding beat. A small woman, probably Polynesian, he thought, parted the beaded curtain and began to bump her way along the dimly lit bar. Passing right by Ziggy as if she didn't see him, she moved quickly to the far end of the bar where several other men were seated. She paused in front of each one, staring them down one by one while moving sensuously to the lazy, cymbal-punctuated beat. Then she swirled around, and the sheer veil she wore fell to her feet. Standing with her legs apart, she ran her long painted fingernails provocatively over her tiny g-string.

A few people clapped. She moved her hands upward, curling her fingers as if offering an invitation. The four men at the end of the bar began to applaud loudly and cheer her on.

The tempo quickened as the dancer moved toward the group and began to work her sensuous wiles on them one at a time. She dropped to her knees, pumping the flimsy g-string as close to their faces as she dared. They began to stuff money under a bright red garter. One man waved a twenty and was invited to tuck it directly into her g-string. As he lingered, she leaped to her feet and shook her finger, mockingly scolding him.

She moved down the bar, pausing to go through the ritual with two more customers. Then, only Ziggy was left. The trio played a wild, loud, final few beats. Then she spun around, twirling the g-string over her head, ran down the bar and disappeared behind the beaded curtain. She didn't even notice the fifty dollar bill Ziggy held in his hand.

Ziggy had been in strip joints before, but always as an obscure customer hidden in the crowd. His mother had threatened once to kick him out of the house if she ever caught him on Bourbon Street. Now, loaded with money and eager to participate, he had been rejected. It puzzled him. Was he really that ugly? He looked enviously at the group at the other end of the bar.

"And now, presenting the pride of Bourbon Street, the steamy, hot, hot, hot, Flo Dupre!" A gravel voice boomed from a hidden speaker. Ziggy felt a lump rise in his throat as the curtain parted and his statuesque new friend undulated down the bar, staring all the while at him only. She paused in front of him, jiggled and bumped, winked, then moved down the bar.

Ziggy sat up straight and glanced around. People were actually looking at him, probably wondering who he was. Maybe they were envious of him! He sipped nervously at the long-empty beer bottle and watched Flo work the customers. Two bright pink garters were already stuffed with money, and several tens and twenties hung from the tiny g-string. She was even more beautiful than she had been at Louisiana Downs.

Finally, she returned to him. She moved sensuously as the band began to build toward her finale. The tempo increased as she sank to her haunches, knees wide, grinding her pelvis just for him. Ziggy stared at all the greenbacks stuffed into the g-string, mentally cursing the men who put them there. All the money now served only to obscure his view of the intimate features.

She glanced at the fifty dollar bill he clutched in his hand and then quickly vaulted to the floor. She grasped him by the hand and led him to a table in the corner and pushed him into a chair. She stood on the table in front of him and began to dance with the slow, pulsing beat of the rejuvenated band. Then she pointed to the fifty dollar bill and rubbed the spot at the center of her g-string that she had held away from all the others. The crowd cheered wildly as he slid the fifty under the elastic. She permitted his hand to linger just a moment and then pulled away to bound from the table and run toward the beaded curtain. Ziggy ordered another beer. He had never spent a night like this one.

He felt a tap on his shoulder and turned to see Flo standing beside him, dressed now in a loose silk wrap. She sat down, pulling her chair close to him. The scent of lilac he had noticed at the racetrack was pervasive, even in the smoke-clouded room.

"Thanks for the tip, Ziggy," she whispered. "That was nice. Do you like how I dance?"

"You're terrific."

As he spoke, she let the flimsy wrap drop open, and looking down he could see that all the money in her garters and g-string had been removed except for the fifty he had given her.

"That's too big a tip for you, Ziggy. You're my friend. Please take it back."

"Oh no! I have lots of money." Ziggy pulled the roll of bills from his pocket. "I made a big bet today, and the horse came in."

Flo gaped at the wad of money. She could see several hundreds. "That's wonderful, Ziggy. How did you do it?"

"The same system. This guy carries a small briefcase with thousands in it. I've watched him for weeks. He has good connections with horse people. Today, I finally saw him make a big wager. He bet over four thousand during several trips to the window, all of it on the same horse."

Flo took Ziggy's hand and placed it on the fifty dollar bill still tucked in her g-string. "Do you mean that this guy always carries a briefcase full of money?"

"Sure. There are lots of people like that around the Downs. The trick is to see them actually betting a bundle on a horse." As he talked, braver than he had ever been, he slipped his fingers into her g-string, beneath the fifty. He felt her legs part in slight accommodation.

"I want you to take me back to the racetrack, Ziggy. It's so exciting. I want to see you make a really big hit. I want you to show me all the guys who carry around a lot of money. Will you take me on Saturday, Ziggy?" She parted her legs further and gazed innocently at Ziggy, who was sweating profusely as he continued his earnest exploration.

"I . . . I had planned to go on Saturday." He was trying to find words as he stared down into her lap. "Sure . . . sure, I want you to come with me." He paused to savor a desire he had never felt before. "Yes, tell me where to pick you up. We'll take a cab. . . . We'll have to get there early."

"Ziggy!" She brushed a lilac-laden kiss against his cheek. "If we win a lot of money, you can do anything you want with that."

"With what?" Ziggy asked, puzzled.

"With what you're holding in your hand, silly." Flo giggled softly as he reddened. "I'll bet you'd like to kiss it."

"What!"

"I'm sorry, Ziggy. I didn't mean to offend you. I watch faces when I dance, and of course I was watching yours. As I said, anything goes, if we win big. How about the Cafe du Monde, at ten on Saturday?"

"I'll be there." He slipped his hand out and watched as Flo walked to the rear of the club and disappeared behind the beaded curtain.

The next day, Florence Dupre waited until noon to call Santa Monica, California. She didn't want to awaken Ellie-Jo too early, but she had to reach her at home.

"Flo! It's been a long time." Ellie-Jo's voice was filled with enthusiasm.

"Ellie-Jo. I've found a goose that is going to lay some golden eggs for us. He's kind of a nerd and an oddball, but he's for real."

"What's the venue, vision?"

"Right here in New Orleans, Louisiana Downs to be exact."

"Wow! You wouldn't believe that Hacker and I were just talking about New Orleans the other day. How good does it look?"

Flo filled her in on the details.

Ellie-Jo saw the possibilities immediately. "I'll run it by Hacker. Maybe we'll come out there in a couple of weeks. Let me know about Saturday at the Downs. Are you keeping a close rein on this Ziggy creep?"

"Real close, right between my legs. He ain't going no place."

"Good girl! Hey, doll, you still taking off your clothes in your spare time?"

"You bet! Want to do another gig when you're out here? You'd drive 'em nuts."

"No thanks, Flo. It's all business these days."

"How's the company doing?"

"We just opened our fifty-ninth restaurant, Seattle Waterfront. The formula's working, babe."

"Hell, you'll soon be shutting down your fun and games on weekends."

"Not a chance, doll, not a chance. That's where Hacker and I get all our kicks. See you in two weeks."

7

The DC-9 touched down so softly at Los Angeles International Airport that Willy Hanson didn't even stir until the reverse thrusters jarred him from a deep sleep. He looked at his watch. The flight from Reno had taken just a little over an hour.

The coast was cooled by a morning fog, a welcome relief from the desert heat of the past few days. He knew that once the sun burned through, the day would be a real scorcher.

He picked up Ginny's Porsche, which he had parked at the airport. She would be in Seattle for another ten days, so he had plenty of time on his hands. This would be a perfect day to drive down to Laguna Beach to see if he could locate Doris Hackley. He knew the odds were against him finding her. Even if he managed to trace her, she might be away on her honeymoon.

He angled off the San Diego Freeway onto the

Pacific Coast Highway near Newport Beach for the last few miles to Laguna. By then the haze had burned off and the Pacific was a leaden chop against a horizon of brilliant blue.

His first objective was to find a telephone book. He parked the Porsche near an old hotel that had several payphones in the lobby. Under one of them was a battered local directory. There was no Doris Hackley listed. His hopes sinking, he flipped to the business pages and was delighted to see a small ad: Hackley Flowers—Flowers for all occasions. The address was on Pacific Coast Highway, a couple of blocks away.

The walk took only minutes. He glanced through the glass front door and saw a young woman wearing cut-off denim shorts and a man's white shirt knotted at the waist. When he went in, she greeted him with enthusiasm. "Hi, there! You are just in time. I was getting ready to close for a bit of lunch. What can I do for you?"

She was a scrubbed California blond with a few freckles and a smile that made you want to buy something. She was young, maybe sixteen or seventeen. Willy hesitated, looking around the shop.

"I'm sorry I don't need flowers. You have a magnificent selection."

"I'm sorry, too. All we've got is flowers." She extended her arms with obvious pride at the display. "If it isn't flowers, what is it?"

"I thought Doris Hackley might be here."

"Uh oh. I guess you haven't heard. I hope you aren't another former boyfriend. I don't like to be the bearer of bad news."

"Oh no, nothing like that." Willy smiled. "I hope the news isn't too bad."

"Doris got married about a week ago. She's in Cabo

San Lucas on a honeymoon. Lucky girl! He's a great guy."

"Well! That's not bad news at all." Willy grinned, elated that his slim lead had panned out. He decided to get right down to business.

"I was really looking for her brother." He watched as the girl's demeanor suddenly darkened.

"Hacker? You looking for Hacker?" The girl shook her head. "All I know about Hacker is that's what people call him. He doesn't come around much. When Doris found out he was going to her wedding, it surprised the hell out of her."

"Well, Hacker's not a bad guy," ventured Willy, trying to draw more out of the girl.

"Really! You're the first person I ever heard say that." She leaned forward to whisper, even though no one else was in the shop. "I think he's a creep. He's only been here a couple of times. When he talks to Doris he uses language that would curl a truck driver's hair."

Willy turned more serious. "Old Hacker gets worked up sometimes. By the way, where is he now?"

"Same place as always, I guess. He's got a restaurant up in Manhattan Beach. I couldn't even tell you the name of it. If it belongs to him, it's probably a dive." She put her hands over her mouth. "I really shouldn't say things like that."

Willy smiled. "Don't worry about it, kid. Honesty is the best policy. I won't breathe a word to anyone."

"Thanks. How's a nice guy like you mixed up with a guy like Hacker?"

"I just wanted to ask him about a mutual acquaintance." The image of the bloated corpse of Lefty Grogan flashed across his mind.

"Maybe Doris would know where to find him. Want to leave a number for when she gets back?"

"No, thanks anyway. I may drop in when she is back. Or maybe I can find him in Manhattan Beach."

Willy left the flower shop feeling elated. His only lead had been a live one. He headed the Porsche northward along Pacific Coast Highway. He decided he might as well spend the evening poking around to see if he could find Hacker's joint. He remembered Manhattan Beach as a fairly compact little community.

When he got to Manhattan Beach, he parked the car near a cluster of businesses along the highway that included several bars and restaurants. He'd walk for a few blocks and see if he could get lucky.

Everywhere he stopped, he asked the same question: "Is Hacker in?" And the answer was always the same: "Who?"

"Hacker. I thought he had a piece of this place."

"You got the wrong information, buddy. Nobody like that here."

Coming up empty after walking a dozen blocks, he turned back. He stopped to check for "Hackley" in the phone book, but there was none listed. He got back in the Porsche and began to explore the side streets. He parked in front of one particularly seedy looking establishment called the Pair-a-Dice Club and went in.

"Hi, pal, is Hacker in?"

The bartender, busy toweling some cocktail glasses, stopped abruptly, pulled his eyeglasses down to the end of his nose, and looked out over them.

"He ain't here today. In fact, he'll be gone through the weekend. Who wants to know?"

"We have a mutual friend who got into some big trouble. Just wanted to gab with him. Nothing important." Willy was still sweating from his long walk in the hot afternoon sun. "I'll take a cold draft, if you don't mind."

The bartender turned to pull a draft from the tap.

Willy's eyes began to adjust to the inside light. Just over the center of the bar was a large glass or plastic cube tilted toward the bar. A pair of dice were glued to the bottom. The dice showed a five and a two.

The bartender pushed the beer in front of Willy, then turned to look at the glass cage that still had Willy's attention. "The boss went to Vegas once and made twelve passes in a row at the crap table. Claims he won enough money to buy this joint. Do you believe that?"

Willy thought the question was rhetorical, then realized the bartender was waiting for an answer.

"Hell, I don't believe that. Twelve passes in a row? Who in hell is he trying to kid?" The bartender slapped the towel against the bar.

"There's no accounting for luck," replied Willy. He stuck out his hand. "By the way, my name's Lefty," he lied.

"I'm Al. I've been around this place forever. Used to be one of the nicest places in town, a quiet place for a couple to have a drink. You should see it at night now, when all the bikers and their gals pile in here. The music'll knock you right off your feet."

"Hacker must be making some bucks," Willy ventured.

The gaunt bartender shrugged. "I liked it the old way." He walked away and resumed shining glasses. "Hacker will be back Monday afternoon."

"Thanks. If I'm still around, I'll drop by."

"Hey, Lefty, you're not a cop, are you?"

"Never been accused of that. I try to keep my distance. By the way, is Hacker still kickin' around with Ellie-Jo?"

Up to that point the man had been pleasant, almost grateful to have someone to talk to. But now, his expression turned to a deep scowl. "You ask too many questions, Lefty. Finish your beer and get out of here. I don't want any trouble. Ellie-Jo is Hacker's business. He'll punch your fuckin' lights out if you start blabbing about Ellie-Jo."

"Sorry I asked, pal. I'll come back sometime when Hacker's here."

"Yeah, you do that." The bartender walked down to the far end of the bar. Willy left his beer and walked out.

8

Ellie-Jo stared at herself in the mirrored ceiling of the plush Las Vegas suite. The light that filtered through the sheer drapes flattered her. She fluffed her hair out over the pillow until it surrounded her head, then clasped her hands behind her neck. Legs slightly apart, she studied the perfection of her nude form, until her eyes came to rest on the red mark on her thigh. It was surprising to see that it was so noticeable in the dim light. She hated the sight of it. That goddamn Hacker and his hickies! It must be some hangover from his high school dropout days, she thought. Vulgar. But then everything about Hacker was vulgar.

She stretched her arms out to her sides, unintentionally letting one hand fall on Hacker. She pulled away quickly, but it was too late. Hacker stirred and then rolled over to face her. She kept looking up at the mirror, not really wanting to engage in another one of Hacker's five-minute sessions. He had to be the most insatiable, lousy lover in existence. Six times a night, five minutes each. That was his style.

Once in a while, she began to feel herself responding. Then there would be Hacker's convulsing and groaning, and it was all over. She was left tight as a drum. Once in Miami she had bought a popular sex manual, fully illustrated. He had looked at a few pages, then flung the book across the room saying, "I don't want you buying any more stupid books for queers, baby."

Hacker stirred again. She tensed, waiting for the inevitable. "What time is it?" he asked.

"It's eight-thirty, Hacker. P.M."

He sat upright on the edge of the bed, rubbing his eyes. "We gotta move, baby. Your big honcho will be on the crap table soon."

She relaxed. Hacker's mind was on the business at hand. It was getting close to the kill. They had studied this guy for thirty-six hours.

Hacker bounded out of bed and headed for the shower. Ellie-Jo began to run over the plans for the night ahead. Dr. Edward Fears was a surgeon attending the convention that packed the hotel. He was a high roller, and he was alone. Last night he had cashed in at least twelve thousand, all in black chips. Hacker said he knew there must be a lot more if the guy could wager at that level.

Dr. Fears was clearly infatuated with Ellie-Jo. His eyes followed her as she wandered around the casino. When he had gone to the sports book to bet a couple of horses, Ellie-Jo had sat down beside him. He had positively drooled over her every word and movement.

Hacker's shower was still running. Ellie-Jo stretched her legs and began to undulate her hips slowly as she thought of her sojourn into Dr. Fear's suite the night before.

She had cased his room first, collecting all the pertinent details for the checklist she and Hacker had contrived. Then she had spent two glorious hours in the doctor's arms. No wham-bam man was he. Too bad Hacker couldn't take lessons. She had returned to her own suite by eleven o'clock, showered, and waited for Hacker. She had hoped that he might stay on the blackjack table all night—no such luck.

Hacker emerged from the shower and dressed in a flash. He wore no socks or underwear. A loose-fitting Hawaiian sport shirt concealed the silencer-equipped .22 automatic strapped under his left arm. Dark trousers and a pair of black sneakers completed his ensemble.

"Got everything straight, baby? How much do you think this dude carries tonight?"

"Maybe twenty G's, maybe more. He may leave some in the hotel safe." Ellie-Jo didn't like to be grilled at the last minute. Sometimes Hacker seemed to forget who was boss. "I don't think he'll leave much in the safe, because he expects a busy night. It's his last night in town."

Hacker stared at her, his face as hard as stone. "It's not only the dumb bastard's last night in town, it's his last night. That's a fact, baby."

That was Hacker's favorite expression. Something was always a fact. Someday she would tell him, "You're a lousy lover, baby, and that's a fact."

"See you in an hour and a half, Hacker. Be sure you're on time."

He scowled. "I'm always on time."

"I know, Hacker, that's a fact. In fact, you're usually early."

He replied with his perpetual scowl and exited their room.

A half hour later Ellie-Jo went to meet Dr. Edward Fears in the sports book. But first, she studied him from a distance. He was watching several different baseball games at once on multiple monitors.

He was a tall man with short, dark, wavy hair and a neatly trimmed moustache, which he stroked slowly as he watched the television screens. Handsome! she thought to herself. Why couldn't hit-men look like that?

"Hi, Eddie."

"Ellie-Jo!" He rose to kiss her on the lips. "I thought maybe you had chickened out."

"Not a chance. Not after last night. Not in a million years. I'm sorry I'm a little late. The traffic on the strip tonight was murder. What are we watching?"

"I have a small sentimental wager on the Phillies. It's only the fifth inning. But I'm anxious to meet your friend, the pit boss up at the Grand Pavillion. Outside of this place and Caesars, I'm a stranger here in Vegas."

Ellie-Jo glanced up at the scoreboard. The Phillies were losing, eight to nothing. "Eddie, I love your confidence."

"As Yogi says, 'It ain't over til it's over.' " He watched her appreciatively. Her skimpy black silk dress clung provocatively and her braless torso jiggled teasingly. "First we're stopping at your place, right?"

"That's right, Eddie. My place for cocktails and dessert."

"We just might spend all night, you know." His eyes came to rest on the auburn-haired beauty's endless legs.

Ellie-Jo smiled broadly. "Don't forget, you promised to teach me how to make a bundle on the crap table."

"It's a bad habit, Ellie-Jo. It takes many misspent years of study, and even then it's still a gamble." Fears pulled out a chair for Ellie-Jo. "Let's catch another half inning. The Phils have the bases loaded. What are you drinking?"

"I'll have a margarita. They turn me on." She studied the handsome doctor, his eyes again riveted to the TV screen. She had to be careful not to move too quickly. But Hacker was down the strip, waiting.

"A grand slam! How do you like that? Ellie-Jo, you bring me luck." He leaned over to kiss her lips.

"Aren't they still four runs behind? You still need a miracle."

"Ellie-Jo, you're my miracle tonight. You don't get two miracles in one evening. Let's drink up and get out of here."

The doctor always said the right thing. It was a real talent, but a dangerous one. His glib flattery was destined to get him killed. She suddenly decided she disliked him. In reality he was just like any other guy trying to maneuver her into a bedroom. Maybe Hacker wasn't so bad after all, she thought. At least he was up front with her.

The casino floor was jammed with people as they pushed their way through the crowd to get to the parking valet. Dr. Fears stopped briefly to study the action at a crap table. After observing for several moments, he laid a neatly folded hundred dollar bill on the pass line. The dice rolled and the hundred was immediately replaced by two black chips. The doctor stuffed them into his pocket and grinned at Ellie-Jo.

"See, you are lucky. Let's get out of here. Lead me to the action."

Ellie-Jo grasped his hand and led him quickly

through the crowd. She handed the parking valet a voucher and continued to lead the doctor outside to wait for Hacker's specially equipped Ford Bronco.

Ellie-Jo climbed in behind the wheel when the Bronco arrived. Dr. Fears shoved a couple of bills at the attendant and got in on the passenger side. Ellie-Jo made a right and wheeled southward along the Strip. Traffic crawled, especially in front of the Mirage, where the usual crowd was watching the eruption of the man-made volcano.

Fears gaped at the miracle created with fire and water. "This is a crazy town, Ellie-Jo. Don't you get tired of all the noise and confusion sometimes?"

"Doc, you ain't seen nothing yet."

Fears stared at his exotic companion as she aggressively steered her way through the impossible traffic. She fit in perfectly with the garish neon of the Strip.

Unexpectedly, she made a left turn and swung onto a ramp leading to Interstate 15 south toward Los Angeles.

"You really know your way around this zoo, kid," Fears murmured.

She reached for his hand, pulled it toward her, and pressed it firmly to her exposed thigh. "I love this zoo, Eddie. It's dynamite!"

Within minutes, Ellie-Jo pulled off the freeway and drove past a colony of motels lining the road. She came to one named Casa El Bandido. The ornate motel was obviously still under construction. She turned between two rows of unfinished units into an unlit parking area. She could see Hacker's bright orange *aloha* shirt about a half block away. He was sitting on the steps of a construction shack.

Dr. Fears nervously pulled his hand from between Ellie-Jo's thighs, where she had tucked it. "Where the hell are we, Ellie-Jo? Are you lost or something?"

"Yeah, I'm sorry Doc, I think I am lost. There's a watchman or someone over there. He'll probably give us hell for bothering him. Let me handle this."

Hacker was standing by the curb holding his arms up, as if to signal them to stop. Ellie-Jo stopped and doused the lights. As she exited the Bronco, she activated a hidden door-locking switch, stepped out, and walked right past Hacker who was standing on the curb.

Hacker swiftly circled the van to face Dr. Fears, who was now yelling at Ellie-Jo, trying to make himself heard from inside the sealed car. Hacker activated a remote switch to pop the passenger door. He stuck the silencer-equipped .22 automatic against the forehead of the emerging doctor and sent one carefully placed bullet into his skull.

Hacker shoved the slumping form of Fears back into the seat and slammed the door. He circled the van, climbed into the driver's seat, and drove slowly out of the parking area. He turned onto the ramp leading south on I-15. The whole operation had taken only about thirty seconds.

Ellie-Jo stared at the disappearing vehicle. She spoke into the darkness of the parking lot, "God, Hacker. You're good!"

The next morning, Ellie-Jo tried to doze as Hacker drove the Bronco along the barren highway toward Los Angeles. Hacker had been insatiable. All night long he had pestered her with his selfish two-minute attacks. A killing always made him that way.

Ellie-Jo turned the radio on softly, hoping the music would lull her to sleep. As she started to drift off, a sports announcer gave the scores from the night before. The Phillies had beaten the Giants ten to eight.

Ellie-Jo reached for the plastic bag that Hacker had

stuffed the loot into. Tucked into a pocket of his wallet was the neatly folded betting slip from the sports book. Dr. Fears had bet five hundred dollars on the Phillies to win. She noticed that there were no proprietary markings on the betting slip.

"What was the take, Hacker?"

"Twenty-six thousand in cash and chips."

"Make that twenty-six five." She waved the betting slip in front of Hacker's face. "It's got to be cashed within thirty days. It says so right on it. When I met him in the sports book, he told me he made a bet on the Phillies. They were losing eight to nothing at the time."

"You know, Ellie-Jo, Dr. Fears was one lucky son of a bitch. That's a fact."

"Yeah, Hacker. By the way, where did you put him?"

"I stuffed him down an old mine shaft, way out in the boonies."

For a fleeting instant, Ellie-Jo saw his face contort with a hint of a smile. "You really love your work, don't you?"

The dark scowl returned. "It pays good, Ellie-Jo, and that's a fact."

9

Fresh Maryland crabmeat, sitting on a scone that more resembled an old-fashioned buttermilk biscuit slightly overbaked. Topped with a spicy Thai sauce, then sprinkled with feta cheese, the crabmeat had been flown in, along with meticulous instructions for its preparation as an appetizer, by the chef of Waterfront, Inc.'s, Baltimore kitchen.

Sheldon Blake stood in the tower of Waterfront, Inc., headquarters and surveyed the panorama of noonday activity along the San Pedro Harbor. He munched on the Baltimore delight.

"Ms. Lambert, this is very good." He spoke in a loud baritone. "It belongs on the menu in all fifty-nine locations."

This was the monthly directors' meeting of Waterfront, Inc., one of the most successful restaurant enterprises in the history of the business. Ellen Lambert, standing at Sheldon Blake's side, was the center of attention. She was a tall, striking woman, even though her style of dress was severe.

Ellen Lambert wore a pinstripe black suit this day and, as usual, no makeup. Shiny auburn hair was pulled tightly back from her face and wound in a bun held in place by a string of pearls, the only jewelry she wore. To most people, she was intimidating. Penetrating green eyes commanded attention whenever she spoke. Some of the women in the office gossiped, insisting that the startling appearance was abetted by specially tinted contact lenses.

Everyone respected her business acumen. Since Sheldon Blake had stepped aside to become Chairman of the Board, he had given her a free hand in company management. In just two whirlwind years she had transformed Waterfront, Inc., from a struggling chain that was little more than a sophisticated fast food operation, to a highly acclaimed network of seafood houses that dotted the coasts of Baltimore down to the Gulf, and of San Diego to Seattle. Even the severest of critics begrudgingly agreed that Waterfront, Inc., served the best food, matching or surpassing the prestigious long-time family-owned seafood houses in the country. Reservations for most of their locations had to be made days or even weeks in advance.

"Sheldon, I agree. We'll vote on it after everyone has had a sample." This was Ellen's usual way of handling things. She collected votes on everything, then made the final decision herself. It wasn't democratic, but it worked. Ellen Lambert never lost control.

At the conclusion of the meeting, Sheldon Blake approached her as she gathered her papers into a briefcase. "Ellen, I would like you to meet Armand Hauser." Ellen looked up and held out her hand to the gentleman. "As you know, Armand managed our unit in Galveston before we brought him back to the ivory tower."

"Armand, welcome! We met briefly in Galveston about a year ago."

"Yes, I remember that quite well. Your comments to me that day were very useful."

Sheldon excused himself and left them alone.

"With all due respect to Sheldon, I hope this will not be an ivory tower for you." Ellen Lambert eyed the man carefully: midthirties, thickset, but trim. He had neatly styled blond hair cut even with the collar in back, and a neatly trimmed moustache, an inverted V that drooped just slightly around the corners of his mouth. Probably German or Dutch, she thought. He looked right at her when he talked.

"Not a chance, Ms. Lambert. If that were to happen I would be of no use to you."

"Well put, Armand. That is a good thing to remember. Sheldon and I watched in utter amazement as you turned the Galveston property around. I'm sure you didn't accomplish that by locking yourself in your office on the Galveston waterfront. What did you think about our little meeting here today?"

"It was fascinating. I must confess that I did vote against your decision to reject the Baltimore appetizer. It was delicious. The chef there should be complimented."

"And will be, Armand. In fact, I believe it will make a fine entrée. It's a bit too spicy to achieve volume sales as an appetizer, but it would be a successful entrée for more selective palates. I intend to make that happen."

"Ah, that's wonderful!" exclaimed Armand.

"Armand, I hope you will always speak your mind. The fact that you voted for the appetizer doesn't mean you were wrong. It just means that you weren't totally right." Then, much out of character, she winked at him.

"Ms. Lambert, it is a small matter, but I still disagree with you." Armand returned her wink with a broad smile.

"Please call me Ellen. We will be working too closely together to bother with formalities. Are you free for dinner tomorrow evening?"

"It would be a pleasure."

"We will drop in on our restaurant in Santa Barbara. You can compare it to your wonderful place in Galveston. We'll drop in unexpectedly. That always shakes them up!" She said it with a wry smile, mostly with her eyes.

"Perhaps you would be willing to offer suggestions regarding living quarters here. I plan to sell my home in Galveston."

"I will do my best, Armand. There are many possibilities here that might escape the attention of a stranger."

"I would love your advice."

As he excused himself, Armand's feelings were upbeat. Leaving his beloved Galveston had not been an easy decision for him, but Ellen Lambert was making him feel more comfortable about it. The invitation to dine with her in one of Waterfront, Inc.'s, local units constituted a royal welcome.

Sheldon Blake cornered him moments after his conversation with Ellen ended. "So what do you think of your new boss?" he asked. Before Armand could reply, he continued. "I'll tell you what I think. She is a genius. She can turn a grain of sand into a diamond."

"Ah! I will have to take her to the beach someday," Armand said with a smile. "I like her. She seems decisive, yet open to new ideas."

"That she is, my boy." Sheldon Blake, probably thirty years Armand's senior, put his arm lightly on the shoulder of their new recruit, and lowering his voice, went on. "Tell me, Armand, did you notice that she is a woman?"

"Oh yes sir, absolutely." Armand snapped out the answer sharply, but wondered what Blake was trying to convey.

"Young man, I think your perception is very good. When I selected Ellen to take my place, you can't imagine how it shocked a lot of people. Many of them were at this meeting today." The old man paused, and looked around the room. "She made believers out of all of them." He sipped from his snifter of cognac, raised his eyebrows knowingly, then left Armand and turned to his next conversation.

Armand stayed on to talk to as many members of the management group as possible. One chap introduced himself as systems director. Kevin Billingsly had sat next to him at the luncheon. "I'll drop by your office sometime after your personal computer has been installed. If you have any questions then, please fire away," he offered.

"Thanks," replied Armand. "I'm always glad to have help in that department."

"You must have impressed Ellen Lambert a great deal. I heard her invitation to you. I don't think any of us have been out with her socially before, except perhaps Sheldon Blake."

"Well, perhaps I should feel flattered, but we are going to Waterfront in Santa Barbara. More business than pleasure, I suspect."

"What do you think of her?" Kevin asked bluntly.

"I was certainly impressed with how she ran the meeting." Armand decided not to say anything more.

"She's a very private person. No one ever sees much

of her, except at the weekly meetings," Kevin volunteered.

"I'll bet that's because people do their jobs very well. If it were otherwise, I'm sure they'd hear from her."

"Maybe so." Kevin paused thoughtfully for a moment. "Well, let me know if I can help you with understanding our systems."

Kevin walked away then. Armand suspected he had been fishing for gossip and was going away disappointed.

10

Willy Hanson arrived at Wally's Westside Cafe and waited. He and Coley Doctor went back a long way. The black, six-foot-six, All-American basketball player (turned lawyer, turned private investigator) was one of Willy's closest friends. When Willy had called that afternoon to arrange dinner, they hadn't spoken for several months. Coley had given him hell about that, and rightfully so. Willy was the nomad. Coley had a permanent address.

It was 7:30 P.M. before Coley showed up. He immediately took the offensive. "Where in the hell have you been? You spend six months sailing to Hong Kong, and when you get back, you don't even bother to call. I could have been dead or in big trouble, but obviously you don't give a damn." Coley clearly enjoyed needling Willy. "Where's Ginny? She finally discovered the true Willy who forsakes his friends for months at a time? She's probably got a beau who appreciates her. I'm

56

disappointed. I told her to call me if you guys ever broke up."

"Okay, Coley, okay! I'm sorry. Ginny's fine. She's visiting some folks in Seattle for a couple of weeks. We both needed to catch up with our friends on land."

"If I were you, I would never let her out of my sight. She can do a lot better than you."

"I'm happier than hell. Please, don't tell her about that."

The light banter continued back and forth over dinner as they caught up on each other's lives. Coley was prospering. He had several investigators working for him now, and his business was attracting some major clients with a lot of money. "Of course, most of it is pretty tame stuff; suspicious wives, suspicious husbands, or missing persons who usually want to be missing. Once in a while a gig for the DA comes along. It's nothing like the life and death stuff you and I used to see, Willy."

It was not until both had pushed their chairs back from the table and crossed their legs, comfortably sipping brandy, that Willy told him about Lefty Grogan. He told him the full story right up to his visit to the Pair-a-Dice Club.

Coley stared at his friend. "Man alive, I never saw anyone else who had such a reliable nose for trouble. You go on a nice fishing trip in the Sierras, and murder shows up. Sorry about your friend, but why don't you call Ginny, get on the boat, and stay there? Sail around the world or something?"

"It's hard to just walk away, Coley. Lefty was a pal. You would have liked him. But I've taken this thing about as far as I can go until Doris Hackley returns from her honeymoon or until Hacker gets back in town Monday from wherever he's spending his weekend. What do you think?"

"First of all, I think you're grasping at straws. I don't think you even have a lead that makes sense. It's a common story, you know. Somebody flashes a lot of money and then gets done in by some opportunistic punk. That's the USA today, man! It's a way of life. The desert is chock full of bodies nobody will ever find. Every now and then somebody stumbles on a skeleton picked clean by the varmints. The investigation is cold and nothing ever happens."

Willy listened. No doubt Coley was right. Was it really likely that two people on the way home from a wedding would commit a crime like that on the spur of the moment? Not hardly.

"Coley, these people may not be involved at all. But maybe they saw someone else."

"What did the bartender say at the Old Silvermine?"

"He said there was no one else in the place that night except the help."

Coley rubbed his chin in deep thought. "This Hacker guy seems to get bad reviews from everyone you've talked to. Maybe that's just his style. Everybody isn't peachy keen like you and me."

"I guess you're right. But I've got to confront Hacker just once, to see if he blinks. You have to remember, Coley, I talked to Lefty on the phone hours, or even maybe minutes, before he died. I've got to follow through."

"You may have already blown that possibility, Willy."

"How do you figure that?"

"You told his bartender that your name was Lefty. Now if Hacker doesn't know many other Leftys, you might have touched a raw nerve. I'm ashamed of you, Willy. Why did you do a thing like that? This ain't a TV private eye show, it's real life."

"Yeah. It just seemed logical at the time. A way of making Hacker seek me out."

"You can bet that he ain't gonna do that. If he did kill Lefty, he knows that he's dead, and any other Lefty wouldn't matter. How about this Ellie-Jo? If she was drinking with Lefty, she might have more to tell than Hacker."

Willy's thoughts flashed back to Lefty's description of Ellie-Jo on the telephone. "That's right, but there is absolutely no lead on her other than through Hacker."

"Pal, rather than to see you continue on this wild-goose chase, let me nose around just enough to make sure Hacker is a dead end. Maybe I can find Ellie-Jo and see if she is worth dying over. I'll do it for old times' sake, Willy. No charge, I'll put it on the tab of some unsuspecting rich bitch with a cheating husband."

Coley paused for a few moments to scribble a few notes on a pad he had withdrawn from his jacket. "How about shootin' some buckets next Saturday? We can work up a sweat, shower, and then go out and try to flush out a covey of quail. There's this new spot down in Pedro."

"I like the shootin' buckets part of your plan. See you down at the old basketball court on Saturday. Ten A.M.?"

"Okay. I think I'll have your problem solved by then."

"Coley, we didn't talk much about William Merton, Doris Hackley's new husband up in Santa Barbara."

"Look, pal, don't start stirring up trouble with the happy bridegroom. As far as we know, he was nowhere near Tonopah. You could destroy a happy honeymoon and get your nose punched in."

Willy drove back toward Dana Point to spend the night aboard the *Tashtego*. The ketch had been secured for over a week now and needed airing out. The new slip was on the end of one of the marina fingers. It would be quiet.

After climbing aboard and opening the hatches, he decided to have a brandy out by the taffrail. He gazed northward along the endless string of lights that marked the coast.

He couldn't get Lefty off his mind. He decided Coley was right; he shouldn't confront Hacker right now. Instead, he would tail him. He would personally stake out the Pair-a-Dice Club on Monday and follow Hacker around. Maybe he would lead him to Ellie-Jo.

He tossed down the last swallow of brandy and went below to turn in for the night.

11

I'd better drive, Armand." Ellen Lambert had rolled down the car window and was leaning over to speak to Armand Hauser, who stood waiting outside his hotel. "The freeways out here are a little intimidating. You'll get to know them in time."

"Thanks. I think we'll both feel safer this way." Armand climbed inside the black Mercedes. "People drive your freeways like they all had a death wish. Where is all that laid-back attitude I hear about?"

"Oh, that attitude applies to everything here except driving cars, business, and sex. *Those* things are absolutely frantic." Ellen smiled faintly as Armand struggled to get the seatbelt in place.

"I'll file that away for future reference." Armand studied his green-eyed companion. Her hair was again tied neatly in a bun, held secure with a string of pearls. She apparently work no makeup, and had chosen to wear a long black cocktail dress. The dress however was anything but conservative. The slit up the right side was to the top of her leg, providing Armand with a provocative view of shapely calf and thigh as she sat at the wheel.

She accelerated rapidly and drove several blocks before turning north along the coastal highway. "This route will take a little longer, but I thought you would enjoy the view. Actually, you would do well to locate in one of the communities we pass along the way to Santa Barbara. Are you bringing your family with you, Armand?"

"No, I'm not. I do have family in Houston and Galveston but no wife or children."

Once through the traffic congestion in and around Malibu, Ellen proceeded to pick Armand's brains. She knew nearly as much about the unit in Galveston as he did, but questioned him in great detail about the kitchen and bakery. She inquired about his purchasing of fresh produce, fish, meat, and wine. She complimented him on maintaining crucial inventory levels with a low waste factor. She was more curious about the flow of money through the establishment—who was accountable at every level before the money reached the bank.

"After all, that's what this is all about, isn't it Armand? To you, having started as a chef, it may seem to be about food. But for me here in the home office, it is about money. All the other factors can be controlled through prescribed standards of excellence. But money appeals to the basest of instincts, and a crooked hand on the receipts has wiped out many a fine restaurant.

"Do I bore you, Armand?" She reached across to pat his hand, which lay on his leg.

"No, no. I am not bored at all. I think you are absolutely right. I recently had to dismiss a bartender and a cashier whom I had regarded not only as honest, but as friends of the family. Costly revelations like that are always very disappointing."

"Armand, I must tell you that I am very concerned about the Santa Barbara location. Jorgé Sanchez is the manager. Like you, he started in the kitchen. He is personable, works long hours, and all the costs seem to be in line. Yet at the end of the month, the profit per customer is one of the lowest in the whole group. Tonight, when you are there, I'd like you to keep your eyes open. Who knows? You might notice something that would provide the explanation."

"I'll do my best, Ellen, but finding the solution during one evening of casual observation seems unlikely."

All at once she hit the brake pedal as she approached a rapidly slowing car. "Oh, damnit!" she exclaimed, glancing toward her lap. "I'm afraid this skirt is not sensible for driving. Well, we'll fix that." She reached down and unfastened a snap that loosened the top of the long slit.

"I hope I am not embarrassing you, Armand, but freeing my legs is far better than having an accident."

"Not at all!" Armand replied. "Don't worry about me. It's important to be comfortable when one drives. Actually, I don't mind at all." Armand wondered about the immodest display by his new boss who seemed so otherwise prim. But, he decided, it was probably a simple act of logic and safety performed by a woman who possessed a great deal of self-confidence. Silently, he vowed to keep his eyes straight ahead.

They arrived at the Santa Barbara Waterfront, Inc., just as the evening rush was at its peak. Jorgé Sanchez spotted Ellen Lambert immediately and came rushing toward them. He was gracious but flustered. "Ms. Lambert, what a welcome surprise! You should have given me some notice. But I will fix you up quickly."

"No, Jorgé, don't rush. We are in no hurry at all. Just pretend we are customers who happened along. We did have a rather harrowing drive though, and I think Armand and I would like to relax over a drink for a while."

Relieved, Jorgé showed them to the bar. "Chico here will take good care of you. Would you prefer to wait for a nice table along the windows?"

"Absolutely, Jorgé. Thank you. And please stop by to chat with us later. Armand Hauser here is a new recruit for our staff. He formerly managed our unit in Galveston."

"Mr. Hauser, welcome!" He shook Armand's hand firmly. "Ah, you will enjoy the view of the sea tonight. Dolphins have been passing by the hundreds. Everyone is much excited with the view."

"Poor Jorgé!" Ellen said after the manager had left. "I'm afraid our choice of restaurants tonight has him a little flustered. Perhaps I should have thought better of it, but I felt it was a perfect way to welcome you to the home office."

"He'll settle down now, I'm sure. And you're right. It is a delightful way to spend an evening. I can't tell you how much I appreciate your choice." As he spoke, he noticed that Ellen had not reclosed the snap on her skirt. Well, he thought, if she was comfortable, it was okay with him.

They spent nearly an hour at the bar. Ellen drank Glenlivet neat, sipping it from a rocks glass. Armand noted that it took her a long time to consume a drink. It was more a frequent wetting of lips than consumption. Meanwhile, Armand had ordered a second drink. He reminded himself to slow down as he watched

Ellen provocatively lick her lips after each miniscule sip. Their discussion was pure business.

Once seated at their table, however, the conversation turned more personal. "So what are your pleasures in life, Armand? As exciting as our business is, an intelligent man like you must have other interests. Sports? Reading? Tormenting the ladies?" Ellen Lambert's sudden warm smile captivated him.

"Well, I'm not much of a sports fan, maybe a little football, although with the Oilers, that gets pretty frustrating. I play a little handball, and I read some nonfiction, mostly biographies. I never, never torment a lady."

"Come now, Armand. You are a handsome fellow. I can't imagine that you haven't led more than a few women on a merry chase."

Armand ignored her remark. "I do enjoy the rather solitary and lonely hobby of collecting rare coins. Regrettably, I don't spend much time at that anymore. Once in a while I do go to a coin show or convention."

"Fascinating! Some day we will set aside time so you can tell me all about that." Her wide-set green eyes bored into his own until, flushing, he had to look away.

"And you, what do you do with weekends or spare time? I'll bet you are a restaurateur seven days a week." Armand hoped to turn the attention away from himself.

"My weekends are off-limits to the rest of the world, Armand." She paused to stare at a school of dolphins rolling southward along the coast. "My spare time is spent doing what we are doing now. I hope you might share more of that time with me."

Armand was relieved to see their waiter approach.

"Did you notice anything about our little problem with the restaurant, Armand?" Ellen asked the question later as they were returning southward along the coastal highway.

"Yes, I did," Armand replied evenly. "I noticed a few things. First, you'll have to get rid of Chico."

"Chico!"

"Chico is a mathematician. When he gets an order for five drinks at the same time, he rings up only three of them. I saw him do it twice. Later, when making change, he pulls the accumulated surplus from the register. People as slick as he is do that when the bar gets very busy. Anyone watching would find it difficult to follow the fast cash transactions. He's very good."

"Are you sure?"

"Sure I'm sure. As I said, I watched him do it twice. Chico could clip you for maybe a hundred or even two hundred on a very busy night."

"Why wouldn't the liquor inventory be short?"

"Because once he gets the scam rolling he starts pouring light drinks to people who have had a few. Chico is a very slick crook."

Ellen pulled the Mercedes off on the shoulder of the road paralleling the beach and turned off the engine. She leaned across the console to kiss Armand's cheek. "Mr. Hauser, I think you are pretty slick yourself. Welcome to Waterfront, Inc.! I think it's time to celebrate."

"I thought we just did, over dinner," Armand mumbled as she planted another kiss, this time on the corner of his mouth.

Then she bounded out the door, walked around the car and opened Armand's door. She took off her high heels then and tossed them into the back seat, and slipped off the troublesome wraparound dress, and tossed it on top of the shoes. She grasped Armand's arm with both hands and pulled him from the Mercedes.

"Armand! It's time to go walking on the beach." She raced ahead toward the lonely beach clad only in flimsy bikini panties that shimmered in the light of a wedge of new moon.

Armand grinned broadly in disbelief at the unlikely sight. Then he ripped his shoes from his feet and tossed his jacket into the Mercedes with them. He tore across the beach until he reached the now waiting Ellen and wrestled her to the sand. Pinning her, he looked directly into the glistening green eyes and began exploring her face and mouth with his eager tongue and lips.

Putting her hands behind her head, she twisted at the confining string of pearls until the heavy mane of auburn hair fanned out in the sand behind her head.

"Welcome to California, Armand," she whispered. "I guess I'm on the menu now, huh?"

12

It was 7:00 A.M. Saturday morning. Ellen Lambert stretched to reach the radio alarm button that blared loudly with the morning news. She had to roll over to punch a change of stations that filled the condo with the soft measured strains of a Bach concerto. She laid back on the cool silk sheets for just a few precious moments to reminisce idly about the past two evenings. It was very difficult for her to get Armand Hauser off her mind. The intense feeling she had for this man was both elating and confusing. She really knew very little about him. She tried to convince herself that it was all physical. Passing time with him was like reading an absorbing novel. Before you knew it, hours had passed in a gentle exhaustive passion that neither wanted to end.

Finally, she pulled herself to a sitting position on the edge of the bed. The digital clock now shone 7:23. My God! she thought to herself, she had to be ready in less than an hour. They would go to the airport at 8:15. Four hours sleep would have to do. Maybe she would be able to nap on the plane to New Orleans.

She walked across the condo to slide open the glass doors to the terrace. The foggy morning air was cool and exhilarating. She turned and stretched, letting her hastily donned robe fall to the floor. She noticed the red lights blinking on both answering machines. Reluctantly, she punched the playback button on one of them.

"Good morning, Ellen. Armand here. Just checking to see that you made it home safely. Last night was just super. It's going to be a chore getting my mind to focus on sautéed shrimp, rack of lamb, and all that. But of course, I will. Thanks again for a beautiful evening. I hope you will forgive this intrusion on your weekend. I won't do it again, I promise."

Ellen smiled and stretched languidly. Yes, Armand, she thought, you have already broken one of my rules. But I'll forgive you. She took great care to erase the message.

She pushed the playback button of the other machine. Predictably, it activated the surly voice of Hacker. "Ellie-Jo, where the hell have you been? I've been trying to get you for two days. I don't like this, baby. It's my ass on the line, you know. We may have big trouble. Some creep who calls himself Lefty has been askin' around for you and me at the Pair-a-Dice. Makes no fuckin' sense. See you at eight A.M."

Ellie-Jo felt a chill run down her spine. Her pulse quickened. Lefty, she thought. A vision of the helpless gambler in Tonopah crossed her mind. "No way," she said aloud. Her anxiety ebbed, almost as quickly as it had risen. It was Hacker being paranoid again. There was no way, she assured herself, that anyone could trace the events of that lonely night in the desert back to the Pair-a-Dice Club.

The irksome call catapulted her into action. It was only 8:05 when she stood on the terrace again, this time stuffing her hair under a Dodger's baseball cap. Then she heard Hacker's big Harley.

She walked out onto the terrace to wave. If Hacker saw her, he gave no indication. "Dumb bastard," she muttered.

Hacker activated the automatic door to the garage below and pulled the big Harley inside. When she reached the garage, he was still sitting on it, waiting, dusting some invisible speck from the fuel cell.

"Hacker, if you only took care of your woman like you take care of that Harley, you'd be in better shape."

"Now what do you mean by that?" Hacker glared. "You look funny today, Ellie-Jo."

"Thanks, Hacker. That's the nicest thing you've ever said to me." She tossed him the keys to the Mercedes. "Be sure you lock the garage when you get back from the airport. There have been some problems around here."

"With who, Ellie-Jo?"

"Crooks. You know, people like us, Hacker."

Hacker came as close as he ever did to smiling. "You're real funny today, Ellie-Jo, and that's a fact. Ain't you gonna wear no makeup?"

"Thanks again, Hacker. I've got three hours on the plane to New Orleans to worry about makeup. It's nice that you noticed, though."

"Noticed what?" Hacker scowled again.

"Forget it! Let's go."

Hacker backed the Mercedes out of the garage, took one last glance at his treasured Harley, then pushed the button to lower the door. Ellie-Jo closed her eyes, hoping to doze the few minutes it would take to get to the airport. The dark windows of the Mercedes screened the sun now burning through the morning fog.

Hacker had other ideas. "Ellie-Jo, baby, why don't you lean over here and take care of old Hacker on the way to the airport."

"Hacker, when you drop me off, go buy a dictionary. Look up the word jerk: j-e-r-k. Read it and you'll find a description of yourself."

Hacker's trademark scowl returned. "Hell, Al's wife down at the Pair-a-Dice does that all the time."

"Well, maybe you ought to start hanging around with Al's wife then."

"That's a rotten thing to say. Al is a friend. Sometimes I wonder whether or not you got any principles."

Ellie-Jo closed her eyes again. Then, trying to change the subject, she asked, "By the way, what's the story about somebody called Lefty talking to Al?"

"Some guy came into the club, introduced himself as Lefty, and asked Al about you and me."

"That's strange. But don't worry about it, Hacker. It can't be our Lefty. He's dead, remember?" Even as she said it, the deep feeling of anxiety she had felt before returned.

"He's dead as a doornail, Ellie-Jo, and that's a fact."

"Then let's never mention it again, okay?" She watched as Hacker nodded, obviously still perplexed about the bartender's reported encounter with a man called Lefty. It was strange, she thought. So few people in the whole world could connect her with Hacker, or knew them both.

Before reaching the front of the terminal, Hacker pulled the Mercedes over to the curb. "I should be going with you, Ellie-Jo. I feel a little nervous about bringing a new face in on the Tahoe deal. What if Flo has misjudged this guy?"

"Hacker, from what Flo says about Ziggy Lemon, you would scare him right out of town. Don't forget your deal, baby. I hire and fire. I'll be the judge of Ziggy Lemon. If he has the talent we need, we'll use him. If we don't need him later on, I'll turn him over to our garbage disposal man."

Hacker's brow furrowed in its deepest scowl. "And who might that be?"

"You, baby, you." She leaned over to kiss him goodbye, sliding her tongue gently along his lips. Predictably, it wiped away the frown frozen on Hacker's face. "Be a good boy while I'm gone."

"You're a lousy tease, Ellie-Jo." He edged the Mercedes ahead to the curbside check-in area.

Without another word, Ellie-Jo quickly exited the Mercedes, slung the single piece of carry-on luggage over her shoulder, and strode rapidly into the terminal.

She boarded the big 767 with only minutes to spare. Once aloft, she felt much relieved. She stretched out in a window seat in the first-class cabin, asked for a blanket, and slept most of the way to New Orleans. Once in a while she emitted a low moan when the attentive Armand would appear in a fleeting dream.

13

Henri Belanger had sold his soul the day he married the sheik's daughter. Orchid was as erotically beautiful as the flower for which she was named. In Paris, her popularity had opened many doors for him. She was as much responsible for his short career which had led to the presidency of a bank as he was. The name of her endlessly wealthy father had opened doors for him when all else had failed.

Then came the inevitable job offer from the sheik himself. The sheik would pay him twenty times what he earned at the bank to manage his portfolio. He would travel to all the most fabulous places around the world: Monte Carlo, Paris, Buenos Aires, Rio, New York, Beverly Hills, Hong Kong. Wherever the sheik played, Henri and Orchid would also go and live the life of royalty.

Lately, however, Henri longed for the old days when he had been merely the president of one of the most prestigious banks in Paris. At first, he had actually enjoyed helping Orchid establish her high-fashion shops for the beautiful people. It had started as a fun kind of a hobby, something to keep Orchid busy to make up for the time she would have spent raising the children that she could not bear. At first, she had hung like a jewel on his arm during their world travels. But lately, the project had become the centerpiece of her life. Now, Orchid had her own agenda, hawking the wares of her up-scale shops wherever they went. Henri Belanger found himself alone much of the time.

He looked at the briefcase sitting on the polished rosewood table. It contained seven hundred and fifty thousand dollars. This was the sheik's gambling stake. Like many of his countrymen who found oil spewing out of their sheikdoms faster than they could spend the money, he was attracted to the elaborate gambling meccas of the world.

Next Saturday would be the start of a five-day sojourn to Lake Tahoe. Orchid was opening a new shop in one of the hotels there, and the sheik, loving publicity, had made certain that her plans and his visit were widely publicized. His reputation as a high roller preceded him. This ensured their party the most elegant accommodations, covering the entire top floor of the casino's hotel.

Henri walked over and drummed his fingers on the briefcase. He had become a chattel, he thought to himself, little more than a courier whose sole responsibility was tending to the sheik's gambling stake. Rarely did the sheik consult him anymore. The sheik would remind him that it was important to be the faithful husband of Orchid and to see to it that the ways of life were lubricated. He wanted her to suffer no adversity in a world that was turning more cruel and unpredictable each day.

Henri Belanger looked into the mirror that hung above the ornate rosewood table. He was a strikingly handsome man of thirty-four years. Tall, dark, with a hint of salt-and-pepper showing up in his carefully styled hair, his image was that of a vital man in his prime. But he wasn't—he was a slave to the briefcase that lay on the table.

The sheik and his daughter had taken off that evening to do some politicking at some fancy restaurant in Georgetown. At first, on such occasions, the old man had always asked Henri's permission. He would say things like, "I want to borrow my daughter tonight. She attracts the best of local gossipers. She is a conversation starter, you know." But the sheik no longer asked such permission. Nor did he invite Henri along.

In short, Henri was abandoned. He had become one of the entourage.

After checking the briefcase in the hotel vault, he positioned himself in a restaurant just off the lobby at a table where he could maintain some surveillance of the activity. Henri sat at the table and hated himself. The giddy world of high finance that had occupied his time only a couple of years ago was gone. He felt as if his mind was rotting. Orchid was not a wife, he reasoned. She was a duty. The only facet of her life that he shared anymore was the bedroom, and there she had become more and more demanding. He actually wondered how long he could continue to respond to Orchid's routine, now totally geared to her own personal pleasure. In her, he now saw the sheik. And he hated the sheik.

Henri pulled a small datebook from his jacket pocket. Several weeks ago he had made a small notation next to the planned itinerary to Lake Tahoe. His thoughts returned to Las Vegas, almost a month before. He thought about his brief conversation with the incredibly beautiful woman who had shared a blackjack table with him. The next day when he had gone to the pool to swim laps in the early morning, she had been there, just as she had said she would be.

The tall, auburn-haired woman had said that she was alone, on some sort of business she wouldn't describe. She had stated that she found the hustle-bustle of the big casinos in sharp contrast to her disciplined daily work. A good place to people-watch, she had said.

He had told her a little about his marriage and his responsibilities with the sheik. Over Danish and coffee at poolside, she seemed excited when he told her of his plans to visit Tahoe where his wife was opening a new shop.

"It's a small world," she said. "I will be in Tahoe that very week."

"Perhaps we'll swim together again," he replied. She was a knockout. So full of mystery. She was like Orchid used to be.

He flipped open the datebook to the pages that blocked out the details of the Tahoe trip. There in the corner of one date box he had printed in the tiniest of letters, "EJ".

He stared across the dining room and chuckled aloud. "EJ" for "Ellie-Jo." That was her name, Ellie-Jo.

14

Flo had hired a sleek black limo for their ride to New Orleans International Airport. She pushed Ziggy Lemon into the limo ahead of her. Might as well take him along, she reasoned. Ellie-Jo's time in New Orleans would be short. It was important that she get to know him.

Flo scooted across the spacious leather seat and pushed her scantily clad body next to him. Ziggy shifted uncomfortably as she put her arms around him. Such attention was a first for Ziggy. For him, things like fancy limos and fancy women only happened in motion pictures.

"You sure look nice today, Ziggy." She kissed him on the cheek and studied the little man carefully. He had made a special effort to spruce up. His hair was neatly combed, and he wore a new turquoise sport shirt and a pair of sharply creased slacks. "Are we going to win some money at the track today with Ellie-Jo?"

"I hope so. If the guy shows up as usual, we'll have a good chance." Ziggy was having some trouble finding a place to put his hands. Finally, he let his right hand fall onto Flo's leg. She immediately placed her own hand atop his. "You understand, though, that you and your friend will have to keep your distance. He . . . he might become distracted."

"Ziggy! That's such a nice thing to say." She squeezed his hand. "How come you are so sure of this man, Ziggy?"

"He has big connections, both with stables and the mob," he said matter-of-factly.

"How do you know?" Flo traced her fingers lightly across the back of his neck.

"Oh, I have followed him all over. Once I trailed him for a week. He carries a lot of money that bookies give him to lay off when the load gets too heavy for them to take a risk."

Flo listened carefully. The man was a total wimp, but he knew a hell of a lot about the seamy side of horse racing. "So how does that help you?"

"Once in a while, he will make a real whopper of a bet that looks crazy to me. When he does that and the horse belongs to one of his stable connections, I try to get a large bet down."

"Try?"

"Yeah, he usually does that with only a minute or two left before post time, so the crowd doesn't get a chance to respond. Sometimes I get shut out."

"Oh, that would be a shame," Flo whispered, though it actually didn't matter much. All Ellie-Jo really wanted was the identity of the mobster who was packing a lot of money. From there, Ellie-Jo and her friends would take over. If they won any money betting Ziggy's tips, that would be the gravy.

"Actually, you and your friend could be a big help to me," Ziggy said. "You can both wait in lines at the betting windows. The lines get pretty long. When I pick up the tip, I could relay it to the one closest to a window."

Flo squeezed his hand again. "Ziggy, that's brilliant!"

The limo pulled alongside the curb adjacent to the Delta Airlines arrival area at New Orleans International Airport.

Ellie-Jo exited the plane in a pair of short, ragged, cut-off denim shorts and a see-through, gauzy, yellow blouse that offered a spectacular view of her torso. The prim Ms. Lambert had turned into the flashy, extroverted Ellie-Jo.

Ziggy Lemon was overwhelmed when he saw the two women stand side by side before him. A few days ago he had convinced himself that Flo was the most beautiful female he had ever seen. Now he wasn't so sure.

After Flo hugged Ellie-Jo, she turned to Ziggy. "Here, meet Ellie-Jo."

Ellie-Jo extended her hand, which was feebly caught up in Ziggy's limp grasp.

"This is Ziggy Lemon," Flo snapped quickly. "Ziggy is a genius. He's going to show us how to make a lot of money at the Downs today."

"Oh, really," murmured Ellie-Jo, gaping at the nondescript looking little man, who turned around nervously without saying another word and led the way down the concourse.

"Flo, you've got to be kidding. This is the guy you brought me two thousand miles to see?"

"Wait until you see him in action, doll. He can sniff out money like a dog can sniff out crack."

Ellie-Jo grinned. "Can he handle both of us?"

"Doll, we can sure find out. I'm not sure he quite knows what women are all about. Maybe we can teach him."

"I'd rather teach Hacker," mumbled Ellie-Jo as they made their way to the limo outside.

"Still having trouble with that bastard?"

"Yep. But he is still the best there is at what he does."

"What does he do?"

"Flo, you don't want to know. Don't ask again. Okay?"

The limo driver stood at the open trunk. "Any bags, miss?"

"Just what's in this big purse. I don't wear very much, as you can plainly see."

Flo steered Ziggy into the limo first, maneuvering him so that he was between Ellie-Jo and herself. Ziggy, wedged between the two, crossed his hands in his lap trying unsuccessfully to avoid contact with his two gorgeous companions. Not staring at the legs of the two women was impossible. Try as he did, his eyes always returned to them.

"Flo says you know all about racehorses."

"Well, I know a little bit, but I know a lot more about how to win, and it has a lot more to do with people than horses."

"And you're going to be our teacher." Ellie-Jo watched the little man who was now gaping at her see-through chiffon top. "I'll tell you what, Ziggy, if you give Flo and me a big winner, we will give you something special."

"Like what?"

"Anything you want, Ziggy. How's that?"

"Maybe we could go to Brennans for dinner."

"Really! Ziggy, is that the most special thing you can think of?" Flo hugged him close to her, realizing that he had probably never received such attention before in his life.

"Flo, I think we have time to go back to your place. The plane got in early. I'd really like to freshen up. I don't think Ziggy approves of my blouse. He keeps staring at my boobs."

Ziggy flushed, trying mightily to keep his eyes straight ahead.

"We'll go back to my place and change. We have plenty of time to get to the Fairgrounds. That way Ziggy can brief us on what we are to do this afternoon. Okay, Ziggy?" She pulled away from him as far as she could, sensing that he was too flustered by their teasing to muster any speech.

He nodded his assent and finally found words. "I think you are both so sexy that everyone will be staring at you all afternoon. But that's okay. No one will be looking at me. In fact, maybe you shouldn't change at all."

"Atta boy, Ziggy!" Ellie-Jo squeezed him, pulling his face against the thin chiffon of her blouse. "After awhile you will think of us as just a couple of guys."

"Oh, I could never do that," he said, flushing again as Ellie-Jo hugged him even closer.

"Just pick us a couple of winners and Flo and I will show you how to celebrate. Okay?"

"I'll do my very best," Ziggy mumbled, hoping to hell this would not be one of the rare days when his information produced no winners.

The limo driver soon pulled up in front of Flo's courtyard apartment on Royal Street deep in the French Quarter. The ironwork balconies running the length of the street jutted out over drably painted green doors that gave no indication of the elegance beyond them. Ziggy gave a low whistle as he followed the two women inside. A highly polished grand piano stood on an ornate Persian rug that covered most of the hardwood floor. Original oil paintings hung on the walls. French provincial furniture gave the spacious apartment an aura of expensive elegance.

"Wow!" Ziggy exclaimed, bug-eyed. "I've never seen anything like this. Flo, you must be rich already. I don't think that you need me."

"I have a lot of generous friends, Ziggy. Wait until you see my boudoir." Flo opened drapes and flipped on the light of her dazzling bedroom. A king-size bed with a lush pink brocaded spread was liberally sprinkled with bright satin pillows. Mirrors on the ceiling doubled the erotic power of the room. "This is where it all happens, Ziggy."

"What? What happens?"

"Life, Ziggy. Life here in the French Quarter. This is where we will celebrate after winning all that money at the races."

As Flo talked, Ellie-Jo was busy peeling off her clothes, preparing to take a quick shower. She totally ignored Ziggy's presence in the room.

Ziggy turned toward the living room, overwhelmed by what he was seeing. He sat for a moment at the grand piano and lifted the panel covering the keys. Tentative at first, he touched on several keys lightly. Then he squared himself and, sitting erect, started to play. The strains of "Amazing Grace" filled the apartment.

Flo finished mixing a batch of daiquiris in the kitchen, then went to the sitting room, pitcher in hand. The unexpected sight of Ziggy Lemon playing the old hymn flawlessly was startling, to say the least.

"Ziggy! Where on earth did you learn to play the piano?" She looked at him in disbelief.

"I just always knew, I guess. Mom had an old piano at home. I just started to play it when I was a kid." He paused, running his fingers over the polished ebony wood. "Of course, I have never played a piano like this one. I saw a piano like this in the old opera house in Biloxi once."

Ellie-Joe emerged, swathed in a huge towel. "Ziggy darling, was that you? I don't believe it. Play me something. Please."

This time Ziggy launched into a jazzy medley of Gershwin tunes. Ellie-Jo walked over to stand next to him at the piano, drying her hair vigorously with the towel, not bothering at all to conceal her nudity from Ziggy, who stared at the oil paintings on the wall in front of him.

Then, fleetingly, he glanced over at Ellie-Jo's nude perfection. Without missing a beat he switched again to "Amazing Grace," this time the volume soaring, filling the apartment and the courtyard with the inspirational strains of the mighty hymn. He stopped abruptly and carefully closed the panel of polished wood over the keys.

Ellie-Jo wrapped the towel around herself, then leaned over and kissed Ziggy squarely on the forehead. "Thank you, Ziggy. Maybe you can play for us later. Right now, we'd better all get ready to hustle out to the racetrack. Maybe I ought to wear a nun's habit or some such thing. What do you think, Ziggy?"

"What you are doing is not nice!" Ziggy snapped the words harshly toward Ellie-Jo.

"Oh, Ziggy. Okay, I'm a bad girl. I'll try to do better." She rubbed her fingers through his hair, shrugged toward Flo, and walked into the other room to dress.

"Ziggy, you play beautifully." Flo wanted to cajole

Ziggy out of his dark mood. "Do you ever play any modern stuff? You know, like the stuff you heard at Threes Are Wild, while I was dancing."

"Oh sure. I can play almost anything if I hear it a couple times. I guess I haven't touched a piano in a long time though."

"Ziggy, you can drop by and play my piano anytime you like." Flo smiled and looked away, hoping that he wouldn't catch the double entendre in her remark.

The limo that Ellie-Jo had decided to hire for the weekend was now waiting outside. The driver opened the door for the threesome.

There were few words exchanged during the trip to the Downs. Ellie-Jo sat quietly, wondering why Flo had developed so much confidence in Ziggy so quickly. The thought of her taking him to Tahoe in a couple of weeks just to tail Henri Belanger seemed a mistake. She decided that he must learn nothing about the real work they were doing. He must believe that their total interest in him was to have a ball at the races.

Ellie-Jo finally broke the silence. "Ziggy, what's the name of the man who walks around with all the money, laying off big bets?"

"Sammy Lasker. That's his name. He owns pieces of some pretty fine horses, owned by some of the most successful horse people."

"How do you know he will be there today?"

"He's almost always there. Also, he has an interest in a couple of horses that are running today."

"You'll point him out, of course."

"Sure. Stay away, though, when you see me hanging nearby him. I don't want to interrupt his routine."

"Gotcha, boss." Ellie-Jo saluted Ziggy, causing Flo to chuckle.

"He'll be looking at you, anyway." Ziggy cast his

eyes downward to glance at the exposure of thighs offered by the two women.

"Why do you say that?"

"He always looks at the women. I've studied him for a long time."

Ellie-Jo watched Ziggy's face carefully as he talked. She decided that he was strange, but no dummy. His eyes were beady, like those of a starved, hungry rat.

A sizeable crowd was already beginning to accumulate when they entered the betting level of the grandstand. In a low voice, Ziggy began to instruct his two beautiful cohorts. He supplied them with programs for the day's racing card, then led them to the refreshment stand nearest the betting windows. Ellie-Jo noticed that he did not have a racing program for himself.

"Hang around in this area," he said. "Act like you are studying the program. I'll go on about my business. You should both get in different betting lines about five minutes before each race. When it gets time to bet, I will find you about two minutes before the start of the race. The clock indicating the number of minutes to post is right over there." Ziggy nodded toward the odds board located within the betting level.

"What if you don't show up, Ziggy?" Flo asked.

"Then either get out of line or bet a couple of bucks on any old horse you want. When Lasker makes his big bet, I'll tip you off."

"Ziggy, there are ten races. We could be standing around here all afternoon."

Ziggy groaned audibly. "Maybe you would like to go sit in the clubhouse and let me handle everything. The danger is that once I get my information, I may have only a minute or two to bet. I could get shut out by the long lines unless you are near a betting window." Ziggy was perspiring and obviously irritated. "I thought I explained all of that to you before."

"Okay, boss. I've got the picture. Flo and I will be good soldiers." Ellie-Jo grinned and again gave him a quick hand salute.

Ziggy stared at Ellie-Jo for a second, his face breaking into a feeble smile of relief. Then he turned and walked away to be quickly swallowed up by the crowd.

Flo glanced at the odds board. It was eleven minutes until post time for the first race. She was already conscious of being ogled by some of the patrons. "I think maybe we should have worn army fatigues."

"Wouldn't have done us any good," Ellie-Jo said. "This is a hungry group." She scanned the crowd jammed in the betting level, unsuccessfully looking for Ziggy. "You know there must be ten guys for every woman in this place."

"Yeah, but they've mostly got their minds on horses, except for that guy over there who is about to lose his eyeballs." Flo stared and frowned back at him until he broke his gaze. "Wimpy creep! Hell, he hasn't got the guts to be a winner. You know, it's not much different here than it is at the Threes Are Wild Club."

The announcer blared out that it was five minutes to post time. Flo and Ellie-Jo got on parallel lines in front of the betting windows.

When the clock read two minutes until post, Ziggy emerged out of nowhere to find the women a half dozen patrons away from the window. He sidled up to Flo and opened his hand to reveal the message written on the flesh of his palm. "Number 7, bet heavy." He moved casually to Ellie-Jo and repeated his disclosure by flashing his palm again. Then Ziggy turned and vanished again into the crowd.

The two women got their bets down and made their

way outside through the throng where they could watch the race. Ellie-Jo glanced at her program. Number seven was a three-year-old filly named Tiger Blood. She was fifteen to one in the morning line. Her spirits sank. She had just bet two hundred dollars on a long shot. She couldn't wait to give Ziggy a piece of her mind. She shrugged toward Flo who was also looking grim.

When the horses thundered across the finish line, however, the big number seven was five lengths ahead of the field and the women were screaming with joy. Tiger Blood had paid over eleven to one. Ellie-Jo had won over twenty two hundred dollars and Flo had won over a thousand.

"That sweet little bastard," squealed Ellie-Jo. "Where did you find him?"

"Right here at the race track, a couple of weeks ago. He's a wonder, but you've got to remember that his talent is not picking horses, but tailing people and eavesdropping. As you can see, he doesn't even buy a program."

The two walked back under the grandstand to look for Ziggy near the designated refreshment stand. After both had scanned the crowd unsuccessfully for a few moments, he materialized out of nowhere almost right in front of them. He was smiling slightly. A forced smile, as if someone were about to take his picture.

"Ziggy! We won a bundle! You are too good to be true." Flo squeezed him around his narrow shoulders until he flushed and backed away, the smile now gone.

"How much did you bet?" asked Ziggy.

"I bet a hundred and Ellie-Jo bet two hundred."

"Really? That's a lot of money." The little man shook

his head, looking awed that they had plunged that heavily on his tip. "I never bet that much."

"How much did you win, Ziggy?" Flo persisted.

"I didn't bet. I got the tip too late and the lines were too long. I was going to bet ten dollars."

They could tell that he was disappointed.

"Consider it done, Ziggy. Flo and I will pay you out of our winnings."

Again came the affected smile. "Thanks. That's very nice of you." He stared off into the distance. "Hey, there he is."

"Who?"

"Sammy Lasker. He is going to bet one more horse, in the third race, and then he is leaving."

Ellie-Jo stared at Lasker, who was now eyeing her. "How do you know that, Ziggy?"

"Easy. I heard him tell the clerk he was leaving after the third race."

Ellie-Jo started walking toward Lasker, turning her eyes downward to read the program as she walked. To Ziggy's amazement, she walked right into Lasker, knocking a drink from his hand.

"Oh, gee! I'm so sorry! I'm a real klutz." She dabbed at the droplets on his shirt with a tissue.

"That's okay, baby. It's just lemonade. No harm done." Lasker stood solidly right in front of her. "I'm Sammy Lasker. Who are you, besides being the most beautiful woman in the world?"

"I'm Ellie-Jo, and I'm so sorry about your shirt. I was so excited about winning that I guess I was not paying much attention to where I was walking."

The man's beaming smile seemed to darken for just a moment. "What in the hell gave you the courage to bet on Tiger Blood?"

"How could he lose with a name like Tiger Blood?"

Lasker again broke into a broad grin. "Ahhh, I see

you are a scientific bettor." Then came a deep laugh. "I'll tell you what. If your system is lucky, it's the best system in the world."

Ellie-Jo began to appraise Lasker as he turned to his program. He was a dark, muscular man, probably in his late thirties. He had thick black hair that curled at the tips. She decided that he would look better with a haircut. He wore a black golf shirt that hugged his muscular frame tightly. His gut had no paunch and he smiled with gleaming white teeth. She decided that she liked his sense of humor.

"Ellie-Jo, I sure don't want you feeling bad over a bit of spilled lemonade." Lasker looked around them to make sure no once else could hear. "Here's a little tip for you." He tipped his program so she could read it. He had penciled a circle around a horse named Creole Gal in the third race.

"Hey, thanks." She checked the horse on her own program. "Guaranteed?"

Lasker looked serious for a moment, then broke into a big smile. "Hell, lady. I never found anything in my whole lifetime that I would guarantee. Say, are you here alone?"

"No, that's my girlfriend over there." She nodded toward Flo. Ziggy was nowhere to be seen. "Come on over. I'll introduce you."

Sammy Lasker didn't hesitate.

"Flo, this is Sammy Lasker. I spilled lemonade all over his silk shirt. Sammy does horses."

"Oh, really? Who is going to win the second race?"

"I have no idea. I'm holding off to bet Creole Gal in the third."

Flo glanced at her program. "Can't make any money there. She is a heavy favorite."

"Well, I can see you gals really don't need my help.

Your pal here tells me she hit the big long shot in the first race."

"Did you have it?" Ellie-Jo snapped back quickly.

"Nah, he was too far out for me," Lasker lied.

Just then, Ellie-Jo spotted Ziggy a few yards away. But he disappeared quickly, obviously not wanting to be noticed by Lasker.

"I think you two ladies should join me in the clubhouse. I'd like to know how you pick longies like Tiger Blood."

Ellie-Jo mulled over accepting the offer but decided against it. "Sammy, we'll take a rain check. Flo and I have to leave soon. Why don't you come down to the Quarter tonight? You can buy us a drink and we'll dance for you."

Sammy's eyes lit up. "Ah! I should have guessed. Tell me where and I'll be there."

"The Threes Are Wild Club. It's kind of a kinky dump. But Flo and I will take your mind off the atmosphere."

"And put it on what?" Sammy was now blatantly eyeing the figures of the two distracting women.

"Wherever you want to put it, Sammy. Wherever you want to put it." Ellie-Jo smiled seductively at him. "See you tonight. Good luck in the third."

Ellie-Jo turned abruptly to walk away and Flo followed. Sammy Lasker stared at the two women until they disappeared into the crowd.

When it became time to bet the third race, Ziggy materialized right on time. Ellie-Jo and Flo were standing in line at the betting windows at two minutes before post time. Ziggy wandered toward them in casual fashion and opened his palm. It read, "number 5, bet heavy."

Ellie-Jo looked at her program. Number five was a ten-to-one long shot named Married Bliss. Lasker himself had told them to bet on Creole Gal. She wanted to question Ziggy, but again he was nowhere in sight.

Flo shrugged and looked wide-eyed at Ellie-Jo. "What in the hell do we do now?"

"Doll, Ziggy's a proven winner. Sammy Lasker is a proven liar, albeit a charming one. It's gonna be Married Bliss for me."

Married Bliss led from wire to wire as the two women screamed in delight once again.

"I hope Sammy-boy does show up at the club tonight," said Ellie-Jo. "I want to talk to him about Creole Gal. I'm going to make the guy squirm."

"He's a creep, Ellie-Jo. You see a lot of his kind in the Quarter."

"Yeah, I guess you're right." She thought to herself that it didn't matter much what she thought about Lasker. Hacker would make him history in a couple of weeks anyway.

15

Coley Doctor slumped down in the seat of the dusty, old, dark green Chevy Monte Carlo. It had more dents than could be counted. But the LAPD detective who had loaned it to him had kept the engine in fine tune. The windows were darkly tinted. It was difficult to tell if anyone was in the vehicle, much less to make out their identity. The Pair-a-Dice Club was in the middle of the block on the other side of the street. Coley nursed a cup of coffee, determined to stay where he was for most of the day if he had to. He had read through the newspaper twice, and now he rubbed vigorously at his eyeballs, trying to stay awake. It was shortly before noon and only four people had entered the establishment.

A big Harley rumbled down the street and paused in front of the club. The dark, lean, tough-looking man astride the bike wore a green tank top and a pair of baggy black shorts. A thin cigar jutted from his teeth. The man, probably a hundred feet from where Coley crouched in the car, motioned vigorously to someone inside, then gunned the engine on the bike in two loud bursts of power. The door opened wide; the bike jumped the low curb and rumbled inside the Pair-a-Dice Club.

That must be Hacker, Coley thought to himself. If it was, Willy's description had been accurate. It looked like a rough joint, but even so, who else but the owner would drive his Harley inside?

Coley unfolded his six-foot-six frame from the car, stretched, and walked toward the club door. It was still propped open and loud conversation could be heard from within. Just before Coley reached the door, Hacker emerged. He pushed another man in front of him and then shoved him off the curb into the street.

Hacker took the cigar from his clenched teeth and jabbed it toward the man repeatedly to emphasize each word he spoke. "You fuckin' thief! If I ever see you near here again, you'll be dog meat."

The man struggled to his feet, shook his head, stared at the enraged Hacker for a moment, then walked rapidly down the block. He turned once to shake his fist at Hacker and then continued on.

Coley followed Hacker inside. Hacker went behind the bar and turned to stare at Coley. His menacing dark eyes and perpetual sneer would have frightened most potential customers away.

"Nice bike," Coley commented, nodding toward the big Harley now parked along the wall across from the bar.

"You want to drink, or you want to talk? If you want to talk, you might as well beat it. I've had enough conversation for today."

It was obvious to Coley that Hacker didn't build his

business with his warm personality. "I'll have a draft if it's cold."

"The beer is always cold," Hacker said.

"Good. Havin' a little trouble this morning, huh."

"Trouble? What trouble? The man's a fuckin' thief. I should have ripped his nuts off."

"Man, you sure pitched his ass out of here. I betcha he won't come back," Coley prodded, hoping to start a conversation.

"That's Al. Crooked Al. The bastard's worked for me for seven years. Today, I come in here and find him stuffing money into his pockets. I take one look at the register and he hasn't rung up a damn thing since he got here this morning." Hacker slid the beer across the bar, then walked down to the far end and picked up a newspaper.

Soon two other people came in. Hacker served them silently and returned to his paper. After a few moments, he folded the newspaper and slung it toward a wastebasket, missing the target. He picked up a telephone on the back-bar and dialed, reading from a list of numbers posted behind the bar. After dialing several times, he slammed the phone into its cradle. He walked behind the bar and began rinsing glasses.

Coley shoved his empty stein toward him. Scowling, Hacker drew him another draft.

"Hi, Hacker. Sorry I'm a little late."

Coley turned to see a pert young blond woman walk around the bar, open a cabinet door under the back-bar, and stash her purse.

"Lee Ann, don't bother to put on an apron. You're working the bar today." Hacker practically growled the words.

"You can shove that idea, Hacker. You know I can't make any tips at the bar. Where the hell is Al?" Coley was amazed to hear the woman's sharp response to the intimidating Hacker.

"I just canned the son of a bitch. His filthy fingers got stuck in the cash register. Please help me out, Lee Ann. I'll make it up to you." Lee Ann walked on back toward the kitchen without answering.

Coley stared at Hacker. "Hey, Mr. Hacker, this is your lucky day. You're looking at the best bartender on the coast, any coast."

Hacker walked around the bar, sizing up the lean, six-foot-six black man. He looked clean and sharp. Coley always looked sharp.

"Where'd you ever tend bar?"

"Lauderdale, Palm Beach, Miami. All over Florida." It wasn't a lie. Coley had tended bar in many places while going to school in Florida.

"What are you doin' around here?" Hacker was giving him his full attention now. "What's your name?"

"My name is Coley. I came west to check out my sick mother up in Redondo. I'm going to have to stay awhile." Coley was now aware that this was Hacker's version of a job interview. He decided to push it and see if he could pass muster. "Give me time, man, and I'll give you all the references in the world. I hate to see a man in a tight spot. Maybe I can help you out for a few days."

Hacker walked back behind the bar, bent down, and pulled a couple of employment forms from a cabinet. "Just your name, address, and phone number. That's all we'll need right now. You get forty bucks a day. If you get any tips, you share 'em with Lee Ann. You're off the books. If I ever catch you with sticky fingers, you wind up as hamburger." Hacker strolled back toward the kitchen.

Lee Ann had walked back to the bar area and caught the tail end of Hacker's proposition. "Charmer, isn't he? Mister, if you take that deal, you're crazy. Bartenders here are also bouncers. It's a rough joint sometimes."

"Miss, thanks for your advice. But I've got a little time to kill and this looks amusing."

"Amusing! You'll soon change your mind about that."

"I can always walk away. What's buggin' your boss, anyway?"

"Hacker's nuts. But once in a while he gets generous. It still doesn't make up for what you have to put up with." Lee Ann smiled warmly, shook her head and walked away.

Coley watched her go. Lee Ann was a looker. Had a lot of zing. He couldn't imagine her being mixed up in anything nefarious that Hacker might be involved in.

He filled out the forms, careful to give only the sketchy information Hacker had requested. He slid them across the bar and sipped at the cold beer. Hacker returned, glanced at the forms, and tossed them into a drawer.

"When do I start?" Coley asked.

Hacker picked up the phone and dialed a number. He let it ring several times, then hung up.

"How about right now. It'll be slow for a while. Lee Ann can fill you in if you have any questions." Hacker tossed him an apron.

It was the quickest job interview he ever had. Coley felt his heart pumping. If he was careful, he would know a lot more about Hacker in a day or two.

Coley was totally unprepared for his first customer. He was stooping down to inspect the row of beer coolers under the back-bar. When he straightened up and turned around he was staring straight into the eyes of Willy Hanson.

Willy wiped the look of complete shock off his face

instantly and seated himself at the bar. "I'll have a strawberry daiquiri," he said, with a mere hint of a smile.

Coley looked to see if Hacker was anywhere around. "Bullshit! You'll have a draft beer."

"Thanks. That's just what I want. I think you'd better buy a bartender's guide at the local drugstore. What in the hell are you doing here?"

"You better ask yourself the same question." He leaned over the bar to speak in a low voice. "Hacker's here. He drives the Harley over there. Get the hell out of here. I'm the detective. Remember?"

"Where's the old bartender?"

"He got canned, lucky for you. Now drink up and get out. I'll call you tomorrow." Coley turned to see Hacker returning from the kitchen.

Hacker eyed Willy. "What's all the chitchat about?"

"Our customer here was just inquiring about Monday night football. His TV is on the fritz and he's lookin' for someplace to watch some games."

"Oh, another football nut. Yeah, we turn the games on with the sound off. Somebody might want to dance to the music."

Coley walked back to Willy. "Sir, we do turn on the football games. Come on in Monday night and have a look-see."

Willy quaffed the rest of his beer. "Hey, that's great. I'll do that." Willy slid a dollar tip across the bar, grinned at Coley, then walked out the door.

Coley turned to see Hacker scowling at him. "Hey, look. There's one nice guy. My first tip." Coley waved the dollar at Hacker.

Hacker pointed to the tip glass beside the cash register. "That goes in there, pal. You split it with Lee Ann."

Hacker watched him stuff the dollar bill into the tip

glass, then scowled toward the door. "Coley, come here. I'd like to tell you something."

Coley moved down the bar toward Hacker who was now seated, sipping at a glass of ice water.

"I want you to keep an eye on the people coming in here. We get a lot of nuts that can make trouble. They prowl around the beach after dark." Hacker paused. He seemed to be mulling over something. "I have an old biker friend. Name's Lefty. If he ever comes in here and asks for me, be sure you hold him for me. We got something to talk about."

Coley had to concentrate on keeping his expression steady. "Sure, boss. Lefty, you said?"

Hacker nodded. "That's right, Coley. Try to remember that."

"Sure thing, boss." Coley hadn't expected to hit the jackpot so quickly.

16

It was a roaring Saturday night in the French Quarter. Streets were blocked off. Pedestrians along Bourbon Street spilled off the sidewalks and milled around, drinks in hand, seeking whatever thrills lay hidden behind the doors of the scores of bars and clubs. Several conventions were in town.

The sidewalk barkers were doing their jobs. "Come on in, pal! We try to keep the young ladies from taking it all off, but sometimes they just won't stop. No cover! No minimum!"

Alex Pearson, publishing executive from New York, followed by an entourage of meeting-weary salesmen, peeked through the doorway of the Threes Are Wild Club to see Flo Dupre twirling amid her veils of see-through splendor.

"Come on in. You ain't seen nothin' yet!" The shill whispered, "We ain't got nothin' in there but cold beer and hot pussy."

Pearson led his group inside, where they filled up the few remaining barstools and tables. Flo, now performing in front of a packed house, tossed the sheer veil covering her legs to the drummer in the band, who rewarded her with the perfect beat for bumping and grinding her way down the length of the bar. Flo was a master at working the crowd. Eager customers lining the bar were busy stuffing money into her g-string.

Ellie-Jo watched the raucous but appreciative crowd through the beaded curtain leading to the dressing room. She was on next. It would be her second performance of the evening. Though it was still fairly early, she saw no sign of Sammy Lasker and was beginning to wonder if he would show up at all.

There was the usual wild finale, a drum solo finely tuned to each bump and thrust of Flo's sleek pelvis, and then the dropping of the last bit of nylon, leaving only the thin ribbon of a g-string, now bulging with money. Then came the shouts of "More! More! More!" Flo began slowly removing each bill from the ribbon, teasing the crowd with a little bump every time she collected a dollar bill. Finally, there was a blinding flash of strobe lights and an ear-splitting crash of cymbals, then darkness as she ran into the dressing room.

Ellie-Jo hugged her perspiring friend. "Wow kid, that's a wild crowd out there. How the hell do I follow that! You were terrific."

Flo smiled, still breathing heavily. "Yeah. You know I actually got turned on watching those jerks. That hasn't happened in a long time. Watch out for that one guy who just came in with his buddies. He thinks he's a gynecologist."

"But no Sammy Lasker?"

"Oh, sure he's here. Over in the corner, all by himself. He never took his eyes off me. He just kept staring, no expression at all. I think he doesn't want to be noticed."

"Really? He looked like the kind of guy who has been everywhere and done everything."

"I think he's a hood who wants to keep a low profile. Can't expect him to act like a tourist."

"Not really, though it would be easier if he did. He's a sharp guy. We're going to have to handle him with care."

Ellie-Jo heard the band playing her intro. She did a little pirouette, and picking up the beat, she parted the beaded curtains and started down the runway toward the bar. Strange, she thought, that Flo didn't get turned on by this nonsense very often. She always did. Eyeing the wall of gaping eyes, her thoughts unexpectedly drifted to Armand Hauser and their last night on the beach near Santa Barbara. Her eyes fixed on Sammy Lasker, dimly visible in the corner. She imagined that he was Armand, and that she was still on the beach. Her torso swinging, her derriere snapping to the tempo of the drums and clash of cymbals, she let the flimsy wrap that she wore fall to the floor. Hands reached out to her, waving greenbacks. She ignored them for the longest time until Sammy Lasker finally acknowledged her by giving a fleeting thumbs-up salute.

Ellie-Jo moved along the bar, skillfully working on each customer until her g-string was crammed with their gratuities.

Flo was all smiles when Ellie-Jo finally returned to the dressing room. "God, Ellie-Jo, I'm glad you don't live in New Orleans. You'd take my star billing away from me."

"Don't be silly. You're the best. If I had to do that every night, I couldn't handle it. I'd get so keyed up you'd have to take me out of here in a straight jacket. In fact, doll, I've had it for tonight. I'm going to dress and go out and sit with Armand."

"Who?"

"Oh God! I am losing it." Ellie-Jo tossed her head back and stared at the ceiling, closing her eyes for a moment. "Sammy Lasker. I'm going out there and see what makes Mr. Lasker tick. He doesn't know it, but he's going to have a hell of a party two weeks from today."

Flo became serious. "I hope you know what you're doing, Ellie-Jo. I think he's a rough customer. He has sleazy connections if we're to believe Ziggy."

"That's Hacker's problem. You and I are just innocent little lambs who have lost their way."

Ellie-Jo became very quiet. She had to remember that Flo was not a person to confide in. They had met about six months previously at a party in the Quarter. Since then, they had met several times and had some outrageous parties. Ellie-Jo had paid Flo thousands of dollars for just being around. "You're my New Orleans party girl," she had told her. "Just never mix your personal life up in what we do together. Never ask questions. If you like that arrangement, we'll have a ball and make a lot of money." So far Flo had stuck to the agreement.

"Who is Armand?"

"Armand?"

"Yes, you just mentioned him, when you meant to say Lasker."

"Did I really?" Ellie-Jo paused and smiled, staring off into a corner of the cramped room. "He's an old beau. I haven't seen him for years. I guess someone out front must have reminded me of him."

"Wow. That's heavy. He must have been something special."

"Forget it, Flo. Thinking about the past, things that you can do nothing about, only makes you sad. All the important fun and games are in the here and now."

Ellie-Jo got up from the edge of the small dressing table where she had been sitting and wrapped herself in a silk kimono. She walked over to where Flo was standing and kissed her tenderly on the cheek. "Hey, kid, get ready to turn it on. Those lousy creeps out there are screaming for action."

Ellie-Jo pushed through the beaded curtain, made her way to the corner of the show room, and sat down next to Sammy Lasker. "Hi, baby. Thanks for nothing. Your last tip at the track was a stinker."

"Sorry. I tried, Ellie-Jo. You just can't win them all."

Yes, you can, Mr. Lasker, she thought to herself. Ziggy heard you pick the winner. She snuggled close and kissed his clean-shaven cheek. "You like my dirty dancing?"

"Dynamite, Ellie-Jo. What the hell you doing in this dump? You should be playing the big clubs."

"It's a freebie, Sammy. Just doing a gig for a friend. It's all for kicks. I'm just visiting Flo. In fact, I have to leave town tomorrow."

"Where do you live?"

"West coast. You gonna ask questions or are we gonna have fun?"

"Let's split then. I'd like to show you around a bit. What time does your friend get off work?"

"The wee hours, Sammy. We don't need her, do we?"

"Hell no."

"Give me five minutes to change. I've had enough of those characters at the bar. Flo will understand. I'm staying at her place. Who knows, maybe we'll meet her later on."

Ellie-Jo dodged groping hands to get back to the dressing room. She stepped back into a pair of denim cut-off shorts, slipped on a man's shirt, and tied the tails around her waist, not bothering with the buttons.

"Ellie-Jo, you devil, you're leaving me alone. Are you coming back later?" Flo watched as Ellie-Jo fussed with her hair as she looked into the mirror.

"Lasker wants to show me the Quarter. I'm going to keep him out late and try to set him up for the big party in two weeks. If it all works out, we'll end up at your place about four A.M."

"Oh? And what then?"

"I dunno. I guess we flip a coin. One of us is going to give him the best lay he's had in years."

"Ellie-Jo! That's crazy. You can't even be sure that the guy likes women."

"Yes you can, doll. I've already been exploring." She winked, then kissed Flo on the cheek and hustled out to meet Sammy Lasker.

They walked for several blocks down Bourbon Street to a point where there were no traffic barricades. Lasker hailed a cab and gave the driver the name of a restaurant in Metairie.

"Are you married, Sammy?"

"Not at the moment." He was staring at her in the darkness of the cab. "How about you?"

"Not at the moment. It's been a long time, in fact."

"Good. Then there is no jealous husband prowling around." He continued staring at her as the taxi pulled onto a freeway leading north. "I can tell you're not a dancer. What do you do for a living?"

"Sammy! That's not very complimentary. I thought you really dug my act."

"I did. I loved it because it was fresh and just amateurish enough to be stimulating. You were putting your heart and soul into it. Most of the strippers in the cheap clubs become robots after awhile."

Ellie-Jo decided to smile for him. She scooted closer and kissed his cheek. "Thanks. I'll assume that is a compliment. What do you do for a living?"

"I play with horses mostly. And I dabble around in the stock market."

"Sounds like fun to me. I'm fascinated by horses. I'd love to spend a day at the races with someone who really knows what they are doing."

"Easily done. How about Monday?"

"Can't. I'm off to LA. Belive it or not, I run a computer company out there. We are working on an installation here. I'll be back in two weeks, though, on Saturday."

"Then we've got a date in two weeks, for Saturday at the races. I'll meet your plane."

"It's a deal. But don't bother meeting my plane. I'll meet you at Flo's place at noon. I have a couple of things to take care of before we meet. You don't waste a lot of time, do you, Sammy? I like that." Ellie-Jo snuggled closer, close enough to feel the hardware bulging under his left shoulder.

Sammy Lasker responded with roving hands. She decided to let him take inventory. After all, he would ultimately pay for it.

Ellie-Jo could see that he would not be an easy mark. He was not much taller than she was, but powerfully built. Most significant, there was an intelligence about him that would have to be reckoned with.

After a hurried late dinner, Lasker had the taxi take them to Snug Harbor, a jazz joint a few blocks from the Quarter across Esplanade. It was fairly close to Flo's apartment on Royal Street, so they wouldn't have far to go to meet Flo later.

The musicians played wildly while Sammy Lasker

tossed back drinks and began to loosen up. His hands continued their exploration of Ellie-Jo, and he was obviously pleased by her willingness to play. With each drink his exploratory caresses became more bold.

By the time the jazz combo's last set was finished and the lights were turned up, Sammy Lasker was short on words and big on holding his head in his hands. The antique Jax Beer clock on the wall said 4:30. Ellie-Jo prodded him to his feet.

"Come on, honey. We've got some lovin' to do." Sammy rose to his feet, yawed to one side for a moment, and tried to focus on Ellie-Jo.

"Sure, sure, you've got that right, baby." He managed somehow to get himself out to the curb and into the taxi without falling down.

Ellie-Jo studied her lifeless companion in the back of the cab and hoped that Flo would be home to help her get him inside the apartment.

The cab reached Flo's place in a matter of minutes. "We're home, Sammy dear, it's time to play house."

Ellie-Jo was surprised to find Sammy suddenly lucid. He got out of the cab quickly, shoved a twenty at the driver, and walked to the door in a remarkably straight line.

"Sammy, you bastard! It was all an act. You're as sober as a judge." Ellie-Jo shoved at him playfully.

"I'm as sober maybe as a drunken judge, but judges don't get very drunk." He grinned broadly and winked. "You got a key to this little brothel, baby?"

Ellie-Jo froze. She had to bite her lip to keep from slashing out at him. The words ended the growing tolerance she had begun to feel for him. She backed off a couple of steps and smiled, resolving that no matter how hard this small-time hood might try, he would never get her into bed.

Ellie-Jo pressed the doorbell. She could hear music from inside.

The door came ajar just a crack, then Flo dropped the chain and opened it. She stood before them stark naked. "Come on in, the party's just getting started."

Sammy Lasker beamed as Flo thrust a bottle of champagne at him to open. "Hey, I like your outfit. Now I know what strippers wear at home."

Ellie-Jo looked beyond Flo and quickly spotted the source of the music. Ziggy Lemon was sitting at the piano totally absorbed in his rendition of "An American in Paris." He was bare chested. He wore only a New Orleans Saints ball cap and a pair of polka dot shorts.

Flo turned her palms up and hunched her shoulders. "I gave him a key and told him he could play my piano anytime. As you can see, he took me up on it."

"Crazy, Flo, it's crazy," was all Ellie-Jo could think to say as they walked into her apartment. Ziggy seemed unaware of their presence, as if lost in another world.

Sammy popped the cork from the champagne bottle and began filling the glasses Flo had put out on a service table. He served Ellie-Jo first, then handed Flo a glass, took one himself, and pulled her nude form close. "Here's to slow horses and fast women. May the horses die and the women live forever."

As they all drank, Ziggy began stepping up the tempo. Then, out of the blue, "Amazing Grace" rolled from the keys as the unlikely trio looked on.

Flo hurried over to stand near the piano bench. "Ziggy! Ziggy, you'll have to stop. You're going to wake up the neighbors. It is beautiful, but they might rather sleep."

"Pal, play somethin' sexy. If we wanted church music, we'd all go down to Saint Louis Cathedral," Sammy growled.

Sammy had no sooner gotten the words out of his mouth when Ziggy stopped playing. He stared down at the keys briefly, then closed the heavy wood cover over them.

He waked over to Flo and looked her straight in the eye. If he noticed any other part of her nude anatomy, he gave no indication of it. "Thanks, Miss Dupre. Thanks for letting me play. I'll come back some other time."

"Come back anytime you want, Ziggy."

After Ziggy left, Sammy Lasker stared at the closed door. "You know, I swear I've seen that guy someplace but I just don't know where."

Flo glanced nervously at Ellie-Jo. "I can't imagine. He lives with his mother somewhere on Esplanade. I think all that poor boy has in life is the piano."

Lasker again put his arm around Flo. "Well, now he's gone and the church music is off. And it looks like I'm left with the wine and the women."

"Make that singular—woman," Ellie-Jo said. "I've got a seven A.M. flight, which means I have about an hour and a half to get to the airport. While you guys are havin' a ball, I'll be sleeping on the plane."

Flo was stunned. Ellie-Jo hadn't mentioned anything about the early morning flight. Come to think of it, she had always flown back to the coast on Sunday, but never so early.

Sammy Lasker, Flo naked in his arms, stared glumly at Ellie-Jo. "Too bad. I thought we'd get a little threesome going."

"I know you did, Sammy. But we've been together for hours and you dropped the ball, Sammy. See you right here in two weeks. And then we'll be off to the races." Ellie-Jo straightened herself up a bit before a mirror, picked up the big handbag, and headed for the door.

As soon as they were alone, Flo led Sammy into the bedroom. "For Pete's sake, Sammy, let's get these clothes off you. I'm beginning to think you don't really know how to treat a lady."

"You don't say?"

"Let me tell you something right away, Sammy. There ain't nothing Ellie-Jo can do that I can't do better."

"That includes dancin', kid. She can't dance worth a hoot." Sammy started trailing kisses across her bosom and then stopped abruptly. He looked squarely into her eyes. "I don't want any more surprises. What's this little get-together going to cost?"

"You got us figured all wrong, Sammy. You promised Ellie-Jo a day at the track. That's good enough for me. Let me join you then. Hell, Sammy. We girls just wanna have fun." Flo turned off the lights and walked into the bedroom.

Sammy followed her in disbelief. There had to be a catch. The two babes weren't dummies, he thought to himself. They were obviously in the bucks. "Hey, Flo, I guess you're just overwhelmed with my personality."

"That's right, Sammy. I think you're the nuts. But it's five o'clock in the morning. I want you to get in the sack or go home."

He began unbuttoning his shirt. In all the years he had prowled the French Quarter, he couldn't remember getting a free lunch. But gazing at the exotic dancer, he couldn't think of any reason to turn it down.

17

It was Tuesday morning. Henri Belanger was driving his small rental car to the northern shore of Lake Tahoe. A sign pointed the direction to a small public park located at the water's edge. He left his car and strolled along a sandy path that led to the boulder-strewn rim of the glistening lake. This might be the only opportunity to explore the scenic wonders of the area. The sheik would be arriving late that afternoon at the Golden Palace, Tahoe's newest upscale playground for high rollers. There would be no spare time after he arrived. No time, that is, to select a hideaway for his possible tryst with Ellie-Jo on the coming weekend.

He walked along the shore, recalling their chance meetings, mostly poolside in Las Vegas. Her incredible warmth and intelligence had captivated him. Like strangers expecting never to see each other again, they had poured their souls out to one another.

Yesterday evening he had checked into the Golden Palace. He was, as usual, two days ahead of the sheik and his entourage, which, of course, would include Orchid. Orchid would be an unbearable bundle of nerves, totally consumed by the grand opening of Orchid's Chic, her new shop in the Golden Palace. Happily, this situation had played right into Henri's hands. A banker friend of his from the old days owned a condo on the north shore of the lake near Incline Village. Almost at Orchid's insistence he had cleared the day for a personal visit to this friend. His only official commitment for the day was to be back in the Golden Palace before the sheik's Saturday night foray into the casino.

The cryptic telephone message waiting for him when he checked in sent his spirits soaring. "Saturday, usual time, poolside.—EJ." He had fantasized often about Ellie-Jo, but hadn't dared to believe she would remember their date. Now, barring any last-minute whims of the sheik, he would be doing laps with Ellie-Jo Saturday morning at six.

Henri bent over to select a few flat stones to skip across the mirror-flat surface of the lake. He felt invigorated by the crisp morning air. He tamped down a pipeload of tobacco from the eelskin pouch he carried, and he began to puff casually as he made his way back to his car.

A perfect day, he mused. Orchid was nowhere in sight.

Farther down in the parking area, a quarter of a mile away, only one other vehicle had ventured out to share the early morning in this idyllic spot. Henri Belanger circled out of the parking area and returned to the shoreline road heading south toward the Golden Palace, perhaps twenty miles away. Less than a minute later, the small blue Mazda at the far end of the parking area also made its way up to the main road.

Ziggy Lemon gave thanks that there was hardly any traffic at this hour. He could easily follow the slow pace of the car ahead and have time to enjoy the incredible scenery.

Henri Belanger was a strange man indeed, he thought. He had left the Golden Palace at daybreak and stopped only twice. Once at a motel named the Heavenly House. Maybe to ask directions, he reasoned. Then he had driven to the beautiful little park by the majestic lake, apparently to do nothing more than skip a few stones across the water. Now it looked like he may be returning to the Golden Palace. Oh well, he would write it all down, just as Ellie-Jo had instructed. It was an easy enough job for five hundred dollars.

When Ellie-Jo had called him, he had at first balked at the assignment. She really shouldn't spend all that money, he told her. She had promised him five hundred for the week, a hotel, a rental car, and airfare. All for what? To watch a man skip stones across the water? He would have many pages of nothing very interesting to turn over to Ellie-Jo on Friday night. This was a very nice vacation, but he missed Flo's piano.

Ziggy glanced down at the small pad of paper on the seat beside him. Occasionally, he would add a new song title to the list which he intended to play on Flo's piano.

The balance of the morning sojourn yielded no surprises. Henri wheeled into the Golden Palace, avoided the parking valet, and parked his car himself, far away from the building. He climbed out of the car and looked up at the hotel for several seconds. Ziggy figured that he had parked in a spot where he would be able to see the car from his room. Right then Ziggy realized that Henri Belanger was quite different from the heavy bettors he tailed in New Orleans. Belanger was a keen observer, perhaps as keen as Ziggy himself. After all, it was his job to bodyguard the sheik and protect his money. Ziggy smiled faintly. This was a game he relished. He had to spy on someone whose job it was to spot and identify people like himself. He wrote that thought down on his report, hoping that Ellie-Jo would be pleased by his observation.

He followed Belanger inside the hotel and watched him enter an elevator. Ziggy had taken a chance the night before, ridden the crowded elevator with Belanger, and determined that his room was 1821. Now Ziggy watched the lights above the elevator door blink on and off until the cab predictably stopped on the eighteenth floor.

Ziggy returned to the glitzy casino. At this time of morning, there were few customers trying their luck. The blackjack tables, roulette wheels, and crap tables, neatly arranged in the center of the huge room, were ringed by slot machines along the outer walls, most of them several steps up on a higher level. After circling the entire room, Ziggy settled himself in front of a row of nickel slot machines. The vantage point from this area was exceptional. Not only could he look down between the rows of crap tables where the big action would take place, but he could also see into the elevator alcove. If he turned his head ninety degrees he could see clearly through the lobby to the front entrance of the hotel.

Ziggy decided that this would be his headquarters in the casino. He sought out a change girl and bought five rolls of nickels. By playing them one coin at a time, and then recycling the winnings, he was able to play for a little over an hour. He considered it cheap rent for such a vantage point. And it was a lot more fun than standing around at Louisiana Downs in New Orleans. The red leather seats in front of each machine were comfortable. The only thing better than sitting there would be to sit in front of Flo's piano back in the Quarter.

Suddenly, Henri Belanger emerged from an elevator. Ziggy stood up and sauntered between the rows of slot machines toward him. He watched Henri have a brief conversation with a leggy change girl, ultimately buying a roll of dollar tokens. He fed those three at a time into a nearby machine, playing off several small winners, and then proceeded to the gift shop. He eventually emerged with a newspaper and returned to the eighteenth floor. Ziggy shook his head in amazement. The man had just spent at least twenty-one dollars for a Sunday paper. Already this morning he had seen enough money stuffed into the machines around him to buy a very fine piano.

Ziggy saw Henri six more times throughout the day. There were two trips to the coffee shop, two trips to the security desk that handled the guest's safety deposit boxes, two hours at the swimming pool, and a long dinner alone.

It was easy for Ziggy to zero in on Henri's weak spot. On each swing through the lobby, he sought out the same leggy change girl and purchased a roll of dollars from her. With each purchase he spent a little more time in conversation with her. That night, at about eleven o'clock, Henri met her in the parking lot and drove her to a motel about six blocks away.

Ziggy's respect for Henri Belanger took a nosedive. He was vulnerable. A woman like Ellie-Jo could easily wrap him around her little toe.

By the end of the following day, he had Henri completely figured—he was a creature of habit. At eleven o'clock he met the same change girl in the parking lot and took her to the same motel.

Ziggy would have one more day to study Henri's habits before Ellie-Jo arrived. Ziggy wondered whether or not to tell her about the change girl. He finally decided that he would.

18

Willy Hanson sat slumped down in the seat of Ginny's Porsche, trying to be inconspicuous. He was parked about a half block away from the Pair-a-Dice Club, across the street. It was midafternoon. Once, Coley had emerged from his duties as bartender to fiddle with the awning out front. He frowned as he glanced in Willy's direction. Willy knew he was getting under Coley's skin. His friend had told him that it was a bad move to try to follow a bike with a car. "All you can do is get yourself in trouble."

Ginny had called him that morning. Her friends in Seattle were sailing up to Victoria on a ketch very similar to the *Tashtego*. She was being pressured to stay another week and to make the trip with them. Willy encouraged her to stay. This would give him a little more time to follow the slim lead until it petered out, or until perhaps it led to the killer or killers of Lefty Grogan.

Fighting sleep, he envisioned the ketch heeling over under a brisk breeze through the Puget Sound, and he wished that he could be with Ginny. His reverie was abruptly interrupted by the staccato roar of Hacker's Harley. Willy bolted upright.

Hacker eased the big bike off the curb and made a left turn. Willy followed. A block and a half later, pausing for only a moment at a stop sign, Hacker turned left onto the Pacific Coast Highway and sped north, weaving easily through the light traffic. Willy cursed as he tried to keep the Harley in sight. He hadn't realized how hard it would be to tail a motorcycle. Once he had to stop at a light when the cars in front of him slowed down with the yellow light to make the stop. Hacker roared right on through.

Willy was able to track him past El Segundo, LAX, and Marina Del Rey. He saw Hacker far in front making a right on Wilshire, but by the time Willy got there Hacker had vanished. He drove as fast as he dared up and down the streets of Santa Monica, but the big bike was nowhere in sight. He pulled over and sat for ten minutes or so, his eyes glued to the intersections ahead. Then finally he gave up.

Willy headed the Porsche back to Manhattan Beach and parked a couple of blocks away from the club. When he walked inside he saw Coley standing behind an empty bar. Several customers were sipping beer around a pool table in the rear.

"I'll have a cold draft."

"Sure. It's on the house," Coley said, glancing around to make sure there was no one within earshot.

"I tried to follow Hacker just now," Willy said in a low voice.

"I betcha I know where you've been."

"Where?"

"Santa Monica. Maybe on San Vincente."

Willy groaned. He had remembered seeing that intersection leading off to the left. "For Christ's sake, Coley, if you knew that, why didn't you tell me?"

"Fresh information, pal. I have a friend who has a friend at the phone company. Hacker made a bunch of calls last month to an unlisted Santa Monica phone number."

"So what does that mean?"

"Maybe nothing. But he doesn't make very many phone calls other than strictly local. Now if you had a babe that was a looker like Ellie-Jo is supposed to be, you'd call her pretty often, wouldn't you?"

"Did your friend of a friend get a name?"

"He says that a party named Ellen Lambert gets billed for the phone. The address is a posh, upscale condo right off San Vincente."

Willy mulled over the information for a few moments. "Ellen? Not Ellie-Jo?"

"Hey, man, how close do you need? Ellie-Jo could be a nickname. Anyway, it's something to check out. Even if it is Ellie-Jo, we still haven't got anything."

Willy looked at his watch. "When is Hacker supposed to be back here?"

"He said around five o'clock, but he ain't very reliable."

"We've got a couple of hours. I'm going back up to the address on San Vincente to stake it out. I'd love to see Hacker come out of that condo."

Coley groaned. "So you're gonna play detective again? Hacker already knows what you look like. He saw you in the bar yesterday. He'd think it was damn funny if he saw you sitting in a car up in Santa Monica. You've got to keep it real cool and keep your distance."

Willy stood up and downed the last few swigs of the draft. "Getting excited, aren't you, Coley?"

Coley smiled. "I only ask one thing—stay away from that Lambert woman. Let me poke around and find out about her. I don't want her to have an inkling that we're nosing into her affairs. We'll know in a day or two if we're on to anything."

"You've got my word, pal. I've got all the beautiful women in my life I can handle." With that, Willy went outside and climbed into the Porsche.

The drive back up to Santa Monica seemed to take forever. The rush of traffic was at its peak, and it was well after four o'clock when he made the turn onto San Vincente. He hadn't reached the condo yet when he saw Hacker's Harley zip by, going in the opposite direction. There were two on the bike. A woman sat behind Hacker, her bronzed arms wrapped tightly around his waist.

The woman was a classic beauty: long legs, short shorts, and a flawless body. Her eyes were hidden by wraparound black sunglasses. A thick mane of auburn hair whipped in the wind, dipping well below her waist at times. The superlatives of the bartender in Tonopah and the description offered by Lefty Grogan came to mind as he stared at the couple in his rearview mirror. It had to be Ellie-Jo.

19

Armand Hauser felt more than a little disappointed. Ellen Lambert had paid him scant attention since her return from the weekend. The flowers he had left on her desk had drawn no response at all from her when they had discussed business matters in her office. Their wild night on the beach had no doubt been too unorthodox a way to start a business relationship. He had to find out if she was sorry it had happened.

It was late in the day when he returned to her office to discuss a wine inventory report. At the conclusion of their brief meeting, he decided to broach the subject. "Ellen, I've found a restaurant that I think you should see. They have woven some genuinely new ideas into their presentation. I'd like to take you there Friday night."

"Armand," she said abruptly, "I'm going to be tied up Friday. I'll be leaving town. Perhaps we can make it another time. My schedule for the next couple of weeks is booked solid. Perhaps you should write up your observations about this restaurant and give me a report."

"Of course, I'll do that." Armand searched her face, wishing for a more personal reaction. "I confess, I have an ulterior motive. I would like to repay you for the beautiful evening we had together in Santa Barbara."

Ellen Lambert slipped the papers she had been studying into a file folder, then folded her hands on her desk. She stared blankly at him for a moment, then broke into a warm smile. Armand was delighted. It was as if she had pushed a button and a new personality had emerged. The prim business demeanor vanished and she suddenly radiated the warmth he had felt that night on the beach.

"I'm sorry, Armand. It has been a long, busy day." Still smiling, she stretched languidly. "I'm afraid I was naughty that night, wasn't I?"

"You were wonderful. But you know, I was afraid until now that you had forgotten all about it. Or, worse yet, I thought that you might have found me too brash, not very sober, and perhaps out of line."

"No, no, no, nothing of the kind. We *did* have a lot to drink that evening. But that had nothing to do with what happened, Armand. One night we will have the same kind of adventure when we are cold sober." She continued to smile warmly.

"Well! I feel much better," Armand replied, though he was still perplexed by her change of character. "I'm only sorry that our return engagement will have to wait."

"Please bear with me, Armand. We'll try to make the wait worthwhile. Sometimes anticipation makes things even better."

Armand stood as Ellen punched up an incoming

call. The prim executive look returned to her face as he turned to leave the room.

"Armand!" She called after him, holding her hand over the mouthpiece. "Thank you for the lovely flowers."

Armand smiled, nodded, closed the door behind him, and walked back toward his office. He felt invigorated yet vaguely uneasy. Ellen Lambert was no ordinary woman. He made a resolution to be patient, recalling something from Balzac, or some other social commentator of those ribald times. Someone had said there was no pleasure greater in life than exploring the depths of a new lover.

Ellen Lambert continued working at her desk until everyone else in the company went home. She turned down the lights in her office and opened the drapes that covered the full length of one wall. Outside, in the dusk, thousands of lights twinkled in a great circle sweeping from Malibu to the Palos Verdes peninsula.

As happened so often lately, her thoughts traveled back to Texas and the family ranch near Amarillo, where great flat plains stretched for hundreds of miles in every direction and big sky ran from horizon to horizon with no perceptible rise in the landscape. Life had been simple and safe when she was a small child back there. Only the sometimes merciless weather that affected the size of her father's herds and the growth of the crops had complicated life to an appreciable degree.

Ellen had no memory of her mother. She had died when Ellen was only four years old. A painting of her hung above the fireplace in the old ranch house. It looked amazingly like Ellen. Sometimes Ellen liked to copy her mother's prim hairstyle and to use the same string of pearls to secure the tight bun.

Preston Lambert once told Ellen that her mother had died of pneumonia during a severe winter. But Ellie-Joe had learned early never to believe her father. He lied a lot—about money, about gambling, and about the womanizing he indulged in all his life. The gossip burgeoned all around her. People seemed to hate Preston Lambert enough to go out of their way to gossip about him, always just loudly enough for Ellen to hear.

After her grade school days, Ellen was sent away to a fancy boarding school in Dallas and, after that, to a college in Houston. Preston Lambert seemed intent on keeping her away from Amarillo, and as she grew older, she sensed why. She cramped his lifestyle.

College in Houston had changed her life. Her incredible physical attractiveness opened doors for her that would forever remain closed to most of her friends. Added to that was her wealth. Seemingly boundless, it had evaporated overnight when Preston Lambert, owner of the Double Lazy R, died in a Dallas parking lot. The panhandle papers said he was a victim of gunshots, shot by an assailant who had fled with Preston Lambert's wallet. Privately, Ellen heard the speculation about which of several jealous husbands might have done him in. The lawyers said soon thereafter that a combination of bad times and a gambling habit had wiped out the holdings of the once successful rancher.

Ellen Lambert stared at the steady stream of aircraft pouring into LAX in the distance. It seemed like forever since she herself had first arrived, fresh out of Texas. The little money she had brought with her had run out quickly. The job offer she had accepted during her last semester of college, a legal assistant in a small firm, turned out to be a dead end. After a few days on the job, it was obvious that her only function was to decorate the reception area and provide companionship for the firm's clients. Within a month she had resigned. She refused to be anyone's whore.

Standing at the window, she looked out over the sweep of lights and tried to pinpoint the location of the sleazy Pair-a-Dice Club. Somewhere down there was Hacker. Walking back to her desk, she unlocked the bottom drawer. Reaching to the back, she removed a clam-shaped leather bag. She withdrew a small, nickel-plated .22 automatic and put it in her purse. The gleaming weapon had been a present from Hacker. "Don't ever let any of those fancy creeps go too far," he had said.

After she had left the law firm, she had taken temporary jobs waitressing, hostessing, or doing whatever came along. Then came the ill-fated night when she had gone to Las Vegas with a customer she barely knew. He seemed suave and sure of himself.

"Come on, kid. I'll stake you. If you win, the gravy's all yours. If you lose, we'll both have a big laugh," he had said.

The man was a hopeless bastard. They had made a round of several casinos. He lost heavily, and she managed to lose several hundred dollars. She dreaded the thought of spending the night with him. He became surly and insistent, and she walked away from him in the parking lot.

Then he became a brute. Out of the blue, he shoved her against a car and slugged her. She fell, out cold for a few moments. Then she remembered someone shouting, a furious struggle all around her.

Finally, someone knelt beside her, and she felt arms surround her. She looked up into the eyes of Hacker.

"Don't worry, lady. He ain't never gonna bother nobody again. Come on. We gotta get the hell outa here."

He helped her to her feet. The man lay beside the car, his face pulp; blood ran all over the place.

Hacker put her on the back of his bike and told her to hang on. They stopped at a truckstop a few miles out of Vegas, where she cleaned herself up. Then they went on to Barstow, where they stopped again and had breakfast.

Hacker pulled a big wad of bills out of his pocket and counted it. There was almost five thousand dollars. He split the roll in two halves, stuffing one half into her purse. "There, baby, you earned it. That son of a bitch back there will never miss it."

This was the beginning. Already an accomplice to homicide, she became Hacker's girl.

She played his game for a short time, and the money began to pile up. It was simple. They would ply the big gambling meccas. She would wait, usually not very long, until some drooling creep who obviously had a lot of money came along. She would lead him to Hacker. Usually, within a matter of hours, they were on their way back to LA with the guy's bankroll.

They had played their scam a dozen times now. For a while, Ellie-Jo had no idea Hacker was actually killing most of their targets. Until recently, she had never been around when Hacker did his thing. He was swift, decisive, and didn't leave any footprints. "You got to forget about these patsies, Ellie-Jo," he often said. "They're garbage anyway, and that's a fact." Hacker always called her Ellie-Jo. He had misunderstood her when she first gave him her name. She just let it ride.

In just a few months, she set herself up in the condo in Santa Monica. She answered an ad in the paper seeking a publicist. Sheldon Blake, CEO of

Waterfront, Inc., was very impressed. So was she. He was the only guy she had ever worked for who hadn't tried to get her in the sack. She dug in and made Waterfront, Inc., an incredible success.

But at the end of the week, she always returned to Hacker. It would be Ellie-Jo and Hacker going out on another scam.

Two months ago they had gone on a bike ride that ended on an overlook up on Mulholland.

"Hacker, some day we are going to get caught," she had said. "You're good, but you're also lucky."

"You make your own luck, Ellie-Jo. That's a fact."

"What do you want out of this, Hacker?"

"I want a million bucks, tax free."

Ellie-Jo decided to take charge. "Then we're going to have to work harder. We keep going for peanuts. If you don't mind, I am going to set up some really big hits. When we get your million, we're gonna stop. Deal?"

Hacker came as close as he ever had to smiling. "You got my word, Ellie-Jo. And that's a fact."

She jammed her hand into the purse to grasp the handgrip of the shiny .22. This weekend it would be Henri Belanger, if everything worked out. Next week it would be New Orleans. After that, they would be well on their way to Hacker's pension fund and her freedom.

20

Doris Hackley entered her flower shop in Laguna Beach and walked right into a big hug from Maggie.

"Wow, look at you! I can tell the honeymoon must have been super. You look so beautiful!"

"Maggie, Cabo San Lucas was just gorgeous, and of course Bill was even more gorgeous. I can't wait to fill you in on everything." Doris Hackley couldn't resist a big grin. "Well, almost everything."

"Let me tell you, Hackley Flowers has been busy. People have been falling in love, marrying, and dying so fast I can hardly keep up."

"Oh, Maggie, I wish there was some way to do it without the dying part, but I guess that's part of the territory. Say, you look terrific yourself. I bet you've been doing the falling-in-love part."

"No such luck, but things are pretty keen anyway. Bucky wants to take me and his surfboard to Hawaii for the big tournament there. But Mom says no."

"Wise mom! Speaking very selfishly, I need you here. Anything urgent while I was away?" Doris Hackley went into the back room and began picking at the large stack of mail that had accumulated while she was away.

"Not really. Most of that stuff is just junk mail or bills. There's a couple of things marked personal."

She flipped through most of the mail quickly, tossing anything that looked important or interesting into a separate box. She came across two large brown envelopes, both mailed from Pasadena. She slit open the one bearing the latest mailing date. An index card dropped out.

Dear Ms. Hackley,
  I have been trying to reach your brother, Hacker, concerning a matter important to both of us. Would you please have him call Lefty in Tonopah, Nevada. He knows where he can find me.
                    Thanks,
                    Lefty

The note was typewritten, signed with a heavy marker pen. The second envelope contained another index card with the identical message.

"Someone's trying to reach my kooky brother." She flipped the card across the desk for Maggie to examine. "That's a strange way to do it, wouldn't you say. I wonder how they got this address. We don't have many friends in common. In fact, if Hacker has a friend in the world, I don't know him."

Maggie picked up one of the envelopes and then the other. On both, the return address was smeared beyond readability. Someone had either been very careless or had smudged them on purpose. "Can't read the return address. Your brother probably knows who it is."

"Well, I guess I'll have to call him." Doris put the two envelopes and the cards aside. "If he wants them, he'll have to come down here and get them."

"I just remembered something, Doris. Just after you left on your honeymoon, a guy came in here looking for Hacker. He seemed like a real gentleman. That surprised me. The only time I see Hacker is when he comes through town with his biker buddies. Anyway, I told the guy that Hacker had a club up in Manhattan Beach. I couldn't think of the name of the place."

"So what'd he say?"

"Nothing much. I got the impression he was going to go up there and look for him. If his name was Lefty, he didn't say so."

"Well then, maybe he's found Hacker by now. Oh hell, I'll try to reach him. Hacker would blow up if it was important and I didn't tell him." Reluctantly, she dialed the number of the Pair-a-Dice Club.

"Hi, this Al?" The voice she heard was neither Al's nor Hacker's.

"Nope. This is Coley, the new bartender. Al ain't here anymore."

"Is Hacker there? This is his sister."

"He's standing right here, ma'am." He passed the phone to Hacker.

"Look, I'm real busy now, Doris. What's on your mind?"

He's a real charmer, Coley thought to himself. Here is his sister coming off a honeymoon, and he tells her he's real busy.

"What! That's nuts, Doris!" exploded Hacker. "I

don't know any damn Lefty." Hacker's free hand clenched in a tight fist.

Coley wished he could hear both sides of the conversation.

"I don't know anybody named Lefty in Tonopah, Nevada, and that's a fact. You got that straight?" There was another prolonged silence as Doris told him about the man who visited the flower shop.

Coley was trying to stay close to the phone, but Hacker had walked away from the bar trailing the cord after him. Then he started to shout.

"Look, Doris, I'm a busy man. Don't pester me with bullshit. If the turkey shows up again, tell him to come and see me. I'll punch his lights out." Hacker slammed down the phone.

"Hey, boss," Coley said, "calm down. You're gonna blow a gasket."

"You mind your own fuckin' business, Coley. That screwed-up sister of mine pissed me off." Hacker started to wheel the big Harley through the front door. "Take care of things, Coley. I won't be back until late." Hacker then paused, staring out the door as if in deep thought. "Did I tell you about Friday?"

"Nope."

"I'm goin' up north. You'll have to work the late shift on Friday."

"Sure, boss. I can use the bucks. Where you going?"

"Coley, you don't listen too good. I just told you I was goin' up north."

"Hell, man, north runs all the way to the North Pole." Coley found himself chuckling at his little joke all by himself.

"Coley, you talk too much and you ask too many questions, and that's a fact." Hacker stared at him as he revved the engine of the Harley. "Think about that, Coley."

Hacker bumped over the curb and turned left toward Pacific Coast Highway. From inside the bar, Coley heard him gun the engine and roar northward toward LA.

21

It was six o'clock on Friday morning. Ellen Lambert picked up the phone and dialed Henri Belanger's number at the Golden Palace.

"Hello, Belanger here."

His voice was crisp, surprisingly alert for the early hour. "Henri, can you talk? I'm sorry to wake you. It's EJ," she said softly.

"Of course, Ellie-Jo. What's up?"

"I have good news. I will be flying in this evening instead of tomorrow. I'm hoping we can get together."

"Perfect! I can't wait. Orchid and the sheik won't be in until late tomorrow. We will have all that time to explore the lake."

"Henri, you make it sound so legitimate, like we will be truly exploring the lake." She laughed softly. "But seriously, Henri, I have a problem with meeting you in the hotel where your wife will be staying. I don't think it wise."

"Darling, I've thought of that. I made reservations for the morning up on the North Shore. I'll tell them we will be arriving tonight instead. Can I meet your plane?"

There was a rather long pause. "No, that wouldn't be practical. I'm meeting some business people in Reno. It's going to take some time. I'll meet you on the North Shore. Tell me where."

"It's a ski lodge near Incline Village. Absolutely elegant. It's called Heavenly House. We'll be very secluded there this time of year. I'll have you all to myself, if you can stand that."

"It sounds exciting, Henri. I can hardly wait."

"Are you going to be driving from Reno? Why don't you fly straight into Tahoe."

"Henri, dear, I have business in Reno. The drive is lovely. I've done it many times before."

"Okay, listen carefully. Get on the lake road going north through Incline Village. Keep going until you reach State Road 431 going north. There is a large parking area next to a row of shops on the righthand side of 431. I'll be there waiting in a black Cadillac, last three plate numbers are six, nine, one."

"Oh, my poor Henri. What will you be doing while you wait?"

"I'll probably be enjoying an ice cream. There is a delightful little shop nearby."

"Remember, Henri, you are going to teach me baccarat and craps. Will we have time for that?"

"Of course, my dear. There is a hotel casino on the North Shore where we can test your luck. I really don't think we should be seen together in the Golden Palace. The sheik already has other people in the hotel. I saw his valet last evening."

"How much money should I bring?"

"Don't worry your pretty head about that."

"I will have great fun watching you break the bank, Henri."

"I like your confidence, but that never happens, Ellie-Jo. Remember now, six-thirty. And drive carefully. The road can be treacherous sometimes."

"I can't wait! Goodbye, love."

Ellie-Jo glanced at her watch as she hung up the phone. She had a lot to do. She had to call Hacker first. He had driven his Bronco to Truckee, a few miles north of Tahoe, where he was to spend the night. He would bitch about the change in plans, but he would just have to live with it. She guessed there was time for her morning jog and for a shower before taking a leisurely breakfast.

Outside Ellen Lambert's condo, Willy Hanson and Coley Doctor sat in the Porsche about a hundred yards down the street. They sipped coffee and chowed down on some ridiculously sweet and sticky apple turnovers. Their vigil was already two hours old.

"Your choice of breakfast was terrible," Willy mumbled, wiping his sticky fingers on a stack of napkins. "We're going to have to get down to Long Beach State and play a full day's worth of one-on-one to work this crap out of our system. Do you eat this stuff all the time?"

"What did you expect, eggs Benedict? If this fancy car had a hotplate like Hacker's Bronco, I'd whip us up something really good."

"How do you know about the inside of his Bronco? You guys getting to be buddies?"

"Hell, man, he shows it off all the time. His whole life is wrapped up in his Harley and that Bronco."

"And Ellie-Jo."

"Yeah, and Ellie-Jo. What the hell does she see in him, anyway. Do you know that Ellen Lambert is president of a big restaurant network? They have their offices on Santa Monica, near the Coast Highway. Something called Waterfront, Inc."

"You're kidding! That's a huge outfit. They've got a place near San Clemente that's *the* place to go. How did you find this out?"

"Just say I have some connections down at the tax office. You see, Willy, I'm a genuine, real-talented gumshoe. Amateurs like you wouldn't understand that. It comes with the territory when you get to be big time." Coley groaned as he tried to stretch his legs in the Porsche. "They didn't build this fancy car for guys six foot six. I'm going to have to get out and walk around soon. Maybe this is a wild-goose chase anyway."

"Hey! There she is! That's the gal that was on Hacker's bike the other day when I came up here." A jogger dressed in short shorts and a baggy sweatshirt came out of the building and started jogging uphill, away from them. The long mane of auburn hair swung from side to side as she dug in at a fast clip.

"Holy smoke." Coley whistled appreciatively. "Now that's some bod!"

"What do we do now, Mister Detective?"

"We just sit here, pal. She'll be back. That's the way with joggers. They just run around in circles. Besides, there ain't no other way into that building."

It was about twenty minutes before they spotted Ellie-Jo coming out of a side street ahead of them. Without breaking step, she turned into the walkway and re-entered the condo. It gave them a chance to study her facial features for a few moments, though at a distance.

"She's a ten, Willy. But now it'll be at least an hour before she comes out. She'll have to shower, dress, and pretty herself up. She may even have breakfast."

"So we just sit here?"

"Yep. Maybe we better move up a few yards. She'll be heading back toward Santa Monica when she goes to work."

Forty-five minutes later, a commercial limo pulled into the circular driveway in front of Ellie-Jo's building. The limo driver entered the building, then quickly emerged and lit a cigarette.

"I'll make a bet that's for Ellie-Jo," Coley said. "If I had her bucks, that's the way I'd commute."

No sooner had he spoken than Ellie-Jo emerged from the building dressed in a white jumpsuit and carrying a large, tooled-leather handbag.

"Suit fits like it was sewn right to her skin, doesn't it?" Coley shook his head and smiled in approval as the limo moved away from them. "I want a job where women come to work looking like that."

To their surprise the limo turned left off Santa Monica and kept on going.

"She ain't going to the office this morning," observed Willy, as they left Santa Monica behind them. Eventually the limo pulled into a line of heavy traffic filtering into Los Angeles International Airport.

"Suppose she's flying or meeting somebody?" Willy asked. The limo entered the departure level, made a big circle around the U-shaped terminal, and stopped in front of a sign marked Reno Air.

The limo paused for a moment. Ellie-Jo got out, handed the driver several bills, and walked into the terminal as the limo pulled away.

"Oh hell, man. She's flying away from us." They stared at Ellie-Jo now walking away, still visible inside the glassed-in terminal.

Coley sprang from the Porsche. "See you soon, boss. I'll call you from someplace."

"Coley!" Willy yelled several times, but Coley paid

no attention. The cars behind him soon began honking their horns, and a police officer motioned emphatically, ordering Willy to move ahead. He had no choice but to circle and find a parking spot in the terminal garage.

Inside the terminal, Coley got in line, three people behind Ellie-Jo. He watched closely as the clerk handed her a ticket.

"That will be gate thirty-nine. Are you checking any luggage?"

She shook her head and quickly moved toward the concourse security gates.

"And where are you going, sir?" the ticket agent asked Coley when it was finally his turn.

"What have you got going from gate thirty-nine?"

The clerk looked puzzled. "Well, sir, most of our flights leave from gate thirty-nine. Our next is to Portland, with a stop in Reno. It leaves in thirty minutes."

"Okay. I need a ticket." Coley shoved a credit card at him.

"Shall it be Portland or Reno?"

Coley hesitated. It was a perfectly necessary question. "Make it Portland," he finally said, thinking that if Ellie-Jo got off in Reno, he'd get off too.

"Okay. I'll tell you what I'll do. Since you are such a tall fellow, I'll put you in an exit row. Lots more leg room there."

"Hey, thank you very much."

Boarding pass in hand, Coley moved quickly through security and strode rapidly down the concourse. The gate was the second on the left. Ellie-Jo was waiting quietly in the lounge, legs crossed, reading a *Wall Street Journal*.

The gate was directly across from a fast food restaurant. Coley ordered a cup of coffee and another apple turnover. Then he took a seat in the departure lounge far away from, and behind, Ellen Lambert. She kept her face buried in the *Wall Street Journal*.

He boarded the plane before she did and took his seat in the rear exit row. When Ellen Lambert boarded, he breathed a sigh of relief when she took a seat a half dozen rows ahead of him. He had never met her, so there was no reason for her to recognize him. But if he were to continue to follow her, there would come a time when she might notice him because of his size.

Their plane took off right on time. The flight was to take less than an hour. Once, Ellen Lambert got up and passed Coley on the way to a rest room in the rear. He hunched over and focused his eyes on the airline magazine. There was an article singing the praises of Reno showgirls in all the big clubs. Scrutinizing the photos carefully, he decided that Ellen Lambert had them all beat.

As she returned to her seat, Coley got an eye-level look at the neatly packaged jumpsuit. No question about it, she was at least an eleven. The sharply dressed businessman across the aisle grinned at Coley when he caught him appraising her.

He leaned over toward Coley. "Thank God for good eyesight," he whispered.

Coley acknowledged his comment by returning his smile, then engrossed himself once again in the magazine. Coley was dozing when the roar of the jet's reverse thrusters signaled that they had landed. Ellen Lambert stood the instant the seatbelt light went off.

She would have a head start. A dozen passengers ahead of him seemed to take forever fussing with their luggage. By the time he left the jetway, she was turning the corner at the end of the concourse. When he reached the escalator to the main terminal, she was out of sight. Rejecting the escalator, he bounded down the stairs.

Thank God for the white jumpsuit, Coley thought. It was like a beacon in the crowd of people. She was exiting through the doors at the front of the terminal.

He raced through the crowd toward the exit but stopped abruptly when he saw her standing outside. While still inside the terminal he watched a small, slight man approach her. He was dressed in a plain gray sweatshirt, dark pants, and sneakers. His unkempt, short, mousy-colored hair was dishevelled. She hugged him affectionately for several moments. The little man looked embarrassed by her attention: his hands remained woodenly at his side.

He pointed across the street to a parking area, and she followed him as he led the way on the crosswalk. Coley's hopes began to sink. There was a cab stand at least two hundred feet to the right, with a long line of people waiting.

Coley walked rapidly onto the crosswalk and between rows of cars on the other side, trying to keep their backs in sight.

The small fellow opened the door of a blue Mazda sedan for Ellen Lambert, then circled the vehicle to climb behind the wheel. As the driver dipped into the car, he glanced around the area nervously. If he saw Coley, it was only for a second.

He made a mental note of the license plate number of the Mazda that was sitting in an Avis space. Then they were gone. He looked frantically for a stray taxi, but there was none. He stared at the blue Mazda as it moved northward from the airport and, finally, out of sight.

Reluctantly, Coley returned to the terminal and stood in line at the Avis counter. He cursed himself as he waited. Catching the plane on the spur of the moment had been a hair-brained decision. What had happened was bound to happen, though he'd hoped she would have gotten into a taxi or a hotel courtesy van.

"Sir, can I help you?"

"I have an odd situation. I hope you can help me." Coley smiled at the young woman behind the rental car desk. She looked intelligent. Maybe she *could* help.

"That's what I'm here for. A big guy like you needs a Caddy to stretch out in. We have a weekend special rate on one."

"Say, that sounds pretty good. But before I rent a car, I have to find out whether or not someone is outside waiting for me. My name is on the paging system, but so far I've gotten no response. Someone in an Avis blue Mazda with this license plate number is supposed to meet me. It's weird, but I don't know the guy's name, and he evidently doesn't know mine. I've been waiting on the curb out there for a long time and have checked half the cars in the lot. It looks hopeless."

The woman fiddled with the computer for a long time. "Ah, I think I have it, sir. I have to cross-check to identify the plate number. Here it is." She carefully wrote the name of the renter on a slip of paper and pushed it toward Coley.

A Siegfried Lemon, of 1888 Esplanade, New Orleans, Louisiana, had rented the car.

"I wonder where he is staying. I'd like to give him a call. I'll need the Caddy anyway, so you can go ahead and write it up."

The rental clerk fussed with the computer again for a few moments. "He told us he is staying at the Golden Palace in Tahoe, but sometimes people don't stay where they say they're going to."

"Thanks, Sandra, I'll give it a try." He had gleaned her name from the nameplate on her ample bosom. He slid a credit card across the counter.

"I'll bet you're a basketball player," Sandra remarked, as she worked on the rental contract.

"No, I'm a chipmunk rancher. I raise the little suckers by the thousands," offered Coley, quite seriously.

Sandra chuckled. "And what do you do with them?"

"I don't know. I haven't figured it out yet, but when there is a big demand for them, I'll have a corner on the market. Maybe you'd like to visit my ranch sometime."

"Maybe someday, Mr. Doctor. Come back soon and tell me about it." She beamed as she handed Coley the rental contract for the Caddy.

Coley made his way to the lot and glanced at his watch as he climbed into the Caddy. He was a full forty minutes behind Ellen Lambert and Siegfried Lemon, whoever he was. He refreshed his memory of the area by studying the small map Sandra had provided. What the hell, he decided. He'd try the Golden Palace. If he drew a blank, at least he had another piece of the puzzle, an odd little shrimp named Siegfried Lemon.

22

Willy sat dejectedly in the Porsche parked across the street from the Pair-a-Dice Club in Manhattan Beach. The Reno Air jet had pulled away from the gate by the time he had circled LAX and parked the Porsche in the garage. He had been able to confirm that Coley was a passenger on the flight to Portland, with a stop in Reno. He had little choice but to kill some time and wait for Coley to call.

Might as well check out the Pair-a-Dice once more, he thought. As he entered, he noticed Hacker's Harley parked snug against the back wall. It had a sheet draped over it lettered with a crude Hands Off sign.

A barmaid approached him. She was a pert blond, neatly dressed in slacks and a long-sleeved blouse buttoned to the collar. Although she was bright-eyed, she looked a little prim for Hacker's taste.

"I'll have a Coors draft. That your Harley back there?"

"Oh, heavens no. That belongs to the boss. I guess I'm babysitting it while he's away. You a biker?"

"Tried it for a while when I was young, back east. Too much bad weather. It would be a lot more fun out here."

"Yeah, the boss usually lives on the damn thing. He went someplace up north for a long weekend. I'm surprised he didn't take it." She walked away to draw the beer and then returned.

"My name's Bill," he half lied. Nobody ever called him Bill. "What's yours?"

"I'm Lee Ann. I usually wait tables, but today our bartender didn't show up. He isn't here and the boss isn't here, so I'm just filling in." She shook her head and frowned. "Hacker, that's my boss, hired this big tall guy right off the street. Didn't check him out at all. He shows up for two days, then picks today not to come in. He was a sharp-looking guy, too, but I guess the Pair-a-Dice Club didn't appeal to him."

Lee Ann looked around at the dingy nightclub. "Let's face it, who in the hell would this dump really appeal to?"

"Why don't you get your boss on the phone and yell for help? He'd probably appreciate that."

"I have no idea where he went. Hacker doesn't say much." Lee Ann laughed. "Sometimes I think he doesn't know many words."

Willy's mind raced along as she talked idly about her missing boss and bartender. Chances were that if Hacker were driving to meet Ellie-Jo somewhere, it would be Reno, not Portland. Coley and Ellie-Jo probably got off the plane in Reno.

Willy began to get nervous. He looked at his watch and finished the draft. It was time to get back to the *Tashtego*. He only hoped that Coley would call quickly and bring him up-to-date.

He stood up and waved a goodbye to Lee Ann. "Just remembered, I have someplace to go. Keep smiling, kid. And I hope your bartender shows up."

He left the club and ran across to the Porsche. Catching Coley's telephone call on the *Tashtego* was urgent. If Coley was still tailing Ellie-Jo, he might easily run into Hacker. If Hacker was a killer, Coley could be next.

23

Ellie-Jo had Ziggy pull off I-80 before they had traveled more than a half dozen miles. They pulled into a Denny's restaurant on the outskirts of Reno, and they sat at a corner booth where they could talk privately and still have a view of anyone who might enter the coffee shop.

"Okay, Ziggy. What can you tell me about our Mr. Henri Belanger. First of all, do you suspect he saw you snooping around?"

"Oh, no. I made sure he would never suspect. But he *is* a very observant man. Sometimes he made it difficult. Look what I have for you." He withdrew several folded sheets of yellow legal-size paper from his shirt pocket and unfolded them. They were all neatly hand-lettered with a well-organized listing of Henri Belanger's activities over the past three days.

"Ziggy, you doll. How professional! You should work for the CIA." Ellie-Jo couldn't get over the meticulous detail, all presented chronologically and then summarized at the end of each day. She smiled at the reporting of Belanger going to the men's room on two occasions.

Ziggy watched her face carefully, waiting for her to read about the trysts with the cocktail change girl at a motel down the street from the Golden Palace. If she was in any way upset about that behavior, he could not read it in her expression.

"Do you think he carries a weapon, Ziggy?"

"I'm sure he does. I can tell by the way he wears his jacket. It would be foolish for a man who is taking care of the sheik's money not to. He probably has a permit of some sort. If I suspect that he carries a weapon, the security people in the casino must know about it."

Ellie-Jo marveled at the little man. There was a lot more going on in his brain than most anyone would guess. She read through Ziggy's report again. He had even listed the name of the Heavenly House where Belanger had stopped early one morning.

"Where do you suppose he keeps all the sheik's gambling money?"

"He made several trips to the hotel safe deposit counter. I would imagine that he keeps most of it in the hotel safe so he can draw it out as the sheik needs it. He does carry a large amount of money with him. I saw him wagering heavily at baccarat." Ziggy paused, turning his eyes downward, staring into the cup of coffee.

"Something is bothering you, Ziggy."

"Yes. I was at the hotel for three days. I don't think he noticed me following him. But I can't be absolutely sure. One day he was just strolling around the parking lot. I saw him glance at the blue Mazda. Just for an instant, but he did look at it."

Ellie-Jo reached across the table to hold Ziggy's hands in her own. "I'll tell you what, doll. Your assignment is completed. You've done a fabulous job. I am going to drive you back to the airport right now, and we'll get you on the first plane to New Orleans."

Ziggy beamed with approval of the idea. "Look what I have. In my spare time, I made a list of all the songs I want to play on Flo's piano." He slid the list across to Ellie-Jo. "I will play some of them for you when you come back to New Orleans."

Ellie-Jo found herself wanting to laugh, but she fought the impulse. "Ziggy, that's wonderful. I can't wait!"

His thin face grew solemn again. "How will you get around after I turn in the rental car?"

"That's no problem. I want to use the car for a little while. I'll turn it in when I'm finished."

He looked at her with his dull gray eyes for just a moment. "I guess that will be all right. It drives real well. You'll need to buy gas."

"Okay, let's get you to the airport."

It was almost two o'clock by the time Ziggy was safely on his flight to New Orleans. It was still over four hours before Ellie-Jo would meet Belanger and a little over an hour's driving time to where they would meet. Hacker would probably already be checked in at the Donner View Motel near Truckee. It had been Hacker's idea to meet a few miles north of the Tahoe area to avoid a premature meeting with Belanger. Hacker would want time to go over things.

They had reviewed the plan a half dozen times. Nothing Ziggy had said would change anything. Everything was planned except for the exact location of the meeting with Belanger. The site in the parking area next to State Road 431 would have to be cased.

She drove leisurely along I-80, not wanting to give Hacker any more time with her than necessary. She had decided that a roll in the hay with Hacker, which he would expect, would be unbearable before facing the night's ordeal.

As she drove, she pondered Ziggy's copious notes. Belanger was just another SOB. His trysts with the change girl that Ziggy had reported certainly explained why he hadn't answered the phone the night before. He was just another SOB, and he deserved what he was about to get.

24

The bright warm sunlight and gentle breeze made for a rare Friday in New Orleans. The absence of normal humidity was exhilarating as Flo Dupre walked rapidly from St. Louis Cathedral toward Royal Street. She window-shopped along the rows of antique shops and galleries before turning north toward Bourbon Street. The sidewalks were not yet crowded with the streams of tourists who would be along later.

She remembered the words of her father, repeated many times before he had died. "Steer clear of the French Quarter." He always said that nothing good could come out of spending time in the Quarter. He called it a giant trap, its streets infested with every vice and corruption known to man.

Now she finally believed him, but it was probably too late. She had become immersed in the seamiest part of life in the French Quarter, though she hoped she was streetwise enough to avoid its worst pitfalls.

Six years ago, as a student at Tulane University, she had been amazed by the amount of money she could make just by taking off her clothes. Blessed with a flawless body, she drew top dollar from the clubs along Bourbon Street and, counting tips, could make over five hundred on a single night. Once in a while she supplemented this with carefully screened one-night stands. Always, with the exception of one short-lived phase, she had worked without a pimp.

But it was like rolling dice. She figured she couldn't win forever. Ellie-Jo's successful excursion into the business world gave Flo great hope that she too might one day leave New Orleans and close that door behind her forever. The lying, the drugs, the thuggery, and the disease were all rampant in the Quarter. As careful as she was, she knew that one day she would pay the price.

In some strange way, Ellie-Jo herself had become menacing. Ellie-Jo acted sometimes as if she owned her. She resolved that when she closed the door on New Orleans, she would also close the door on Ellie-Jo.

As she walked toward the Threes Are Wild Club, she began to garner the stares, whistles, and obscenities that went with the territory of a stripper going to work. She never made eye contact, never acted as if she heard any of it. The grossest remark drew no reaction.

As always, Flo chose to ignore those around her as she started to cross Conti Street. But one woman spoke her name. "Flo," she said clearly in a strong voice. "Flo Dupre!"

Flo turned to face a short, squat woman, perhaps in her midforties. Her facial features were pleasant, her graying straight hair trimmed neatly to her collar. She was dressed in a plain, belted, dark dress, full skirted to a point well below her knees. Her round features projected a quiet, friendly demeanor. She could have been a schoolteacher—or a nun out of her habit.

"Excuse me, do we know each other?" Flo asked.

"No, but perhaps we should." The woman hesitated, looking around them. "Can we find a place to talk for a few moments?"

"Look, lady, I really don't have time. I'm on my way to work." Flo looked away and checked the traffic, preparing to cross the street, when the woman touched her arm.

"I'm Mrs. Sammy Lasker." The woman's eyes searched Flo's face.

"Is that supposed to mean something to me?" Flo was at a loss for further words. Ellie-Jo had told her that Lasker was not married.

"Miss Dupre, we both know that the name does mean something to both of us. My Sammy is a very troubled man. He could be a very dangerous man. I would like for you not to see him anymore. No good can come of it."

Flo stepped back from the curb. "Lady . . ." she was trying to think fast. "I don't have any interest at all in your Sammy."

The woman's eyes grew moist. "I want to believe that, but I'm afraid I can't. The French Quarter is like a small town. The gossip flies quickly and people see and hear things." She paused. "You are so beautiful. It is hard to blame my Sammy."

Flo stuck out her hand, feeling a little awkward. "I'm sorry you feel so badly, Mrs. . . . ."

"Please call me Nora. I am Nora Lasker. Sammy has friends who are not nice people. I am telling you this not for my sake, but for yours. If you stay away from him, everything will be fine."

"Thanks for the tip. If I ever run into your Sammy, I'll take your advice."

"It will not be easy. Sammy is very persistent," the woman said flatly.

"Thanks for the advice, Nora. I do have to get to work now." Flo walked away abruptly and crossed the street.

About halfway down the block, she turned. Nora Lasker was still watching. She waved gently, then turned to walk the other way.

Poor woman, Flo thought. It didn't take a genius to discern that Lasker was a heel.

The Threes Are Wild Club had its usual share of customers for a Friday afternoon. There was evidently a football game the next day, and the place was filled with college kids on the prowl. Flo grimaced. A lot of noise, miserable tips. Even though she would get off early, she hated the thought of going through the motions for a bunch of obscene kids.

She did it anyway, as always. The college crowd was loudly appreciative, but they kept their slim wallets in their pockets.

In the middle of her last set, Flo saw Sammy Lasker sitting in the dark corner as usual. She tossed him a smile and slid her tongue lasciviously along her lips. But he continued to stare blankly, not even acknowledging her.

One of the young crowd reached up as Flo turned away and ripped the tiny g-string from her body. The few dollar bills flew into the air. Flo lost her cool, turned sharply, and kicked wildly at the youth, grazing his chin with her dancing shoe. The incensed lad tried to scramble over the bar, while one of his companions held him back by the ankle.

In the corner of the room, Sammy Lasker stood and shouted something in a booming voice. A stocky, bald man in a tank top and jeans sprung from a table near Lasker and was on top of the offending youth in a second. He dug one deep punch into his solar plexus and the youth fell to the floor. The man dragged him to the door and shoved him out onto Bourbon Street.

Sammy Lasker followed Flo into the dressing room. "Come on, kid. Throw some duds on. We're getting out of here."

Flo, still shaking from the unexpected ordeal, felt Lasker's arms around her. "Sammy, who the hell is your bald-headed friend?"

Sammy chuckled. "That's Lazy Boy. He's a nice guy to have around. He was a ranking middleweight once."

"I hope he didn't hurt the kid. He just got carried away. He's not worth any trouble."

"The kid's okay. Lazy Boy could have done him in if he was *really* mad."

Flo wrapped a skirt around herself, then paused in front of a mirror to straighten her hair. Lasker stooped to pick up a small duffle bag he had set down on the floor, then took her by the hand and led her out through the club to the street. They walked a couple of blocks in the growing darkness to Canal Street where Lasker hailed a cab. Within minutes they were seated in a small restaurant in the garden district.

"I've got some good news for your friend, Flo. There will be some big action at the Downs next Saturday. We can all make a bundle."

"That's great, Sammy. You going to share all your good information with us?" Flo thought to herself that it didn't matter anyway, unless it agreed with the information furnished by Ziggy.

Sammy ignored the question. "Hey, I wanna show you something." He reached down for his small leather duffle bag, unzipped it, then quickly glanced around to make sure none of the other diners were watching. "Here, take a look."

Peeking inside, she saw some skimpy lingerie.

"Look underneath," Sammy instructed. Flo moved the lingerie aside, uncovering a pair of handcuffs, a coil of velvet rope, and a small whip. There was other paraphernalia, but Flo quickly closed the bag before taking complete inventory.

"You got the wrong girl, Sammy. In my business, you don't need lash marks and rope burns."

"You got it all backwards, baby. I'm the one who needs the discipline."

"You know, Sammy, you could be right. It'll be my pleasure," Flo said, thinking about her run-in with Nora Lasker. "Now eat your dinner, you crazy bastard."

The dinner seemed to go quickly. Sammy Lasker picked at his shrimp creole and was in a rush to pay the check.

"What's the matter, Sammy?"

"I'm anxious to get started on my proposition."

"What? You're serious about the whips and handcuffs scene."

"Completely serious."

"Your place or mine, Sammy?"

"Let's go to your place. It's close and it's elegant."

And Nora won't be there to get in the way, thought Flo to herself. Actually, Nora might enjoy seeing him get the hell beat out of him. "Okay, let's go. I just can't wait to try on all that outrageous sexy stuff. Did you buy that yourself?"

"Of course I did."

"Are you telling the truth, Sammy?"

"Look, sweetheart, this guy never lies."

"We're going to find out, Sammy."

"How you gonna do that?"

"I'm going to take that whip, and beat the truth right out of you."

"And I'm gonna *love* it." Sammy was starting to perspire. "Why the hell don't you take that last sip of wine, so we can get out of here."

A taxi dropped them at Flo's doorstep. She walked ahead while he took care of the driver. As Flo put the key in the lock, she stopped to listen. The swelling refrain to "Amazing Grace" spilled out from her apartment.

"What the hell is that?" Sammy had stopped behind her.

"What do you know about that, Sammy? Ziggy's back in town."

As they entered the door, Ziggy gave them a quick glance, then went back to his music without even saying hello.

"Well, come on in, doll. He won't bite. In fact, he won't pay the slightest bit of attention to us. We'll have him play something appropriate to accompany our little game."

Once inside, Sammy stared at the little man playing the baby grand. "You know, Flo, I've seen that little guy someplace. I just can't place where. He related to you or something?"

"Of course not. He ran a couple of errands for me one day and then just sat down to play. He's harmless, and he plays fine piano. I like the music, Sammy. Where else can you get your kicks accompanied by the classics?"

Sammy mulled that over as Flo began to disrobe. He noticed that Ziggy seemed oblivious to what was going on. His head was bent down toward the keys.

Flo unzipped the duffle bag and slipped into the flimsy bra and panties, then the garter belt and the long black stockings. For Sammy, watching her dress, each motion slow and deliberate, was as much of a kick as watching her take her clothes off. Flo went into the bedroom and emerged a moment later in six-inch spike heels, whip in hand.

"Is this the way you like me, Sammy?"

"It's outa sight, baby." He was now perspiring freely as Flo menacingly twirled the whip. There was a loud crack as it snaked out and curled around his ankle. Her accuracy was a shock to Sammy. Flo jerked sharply, causing him to tumble to his hands and knees.

"Okay, you bastard! It's time to crawl into the bedroom. It's time to play horsey, Sammy."

"Hey, take it easy!" he gasped.

"Easy ain't my style, you creep." She rapped him soundly on the rump as she rode off into the bedroom, slamming the door behind her.

As the whip cracked over and over again behind the closed door, Ziggy played louder and louder as if trying to drown out the profane mayhem now hidden from his view. He didn't stop until the strange noises stopped coming from behind the closed door. He finished with a rousing rendition of "Piano Man."

Then he rose slowly from the piano and stared for a few moments at the bedroom door. Noiselessly, he lowered the heavy lid over the keys, then walked out the front door, locking it behind him.

25

Coley Doctor circled the parking lot of the Golden Palace several times, looking for the blue Mazda. There was no Siegfried Lemon registered at the hotel. He tried Harrah's and then the other big casinos, one by one, without success. Finally, he returned to the Golden Palace.

He located a public phone in a place where he could keep his eyes on the entrance to the hotel. It was time to call Willy Hanson, though he hated to call with no real news.

Willy picked up the phone after the second ring. "Hey, pal, it's about time you called. Where are you?"

"The Golden Palace Hotel in Tahoe. Fancy joint. Some Arab potentate just checked in with an entourage that looks like something out of a movie. There's a couple of babes tagging along who could have me if they played their cards right."

"Coley, do you realize that Hacker could well be cruising around there in his Bronco?"

"Why do you say that?"

"Because Lee Ann told me that Hacker took the day off and drove north in the Bronco. She is really pissed off, by the way, that her bartender didn't show up. You may have blown your new career already. What in the hell are you doing at the Golden Palace?"

Coley told Willy the whole story of Ellie-Jo and Siegfried Lemon. "They evidently drove to Tahoe in the Mazda. I gave the plate numbers to the rental-car gal, who said they were headed for the Golden Palace. Lemon had rented the car. But they sure ain't here."

"So why the hell don't you get back down here before Hacker spots you?"

"Because the lead isn't stone cold yet. This Siegfried Lemon showed a Louisiana driver's license when he rented the Mazda three days ago. The sweet little rental agent gave me the New Orleans address. Next stop—New Orleans."

"Coley, I want you back in LA first. We've got some talking to do. We haven't got a damn thing yet that we can take to the police."

"I'm going to pussyfoot around Tahoe tonight and fly back in the morning. I got this big Caddy with dark windows that match my complexion perfectly. If Hacker's around, he won't see me."

"Where are you staying?"

"In the Caddy. Don't worry, I won't charge you for one of these fancy rooms."

Willy hung up dejectedly. The New Orleans thing could mean absolutely nothing. Ellen Lambert could know people all over the country. Hacker might just be on a fishing trip. Maybe none of it had anything to do with Lefty Grogan. Maybe he should just confront Hacker and Ellie-Jo face to face and get it over with. He could do it in some public place, watch their reaction and take it from there.

He'd bounce the feeble idea off Coley the next time he talked to him.

26

It was almost dark before Ellie-Jo reached State Road 431 where it intersected with the shore road along the lake. She drove into the strip mall and slowly passed by the ice cream shop. Parked just outside was Henri Belanger's Cadillac.

She could see the outline of Belanger inside. She stopped directly behind him and rolled down her window. Belanger quickly got out of his car and walked toward her.

"Hi, princess! I was beginning to wonder if you had developed a case of cold feet."

"Not on your life, doll. You're stuck with me tonight." Ellie-Jo got out of the car and greeted him with a fierce hug and a probing kiss. He returned her embrace, burying a kiss into the hollow of her neck.

"Mmm . . . Now that's the kind of a welcome I like. Say, are you going to buy me an ice cream cone?"

"I have wine, and cheese, and a Peking duck prepared by the sheik's chef just this morning."

"That beats the hell out of an ice cream cone. Let me park this silly little car and we'll go somewhere and pop the cork." Ellie-Jo noticed him staring at her blue Mazda. She looked up and down the parking area. "I'll tell you what. See way down near the end where there are hardly any cars? I'll go down there and park. Pick me up there. Okay? The car ought to be okay until morning."

"Brilliant," he said with a hint of concern in his voice. "Lead the way."

Ellie-Jo climbed back into her car and moved slowly toward the end of the parking area that abutted a grove of tall pines. Belanger followed close behind. She nosed into the pine grove alongside a Bronco, the only other vehicle around.

"Henri! Just a minute, I've lost an earring." Ellie-Jo got out of the car and began searching the seat and the floor mat. "Oh damnit, Henri, it's a diamond."

Belanger waited for just a moment, then decided to help her. As he turned to open the door, he was met by the butt of a small handgun that cracked hard across his face.

"Move over you bastard, and don't say a word."

Stunned and recoiling in sharp pain, Belanger managed to slip one hand into his jacket pocket and fire one shot from a small automatic.

The return fire from Hacker's silencer-fitted .22 struck Belanger squarely between the eyes. Shoving furiously at the dying Belanger, he pushed the dead weight of his body into the passenger side of the Cadillac and climbed behind the wheel. It was not until he had pulled onto the shore road that he felt the aching shoulder where Belanger's one shot had struck him.

Cursing aloud, he glanced in the rearview mirror and saw Ellie-Jo behind him. He steered the Cadillac onto the side road they had selected earlier in the day. He drove through the woods to the very edge of a sheer drop to the lake, a few hundred feet below. He stripped Belanger of the contents of his pockets and then began systematically searching the car.

In the trunk, he found a heavy vinyl shopping bag and a small leather briefcase that was locked. He set these aside on the ground, then reached into the front, flipped the gear shift of the big Cadillac, and watched it begin to roll.

The car smashed noisily once against a projection of the cliff below, the echo resounding against the surrounding mountains. The Caddy then splashed into the lake and disappeared.

Within seconds, Ellie-Jo had driven them back to the main shore road, and they were leisurely on their way to the wooded parking area where they had left Hacker's Bronco.

Hacker, still cursing, was pulling at his sweatshirt, now blotched with his own blood. "That son of a bitch shot me, Ellie-Jo, and that's a fact."

"Try not to bleed on the car, Hacker. It could cause problems later on," Ellie-Jo said, quietly wishing that the wound would be fatal.

"It was so stupid, Ellie-Jo. It was so stupid. I tried to knock him out, but the son of a bitch was still conscious. I should have shot him first, Ellie-Jo, and that's a fact."

"It would have been better my way. Now they'll know he didn't drown."

"Suppose they'll find him?"

"I think it's a sure thing, Hacker. You better pitch that gun as soon as you get a chance. Look what's coming."

A fire truck and a police car moved past them with lights flashing. Somebody had probably heard the crash. But, thought Ellie-Jo, with the Caddy deep in the lake, they had plenty of time to get away.

Within minutes, Ellie-Jo was back at the small strip mall near Hacker's Bronco. She pulled into a parking spot where the light from the outside shone into the Mazda.

"Okay, Hacker, let's see the shoulder." She quickly examined the gouge in the flesh. "You're gonna live. It looks like the shot went right through the muscle and came out the other side. You'll have to get it tended to back in LA. I don't think it would be a good idea around here."

"That bastard! You just can't trust some people, Ellie-Jo."

Ellie-Jo gave up trying to unravel Hacker's peculiar logic as he continued to ramble. He had lost some blood. She decided that maybe he couldn't bleed like that all the way to LA, after all.

"Hacker, can you drive?"

"Of course I can drive. You know that. You going nuts, Ellie-Jo?"

"Then get in the Bronco and follow me. It's about an hour to Reno. I think it would be a good idea to put some distance between us and Tahoe. We'll check into a motel in Reno, clean up your shoulder and count the loot."

Hacker started to calm down a little. "I like the part about checking into a motel, Ellie-Jo. We need to relax. Ole Hacker needs a little, if you know what I mean."

She stared in wonder at her personal killing machine. After all that had happened, all he could think of was a roll in the sack.

"Not tonight, Hacker. And that's a fact."

Hacker forced a near-grin. "We'll see, Ellie-Jo. We'll see about that later."

Ellie-Jo led the way in the Mazda. Hacker followed, too close for comfort once in a while. Now and then, as they descended the winding mountain road toward Reno, he would drift from one lane to another. She decided that if the highway patrol pulled him over, he would face the music alone.

She selected a small motel just inside the city limits. She rented the room herself, telling the bloodstained Hacker to stay in the Bronco. He parked the Bronco next to the Mazda in front of their room, then bounded out of the vehicle with surprising energy. If the gunshot wound was bothering him now, he gave no indication of it. Hacker was as hard as nails.

"Where did you put the briefcase and the rest of the stuff I gave you?"

"It's all in the back seat, Hacker. I'll get it." She tossed him the key to the room and followed him, carrying the briefcase, the large vinyl bag, and the paper sack that Hacker had used to hold the contents of Belanger's pockets.

Once inside, Ellie-Jo set all the stuff on a small desk. The paper bag felt heavy. Peeking inside, she saw Belanger's gun, along with a wallet, a pocket diary, and several bits of paper.

"Of all the stupid things, Hacker, why did you take his gun?"

Hacker shrugged, wincing slightly at the pain from the shoulder. "You never know when you might need another gun, Ellie-Jo. And that's a fact."

She stared at him and wondered if they would ever distance themselves from this mess. "That was damn foolish. If you would have left the gun in the car and they couldn't find the bullet they might have thought it was suicide. Be sure to get rid of the gun, someplace where it won't be found."

Hacker was stripping the bloody shirt from his body. The wound looked ugly, but the bullet had apparently missed hitting any bone.

"Maybe there's a convenience store or drug store near here. That shoulder ought to be washed out with peroxide and bandaged."

"It will be fine. I'll wash it with tap water and use a towel for a bandage. I've had worse things happen."

"I'll bet you have, Hacker. Well, let's count the loot. I hope Belanger was preparing for a big night. He was going to teach me baccarat."

She tossed Belanger's wallet to Hacker. It contained about fifteen hundred dollars, mostly in hundreds. Hacker stuffed the money into his pocket and flipped the wallet back on the table. "That's chicken feed, Ellie-Jo. Let's see what's in the briefcase."

The briefcase was unusually heavy for its small size. Probably lined with some kind of metal, Ellie-Jo figured. Four small cylinders operated a combination lock. Ellie-Jo fingered them thoughtfully. "Hacker, you got a crowbar in the Bronco?"

Hacker snatched the briefcase from her hands, put it on the floor, and kicked it hard several times with his heel. The leather gave way, revealing a shiny heavy-guage metal. "We'll need a crowbar. I'll go out to the Bronco."

Ellie-Jo peeked into the vinyl shopping bag. There were two bottles of wine, several packages of cheese, some bread, and the cold Peking duck. She was thinking about what might have been when Hacker walked in with a toolbox and locked the door behind him.

Opening the briefcase took some time, but Hacker finally forced a heavy chisel into the seam, popping the lock. Inside were two envelopes. Hacker scowled at Ellie-Jo, realizing it looked like a depressing payday after all.

He ripped one envelope and a packet of one-hundred-dollar bills tumbled out. There were a hundred of them, ten thousand dollars. The other envelope contained papers having to do with the hotel and safe deposit box, along with an accounting sheet on which Belanger had entered a withdrawal of ten thousand dollars against a balance of three quarters of a million.

"Ten thousand dollars! All that trouble for ten thousand dollars. You said it would be a big payday, Ellie-Jo. This is bullshit! What's in the shopping bag?"

"A duck dinner, Hacker. It was prepared by the sheik's chef especially for me and Belanger. I'll share it with you if you cool down. Take off your clothes, take a shower, and clean yourself up. You're a stinking mess. I'm not crawling in the sack with you like that."

Hacker gave her a blank stare. "Hey, now you're talking my language, baby."

"That's better, Hacker. Now take your shower. You've got blood all over your side. That isn't a bit sexy. You know how I get turned on every time you kill somebody, Hacker. Now hurry with the shower."

Ellie-Jo waited until she heard the shower door close and the water turn on. She picked up her purse and took Belanger's gun from the desk. She would drop it in some rubbish bag somewhere.

She rapidly penned Hacker a short note. "Go out on the town and get laid. Lots of bimbos in Reno will do all kinds of crazy things for ten grand. I've got a splitting headache, Hacker. See you in LA."

Ellie-Jo fired up the blue Mazda and headed for the airport, hoping that she would find a late flight to Los Angeles. If there wasn't one, she decided she would take a late flight to almost anywhere in order to put some distance between her and Hacker.

Back at Lake Tahoe, Coley had spent the last several hours methodically searching the strip of casinos and restaurants that ran along the shore road next to the lake. Covering both sides of the street on foot, he had worked his way back to the Golden Palace. Tahoe wasn't really that big. He felt that the search had been thorough, but it was still possible that he had missed them.

He had spotted several blue Mazdas, but none with Siegfried Lemon's plate number. And dazzled as he was by the number of good-looking women living it up in the casinos, none of them resembled Ellie-Jo.

Entering the Golden Palace, he boldly took another walking tour of the casino, peeking in all the nooks and corners. Finally, he bought a couple of rolls of quarters and positioned himself at a video poker machine with a good view of the hotel's entrance and registration desk.

Another hour passed. It was now 11:00 P.M. He hadn't seen Siegfried Lemon or Ellie-Jo since well before noon at the Reno airport.

Suddenly, his attention was diverted by a loud and animated discussion going on in the area of the reservation desk. A dazzlingly attractive woman and several swarthy, dark-haired men in dark silk suits seemed to be arguing with the hotel manager. The manager was standing at one of the computers, searching for some information.

Out of boredom, Coley strolled over near the group. He pretended to be studying an airline timetable he had pulled from his pocket.

"I am Orchid Belanger," he heard the woman declare in a loud voice. "I am Henri Belanger's wife. I

167

was not expected until tomorrow. I demand access to my husband's room. We have tried to reach him for hours. He may be in some kind of trouble."

The manager, nodding, was still staring at the computer.

Coley studied the three men surrounding the woman. Their jackets bulged suspiciously, suggesting that they were security men.

The manager was now introducing the group to a uniformed member of the hotel security force. Coley wandered closer.

"Mrs. Belanger, our man here will accompany you to Mr. Belanger's room. You will see for yourself that it is unoccupied. I am sorry for the delay, but I am sure you can appreciate our wish to be extremely careful about access to our guest rooms. Here is the key-card to the room. We regret that we were unaware you would be joining Mr. Belanger. Perhaps it is our mistake."

"Thank you," the woman said icily. "The sheik will hear of this inconvenience." The group walked toward the elevator.

Coley approached the distraught manager. "The beautiful lady was very excited. I want to congratulate you on your tact."

"Thank you, sir. A large party moved in from one of the emirates today, and they have our whole staff jumping. Can I help you, sir?"

"I need a room for this evening. Something with a king-size bed."

"All of our beds are king-sized, sir. The trouble is that we just don't have any rooms available. I'm sorry." The man turned and walked away.

Coley groaned and walked back to the video poker machine where he could sit and continue his vigil. It had its plusses. The change girl had gorgeous legs.

27

Armand Hauser was both perplexed and delighted by the fax he received from Reno. It was the first time Ellen Lambert had communicated with him on a weekend. He wondered what she was doing in Reno. Waterfront, Inc., didn't have a unit there. Somehow, Reno didn't seem like Ellen's kind of town. He read the short fax again:

> Armand dear: How about doing the unit in San Clemente tonight? I'll break my Saturday rule. We'll scout the restaurant and then, dear, there is a wonderful little beach cove near San Onofre. I'll be looking for you around six. Leave a message if you can't make it. Please don't disappoint me, Armand.

It was Saturday morning and the fabulous Ellen Lambert was at loose ends for Saturday night. He wondered how she would react if he told her he couldn't make it. He decided to accept the invitation. A broad smile refused to be held in check as he looked into the mirror.

Armand was sitting in the office of the temporary quarters he had rented in Marina Del Rey. He couldn't remember giving Ellen his fax number. In fact, he had only given it to a couple of unit managers for their use on the weekend to keep him up-to-date, so he could go into the office on Monday well prepared.

He picked up the phone to make reservations in San Clemente, but he quickly remembered what Ellen had said about surprising everyone by walking in unexpected.

Strange woman, he thought. He ran his hand through his hair, recalling the sand he had brought home from the beach off Santa Barbara. His shoes had been full of it. His clothes also. For a moment, he felt a pang of jealousy. He wondered how often and with whom Ellen Lambert let her hair down.

He called her home number but had to settle for the answering machine. He told her he would pick her up at six. It had been over ten hours since she communicated from Reno.

He spread out a map of southern California over his desk. San Onofre was quite a distance south. Armand had several errands to run, the usual Saturday things, like cleaning, laundry, and a trip to the market. He decided to get them out of the way and drive to Santa Monica early in the afternoon. The area was completely unknown to him, so he would locate her condo ahead of time and arrive later on right on the dot of 6:00 P.M.

He worked at his chores through noon, then found

himself driving past Ellen Lambert's condo in Santa Monica about three o'clock.

He turned around on San Vincente and proceeded slowly back past the condo again. He decided to kill some time at the Waterfront, Inc., restaurant in Redondo Beach. He wanted to get to know most of the local managers and their units well.

About a half a block ahead of him a motorcycle eased into the circular driveway in front of the condo. There were two people aboard. A leggy woman in a tank top and jeans held her arms tightly around the waist of her muscular male partner.

Drawing nearer, he could see a bulky bandage that wrapped the upper arm and right shoulder of the muscular driver. The woman dismounted, shoved her dark glasses back onto her hair and kissed her companion quickly on the lips, molding her body close to his for a moment. The man rested his hands casually on her hips. She moved away, waved goodbye, and walked rapidly toward the doorway of the building.

Armand slowed down and stared, flabbergasted. It was Ellen Lambert! Her face, her figure, and the long mane of auburn hair were unmistakeable. It brought back the vivid memory of their night on the beach when she had let her hair down from the restraining string of pearls.

He drove past as she entered her doorway. He observed the biker in his rearview mirror as he pulled out of the driveway. A few moments later the biker roared past him. The dark, swarthy man in a Raiders ball cap had angular features and what looked like several days' growth of dark beard. His green T-shirt looked filthy. Several quarter-sized spots of blood had soaked through a heavy bandage that extended over his shoulder.

Armand sped ahead, trying to keep Ellen Lambert's

unlikely looking companion within view, but the biker quickly lost himself, weaving and speeding through the heavy traffic.

Armand felt baffled by the scene. It wasn't seeing Ellen Lambert with her hair down. He'd seen that before. It wasn't even the motorcycle. He understood that Ellen had an adventurous spirit.

It was the man. It was the grim, menacing look of the man that seemed so incompatible with the sleek, groomed Ellen Lambert that Armand knew.

He looked at his watch. He had almost three hours to kill before picking her up. There was no way he could satisfy his curiosity unless she brought up her penchant for motorcycles. He resolved to think of a way to do that.

She had kissed the guy. Armand shrugged as he drove. Hell, it seemed like everybody kissed everybody these days. He couldn't draw any conclusions from that. It was the rest of her body language that bothered him most, the way she had permitted the man the fleeting touch of her hips.

28

Sammy Lasker awoke in his own bed plagued by a throbbing headache and a parched throat. Groaning, he made a move to get into a sitting position, but found it impossible. He stared at the leather restraints binding his wrists, each trailing a heavy cord secured to the opposite bedposts. He jerked his arms sharply to no avail. The door to the bedroom was slightly ajar, permitting entry of a shaft of light from the adjoining room.

"Sammy dear, are you awake?" A soft voice came from outside the room.

The persistent throb of his headache made it difficult to think. "What in the hell is going on," he mumbled. Now, slightly more alert, he confirmed that he was in his bedroom, in his own house. The early part of the past evening began to come back to him. The last memories he could resurrect were of Flo—and the whip.

He groaned again and tried to touch the thin lash marks on his chest. He pictured vividly in his mind the image of Flo, in her house. And there had been that crazy piano player pounding away in the next room. Now he had fully regained his wits. But what was he doing lashed to his own bed? He reeked of bourbon and the now sickening aftertaste of pernod.

The voice came again. "Sammy dear, I know you are awake. I can hear you. Just a moment, dear, and I'll be ready."

"My God!" he gasped aloud. It was Nora. He was lashed to his own bed in his own house, with Nora.

This time it was Nora, his own sweet wife Nora, who entered their bedroom carrying an ornate, ivory-handled riding crop. Her short-legged figure, lacking the erotic perfection of Flo, was corseted in the tight garb of a dominatrix, complete with black hose and high heels.

He flailed his legs, trying to rise, only to discover they too were held securely to the bedframe by restraints. "Nora! What in the hell is going on here? Have you gone completely crazy?"

She let the knotted leather tips of the riding crop trail across his abdomen and then downward, with a deft feather touch, as he cringed, expecting a whack from the whip.

"Sammy dear, I think it's time to talk. Remember how it used to be, Sammy? I mean before we were married? We just couldn't get enough of each other, could we?"

"It was great, wasn't it, Nora?" he stammered.

Whack! She lashed out with a snap of the riding crop that left a red line on his thigh. Then she watched him twist on the bed.

"Sammy dear. Poor Sammy. You were never very good at grammar. You used the wrong tense. You said 'was' instead of 'is'." Nora punctuated her remark with another sharp crack of the whip across his bare feet, then sat down on the edge of their bed. "Sammy, I guess it is just a classic case of poor communication. You should have told me just what goes on in that rotten mind of yours. I love you, Sammy. You don't have to run off to your sleazy stripper to satisfy your perverted fantasies." She leaned over his tense form and kissed him wetly on the chest, then smiled up into his wide eyes. "Shame on you. I can do everything Flo Dupre can do, and I can do it better, Sammy."

"Nora, please stop it. I can't believe that you are playing this silly game. Have you gone crazy?" He looked pleadingly at her, but his own arousal gave him away.

"Shut up, Sammy. We are going to be here for a very long time. When I finish with you, you will be of no use to Miss Dupre." Nora stood again and trailed the knotted throngs lightly down his body. "Tell me. Do you have a date with her tonight? Are you picking her up again at the Threes Are Wild Club?"

"Of course not. What the hell has gotten into you Nora?"

The whip lashed out again, this time a stinging streak across his chest.

"Oh, my poor Sammy. You are lying again. You are being so naughty. You'd better stop lying, Sammy. We are both going to stay right here until I *beat* all the lies out of you."

Sammy Lasker stared at Nora in fear. He had never remotely envisioned her like this. He didn't know what to expect. Maybe she had really snapped and gone mad.

Nora climbed on the bed again and straddled him. "My Sammy is a fool. But he is still my Sammy. Everyone in the French Quarter knows about Flo, and the money she makes from her little specialties. Did you expect me not to find out, Sammy?"

His hangover was pounding in his head. "I'm sorry, Nora. I'm really sorry. Flo means nothing to me."

"Are you lying again, my sweet?"

"No! No, it will always be just you and me, baby. You know that."

Nora tossed the riding crop onto the floor. She bent over to kiss his lips, letting her tongue linger as she stared at him. "Oh well, Sammy. That's good to hear, but I guess it doesn't matter anyway. By the time I finish with you, there will be nothing left for her. That's the way it's going to be every day, from now on. I'm not the one who's crazy, my sweet."

"Nora, untie me."

"Not a chance, lover. I will do anything you want me to do, except untie you." She put her weight heavily on his chest.

"You win, Nora."

"Then, Sammy, let us begin. What shall we do first?"

29

Coley's eyes flickered open. The sun was high in the sky. He lay slumped behind the dark windows of his rental Cadillac. As he stretched his large frame and prepared to get out of the car, he became aware of a large commotion in front of the Golden Palace. Several police cars were lined up, all with lights flashing. He got out of the car, stretched again, and walked toward the activity.

The attractive woman who had suffered the altercation at the hotel desk the night before emerged from the hotel accompanied by two of her burly, but immaculately dressed, bodyguards. The woman dabbed at her eyes with a handkerchief as the threesome was escorted to a police car. Then the sheik himself appeared with a policeman who seemed to be in charge of the group. They chatted with those inside the police car for a few moments, then walked back into the hotel. Two of the police cars moved slowly from the parking area and headed north along the shore road with lights flashing.

Coley walked inside the Golden Palace where a number of people huddled around the sheik who was talking excitedly in his native language. Coley spied the change girl with the dazzling legs. He had befriended her the night before during his vigil in the casino. She was sober-faced now, dabbing at her eyes with a cocktail napkin.

"Hey, doll, what's going on here?" he asked.

"Oh, it's terrible. The sheik's son-in-law ran his car off a cliff into the lake last night. They are going to watch them pull it out of the water."

"Was he killed?" Coley asked.

"They think so. I hear that he did not return to the hotel last night. He was such a nice man."

"Oh, you knew him?" Coley watched as the tears trickled from the corners of her eyes. "I'm sorry."

"He was a very big tipper, whether he won or not. He was such a fine man. He treated me like a queen."

Coley watched the woman carefully. He decided she and the man must have exchanged more than rolls of coins.

"Well, look, try to calm down. Maybe he wasn't killed."

"I heard one of the police say that there is someone in the car. It is evidently under about thirty feet of water. The lake is very clear, you know. I guess they can see him."

"Well, let's hope for the best. Maybe it's someone else down there."

"I hope so. He gave me a hundred dollars just to stay near him in the casino."

"Wow! That is generous. The sheik and his people must be loaded. What did you say his name was?"

"Henri Belanger. He was a Frenchman who married

the sheik's daughter. He was so nice to me, if you know what I mean."

"Oh, come on now, you're a knockout. I'll bet everyone is nice to you."

For the first time the woman smiled warmly at Coley. "Are you staying at the Golden Palace?"

"I'm afraid not. In fact I'm heading back to LA today. Next time I come to Tahoe, though, I'll look you up. I promise I'll buy all my rolls of dollars from you. And if I hit the jackpot, I'll split it with you."

"Hey, that's a good deal. Just ask around for Carla." Grinning broadly, she walked back toward her station on the casino floor.

Coley watched the spirited movement of her hips and her nyloned legs until she disappeared into the growing crowd. Carla, he thought to himself, I'll have to tuck that away into my active file.

The drive to Reno's Cannon Airport was a pleasant one. The dazzling sunlight and light traffic made it a fabulous day for looking at the rugged, spectacular scenery. Soon, the winding road broke free of the mountains, and all of Reno was sprawled out below. Coley, dogged by a night of fitful sleep in the Cadillac, found himself continually fighting off sleep. He lowered the windows to inhale the fresh, cool, mountain air.

He felt that he had wasted valuable time. If Hacker, Ellie-Jo, and the little Siegfried Lemon had gone to Tahoe, they had certainly managed to hide well. He had covered the rim of Tahoe like a blanket, several times. The resort community was really not that difficult to scour. All the big clubs were along one street stretching for only a short distance. He had walked the entire area by foot.

He rolled into the rental car return, parked the car,

179

and, finding no attendant, headed for the counter inside to check in.

"Sandra, you've been waiting for me." He smiled broadly. "How considerate of you. You must work around the clock."

"How's your chipmunk ranch?" she asked, reaching for his rental contract and beaming her Avis commercial smile.

"Great! Those little devils multiply like rabbits wish they could. I'm gonna have millions."

"You didn't run into your friend in the Mazda you were looking for, did you?"

"What makes you think I didn't?" Coley waited patiently while she fed the computer the data on his contract.

"Because it was turned in last night about midnight, right before I got off duty. Hey, that was some classy lady. Now I know why you were so anxious to find your friend."

"Siegfried Lemon was a lady?"

"No, it was turned in for him by a lady who had all the guys around here running out of control." Sandra smiled as she handed Coley his receipt.

"Long auburn hair, way down the back?"

"Yeah. She a movie star or something?"

"Nah, she's a chipmunk farmer too. I'm tryin' to teach her how to do it right."

"I bet you are, Mr. Doctor. So when are you going to see us again in Reno?"

"Soon, I hope. You gonna save a car for me?"

"Just let me know, Mr. Doctor."

As Coley ascended the escalator to the terminal, his mind was racing with thoughts of Ellie-Jo. She had evidently been in town only about twelve hours. She hadn't even stayed overnight. Maybe she was a gambler and got tapped out before she even checked into a room. It happened. But what had happened to Siegfried Lemon of New Orleans?

He wondered how long Willy would want to pursue the investigation. Willy was right—for all their efforts, they still had absolutely nothing they could take to the police.

30

Armand Hauser arrived at Ellen Lambert's condo at six o'clock sharp. He entered the vestibule and found a building attendant seated at a small podium.

"Hello, I'm Armand Hauser, here for Ellen Lambert."

The attendant was young. He wore a neatly pressed khaki uniform with short sleeves. He greeted Armand cordially, smiling as he asked him to sign a visitors' list.

"Miss Lambert is expecting you. She asks that you come right up to fourteen-C. The elevator is just around that corner."

Armand had fully expected Ellen to join him in the lobby. As the elevator ascended, he wondered if the raunchy-looking fellow had ever made the trip up to 14C. He knocked on the door, which was slightly ajar.

"Come in, Armand. I'll be with you in a minute."

Entering, he found himself in a foyer, just off a spacious living room. It was all elegantly furnished, but a little frilly for his taste. The drapes were drawn wide, offering a spectacular view all the way to the beach fronting Santa Monica. A few lights were beginning to twinkle on in the distance, and he imagined that it must be an incredible view after dark. He could hear Ellen talking on a telephone in an adjacent room, but could not hear what was said.

When Ellen Lambert finally entered the living room, she very nearly took his breath away. "Armand, you are so punctual. I'll bet you're perfect at everything." She wore a black knit miniskirt with a loose silk jacket, also black but with an overlay of faint silvery print. Her mane of auburn hair was secured in a large bun, wrapped tightly with the usual string of pearls.

"Ellen, you look dazzling."

She embraced him gently and kissed him squarely on the lips, pausing for nearly two full seconds (as she almost always did). "Armand, I've missed you. I'm so happy that you could make it on such short notice. Something has come up that is so exciting I have trouble keeping it to myself. The sooner you know all about it the better. Sheldon Blake will meet us in San Clemente and tell you all about it."

"Sheldon Blake?" Armand felt his spirits sink. He hadn't been told that their evening together would include the chairman of the board of Waterfront, Inc.

"Oh, Armand, don't look so disappointed. We will have our time alone later. You poor dear. Shame on you, Armand. I hope you never play poker. You'd never fool anyone." She kissed him again and walked toward the door.

Armand could only smile. "Believe me, Ellen, I have no objection to having dinner with Sheldon. If I had known this was to be a business meeting, I would have come more prepared. That's all."

"You are prepared, dear. All you have to do is listen." Smiling warmly, she turned to face him in the descending elevator. "Sheldon is an early-to-bed guy. He will have one cocktail, order dinner, make his little speech, and then leave us before dessert. How's that?"

"I say it's wonderful. And I must say further that I am on pins and needles as to what this is all about. I feel very flattered that it includes me."

"That's more like it, Armand. All I can tell you is that we are an unbeatable team, and we are going on an adventure together. Sheldon Blake must tell you the rest."

Armand drove his own car. Ellen Lambert turned slightly toward him, crossing one leg under herself. The abbreviated skirt permitted no attempt at modesty. Armand decided that he liked that.

"Armand, have you visited the San Clemente unit yet?"

"As a matter of fact, I haven't. The numbers look very good, though. They must be doing something right down there." He merged into an on-ramp for the San Diego Freeway, got up to the full speed of the freeway traffic, and maneuvered expertly into the fast lane.

"Well done, Armand. You are already adjusted to our insane driving habits. Out here, aggressive drivers get where they want to go. I guess that applies to other things as well. If you don't take charge, you might as well drop out of the game."

"Ellen, then you will be in the game forever. All those people at Waterfront, Inc., hang on your every word. Tell me, does Sheldon Blake ever disagree with you?" He glanced at her and flushed slightly. The leggy display wasn't fair in a serious conversation.

"Of course he disagrees with me . . . frequently. He's the boss. But even if he disagrees, he never overrules me publicly. He has a talent for projecting his opinions through extended conversation. He might try to change my mind and sometimes succeeds. But he never dictates orders."

"Ah, there's a smart man. He appreciates talent."

"Do you think I'm talented, Armand?"

"Of course!"

"At what?

He glanced at her again. Now an enigmatic smile played along her lips. She was teasing him . . . or was she? "I am certain that you have a flair for handling the manpower that works for you. You also have a magnificent talent for making optimal use of public beaches."

"Armand! Shame on you! One mustn't talk about such things, you just do them!"

"Sorry, I couldn't resist saying that. I was just trying to be candid. Don't worry, I'll behave." He rested his hand on the armrest between them. She responded by clasping her hand over his.

The traffic began to slow down as the weekend traffic along the shore became heavy. From time to time a motorcycle weaved between lanes at high speed.

"Now if we were on one of those things, we would get there much faster, wouldn't we?" Armand hoped to draw comment from her.

"No thanks! People who ride them have some sort of death wish. That nonsense is not for me."

Near San Clemente, Armand abandoned the freeway and picked up the Pacific Coast Highway heading south. Soon, Ellen pointed to a road leading toward a cliff abutting the shoreline. A soft blue neon sign read "Waterfront, Inc.," scrawled in script. The building itself was scarcely visible, below the edge of the sprawling parking lot and on the very face of the steep cliff below. Armand followed the arrow to a parking valet area where they got out of the car.

"Good evening, Miss Lambert. Mr Blake arrived just a few minutes ago. He said you would find him at the bar."

"Sounds good to me. Thank you, Alex."

It was obvious to Armand that Ellen Lambert and Sheldon Blake were well known here.

Ellen touched Armand's arm as they entered the building. "I want you to take careful note of everything here tonight. Sheldon and I think that this is our number one unit, and should be used as a template for other units. The numbers are not only good, as you said before, but everything else about it works. Sometimes we are booked weeks in advance."

Armand was impressed. The ambiance was spectacular. They went directly to the long bar where Sheldon Blake sat awaiting them. Smiling broadly, he hugged Ellen and then extended his hand to Armand.

"You're right on time," he said, glancing at his watch. "Good. We can get to our table right now and get down to business." He turned to Ellen. "You haven't told Armand the big news, have you?"

"Of course not, Sheldon. I want to see the look on his face at the same time you do. Besides, I know very little about it, you know."

Armand's interest was certainly piqued. He followed Ellen and Sheldon through the long dining room to a corner table overlooking the steep cliff to the beach. Frothy whitecaps crashed in a steady procession from the Catalina Channel.

"Magnificent," murmured Armand, as the three of them paused to gaze at the view.

"Yes, it is, my friends," Sheldon agreed. "But after this evening, I hope you will be convinced that it cannot only be matched, but beaten."

Sheldon Blake had a roll of what looked like blueprints, which he stood up on end in the corner next to

their table. Dinner was served swiftly, since Blake
had ordered a mix of house specialties in advance.

Dinner conversation revolved mostly around food.
Armand was queried in depth about his years as a
chef and then in management in Galveston. Once
their table was finally cleared, Sheldon Blake rolled
the blueprints out for them to scrutinize.

Blake launched into his presentation. The first page
of the blueprint was a floor plan for a gigantic restaurant. Though much larger, the layout bore a strong resemblance to the Waterfront, Inc., unit they were now
sitting in.

"Picture out these windows, if you can," started
Sheldon, "mountains across a wide span of water." He
pointed to one lengthy side of the floor plan in the blueprint. "Picture on this side a skyline that runs on for
twenty miles. Picture directly in front of you the most
heavily trafficked harbor in the world. Picture over
here, on a clear day, a glimpse of the largest undevel-
oped marketplace known to man. Picture millions of
people all around you who would give almost anything
to eat in a restaurant just like this one." Sheldon Blake
paused dramatically. "And what do you have?"

"Hong Kong." Armand spoke tentatively. "It could
be several places, but it is probably Hong Kong."

"Excellent! Armand, have you been there?" Sheldon
asked.

"No sir, I'm afraid it was a lucky guess."

"We have secured a long lease near Harbour City,
right on Victoria Harbour, just a few blocks off Nathan Road in Kowloon, Hong Kong."

Both Ellen and Armand listened in silence.

"I have been there many times," Blake continued.
"It has to be the best location in the world. It will be
a ten million dollar project. I want you, Armand, and
Ellen to go over there for four to six months and put

it together personally. Frankly, I expect you to open in four months."

Armand's mind was racing. "Four months," he echoed, shaking his head. "According to my reading of trade journals, Mr. Blake, there are a lot fine restaurants in Hong Kong."

"You are right, Armand. But there are none to compare with Waterfront, Inc. Oriental food has captured America. Now it is time for us to win over the diners in Hong Kong. You know, a Chicago steak house is located very near where we will be. It's been a smash. Our seafood restaurant will be even more successful. It will be the flagship of Waterfront, Inc."

Sheldon Blake stood up, preparing to leave. "I am going to let you two think this over together. I want you in Hong Kong within two or three weeks to start setting things up, so I want your decision within two days. If either of you decides not to go, I'll need your recommendations for others who might be suitable."

"Mr. Blake, I think this would be the most exciting challenge I have ever faced." Armand was talking as he continued to study the blueprints. "I'll get back to you within a day or so."

Ellen Lambert was unusually quiet. She had not expected Blake to set a deadline. "I may need to be here a week or two beyond your two-week departure date. But after that, I'm with you all the way."

Blake frowned for just a second or so, then turned on a smile. "Sounds like you're both behind me. Put your thinking caps on, and get back to me officially next week." Blake bade them farewell, picked up the roll of blueprints, and strode out of the restaurant.

Ellen and Armand sat down again and quietly sipped the remains of their after-dinner brandy.

"I am rather surprised, Ellen, that he would ask

you to go over there and head up this project. Who'll watch over the big picture back in the office?"

"Oh, that's really no problem. Things are in good order here. Sheldon can watch over things for a while. It is not unusual for management to oversee the opening of a new unit. It's usually for a few weeks though, rather than a few months."

Armand studied her closely. She seemed pensive, hesitant. "Something wrong, Ellen? Do you have some reservations about the project?"

"No. If Waterfront is going to spend ten million over there, I damn well better go. Actually, it looks like a winner. Blake has a feel for these things. He has spent a lot of time over there. If he says ten million now, it very likely may end up at twelve or fifteen. Armand, it should be a blast over there. Do you think you could stand me for six months?"

"Of course. Longer, if necessary. I'm ready to leave within a few days!" He watched Ellen as she peered over the water toward Catalina with the same fixed, silent stare he had noticed before.

"Well, I can't," she said softly. "I have a commitment next weekend, some old business to clear up before I can leave for any length of time."

"Anything I can help with?" Armand asked the question, but already knew what the answer would be.

"No, my dear. There is nothing you can help me with. There is something you could do right now, however. It's a beautiful night for a walk on the beach at San Onofre. Are you game, Armand?" She lifted his hand from the table and kissed his fingers.

"I wouldn't miss it for anything."

"It's quite remote there. There may be a fisherman or two. Those fellows have their strange addiction to the yellowtail and the sea bass. But they won't mind if we engage in our own little addiction." She gave the barest hint of a smile and continued kissing his fingers. Then with her other hand she pushed her purse toward him. "Look in there, Armand."

He unzipped the handbag, heavy for its size, and peeked in to see a compact nickel-plated automatic.

"You see, I can keep you safe, Armand."

"Ellen, what are you doing with that? Do you know how to use it?"

"I am an expert. I'll give you lessons sometime. I don't think anyone should be without one these days. Now, shall we go?"

Armand stood and led the way to the parking valet. San Onofre Beach was just a few miles south. They made the quick trip in silence. There were a couple of recreational vehicles in the beach parking area, but that was all.

The light of a new moon filtered through a few weathered beach pines. Jagged boulders were strewn in the tidewater, and soon they were walking along the base of a cliff, notched here and there with tiny sandy coves. Ellen was now carrying her shoes. Then she stopped walking, removed the miniskirt and hose, and stretched her arms to the new moon, unwinding the string of pearls binding her hair. "Take me, Armand. Make me forget about everything but us. Tell me, is there anything better than all this?"

Armand hastily spread the beach towels along the sand. She tossed her purse on one of them, the shiny automatic making it thump in the sand. Then he began to kiss her; first her forehead, then her lips. He circled her, barraging her with kisses, spiraling down her body toward the sand. He knelt, not wanting to miss a part of her, then finally pulled her to the towels. They made love until the new moon sank into the sea.

31

Do you suppose you could get your old job back?"
Willy directed his question at Coley, who sat in a deck
chair with his feet propped up on the transom of the
Tashtego.

"I take it you mean my old job at Hacker's joint."
Coley sighed. "I have no idea. I guess I really left him
shorthanded. Hacker doesn't have any sense of justice
that I can see. I suppose I could muster an excuse
that would be accepted by most normal people. But
Hacker ain't normal."

"He just might be hard up for a bartender. It would
be great to draw him out in conversation about where
he spent the last weekend."

"Willy, you've got to understand that Hacker doesn't
converse. He avoids trouble that way. I guess I can
give it a shot, though. He's about the only chance we
have as I see it, other than that skinny little guy from
New Orleans. I hate to go traipsing all the way out

there just to check him out. There really isn't any indication he and Ellie-Jo were up to anything suspicious. Hell, a bimbo like her probably has a herd of guys hanging around."

"Give it a shot. Maybe Hacker'll just chew you out and give you one more chance. What's the worst that could happen? He wouldn't get tough with a guy like you. Have your pals down at headquarters come up with anything on him?"

"A couple of brawls, a couple of liquor license violations. He never did any time."

Willy began scanning the Monday morning paper Coley had brought with him. "Big excitement up at Tahoe. Some sheik's son-in-law ran his car into the lake. They found a bullet in his head."

"Yeah, I know. I was around the hotel when it all happened. This guy, Belanger, had a wife who looked like the queen of the Nile. He was evidently banging one of the change girls. Maybe the sheik or his wife didn't like that."

"How do you know about the change girl?"

"Just say I know a nice pair of legs when I see them. She was all brokenhearted. Says the guy tipped her hundred dollar bills."

"It says here that he was carrying a lot of money, which is now missing. The sheik isn't too happy."

"Yeah, I read all about it. The police up there have got their hands full."

Willy tossed the paper onto a table. "That's the trouble. Royalty gets knocked off and you got police all over the place. A nobody like Lefty Grogan is forgotten in a few days. By God, Coley, let's give it hell for another week or two. Try to get your job back and stick close to Hacker. We'll buzz out to New Orleans in a few days and check out this Siegfried Lemon. If nothing pans out, we gave it our best shot."

"Willy, we're probably blowing a lot of your dough for nothing."

"So what. Some people spend it playing golf, some people shoot crap and play horses. We look for Lefty's killer."

"What's up with Ginny?"

"She's having a ball. She'll be back in ten days. I miss her, of course. You know what I mean. You've been married a bunch of times."

"Pal, I guess I *don't* know what you mean." Coley stood, stretched, and vaulted over the handrail onto the dock. "Hey, it's Monday. If I get the job back, Hacker will put me to work right away. Come on down to the joint. Remember, Hacker thinks you came in to check on Monday night football. You might as well get one more look at him."

"Good idea. I'll do that."

By the time Coley got to the Pair-a-Dice Club it was late afternoon. He squinted through the window under the Budweiser sign. Hacker, behind the bar, stared right back at him.

Inside, Coley took a stool straight across from Hacker, who was glowering at him. His eyes had a glint to them that Coley had seen before in other mindless goons.

"Sorry, Hacker. It's really been a bummer. My mother died up in Bakersfield. I had to get up there to take care of things." Hacker just stared, arms still folded. Coley thought maybe he had used the wrong ploy. Maybe Hacker had never had a mother, just evolved from a fungus under some scummy rock. "I need my job, Hacker. I'm busted."

"I don't believe you, Coley." Hacker unfolded his arms, then walked around the bar to where Coley sat. He leaned so close, Coley could smell rancid sausage and onions on his breath. Hacker had a thick bandage encasing his upper right arm and shoulder. "I'm a dirty fighter, Coley. Someday I'm gonna bust you all up. You let me down. Now, Lee Ann is gone. She got some dumb idea that my joint wasn't fancy enough. I wonder who put that in her head."

"Search me, boss. Some folks just don't appreciate what you do for them. Hacker, I'll pitch in and help you out. I ain't got nothin' poppin' tonight. I meant it about my mother, Hacker."

"I don't believe you, Coley. Just like I said." Hacker straightened up and took off his bar apron and tossed it to Coley. "No more bullshit, Coley. Now listen. When the football nuts come in to watch their sissy game tonight, keep the sound turned off. They can watch their stupid game, but they ain't gonna cost me the jukebox take."

"That's good thinking, boss. Hey, thanks for everything. What'd you do to your arm?"

Hacker glowered at him again. "Hey, Coley, did anybody give you permission to ask a personal question?"

"Nope, I guess not. Just lookin' out for a pal."

"I want you to keep your mind on the bar trade, Coley. And that's a fact."

A couple of waitresses came in, as did a fat fry cook for the late shift. So far only six customers had arrived to stare blankly at the soundless pregame show. There was a small office at the end of the long bar. Hacker motioned to one of the waitresses and entered the small room, closing the door behind them.

Coley busied himself with two customers who were playing liars' dice for their drinks. Then he glanced around and spotted Willy Hanson sitting at the far end of the bar. He drew a beer and slid it in front of him. "On the house, pal," he said quietly.

"How about turning the sound up on this thing," Willy said. "Might as well hear what's going on."

"Sorry, that's against house rules. Maybe you'd like to play the jukebox instead."

Willy smiled as Coley came closer. "Where is he?"

"He's locked up behind that door at the end of the bar with one of the waitresses. Knowing Hacker, he might be screwing her or he might be killing her."

The door of the little office opened. "Hey, Coley, get your ass in here." Coley nodded to Willy and started off. The waitress pushed by him as he entered the office.

Hacker stood there, bare from the waist up. A roll of gauze trailed down from his shoulder onto the floor. "Shut the door, Coley, and take care of this thing. The stupid broad is useless. Says she was about to puke."

Coley picked up the roll of wide gauze from the floor and tore off the part that had been exposed.

"What the hell you doin', Coley?"

"Germs, man, germs. You gotta put clean gauze on that thing. Did you wash it out with that peroxide?" He spotted the bottle on the desk.

"Yeah, that's when the broad started to puke."

Coley removed the short piece of gauze the waitress had bungled. His eyes widened. There was a small hole oozing blood. On the backside of the muscle there was another small hole crusted over with blood. The whole shoulder, black and blue, was swollen around the small wounds.

"Hacker, you gotta get to a doctor with this. When did it happen?"

"I took a slide on my bike a couple days ago. But it's none of your business, Coley. Now finish the bandage and get back to work."

"Yeah, boss." Coley cleaned the wound again with the peroxide and quickly did the wrapping. "Okay, pal, that will take care of it for a while. You better get to a doctor. Something inside may need sewing up."

"Bullshit, Coley."

As Coley left the room, he saw Hacker's biker jacket hanging from a hook on the office wall. Jammed into the side pocket, he noticed a Delta Airlines ticket folder poking out.

Coley proceeded to work the bar. It was strictly a beer and shot crowd. He worked his way down to Willy, who had positioned himself at the end of the bar.

"What was the closed-door conference about, Coley?"

"I dressed the bastard's wound. Looks nasty. Willy, it's a bullet hole if I ever saw one, and I've seen a few."

"Really?" Willy's eyes opened wide. He resisted the urge to look at Hacker who was now standing at the other end of the bar.

Coley spoke softly, gesturing toward the television set, as if he were talking about the impending game. "Willy, I gotta get back in that room for a few seconds. There's something in there I've gotta see. If and when Hacker goes back to the kitchen, I'll go into the office. If he starts to come back up here while I'm in there, you've got to distract him until I can get out. It shouldn't take more than ten seconds." Hacker was walking toward them.

"What's the big conference about, Coley?" He spoke loudly enough for Willy to hear him.

"Man here was wondering where he could get a bet down on the Raiders. I told him we ain't no bookie."

Hacker looked sourly at Willy. "That's against the law. If you're lookin' for action like that, you should get your ass to Vegas."

Willy nodded. Hacker was still looking at him. Willy wondered if he recognized him from the brief visit a few days earlier. Finally, Hacker turned away and walked back to the kitchen.

Coley immediately went into the small office. Willy watched him standing inside with the door slightly ajar. Whatever he was doing seemed to take an eternity. Hacker was now leaving the kitchen, but then he paused to have some sort of a shouting match with his cook.

When he was finished and again starting back toward the bar, Willy was preparing to drop his beer glass on the floor to get his attention. Luckily, Coley emerged from the office an instant before Hacker came into his view.

A little later, Coley served Willy another beer. He spoke quietly while counting Willy's change. "We got some news. I get off about one A.M. See you down on the boat."

"Thanks, pal. Keep the change." Willy diverted his eyes to the silent TV. From what he could make of it, the Raiders had scored on the opening kickoff. Acid rock started blaring from the jukebox.

He downed his beer, waved casually to Coley, and then left the growing crowd in the Pair-a-Dice Club. No point in hanging around.

Driving down the coastal highway, he smiled as he thought of Coley, trapped in the Pair-a-Dice with the blaring music for the next few hours. As often, when he was tired, the image of the bloated body of Lefty Grogan came to mind. Waiting for Coley would seem like an eternity.

Coley showed up about 2:00 A.M. and found Willy dozing on the aft deck of the *Tashtego*. Willy rubbed his eyes, awakened by the abrupt movement of the ketch as Coley climbed aboard. "Thank God, Coley," Willy said, squinting at his watch in the dim light.

"Long night, eh Coley? I don't know how you tolerate that Hacker. He's some putrid piece of work."

Coley sat down quickly in the cockpit and grinned broadly at Willy. "Boss, we got something. Hacker's flying to New Orleans at three-fifteen, Friday afternoon. I saw the ticket in his office. New Orleans is where Ellie-Jo's pal Siegfried Lemon lives; courtesy of the Avis gal in Reno."

Willy got to his feet and stretched, rubbing his growth of beard. "So what?"

"So there may be a connection. Something's going on in New Orleans this weekend. Siegfried Lemon and Hacker are a pretty unlikely pair, but they both know Ellie-Jo. Maybe Lemon could fill in the blanks." Coley was excited.

"That's a real stretch, Coley. All we've really got is a name. Ellen Lambert has a big job. It takes her all over the country. She must have pals everywhere. The whole thing could be a business situation." Willy paused. "But we've got to check it out. It's all we've got."

"Willy, I'm going to fly to New Orleans Thursday, try to get a line on this guy Lemon, and then tail Hacker when he gets off the plane on Friday."

"What if he spots you?"

"Everything's got its risks. And sooner or later, we've got to take some."

"Coley, I'll come along. If there's a confrontation, I want to be there. After all, Lefty was my friend. If anyone sticks his neck out, it should be me."

"I wish you wouldn't, Willy."

"It's my call, Coley. We can back each other up. But before we go, let's find out a little more about Hacker."

"How you gonna do that?" Coley asked.

"He's going to get another telephone call from a pal of Lefty Grogan. You working tomorrow?"

"Yep, the bastard wants me there at noon."

"I'll call between twelve and one. Keep your eyes open and try to assess his reaction."

"What are you going to say?" Coley was obviously dubious about the whole idea.

"I'm going to advise him to meet me someplace. I'm going to tell him that if he makes it worthwhile, I won't go to the police and tell them all about how Lefty Grogan died."

32

It was five minutes past noon the next day when the telephone rang in the Pair-a-Dice Club. Coley answered. It was Willy.

"Hey Hacker, it's for you." Coley nonchalantly placed the telephone on the back-bar and moved away. Hacker came forward from the kitchen, looking angry and in pain.

"Yeah, Hacker here. It's your dime."

"Mr. Hacker, this is Lefty's pal. I've been contacted by somebody from the sheriff's office up in Washoe County. They want to know all I know about Lefty Grogan. They want to know who it was who dumped him out for dead north of Tonopah. Lefty's gonna have a lotta hospital bills. That's why we gotta talk."

Coley watched Hacker as closely as he dared. He could see the sweat glistening on his forehead. He was clenching and unclenching his right fist as he listened. Then he turned his back on Coley and huddled in with the telephone.

"Sure, make it at ten o'clock." Coley heard Hacker remark a minute later, just before he hung up.

Hacker stared at the wall in front of him for a few seconds. Then he picked up the telephone directory and slammed it against the wall. He clutched his wounded arm and cursed, wincing with the pain.

"What's up, boss? Anything I can help with?" Coley spoke quietly, trying to muster a real attitude of concern for the livid Hacker.

"Coley, you shut up," Hacker shouted. "When I want your advice, Coley, I'll ask for it. And that's a fact."

Coley nodded. Fortunately, a few lunchtime customers were beginning to appear. Hacker bent over and picked up the phone book. He scanned the back cover for a moment and then ripped it off, folding it several times before stuffing it into his pocket.

"You're in charge, Coley. If anybody calls, I'm not in. You got that straight?"

"Don't worry about nothin', boss. I can handle it."

Hacker walked rapidly out the front door and turned left down the block. He turned on Pacific Coast Highway and walked a short distance to the Surfer's Crest Motel. Outside, there was a row of phone booths. He entered one, closed the door, and began to study the list of numbers on the crumpled back of the phone directory. He decided he would sit there until Ellie-Jo took his call at Waterfront, Inc. He didn't give a damn that calling her there was a no-no.

Two hours later, Hacker returned to the club. The lunch crowd was gone, and Coley was alone with two customers. Hacker walked straight into the small office and called out to Coley, "Hey, come in here a minute." His tone was uncharacteristically civil.

Hacker closed the door partway, leaving just a crack so he could keep tabs on the bar. "Coley, I believe you got some brains. Also, Coley, I think you got some balls, otherwise you would have never showed up here again after I reamed you out the other day."

"Why thanks, boss. I try my best to use what I've got." Coley tried to figure out what was coming next. Compliments weren't Hacker's style. He was more predictable as a bastard.

"I have a little job for you. I just haven't got time for it myself." Hacker seemed to be hesitant, struggling for the right words. "Some jerk is trying to cause trouble. He's lookin' for a payoff."

"How can I help, boss?"

"This jerk thinks I am going to show up at the end of the fishing pier down at Redondo at ten o'clock tonight. He'll be wearing a denim jacket and a Chargers ball cap. I want you to meet this guy and tell him if he don't lay off, I'm gonna bust him up and send him home to his mother in a box. Can you deliver that message without getting it screwed up?"

"Sounds reasonable to me, Hacker. Anything else?"

"Tell me just what the guy looks like when you get back." Hacker looked around the tiny office as if someone might be listening, and then he whispered in his raspy voice, "There's a dark parking area near there. You any good with your fists, Coley?"

"Never been whipped yet."

"I want you to work the guy over real good. In other words, get him off my back, Coley." Hacker pulled a fat roll of bills out of his pocket and peeled off three hundred-dollar bills. "Here, Coley. And there'll be a bonus if you come back with a good report. The better your report card, the bigger your bonus."

"I gotcha, boss. Don't worry, you just forget about this jerk. Get him off your mind. He's not your problem anymore." Coley jammed the three bills into his wallet and extended a hand to Hacker. "Thanks, boss. I consider this a big opportunity. Say, did you ever see a doctor about that arm?"

"You did a good job, Coley. I don't need a doctor anymore. Doctors get too nosey about things."

Hacker stuck to him like glue the rest of the afternoon. Once, when Hacker went back to the kitchen, Coley dialed Willy's number, but there was no answer. Coley hardly ever used the phone and, if he did so now, he feared Hacker would get suspicious as hell.

At 9:00 P.M., Hacker nodded toward the door. Coley handed him his apron and headed for the fishing pier at Redondo Beach. It was less than fifteen minutes away.

He climbed the stairs to Tony's bar. From here, he could get a bird's-eye view of the whole pier. There was Willy, leaning over the railing, watching some fishermen at the end of the pier. At about ten minutes to ten, Willy pulled a Chargers cap from his pocket and jammed it onto his head. He turned around and cased the pier in back of him just in time to see Coley descend the steps from his aerial view. Willy was grinning as Coley approached.

"You alone?" Willy asked, when Coley came within earshot.

"I sure hope so. But there's no way to tell. We better not act like buddies out here. How's the fishing?"

"These guys are doing great. I should have brought a rod. Where's Hacker?"

"He sent me to do his dirty work. I'm supposed to find out what you look like and then take you somewhere and bust you all up. Hacker's nervous as a cat."

"What do you think, Coley. Does this cinch it?" asked Willy.

"Cinch what?"

"Do we have enough now to go to the police?"

"We can cause Hacker a lot of grief, but we haven't got anything that will pin a murder rap on him." Coley squinted his eyes and looked back along the length of the pier. Hacker could be there in ten minutes if he were as curious as Coley thought he might be.

"Hacker never told you how he got the bullet hole, did he?"

"Nope. He paid me three hundred bucks, though, to come down here and beat you to a pulp."

"He must consider you a real pal now. Maybe that kind of information would impress the police."

"He likes the way I patched up his arm. It's still giving him fits though. I think it might have taken a chunk out of the bone. Come on, Willy, let's get the hell out of here. I want to get back to the club before Hacker blows a fuse. He's waiting for a report." Coley slipped his nine millimeter out of the shoulder holster under his jacket and jammed it into his trousers.

"See something, Coley?"

"No, but I just don't trust Hacker. He could satisfy his curiosity by leaving the joint and coming down here. It's only ten minutes away. There's a couple of waitresses there who could handle the place for a few minutes." Coley's eyes probed the shadows along the boardwalk ahead of them. "I might have been played for a sucker, Willy. Hacker parted with the three C notes in a hurry."

They left the fishing pier and walked along the boardwalk for about a hundred yards. Most of the shops along the walk were closed for the night. The area in front of them was dimly lit, and the parking lot was at least another hundred yards away.

"Well, well, well. If it isn't Mr. Monday Night Football!" Hacker's voice boomed out of the shadows. He was less than ten feet away. The long barrel of his silencer-fitted weapon poked out from his right hand, pointed directly at Willy.

Coley walked boldly ahead. "Hacker, this here is the son of a bitch that's been causing all the trouble. He claims you killed somebody named Lefty Grogan. He's all mine, Hacker." Coley, standing almost in front of Hacker, turned around and pointed his nine millimeter at Willy.

"Okay, Coley, he's yours. Put him away." Hacker lowered his gun for just an instant.

Then, with a pivot that came right out of Coley's past as an All-American, he spun and crashed the nine millimeter across the bridge of Hacker's nose. He grabbed Hacker's arm as he staggered, sending one silenced round harmlessly into the boardwalk. Coley twisted and wrenched the already injured arm, beating savagely at the wounded shoulder. Hacker's silenced .22 skipped off the boardwalk into the water. Coley dug one more punch into his jaw, and Hacker fell heavily to the boardwalk.

"Enough, Coley! For God's sake, that's enough." Willy stepped between Coley and the fallen man. He bent down to make sure Hacker was still breathing. His breath was regular with short whistling noises coming from his mangled face. "Coley, there are public phones near that restaurant in the parking lot. Let's get the police."

Coley stared down at Hacker. "Are we really ready to open it all up, Willy? The cops will have a million questions, and we haven't got many answers."

"You're the private eye, Coley. Let's get the hell out of here then. There are people walking down the boardwalk." He glanced at Hacker, now groaning.

"Don't worry about him. He'll live. We might actually have done him a favor. If they pick him up, they may take care of that shoulder."

They walked swiftly into the parking lot and climbed into the Porsche. Willy drove Coley back to the underground garage where he had parked his own car.

"I'm going to go back to the *Tashtego* and try to sleep. Want to come along?"

"Thanks, Willy, but the bunks are too small." Coley chuckled. "I wonder what Hacker's fancy girlfriend will think of his new face."

"She may like it, Coley. She evidently thinks ugly is beautiful." Willy gunned the engine of the Porsche after Coley got out.

"See you in the A.M., boss. Between now and then, I'm going to run tonight's festivities past an old pal down at headquarters. No names or places though. We'll get another opinion that way. Hey, look!"

A quarter mile away, lights flashed atop a police car that had pulled onto the boardwalk.

"Let's get out of here," Willy said.

"They'll probably take him for a wino," murmured Coley. "A night in the tank is too good for Hacker."

33

The big Harley roared its way down San Vincente and turned abruptly into the driveway of Ellen Lambert's condo. Hacker reached into his jacket pocket and pressed a button to open the garage door. He snuggled the Harley up next to Ellie-Jo's Mercedes, lowered the garage door, and walked through the door leading to the lobby.

The lobby security guard stared at Hacker for a moment. Hacker was wearing wraparound mirrored sunglasses that concealed much of his face, except for the swollen nose scabbed over a scrape that dug deeply across the bridge. "Miss Lambert is expecting you. You may go right on up."

Hacker grunted and walked to the elevator. On the way up to 14C, he removed the sunglasses for a moment and gaped at himself in the mirrored wall of the elevator car. He pawed roughly at his nose, then set the glasses back on his face, muttering a curse at the image in the mirror.

Ellie-Jo answered his knock immediately. "My God, Hacker! What in the world happened?"

He walked in, flopped down on a couch, and removed the glasses. "We got big problems, Ellie-Jo. Remember that creep I iced up in Nevada? The son of a bitch is alive. His buddies tried to shake me down." Hacker proceeded to blurt out the story of the previous night.

"You told me he took a bullet right through his forehead."

"He did, Ellie-Jo. I swear to God, I killed him."

Ellie-Jo surveyed Hacker. His right shoulder was heavily bandaged. The wrappings were clean and seemed to be professionally applied. "Who bandaged you up?"

"The cops took me to an emergency room at the hospital. The stupid bastards think I was mugged."

"Hooray for them, Hacker. You could be in a much worse jam. What did they say about the bullet hole?"

"Nothin'. It all got ripped again pretty good in the fight. If the doc saw anything, he didn't say."

"Who did it, Hacker?"

"One of the guys was the tall black bartender I hired off the street. The bastard was setting me up all this time. The other guy came in the club once or twice to see Monday night football. I swear, I never saw either of them before."

"Think about it, Hacker. Think about that night in Tonopah. There is no way anyone could connect that with us." Ellie-Jo watched as the wide-eyed Hacker moved his head slowly in agreement. "Unless, Hacker . . . unless you blabbed to somebody."

"Bitch! *Me* blab! You goin' nuts. I don't talk to nobody 'bout nothin'. *And that's a fact!*"

"Then stop worrying. Close the Pair-a-Dice Club for a while and lay low. I can think of only one possibility. It has to be that bartender in Tonopah jumping to conclusions. It couldn't be anybody else. Think about it. Hacker, lay low for a while, and someday when you've got nothing to do drive out to Tonopah and take care of business." Ellie-Jo sat next to Hacker on the couch and put her arm around him. "Remember the night you killed Lefty? Remember how hot we were that night? You couldn't get enough of me."

Hacker turned to accept the gentle kiss on his painful swollen lips. "Yeah, Ellie-Jo, I remember." He put both arms around her and strong-armed her to his chest. "Hey, Ellie-Jo. How about right now?"

"You going to take me with you when you go up there and kill the bartender?" She pulled the tank top from his jeans and began to trail kisses down his chest. "You know how crazy I get after you take care of some jerk."

"Yeah, I know, but how about right now, Ellie-Jo?"

"You got it, Hacker. This is just a sample of what you get after you take care of Sammy Lasker this Saturday in New Orleans. Now relax. For once in your life just try to relax. Let's take our time. Everything is going to be okay."

Within a minute, Hacker exploded in spasm after spasm in premature response to her attention. Ellie-Jo groaned, struggled free, and rose to her feet. He stared blankly at her in momentary exhaustion.

"You bastard! Now what in the hell am I supposed to do?" Hacker's brief climb to ecstasy had probably set a new world record, she thought. She could see a slight smile cross Hacker's face. The broken nose made it look more like a grin than she had ever noticed on him before. "Hacker, do me a favor. Get your kicks somewhere else. Let's keep it strictly business from now on."

"What the hell's wrong? I can't help it if you're such a hot chick. And that's a fact."

"Hacker, there's so much wrong that it would take all day to go over the list." Ellie-Jo walked away, putting some distance between them. She had decided before his arrival to tell him about the Hong Kong thing. "Hacker, I'm not going to be seeing you for a few months. I'll see you in New Orleans Friday. After we're finished there, I'm off to Hong Kong for Waterfront, Inc."

"Hong Kong!"

"That's right, Hacker. We need a break anyway to let things cool off. We're going to have to slow down and be more careful. I'm afraid we'll leave some footprints if we don't. There's this thing with Lefty, and I read in the LA *Times* the other day that a bunch of boy scouts found the doctor in the old mine where you put him."

"So what? Dead men don't talk."

"Yeah, I know. But I hope you left him nice and clean, Hacker. This guy was a high roller and a very big name in his profession. There will be a bigger investigation than usual."

"Hey, I'll tend to my business, and you tend to yours. Don't worry about any stupid cops."

"Idiot! Listen! I tell you, you're getting sloppy! It used to be that when you iced someone, that was the end of it. Now Lefty, Fears, and Belanger have all turned up and been identified. What in the hell has gone wrong? You damn well better have more permanent plans for Sammy Lasker."

"I have, Ellie-Jo, and that's a fact." He leaped to his feet and pinned Ellie-Jo to a wall. "And I'll tell you somethin' else." Now he was holding both of her wrists and grinding his pelvis against her.

"You bastard, Hacker. Let me go!" She tried to wrestle free, but Hacker had a steel grip.

Hacker shoved her to the floor and smothered her with his full weight. Their faces were inches apart. Hacker stared at her with his maniacal grin, made more terrifying by his heavily scabbed nose. "You're gonna take care of ole Hacker one more time."

"Suit yourself, bastard." Ellie-Jo closed her eyes to his furious, brief assault.

As soon as Hacker was out the door, Ellie-Jo showered. She decided to take a short nap. Armand was not picking her up for almost three hours. The brutal assault by Hacker had left her mentally and physically exhausted. His selfish attentions had once excited her, perhaps because of their sheer physical intensity. But now he terrified her and she succumbed to his onslaughts only because she feared disfigurement, or something worse. After all, Hacker loved to kill. Right then, she made a pact with herself to end the relationship with Hacker when she returned from Hong Kong.

With that calming her thoughts, she drifted into a deep sound sleep.

Outside the condo, Coley Doctor sat slumped behind the wheel of a beat-up old Buick he had borrowed from a friend in the LAPD. Hacker had left the building, driving the Harley, over two hours ago. None of the other people entering the condo had aroused any special interest.

Another car pulled up and parked ten yards in front of Coley. A man climbed out and quickly walked to the condo. He was well built, dressed in a dark dinner

jacket, and walked with a spring in his step. Coley
glanced at his watch. It was six o'clock sharp.

At 6:30, the man emerged from the building with
Ellen Lambert on his arm. She was wearing a micro
tight skirt that started at the waist and ran out of
cloth just below the hip line. Her hair was fixed in a
bun at the back of her head. The guy she was with
looked sharp, a distinct contrast to the ugly, grunting
Hacker who had left her apartment building earlier.
Coley wondered if the two men knew each other.

The man drove ahead of Coley slowly, almost tentatively. There seemed to be no danger of losing him.

He veered to the left and entered an on-ramp to the
San Diego Freeway. Suddenly, he sped up. Now Coley
would have a harder time keeping him in view. Darkness was rapidly engulfing the LA basin, but Coley
managed to tail the car until it exited just north of
San Clemente. It entered a parking lot with a low Waterfront, Inc., sign blazing in blue neon.

Ellen Lambert and her companion turned the car
over to a parking valet and entered the restaurant.
Coley watched where the valet parked the car, then
he parked in the main lot where he could keep an eye
on the vehicle. He decided he would let the two get
settled in the restaurant before he went in himself.
He sometimes cursed the fact that he was six feet six
and black. It was difficult to escape being noticed. It
was now completely dark outside.

He released the seatback so he could slump low behind the wheel, just to the level where he could keep
his eye on the other car.

A large vehicle entered the lot and parked in an
empty space two cars away from Coley. It was a silver
Bronco. The driver got out and strolled around the lot.
He lit a cigarette and stared at the building set low
beyond the neon sign. Coley got a clear glimpse of the

driver when he silhouetted himself against the blue neon. It was Hacker!

Coley slumped lower in his seat. He withdrew his Glock from the shoulder holster and held it in his lap. His eyes, now adjusted to the darkness, followed Hacker as he walked toward the car that had carried Ellen Lambert and her companion. Hacker stooped to peek in the windows, then placed the flat of his hand on the hood for several seconds. He stood with one foot on the bumper and puffed on his cigarette for a minute. Finally, he ground the cigarette against the asphalt with his foot and walked back to his van. He climbed in, lit another cigarette, and stared toward the restaurant.

The hood of the car Hacker had touched had to be warm. It had not had time to cool since the couple went in. Evidently, Hacker was settling down to wait for their return. After a few minutes, Hacker climbed out of the Bronco again, now wearing a dark sport jacket and a jaunty black leather cap with the visor pulled down over his brow. He walked back over to Hauser's car and looked over the edge of the cliff ahead of the vehicle. Hacker scrambled down over the edge and then peered out over the parking lot, his head barely visible.

Hacker held this position for a couple of minutes before climbing back up on the parking lot again. He walked toward the restaurant, perhaps two hundred feet away, but continued on past the building toward the cliff behind.

Coley puzzled briefly over Hacker's movements. He had an outlandish idea he couldn't shake. He concluded that Hacker was preparing to set up Ellen Lambert's companion for a killing. Coley rummaged in his coat pocket and found an envelope. He ripped the back off and, in bold letters, he scawled a message. HACKER—FROM NOW ON YOU ARE BEING WATCHED EVERY SECOND. GET THE HELL OUT OF HERE—LEFTY GROGAN.

Coley got out of his car, walked to the Bronco, and jammed the envelope under the windshield wiper on the driver's side, praying to God that Hacker would not show before he got back to his own car. He made it. Laying the nine-millimeter Glock on the seat beside him, he pulled out of his parking space and headed for the narrow road that led back to the coastal highway.

He headed south along the highway for about a quarter of a mile, made a U-turn, and parked on the shoulder with his lights off.

Less than five minutes later, Hacker's Bronco emerged from the Waterfront, Inc., driveway and sped north. He would have loved to have seen the look on what was left of Hacker's face.

Coley pulled back into the parking space he had vacated at the restaurant, and he waited.

Inside the restaurant, Armand and Ellen were sipping cognac and staring together at the endless procession of breakers crashing below them. Armand reached across the table to hold her hand. He looked at her imploringly. "For the life of me, I can't see what the big rush is. We should go to Hong Kong together. Sheldon Blake himself said that a couple of weeks would be fine. Now you say you are leaving Monday."

"Armand, please try to understand and accept. This will be our last night together until I see you in Hong Kong in about ten days."

"Where are you going this weekend?" Armand asked abruptly. He immediately realized that his question sounded much too possessive.

"Armand! That is not your concern." But she then drew his hand to her lips and brushed his fingers with a soft kiss. "We will have at least four months together in Hong Kong. My dear Armand, you will be sick of me long before we come back. For a while you will be my only employee over there. I can be a slave driver, you know."

"Ah! I look forward to it. I can't imagine our adventure being any other thing than glorious and fulfilling." Armand broke into a broad smile. "Monday just seems a little soon. You caught me by surprise. But I know that you are a tenacious woman, Ellen. I fully understand that you are anxious to get started."

"That's more like it, darling. There are so many things I have to do personally in Hong Kong. Arrangements must be made with banks over there. Sheldon is a great one for paying as you go. Credit has to be established, and, frankly, I have much to learn about the monetary ways of Hong Kong. Sheldon has given me much to read. But reading is a far cry from accomplishing. Don't worry. We have time. Plenty of time." Ellen's greenest of green eyes fixed widely on Armand.

"Time for what, Ellen?"

"Time to watch the moon fall into the sea again. I think you missed it last time."

Armand signaled the waiter to bring the check. They gave their compliments to the manager and the chef. Outside, the valet ran to pick up their car.

Coley was still watching from his Buick when the parking valet delivered the vehicle to the front of the restaurant. As Ellen and her escort started down the narrow drive to the main road, Coley fired up the old engine and began to follow. To his surprise, they turned southward instead of heading north toward Los Angeles. They had driven only a few miles when they turned off on a road marked San Onofre State Beach.

He followed slowly, keeping his eyes on the rear-view mirror, still anxious that Hacker and the Bronco might also be trailing them. The car ahead pulled up to a row of heavy timbers blocking access to the beach itself. Coley doused his lights and parked about a hundred yards away. There were only three other vehicles that he could see, two of them sporting rooftop carriers that held surf fishing rods. The moon, low in the western sky, silhouetted the pair as they got out of their car.

Coley gaped as they stood near the trunk of the car and embraced in the moonlight. They stood in their embrace for what seemed an eternity to Coley. "Come on, folks, let's get it on," he murmured to himself. "It's gonna get cold out here."

The man helped Ellen Lambert over the timber, then sat on the timber to hold her bosom against his face. Coley sat transfixed as she tossed her jacket aside, and her companion dropped to his knees on the sand. Then she turned abruptly and started running down the beach; as she passed a rocky crag that towered from the sand, he could no longer see her.

Coley walked toward the empty car. Still checking behind him frequently, he bent over to look in the open window. He removed some papers that were jammed between the console and the driver's seat. He quickly determined they were the car rental contract. He stuffed them into his pocket and proceeded cautiously down the dark beach.

When he got to the giant boulder at the water's edge, the beach narrowed to only a few feet of sand. Every now and then a breaker would wash water over the base of the boulder. He skirted the boulder and then came to a quick stop. On a shoal of sand, a couple of hundred feet away, Ellen Lambert and her companion lay in an embrace. By the light of the moon, they appeared to be naked and totally oblivious to everything around them. Coley gaped at their ardent lovemaking for a few seconds and then backed off, retreating past the boulder again, forced to wade ankle deep in the incoming tide.

Now hidden from their view, he walked quickly back to his car, water squishing in a new pair of dress shoes that were probably ruined. He climbed in and sat quietly for a moment, thinking about what he had just seen. With Ellen Lambert or Ellie-Jo, or whoever she was, surprises and revelations came one right after another.

He combed the parking area carefully. No other vehicles had entered to join him and the fishermen. He shuddered to think what Hacker would do if he had witnessed what he had just seen.

He waited another half hour before returning to the coast highway and driving north toward Long Beach where the *Tashtego* was now moored. He pulled over to the curb in Huntington Beach along the well-lit main part of town.

He looked at the car rental contract. It was a monthly lease made out to "Mr. Armand Hauser, of Waterfront, Inc." Coley couldn't help smiling. Ellen Lambert's peccadillos obviously included sleeping with a fellow employee of the prestigious company.

34

A light was burning in the cabin of the *Tashtego* when Coley arrived. He rapped on the bulkhead as he climbed aboard. "Anybody home?"

"Come on in, Coley. It's only one A.M. Where in the hell have you been?"

Coley entered the cabin, sat down, and propped up his water-soaked shoes on the chart table. He found Willy settled back on pillows in the port bunk, fully dressed, reading the latest Richard Wheeler paperback Western.

"Boss, I got hot news."

"Coley, you were supposed to be here at nine o'clock. Or maybe you don't remember. I was beginning to think that Hacker might have found you and gotten even." Willy stared at Coley's soggy trousers and water-soaked shoes. "Your feet are wet."

"You think I don't know that? Boss, you owe me a new pair of shoes. I tailed Ellen Lambert and Armand

Hauser—he's a Waterfront, Inc., guy—all the way to San Onofre, and I finally closed my eyes when they started going at each other on the beach like two sex-crazed rabbits."

Willy put the paperback aside. "Okay, Coley, you've got my attention. Tell me what happened."

Coley went through the evening in detail, trying to fill him in on everything that had happened with Hacker and with the unexpected tryst on the beach.

"You sure Hacker didn't see you?"

"Yeah, I'm sure. But the bastard must have gone crazy when he got that note from Lefty. He left the place and went north like a bat out of hell." Coley paused a moment, pondering the whole evening. "Willy, we both know Hacker is crazy. I think I have an obligation as your private investigator to turn what we have over to the police, before he kills somebody else. I'll give it to some buddies down at the LAPD. At the very least, they will probably question Hacker, and maybe Ellen Lambert."

Willy stood up and walked over to fish a newspaper out of the side keep. "Maybe you're right. And you might be more right than you think after you read this. What time did you say Ellen Lambert checked in that car at Reno Airport?"

"Sometime around midnight. Why?" Coley paused to read the brief article in the LA *Times*. The gist of it was that an automatic sidearm registered to Henri Belanger, murdered son-in-law of the sheik, had been found in a trash barrel at the Reno Cannon Airport by a maintenance person early the previous Saturday morning. The ornate weapon had Belanger's name etched on the hilt. Coley whistled aloud. "You're thinking Ellen Lambert ditched the gun?"

"Could be."

"Yeah. The police will say it could be, but it also could be a couple of thousand other people."

"That's true, Coley. But it is another circumstantial piece of the puzzle that fits. It's beginning to develop a pattern."

Coley nodded. "Willy, mind if I crash here?"

"Help yourself. Tomorrow, I think it might be useful to go see this Hauser fellow. Maybe he'll slip and tell us something about Ellie-Jo." Willy stretched out again on the bunk. "You say you got a good look at this guy down on the beach. Tell me, did he use a condom?"

"How the hell would I know!"

Willy rocked the *Tashtego* with a roar of laughter, then turned his back to Coley, determined to get some sleep.

"You're just jealous because you missed the whole damn show. I hope you took a good look at these shoes. A hundred and eighty-five bucks down the tube. They go right on the expense account, boss."

Willy turned his head to speak to Coley, now removing the sodden shoes. "How do you plan to confront this Armand Hauser? For all we know, he might not be in on all the activities of Ellie-Jo."

"For starters, I could say I found the car rental contract on the beach. He probably hasn't even missed it yet."

"Those things are not really of much value, Coley. It's not like returning a wallet or something. All that stuff is stored in a computer somewhere."

"Honest to God, boss. Sometimes you forget you've got the sharpest private eye in California working for you. I'll launch right in and sing the praises of Waterfront, Inc., and how much I love their coconut batter shrimp. I can tell him that Ellen Lambert must be some sharp cookie to run a company as fine as that."

Willy looked perplexed. "How are you supposed to know about her?"

"Man, she's been in the papers. Big article in the *Times* financial section a couple of months ago when she made prez. My buddies down at the tax office told me all about it." Coley tapped his forehead. "Have faith, Willy, there's a lot more going on up here than you think."

"I believe it about half the time, Coley. Now let's get some sleep."

"Just one more thing, Willy. Do you still carry that beat-up old peashooter of a .38?"

Willy's hand shot into the port keep and help it aloft.

"Good. Keep it handy. Hacker's somewhere out there, running loose."

35

Flo caressed the bare back of Ziggy Lemon with a deft, light touch that evoked sighs of ecstasy from him. They were snuggled in her big brass bed. Ziggy's unexpectedly affectionate talents had surfaced just a few hours earlier. She had been in bed, ready to fall to sleep, while Ziggy practiced a new arrangement on the piano.

Suddenly, looking up from the piano, he caught her watching him. He carefully closed the lid over the keys and walked into her bedroom. He stripped himself of his clothes, and he carefully folded his slacks and hung them on the back of a chair, then covered them with his shirt. Without saying a word, he lifted the cover and crawled in next to her. Proceeding slowly, and never speaking, he made love to her for over two hours.

When he had started, she had toyed with the idea of walloping him. But then she decided that he couldn't possibly know what he was doing. Then she felt herself actually responding. Finally his deliberate, steady, endless foreplay pushed all rationality out of her mind. He played her like he played a piano concerto, until they were both locked in a frenzied crescendo. After a brief period of quiet exhaustion, he began again.

"Ziggy, where in the world did you—" She stopped in the middle of her question. "You know, I never once suspected that you were attracted to me like that. In fact, I have a confession to make, Ziggy. I thought you might be gay."

Ziggy shifted his position so he could face her. "That's crazy. I would never act like that with anyone but you."

"But why now? What made you think you could just come into my bedroom and take me, just like that?" She snapped her fingers in his face and smiled at him.

"Because the time was right. I could tell you liked my music. I could just tell."

"Oh, I do love your music, Ziggy. In fact, I love lots of things about you. Do you know that I've grown to trust you more than I trust anyone else?"

"Even Ellie-Jo?"

"Especially Ellie-Jo. I'm not at all sure about her. I'll be glad when the weekend is over." Flo paused, staring directly into the eyes of her unlikely lover. "Say, I betcha Ellie-Jo got you into the sack out in Tahoe!"

Ziggy sat up quickly. "Never. I would *never* let her do that." He looked at her like he was genuinely hurt by her suggestion.

"Ziggy, she's so beautiful. I don't think any man in the world could turn her down."

"I could, and would!" he said emphatically. "She is bad. She is very bad. I can tell. You will find out someday."

"What about me, Ziggy? What about those crazy

nights I spent with Sammy Lasker? I'll tell you there have been many others. Am I bad?"

"You are using those people. You are doing all those things to make money. You must hate them, or you wouldn't take their money. I've watched you. I can tell that you are disgusted. You are only happy when they leave."

"You can tell all that, just by watching?"

"Oh yes. I am sure." Ziggy nodded.

"Ziggy, you've made me very hungry. Let's get dressed and go to Cafe du Monde. We'll get a sack of beignets and some coffee and celebrate. How does that sound?"

"I'll buy."

"Okay, lover, you can buy."

In a few minutes they were out the door. The faint first color of daybreak lit the eastern sky. They walked rapidly down Decatur Street. When they got to Cafe du Monde, they joined a sparse crowd of late night revelers from the French Quarter and a few tradesmen on their way to work.

At first they spoke very little, concentrating on the pastries dripping with grease and powdered sugar.

"Ziggy, this will renew all our spent energy. If we can't sleep, we can make love again. How's that!"

"You must sleep. You need sleep so you can stay beautiful."

"Have you ever been to the Virgin Islands, Ziggy?"

"No, I'm not even sure that I know just where they are."

"They're in the Atlantic, east of Puerto Rico. I love Saint Thomas. I love Saint Thomas so much, Ziggy, that I am moving there." Flo paused to brush the powdered sugar from her clothes.

"When?" Ziggy looked as if he had been slapped.

"Soon, Ziggy, soon. You must tell no one, not even Ellie-Jo."

"I'm sorry, Flo. I will miss you very much." Ziggy's eyes moistened and he looked away.

"That's why I want you to go with me."

"Me? To Saint Thomas?"

"Absolutely. I'm going there to run a small bistro in a beach resort. You can help me. And do you know what?"

"What?" Ziggy couldn't believe his ears.

"The resort is beautiful. It's run by a Danish family. I got to know them when they visited New Orleans one Mardi Gras. Since then, I have been there several times. Their son is an engineer, and he is no longer there to look after the bistro. And Ziggy, perfect for you, on a veranda, next to the bistro, is a huge grand piano. It could be your job to play for our customers. You could try to inspire them to romance, like you did to me last night. Will you come with me?"

"When do you leave?"

"Maybe next week. Maybe sooner."

"I will go."

"What about your mother?"

"She would be happy for me. Maybe someday I can send her money."

"I have lots of money, Ziggy. I have been saving for this business for years. And after Saturday, you and I will have lots more money."

Ziggy grinned broadly. "Saint Thomas?"

"Yes, near Charlotte Amalie. That's the capital."

"Just you and me. No Ellie-Jo, and no Sammy Lasker?"

"Yes, but first we have to talk about Saturday, Ziggy."

36

Joe Martin, veteran detective for the Los Angeles Police Department, scratched his unshaven chin as he listened to the story that poured from the mouth of his old friend Coley Doctor as they sat over donuts and coffee at the Vermont Diner. Martin, squat and beefy, scowled at Coley and looked at him intently through steel gray eyes. When Coley finished, Martin shook his head from side to side, pausing to find the right words. The fact that they had been friends dating back to high school days made it tough to say what he was about to say.

"So, Joe, what do you think?" Coley asked.

"I think you need a good kick in the ass. That's what I think." Martin held his empty palms up. "You've got nothing solid. It's a story totally fabricated with coincidence. The one time you had something hot, you blew it."

"When was that?"

"Down on the boardwalk in Redondo Beach, when this Hacker character pulled a gun on your pal, you should have brought me in. You should have sat on his scummy ass til I got there. Instead, you let him go. You caught him making a major mistake. He committed an armed assault, and you let him get away with it. That alone would have been enough to lock him up for days. It would have given us time for a complete investigation."

"I thought about it, but I guess I blew it." Coley recalled the night vividly. "I smashed him up pretty bad. Hell, it even occurred to me that I might have killed him."

Martin frowned and stared out the window at the heavy traffic moving down Vermont. "Then you blew it again. When you found him in the parking lot in San Clemente, you could have let us nail him. A little phone call, Coley. My line is always open to you. You know that."

"Joe, you can still pick Hacker up for questioning."

"Wanna bet? It ain't gonna be easy. Give you ten to one he's on the lam. Look, from what you've told me, the guy may be an animal, but he ain't stupid." Martin studied the dejected expression on Coley's face.

"So you're telling me you can't do anything? We may have a hit man out there doing serial homicides, and you can't do *anything*?"

Joe Martin shrugged his massive shoulders. "I didn't say that. I suppose we could pick him up for questioning if we can find him. I'll make some inquiries with the police in Tahoe, Vegas, and Tonopah and see if they have anything else on this guy."

"Thanks, Joe. I guess it's a wild story to spring on you all at once. My client is a friend. Lefty Grogan was a good pal of his. If it were anybody else, I wouldn't have taken the case." Coley picked up the check, stood, and walked with it toward the cashier.

Out on the sidewalk, Martin had one more question. "You say the guy held a gun on your friend. What happened to the gun?"

"It slid off the boardwalk into the water during the fight. It happened directly in front of Beano's Taco Stand. It was closed."

"Thanks for telling me, Coley. We'll take a peek. Anything else I should know?"

Coley shook his head. "Joe, I'll call you if I think of anything else. Thanks."

Coley climbed into the battered old Buick and drove south on Vermont. He eventually turned north on Sepulveda, heading toward Santa Monica and the main office of Waterfront, Inc.

The top floor of a slick new office building held the offices of Waterfront, Inc. Leaving the elevator on the fourteenth floor, he found himself ogling a sleek blond receptionist with short hair curled under at the tips. The effect emphasized her wide-set blue eyes.

"What can I do for you, sir?"

Coley toyed with the idea of telling her she could do anything she wanted, but decided against it. "I would like to see Mr. Armand Hauser."

"Is he expecting you?"

"No, but he will be glad to see me. I have some personal papers of his that I found and want to return." Coley became lost in the deep blue eyes. "I'll bet this is just a temporary job for you until you get a call from some big-time producer."

There was the flicker of a smile. "I like my job very much, and I hope it is very permanent. But thanks for the compliment anyway." She picked up the phone and dialed. "Mr. Hauser, there is a gentleman here who says he wants to return some lost papers that belong to you."

Coley swept his eyes around the office. Everything was neat as a pin, but the neatest of all was Marissa Chablis. A neat little gold sign at the corner of the receptionist's desk identified her.

"He will be with you in just a few moments, sir. Can I get you a cup of coffee?"

"Hey, that would be nice."

Armand Hauser came walking down the hall before Marissa Chablis returned. He smiled as he eyed Coley's tall athletic form. "Say, I'll bet you are one of our Lakers."

"Oh no, sir, I'm afraid not. I considered that once, but decided I wouldn't know what to do with all the money. My name is Doug Johnson," Coley lied, sticking out his hand.

"Well, Mr. Johnson, what can I do for you? Marissa says you have something I lost."

Coley reached into his jacket pocket and pulled out the Avis rental contract. "I went fishing down at San Onofre State Beach, and I found this in the parking lot." He handed the folder over to Armand.

"Really?" He looked thoughtfully at the folder for a moment. "You know, I hadn't realized that I had even lost it. You shouldn't have gone to all the trouble of bringing it up here to me. I'm sure they must have this all in their computer. But thanks, anyway. I guess if one were to have an accident or something, it would come in handy."

"That's what I figured, too." Coley certainly didn't want to end the conversation right there. "Actually, I had an ulterior motive, Mr. Hauser. I was heading north on the freeway anyway so I thought this might be a good time to drop in and see Ellen Lambert. I saw the Waterfront name on your contract. She did me and a good friend a big favor once, a long time ago. Then we saw the big write-up on her success story in the LA *Times*. I just wanted to say hello and thank her again."

Hauser listened carefully, pausing thoughtfully before replying. "It's a shame, but Ellen Lambert is not in today. She's taking a long weekend."

"Well, maybe I'll drop by Monday. I'll still be in the area."

Armand shook his head. "I'm afraid that won't work either. Ellen Lambert will be leaving for Hong Kong on Monday."

"Hong Kong?"

"Oh yes. Read the *Times* tomorrow and you'll read all about the new Waterfront, Inc., we are building on Victoria Harbor."

"Hey, that is big news!" Coley exclaimed. "Will you pass along a message to her."

"Of course."

"Just let her know that Doug Johnson and Lefty Grogan hope to see her very soon."

Armand turned to Marissa who had just returned with Coley's coffee. "Marissa, will you write that up, and put it in Ellen's pouch for Hong Kong?"

Coley repeated the message from the mythical Doug Johnson and the deceased Lefty Grogan to Marissa.

"Thank you again, Mr. Johnson. I must get back to my work." With that, Armand Hauser walked back down the hall, thoughtfully studying the rental folder as he turned into his office.

Coley sipped his coffee and sat down in the chair next to the receptionist's desk. "Now, you'll make certain Ellen Lambert gets that note?"

"I certainly will, Mr. Johnson."

Coley leaned closer to Marissa. "Say, tell me the truth. Would you actually eat in one of these Waterfront places?"

"Mr. Johnson! Of course I would. They're the best."

"Glad to hear it. Which one are we going to?"

Marissa sat straight up in her chair and laughed softly. "Good try, Mr. Johnson. But no cigar."

"Aw, shucks! Can I call you sometime?"

"Sure. Answering the phone is part of my job."

Coley sighed, got up, and walked toward the elevator lobby. He pushed the button and looked back over his shoulder at Marissa on the other side of the glass doors.

Forming words with exaggerated lip movement, she unmistakably said, "Call me!"

"Doug Johnson, you're a killer," he mumbled to himself.

Coley got back on the San Diego Freeway and headed south. He still had several hours before the flight to New Orleans. He and Willy had decided that Coley would make the New Orleans trip alone to check out Siegfried Lemon. Yet he had plenty of time to get back to the *Tashtego* and bring Willy up-to-date on detective Martin's reaction and the news he had pried from Armand Hauser. He'd give top dollar to see the look on Ellen Lambert's face when she saw the note from Lefty Grogan in her Hong Kong mail pouch.

He zagged off the freeway at Manhattan Beach on a sudden impulse to check out the Pair-a-Dice Club.

He turned off the coastal highway and drove down the block in front of Hacker's joint. A crude sign, lettered on a long piece of craft wrapping paper, read, CLOSED FOR REMODELING. SEE YOU SOON.

Stunned, Coley stopped and read the sign again. He got out of the car and peered through the plate glass window. Not a soul was inside. The Harley was gone and a few empty glasses still stood on the bar. Damnit! he thought to himself. Joe Martin was right when he said Hacker would be on the lam.

37

It was about noon on Friday. Ellie-Jo and Ziggy Lemon sat across a small table from Hacker in a ramshackle little bar a few doors from the Old Blacksmith Shop on Bourbon Street.

Ziggy couldn't keep his eyes off the man with the crooked swollen nose. When he took off his dark glasses once, he could see that both eyes were blackened and bloodshot. "You should go to a doctor with that, Mr. Hacker," Ziggy advised softly.

Hacker ignored the remark. "Maybe you better go over everything one more time, especially about Lazy Boy."

"He is very tough. I've heard he was a middleweight contender once. Now he drives for Sammy Lasker. He picks him up and drops him off everywhere he wants to go. He lives on Toulouse Street at the address I have given you."

"Tell me about the Caddy again."

"Lasker lets Lazy Boy park it in a garage near his house. No matter how late it is, Lazy Boy always polishes the car before he puts it in the garage. He washes it right in the street and then polishes it up."

"Lazy Boy pack a heater?" asked Hacker.

Ziggy looked confused and glanced at Ellie-Jo.

"A gun, for Christ's sake, a gun, Ziggy. Does he carry a gun?"

"I don't think so. All he wears is a tight shirt and jeans. Maybe he has one in the Cadillac."

The surly Hacker nodded toward the door. "You can go now. If you ever tell anyone about this chitchat, you'll wind up in one of those cemeteries I saw driving in from the airport."

"Hacker, take it easy. Ziggy's on our side. He's Flo's friend. Thanks, Ziggy." Ellie-Jo hugged his narrow shoulders. Then he rose quickly and left.

"There's something about that guy I can't stand. I hate wimpy little bastards." Hacker scowled at him until he was out of sight.

Ellie-Jo let the subject drop. They had a lot of details to clear up before she was to meet Flo and send Hacker on his way.

"So what's this chump got in his poke, Ellie-Jo?"

"Ziggy and Flo say it could be sixty G's or more. It's a big race day. He lays off bets for a gambling syndicate. He's had his job for a long time. That means he's good at it, Hacker. So you've got to be on your toes. Lazy Boy sticks to him like glue." Ellie-Jo stared at Hacker's mutilated face. She wished he'd put the sunglasses back on. "Ziggy was right. You should get to a doctor, Hacker."

"I ain't got time for such bullshit. My face doesn't matter, Ellie-Jo. You and I both know what matters. And that's a fact." He grabbed obscenely at his crotch.

"Forget it, Hacker. See you tomorrow at eleven A.M.

You better find time to put an ice pack on your nose."
She arose from the table, pecked him quickly on his
forehead, and walked out the door. Maybe, just
maybe, she thought, tomorrow would be the last time
she'd have to put up with Hacker.

A dozen blocks from the Old Blacksmith Shop,
Coley Doctor walked north on Esplanade until he
came to the house number that had appeared on Siegfried Lemon's rental contract back in Reno. Esplanade
was a broad, tree-lined boulevard that must have
been elegant in the past. Now, the area was being refurbished, numerous old dwellings mingling among
those being revamped to match their original elegance. The address of Siegfried Lemon turned out to
be one of the most deteriorated residences on the
block.

Coley paused, reflexively tapped the Glock under
his armpit, and rapped on the weathered green door.
He kept at it for a while before peeking around the
corners of the house to see if there was any other access. He walked several steps back to the sidewalk,
looked at his watch, then up and down the street to
see if there was a logical spot from where he could
stake out the house. The entire block was residential,
so it wasn't going to be easy to accomplish a low profile stakeout.

"Can I help you, mister?"

Coley turned around to see an obese elderly woman
standing on the porch of the next house. He waved
and walked over to the porch banister.

"My, my! You are a tall brother. You are standin' on
the ground and I am up here on the porch. Yet you are
taller than I am." Her large frame jiggled as she
laughed.

"I can't help it, lady. Sometimes I wish I was more

your size." The jolly soul giggled again at his remark. "Lady, I'm looking for Mr. Siegfried Lemon, who is supposed to live next door."

"Siegfried? Mr. Siegfried?" She laughed again and stomped her foot. "There ain't no Mr. Siegfried Lemon, but there is a Ziggy Lemon who lives there. Ain't never heard tell of anybody calling that little pipsqueak 'Siegfried.' "

"Yeah, I guess that son of a gun is a little pipsqueak, isn't he," said Coley. "I reckon Ziggy is just his nickname. You don't know when he'll be home, do you?"

"You ain't no bill collector, are you?" All of a sudden the woman became dead serious.

"Ma'am, you can see that I'm too tall for that. Everyone would see me comin'!" The woman chuckled again.

"Well now, it really don't matter whether you're a bill collector or not. Either way, you can't see Ziggy Lemon."

"Why not?"

" 'Cause he's gone. He left a couple of hours ago. Ziggy came over here to ask me to check on his mail now and then. He had a suitcase with him and said he was headed for the airport. He walked straight down the street and turned the corner on Royal."

"Well, I'll be damned." Coley's spirits sunk. He had flown all the way from California to miss him by only a couple of hours.

"Did he say where he was going?"

The woman rubbed her chin. "He said he was going to the Islands." She started laughing again. "But, you know, he didn't say which one. I guess there's lots of islands."

Coley groaned. "Did he give you a forwarding address?"

"No, but he said he'd drop me a postcard. He usually does when he goes away. He went to Nevada here a while back and sent me a postcard from Lake Tahoe."

"Does anybody else live in that house?" Coley asked.

"Oh no. Ziggy used to live there with his mother. But she died a couple of years ago. I felt so sorry for him. You know, he stayed in that house most of the time for over a year before he started going out. The poor boy took it awful hard."

"What's he do for a living?"

"Not much. He plays the piano in some of the hotels and bars around the Quarter. Just fills in once in a while." The woman looked thoughtful for a moment, and then snapped her fingers. "You know what? You might check with Flo Dupre down on Royal Street. He tells me he plays the piano in her fancy house sometimes. She might be able to tell you something."

"I really appreciate that. I have some good news for Ziggy if I can find him. He might have come into some money."

"Well, you just walk straight down til you get to Royal. Turn right and go about three or four blocks. There is an antique shop (I call 'em junk shops) called the Clutterbox. The Dupre apartment is right next door. Pretty fancy neighborhood. Of course, in her business, you need a fancy place." The woman started her infectious giggling again.

"What business is that?"

"You go on down there and judge for yourself. It doesn't pay for me to gossip, but lots of gentlemen come and go, I'm told."

Coley pulled a roll of bills from his pocket and peeled off a twenty. "Look, I'd take you to lunch or dinner if I had time. But I haven't. Take this and have a good time on me. Sorry I can't join you."

"I thank you very much, sir. Say, what's your name?"

"Johnson, Doug Johnson," lied Coley. "I'll give you an address in case Ziggy shows up." Coley wrote a box number for his mail service in LA, then waved goodbye to the woman clutching the twenty. When he turned the corner on Royal Street, he noticed she was still watching him.

He peeked through the window of the Clutterbox. It looked just like its name. Next door, a row of apartments were separated by an alleyway blocked by a massive wrought iron gate. At the end of the walkway he could see a courtyard, neatly filled with cobblestone walkways and well-kept gardens. The apartments in this area were all refurbished with great care to duplicate the architecture of the olden days. The wrought iron balconies overhead were freshly painted, and most of the windows were hung with fine drapery. He tried the massive gate only to find it locked. In front of the building, several steps led up to the doorway. A mail slot was topped with a small neatly lettered sign, DUPRE.

He pressed the doorbell and heard a melodic chime from somewhere inside. He pushed the button again and heard someone stir. Then he heard voices. Finally, the door opened as far as a security chain would permit. An absolutely striking woman stood inside. Raven black hair plunged to her waist. A tall, flawless figure stood in front of him sheathed in a leotard.

"You gonna say something, mister?"

"Yes. I'm Doug Johnson. I'm really looking for a Mr. Siegfried Lemon."

The woman stared at him for a moment. "You a cop?"

"Oh heavens, no! I'm just a guy looking for a piano player. My sister is getting married down at the Royal

Orleans in a few weeks. I was told that Mr. Lemon played for you. I'm trying to locate him."

The woman laughed. "Oh, you must mean Ziggy."

"That's right. I guess everyone calls him Ziggy." Coley could hear a shuffling noise in the background. Someone else was inside.

"You're out of luck, Mr. Johnson. Ziggy's not here." She started to close the door.

"Do you have any idea—" Coley started.

"Nope, I said you're out of luck. He's flown the coop. He left town. I have no idea where he is." She shut the door. The trail to Ziggy Lemon ended right there.

The woman was damned uncivil, Coley thought. Maybe it was because she thought he looked like a cop. Other people had told him that. Maybe she was a hooker. Ziggy's neighbor had hinted she was. He felt certain that there were others within her apartment listening to their conversation.

Coley walked to the corner. There was a bar across the street from where he could see the Dupre doorstep. He went in and ordered a rum and coke in a tall glass. He needed some think-time. There was no reason to believe that the raven-haired doll had anything at all to do with Lefty Grogan. Maybe Ziggy Lemon had led him on a wild-goose chase. Yet he had spent Willy's money to get to New Orleans. His plane back to LA didn't leave until tomorrow afternoon. And the only thing he could think of to do was to stake out Flo Dupre's place for a few hours.

38

Hacker parked his rental panel truck in a small lot near where Toulouse Street left the French Quarter. He strolled down Toulouse several times, casing the neighborhood carefully. A few minutes after midnight, a black Fleetwood Cadillac moved slowly down the narrow street. The plate numbers were the same as those given him by Ziggy Lemon.

He lifted the protective glasses and rubbed his swollen eyes. He checked the weapon jammed in his belt. Sure enough, just as Ziggy had said it would, the Cadillac parked alongside the curb. A stocky, bald driver got out, pulled a garden hose from an alleyway, and began hosing down the car. In a few minutes, he turned off the water and started to blot the car with a large cloth. It was when he stooped to shine the wheel covers that Hacker saw his opportunity. Lazy Boy was on his knees, rubbing vigorously to remove all the water spots.

Hacker looked up and down the street. A little farther down Toulouse, where it crossed Bourbon Street, a group of pedestrians crossed now and then, most of them tourists exploring the wonders of the French Quarter after dark. Hacker started cautiously toward the kneeling Lazy Boy, still working on the curbside wheels. About fifteen feet away, he gripped the hilt of the silenced .22 concealed under his leather jacket. He glanced once again up and down the block and saw no one.

"Pfft!" Lazy Boy never knew what happened. The single muffled point-blank shot entered the top of his skull and tunneled down through his head. Hacker picked up the inert hulk and stuffed him in the back seat. Glancing down Toulouse toward Bourbon Street, several revellers carrying paper cups of booze in their hands were coming his way.

Hacker climbed behind the wheel of the Cadillac, switched on the ignition, and pulled away from the curb just as someone emerged from the building where Lazy Boy had returned the hose.

"Hey, Lazy Boy! Hey!" he heard the man yell, but felt certain the man could not see him through the dark glass of the windows. Within minutes he had pulled the shiny Cadillac onto the freeway leading to the airport. He pulled off the freeway after less than a mile and drove into an industrial area he had selected the night before. Moving between two darkened buildings, he popped the lid on the trunk. Within seconds, Lazy Boy was stowed in the closed trunk.

"That was beautiful!" he exclaimed aloud to no one. "That was the best. Ellie-Jo, you should have seen old Hacker do his stuff!"

Hacker drove into the entrance of a long-term parking lot near New Orleans International Airport, paused to get a parking chit from the attendant, then parked Sammy Lasker's Cadillac in the midst of a sea of other vehicles.

Once inside the terminal, he took a courtesy car to the motel across from the airport where Ellie-Jo was supposed to call him later on. He flopped back across the king-size bed and fell into a deep sleep until the phone rang.

"Hacker, that you?"

"Hi, Ellie-Jo. It was a walk in the park. The creep didn't know what hit him."

"I knew you could do it. I got something special planned for you, Hacker. You're going to need all the strength you've got. Hey, lover, ten forty-five A.M. sharp. Everything is all set. Sweet dreams." Ellie-Jo hung up abruptly.

Coley checked into the Royal Orleans about 2:00 A.M. He slept fitfully for about three hours before giving up. The elegance of the charming hotel was wasted on him.

By 7:00 A.M., he had left the room and was strolling out onto the empty sidewalk. He walked idly along Royal Street, half-looking at the real and phony antiques in the line of shops that seemed to go on forever. At nine o'clock he entered the bar a half block from Flo Dupre's place and started his vigil again.

The bartender scrutinized him. "You been up all night?"

"Nope. It just feels like it."

"Rum and coke?"

"Why don't you just make that an orange juice. It's a little early for rum and coke." Coley still had the taste of rum in his mouth from the night before.

"Hell, some people drink 'em around the clock. But then, they're crazy." Having served him, the bartender pushed a *Times Picayune* at him. "Help yourself to the news. It's all bad."

Coley scanned the paper, glancing down the block once in a while toward the Dupre house. At about ten o'clock, a taxicab pulled up in front of her doorstep. A well-dressed man in a smartly tailored suit got out carrying a briefcase. He climbed the three steps and was admitted to the house almost immediately after pressing the doorbell. The cab moved on.

Coley decided it was time to take a little stroll and get a closer look at the house. As he passed the iron gate, he could hear a piano. Classical music wafted out onto the street. Coley's pulse quickened. Maybe, he thought, Ziggy was there after all. He retraced his steps, and after some hesitation, pushed the doorbell.

A curtain on the door was pulled aside just a little, and after a moment the door opened to the limit of the security chain. There was the same raven-haired beauty staring at him. But this time she was stark naked except for a pair of high heels.

"Oh, it's you again," she said without a trace of surprise.

Coley eyed the statuesque beauty, momentarily at a loss for words. "Well, you see, I just happened to be passing by and heard the beautiful piano music. I thought maybe Ziggy was back."

"Not a chance, mister. It's just a tape. I told you once that Ziggy isn't here. If you come back again I'll call the cops. Now beat it! We're hard at work in here." She slammed the door and threw the dead bolt.

Coley walked several steps and heard the sound of laughter from inside. Now he knew there were at least two women and one man inside, all "hard at work." He smiled to himself. The dude in the fancy suit must be getting the works.

Coley walked a couple of blocks and took up his vigil again, next to an artist at work painting his version of the ornate old French Quarter. The painter didn't seem to mind having an audience.

Inside the apartment, Sammy Lasker looked up helplessly from the brass bed when Flo slammed the door.

"Who the hell was that?" asked Ellie-Jo.

"Some guy looking for Ziggy. He wants him to play for somebody's wedding in a few weeks. At least that's what he says." Flo was eyeing Sammy's briefcase as she started to dress. "Who knows? He might just be some creep who followed me home from the club one night."

Ellie-Jo turned her attention to Lasker, now bound securely to the bed. "Sammy! What are all these welts?"

"It's Nora. She's gone off her rocker."

"Poor Sammy. Let me kiss them and make them all well." Sammy tensed, not knowing when or if she would unleash the whip she held in her hand. "What's the matter, Sammy? You're not your depraved old self this morning."

Sammy shook his head. Ellie-Jo could see that he was not responding to her attention.

"The whole world is going nuts," rasped Sammy. "Lazy Boy has disappeared with my Caddy. It's the first time in ten years he's done some fool thing like this."

"Poor Sammy," whispered Ellie-Jo. "Relax and enjoy, baby. Lazy Boy probably just got the time wrong." Ellie-Jo moved to straddle him and then pulled the silk spread over both of them, forming a tent with the coverlet.

Flo, now finished dressing, picked up Sammy's briefcase, took it into the other room, and set it down by the door leading to the courtyard.

"That bastard Lazy Boy. My car wasn't even in the garage. He's been out all night with it."

Ellie-Jo threw the coverlet off and slapped him hard across the face. "Sammy, you selfish creep." She slapped him hard again. This time it really hurt. Blood ran freely from the corner of his mouth. "Lay there a while, lover, and think about your Cadillac and Lazy Boy. I'm going to take a walk."

She went into the next room, leaving Sammy Lasker staring at himself in the mirrored ceiling. It was 10:40. Flo and the briefcase were gone. Ellie-Jo dressed quickly, discarding the abbreviated leather dominatrix garb, and donning a black sheath dress. When the doorbell rang she was putting on makeup to replace the exaggerated version of herself that she had prepared for Lasker. She opened the door to admit Hacker at exactly 10:45.

Outside, Hacker had lowered a large packing case from the panel truck on a tailgate lift. When she answered the door, he was maneuvering it onto a hand truck. Within seconds he had it inside the house.

Ellie-Jo nodded toward the closed door of the bedroom. "If you don't mind, Hacker, I'm going to take a stroll in the courtyard. See you later, baby."

"You got the loot?"

"It's safe and sound, honey. We're a hell of a team."

Hacker opened the door to the bedroom and walked in. Lasker stared wildly at Hacker's grotesque face pushing out from under a dirty felt hat pulled down over his brow.

"Who in the hell are you?" screamed Lasker, jerking savagely at the restraints on his wrists and ankles.

"Ellie-Jo says you like to be worked over good. Now you're going to get a real professional job." Hacker pulled a heavy pair of brass knuckles from his jacket and put them on his right hand. He walked over to the bed and, without hesitating a second, he jabbed his hardened fist into Lasker's temple with all the brute force he could muster. Scrambling up on the bed, Hacker teed up his head with his left hand before letting a vicious right explode into his Adam's apple. Lasker's body twitched spasmodically for several seconds and then became quiet.

Hacker went back into the living room and dragged the large wooden packing case into the bedroom. It was the kind of shipping crate that one would expect to be used for heavy machinery. He lifted off the large, heavy lid and leaned it against the wall. Hacker dragged Lasker's body over to the crate, and, in one powerful effort, bent his torso inside and then flipped his legs over the top. He pulled a hammer from his belt and a half dozen large nails from his jacket, stuffing them into his mouth. After nailing the lid down tightly on the packing case, he tossed the hammer aside and put his foot on the axle of the hand truck. Then he swiftly moved the heavy load out the front door.

Within a few seconds, he had the crate balanced on the lift gate and into the truck.

Coley, a full half block away, had watched the driver exit the house with the case, obviously heavy as it thumped down the three steps. Now the driver, a muscular man in a loose denim jacket, climbed behind the wheel and started driving down Royal Street toward where Coley stood watching the artist, still waiting for one of the women to come out of the house.

The truck picked up speed rapidly as it passed Coley. He got only one quick glance at the driver. The man had a felt hat pulled down low on his forehead. He had a protruding, ugly nose. From what little he could see of him, he bore an amazing resemblance to Hacker.

Coley watched the truck until it turned left on Esplanade. He tried to remember the driver. His felt hat and denim jacket didn't fit Hacker's image, but the man was strong, like Hacker. He had maneuvered the heavy packing case rather easily. His look at the driver was fleeting. He decided it could have been Hacker, but probably wasn't.

He walked past Flo Dupre's doorway again and went back to the bar. He decided he would continue to wait until one of the women he heard talking, or the man in the silk suit, came out of the apartment.

Hacker drove the rental truck down Airline Highway, watching the traffic lights and speed limit very carefully. It was all he could do to keep his mind on his cargo. He was sweating profusely and feeling chilled. The wound in his shoulder throbbed with pain after having moved the heavy packing case.

That bastard, Coley Doctor! he cursed to himself. Here in New Orleans. How? Why? He should have killed him back on the pier in Redondo. Now, somehow, he had tracked him to New Orleans. He was either a cop or a nut out to avenge the murder of Lefty Grogan. Hacker vowed to himself that Coley would be next on his list.

Hacker pulled off the highway and turned slowly into a driveway leading to a long, narrow building. A large sign on the building proclaimed that it was the Bayou Quick Storage Company, from thirty-five dollars up per month. He pressed the code number on the box at the gate. The same attendant he had met the day before glanced at him through a window. He waved casually as he drove alongside the long building, which must have had over a hundred storage rooms.

He backed the truck up to a storage room with a big number 79 on the door. Hacker unlocked the eight-by-ten cubicle and slid the big crate holding Sammy Lasker across the floor until it was snugly tucked against the rear wall. "Sweet dreams, you dumb bastard," Hacker cursed. "You can thank old Hacker for the six months free rent."

Much relieved at having shed his cargo, Hacker toyed with the idea of driving back downtown to see if he could find Coley. But Ellie-Jo wouldn't like it if he didn't get to LA as planned so he could meet her plane later in the day. And then, there was the matter of the loot, which they were to divvy up at LAX. Coley would have to wait.

Hacker returned the rented panel truck near the airport. It was still over an hour before his flight. The sun was blazing through the haze and soon he was cursing his decision to walk to the terminal along Airline Highway, fighting dizziness with each step. His injured shoulder throbbed again with pain. Sweat rolled off him in a steady stream. He decided he would have to see a doctor when he got back to LA.

Meanwhile, Ellie-Jo paced the floor in Flo Dupre's apartment. The plan had been for Flo to exit through the courtyard and then through a neighbor's apartment on the next block. She was to lay low until Hacker had left with the panel truck and then to come back to split the loot. She should have been back long before now.

She became uneasy, not really willing to acknowledge her deepest fears. Flo had always been reliable. Where in the hell was she now?

Ellie-Jo began to explore the apartment. She

opened the ornate jewelry box on a dressing table next to the bedroom. It contained only a few pieces of costume jewelry. The few fine pieces that she had seen Flo wear were all missing. Suddenly panicked, Ellie-Jo ran to the large closet. Many of the chic clothes that she sometimes borrowed on her visits to New Orleans were gone. Flo had taken off, damnit! she screamed to herself. The bitch had flown the coop with everything worthwhile, including Lasker's brief-case, with over a hundred thousand inside. Furious, she began to open drawers and rifle through the contents. There was nothing worthwhile anywhere. The bitch had been planning her exit for a long time.

Coley Doctor was sitting in the corner bar sipping a rum and coke. The bartender had assured him that the hair of the lip theory was a good one. Sooner or later, one of the three people he thought to be in the apartment had to come out. A few minutes after 2:00 P.M. he was rewarded.

A tall, shapely woman left the apartment and slammed the door so hard that Coley could hear it from where he sat. She strode rapidly away from him, down Royal Street. A long mane of auburn hair tumbled to below her waist, whipping saucily from side to side as she moved.

Coley stared, having expected the raven-haired Flo Dupre. But this woman was a carbon copy of Ellen Lambert! Coley shoved a few bills at the bartender and started in pursuit of the auburn-haired beauty the instant she turned the corner and headed toward Bourbon Street.

After three blocks of following her, he pulled alongside. "Ellen Lambert! I know you. Please, we have to talk."

She turned to face him with fire in her blazing

green eyes. "I don't know what in the hell you are talking about. I tell you this, you better quit following me or you'll wind up in jail. Now leave me alone!" She resumed her rapid pace.

Coley hustled alongside her. "Miss Lambert, Ellie-Jo, or whoever you are, I ain't going to let you out of my sight until you tell me all you know about Lefty Grogan and your pal, Hacker."

"Listen, jerk! Do you know what they do to guys in this town who stalk women and make a nuisance of themselves? If you don't leave me alone, you're going to find out."

"Look, Miss Lambert, we've got to talk. And I'll tell you something else. I'll be the one going to the police if we don't."

"We'll see! Buster, I've got to get to work." She again started rapidly down the street. She glanced over her shoulder and then unexpectedly turned into the Threes Are Wild Club, one of the strip joints that lined that block of Bourbon Street.

Once inside, Ellie-Jo walked past the bar, on through the club room, and into the dressing room. Hesitating for a few moments, she peeked out from the curtain on the dressing room door and saw the tall black man seated at the bar. She was actually trembling. Hacker! That bastard hadn't taken care of business, she thought to herself. How in the hell did this guy know who she was? And how did he know anything about Lefty Grogan?

"Ellie-Jo, what's the matter? You're upset." It was Maria, the stripper working the afternoon shift.

"Nothing that matters, Maria. Just some creep sitting out there who's been following me."

Maria shrugged. "Welcome back to the French Quarter. I'd say to sic Lazy Boy on him, but I haven't seen him today."

Nor would she ever see him, thought Ellie-Jo. She glanced once again through the curtain, and then when Maria went out for her act, she opened a door at the rear of the dressing room that led to an alley. She hurried quickly through the alley, and turned left on Dauphine Street. At Canal she hailed a taxi.

"Driver, take me to the airport." She looked at her watch. Waiting for Flo might have made her miss the plane. It was forty minutes until takeoff.

Coley waited and waited. Finally, when Maria finished her act and began circulating around the bar, Coley asked her when Ellie-Jo was coming on.

"Ellie-Jo? She left a long time ago, mister. She went out the back door. You better leave her alone, fella. She was really pissed off that you were following her."

"Strike three," muttered Coley to himself. He smacked his fist into the palm of his hand. Maybe I'm not really cut out for this work, he thought. He had let Ziggy Lemon, Ellie-Jo, and Hacker all slip through his fingers.

Wanting to make absolutely sure that Ellie-Jo was no longer in the club, he walked to the rear, chanced walking through the empty dressing room, and opened the door into the alley. Maria came screaming into the dressing room. Coley slammed the door behind him and escaped down the alley.

He decided to check the apartment on Royal Street once more and then head for the airport. There was no doubt in his mind that the woman he had followed was Ellie-Jo, and that the man who looked so much like Hacker, was Hacker.

39

Ginny Dubois sighed deeply as she sat down on a main cabin bunk aboard the *Tashtego*. "I'm back at last, Willy. God, it feels so good to see you again."

Willy tossed her last piece of luggage into the forward cabin, then returned to sit beside her. Their initial embrace found them sinking slowly but inevitably to a horizontal position in the narrow bunk. "Willy, that's the last time I go sailing without you," she managed to say between kisses.

The *Tashtego* bobbed gently against the dock and, for the next hour or so, no words were spoken by either. Finally, wrapped in each other's arms, they watched the evening lights twinkle on around the marina.

"Ginny, we have a lot to talk about. I want to hear all about your trip, but I also need to bring you up-to-date on things happening around here. You up to going out to dinner?" There was a serious edge to his voice.

"That's a great idea. It's early yet. I'll pull myself together, and we'll be off."

"We'll go to the Waterfront, a new place Coley discovered near San Clemente."

"Coley must have seen some good-looking babe there." Ginny smiled at the thought of Coley. "Where is good old Coley these days?"

"He's in New Orleans right now. But I'll tell you about that later."

Willy chose the Pacific Coast Highway rather than the freeway. He drove slowly, telling the story of Lefty Grogan from the beginning, trying not to leave anything out. It was important that Ginny understood the details that had driven him to vengeance over the slain Lefty. Ginny listened intently. By the time they arrived in San Clemente, the details of events in Tonopah, Tahoe, Las Vegas, and now New Orleans were all swimming about in her head.

At dinner she was full of questions. "How about the police, Willy? What do they think?"

"Coley is working with Joe Martin, an LAPD detective who has contacted the police up north. He says they've got nothing to merit an arrest. They will try to bring Hacker in for questioning, when and if they find him."

"How about Ellen Lambert?"

"No grounds to bring her in. Besides, she's off to Hong Kong for an extended stay for Waterfront, Inc."

"Hong Kong!"

"Yep. And I have to go after her, Ginny. I can't wait until she returns. The whole case might dry up."

"Willy, that's crazy!" Ginny was quiet for a few moments. "It's crazy, Willy, but I can't wait to go to Hong Kong. I've been there a couple of times. This time I can really help."

"Ginny, I don't want you to go. You've put yourself in harm's way for me before. But not this time. You didn't even know Lefty Grogan."

"It's not even up for discussion, Willy. When do we leave?"

"I leave in two days. You can't get ready that quickly."

"Hell, lover, I'm already packed. I could leave tomorrow and have everything scouted out before you get there." Ginny beamed her toothpaste-ad smile. She knew he would ultimately give in to her. "Besides, I have mucho shopping to do. And Hong Kong is the best place in the world to do it."

"Sleep on it, doll. Maybe you'll change your mind. I have no right to drag you into this."

"Hey, we're partners. Remember? Besides, you are going to Hong Kong to talk to a woman. The way you describe Ellen Lambert, I damn well want to be nearby."

Ginny stared out across the water where Catalina was silhouetted by bright moonlight. "Just one thing bothers me, Willy. It doesn't make sense that Ellen Lambert and this Ellie-Jo are one and the same person. It seems like there's no way that Ellen Lambert, the business woman, could be a bimbo like Ellie-Jo."

"Coley has seen them both, and he says they are."

"Coley also is easily mesmerized by short skirts, and maybe that's all he sees sometimes."

Willy nodded his understanding of her observation. "You know, Ginny, I've thought a lot about it too. But I am convinced they are the same woman. Look at our society today. You've got people in this world, and especially in LA, who have tried everything. And that isn't enough for them. Morality has flown the coop. It just doesn't exist in the minds of a hell of a lot of people." Willy prepared to take care of the check, thinking all the time about the trip to Hong Kong. Maybe it wouldn't be so bad after all. The thought of turning around and seeing Hacker's ugly face wouldn't bother him day and night. He'd leave Hacker to the police. "Okay, doll. Let's go. Let's forget about all this, go back to the *Tashtego*, and do something special."

40

Ellen Lambert spent the first ten hours of a Cathay Pacific flight to Hong Kong in almost continuous sleep. The hectic events in New Orleans had taken a lot out of her. She awakened to the aroma of breakfast being served in the first-class cabin. The deep sleep had been one of exhaustion. Now, preparing for breakfast, all unanswered questions of the past two days returned.

Where the hell was Hacker? He hadn't met her plane from New Orleans. Nor had she heard from him while she was at her apartment packing for the Hong Kong flight. Flo, that bitch! Where was she? And where was Lasker's hundred grand? Being duped by Flo irritated her more than anything. Someday, she vowed to herself, Flo would pay dearly.

All the uncertainty gnawed at her. When her breakfast came, she could take no more than a few bites. The coffee snapped her wide awake. She stared at the other passengers in the cabin. Some were eating, some still sleeping and others reading; normal people doing normal things. There were still five hours remaining on the flight. She got up and decided to take a walk around the big 747.

At the last minute, she had called on Armand to take her to the airport. He had jumped at the chance. Nice, she thought, but Armand set her ill-at-ease. He was one of those meant to live in a normal world with normal relationships. She would use him like she used all the others, until his usefulness had burned out. He must never suspect what her real objectives were in Hong Kong. In a pinch, Sheldon Blake would take him off her hands.

Ah, dear sweet Sheldon, she thought. He was the only man she had ever known who could separate business and pleasure efficiently enough to treat her like a complete woman.

Finishing up her leisurely circuit of the 747, she paused to chat with several flight attendants near the galley. They supplied answers to her questions about Hong Kong. She had been there before, but never on business. Her chief activity had been exploring the shopping meccas of Nathan Road and Stanley's open markets.

Returning to her seat, she opened the overhead compartment to locate the pouch of correspondence Armand had given her. At first she had told him just to send it along by express, but then she had changed her mind and taken it from his hands at the last minute. Now she was glad she had. It would help kill the time until she reached Hong Kong.

One by one, she read through the papers in the hefty sheaf of correspondence, and she started to relax. She studied with great care the list of banks she would be dealing with. There was a big red circle around the Bank of Macau, destined eventually to hold most of the funds forwarded from Los Angeles.

She rested her eyes, looking out across the endless Pacific. The large electronic map on the cabin bulkhead slowly traced their route across the ocean. She decided the large land mass out her window to the south must be Taiwan. Her thoughts skipped to a previous visit to Macau when she and Sheldon Blake had made the run just to gamble in the casinos. She remembered the late-night trip back on a hydrofoil through uncomfortably heavy seas. Now she was destined to make the run to Macau frequently, perhaps often enough to anticipate and become less fearful of the boulders and small islands that dotted that portion of the South China Sea.

Leafing on through the sheaf of papers, she came to a small envelope with her name typed on it. Inside it was a note from Marissa Chablis. Marissa was such a bright mind, so thorough and well organized.

The note was brief: "Doug Johnson dropped by the office. He told Armand that he and Lefty Grogan hoped to see you again very soon. He said you would remember them. Johnson is some man! Must be about six-seven. Armand thought he must be one of the Lakers! Best—Marissa."

Ellen's anxiety abruptly returned. The name Lefty Grogan had surfaced again, thousands of miles away from the Nevada desert.

Doug Johnson? The image of the tall, athletic-looking black man who had pursued her in New Orleans came instantly to mind. He knew who she was and had somehow managed to communicate with her through the Waterfront, Inc., mail pouch. He must have seen her with Hacker in Tonopah. He must be the same guy who had been pestering Hacker. Maybe that's why Hacker disappeared, she reasoned. Maybe he's out right now taking care of that tall son of a bitch. Still, she was concerned. In their early days together, all their plans had worked out perfectly. Now she was preparing for the biggest kill of her life, and some guy named Doug Johnson was ready to cause big trouble.

"Damnit, Hacker!" She unwittingly muttered the words aloud, causing the man across the aisle to glance at her. She shrugged and smiled at him, then crossed her legs provocatively. The gentleman's face reddened and he turned quickly back to his newspaper.

The final approach to Kai Tak Airport in Hong Kong was a nail-biter, as usual. The big 747 lumbered in between the tall apartment buildings. She wondered how the people living in them ever got used to the deafening passage of so many aircraft. Soon the plane thumped down on the short runway. When the 747 slowed enough to abandon the runway, it was scarcely a hundred yards from the edge of the South China Sea.

Once cleared through customs, Ellen was met by Lee Ching, a contact selected by Sheldon Blake to facilitate her moving around in the dense metropolis. Lee would be at her disposal as interpreter and guide both in Hong Kong and Macau.

"I will take you to the Peninsula Hotel first. It is in Kowloon, on Salisbury, very near Harbour City," volunteered Lee. "It is early in the day. Perhaps after you get settled there, you would like to go to Harbour City and see the Waterfront location for the first time."

"I would love to do that, Lee. Sheldon said it was within walking distance."

"It is quite close, but perhaps I should drive you

there the first time and show you the best way to come and go. You will be doing that often, I suppose."

Ellen guessed that Lee was Chinese, with some European heritage mixed in. He was a robust man, broad chested and fit. His black hair was fringed with a touch of gray at the temples. Just as Sheldon had described, he seemed able, intelligent, and trustworthy. She wondered how much Sheldon might have confided in him.

"Miss Lambert, at Mr. Blake's suggestion, I have arranged for several representatives of the Hong Kong Western Bank to meet with you at three this afternoon. They are located in Central District. I can drive you there, or we can take the Star Ferry from nearby your hotel. It is a lovely day. Perhaps you would enjoy the ferry."

"Suits me fine. Lee, please call me Ellen. I want everyone to call me Ellen."

"Yes, Miss Lambert," he replied, as if he had not heard her.

"Lee, please refresh my memory. What is the most convenient way to get to Macau? I have a friend there I would like to surprise," she lied.

"Oh, it is very easy. Hydrofoils and jetboats run quite often. Just be sure you make a reservation in advance, if you plan to stay overnight. It is very crowded, especially on weekends. Everyone flocks to the gambling casinos." She saw Lee studying her intently, probably wondering if the casinos interested her. "Hotel Lisboa has a large casino. If that does not appeal to you, there is a Hyatt across the causeway on Taipa."

"I do remember the hotel on Taipa. But if I stay at all, it will probably be with my friends." She decided then to change the subject. "How long have you known Sheldon, Lee?"

"I met him about a year ago when he was looking for a location for his new restaurant. I then didn't hear from him for a long time. I thought perhaps he had given up on his plans."

"Not Sheldon, he is still very excited about them. I am too."

"That is good. So many foreign business interests are not so excited about Hong Kong right now. They worry about 1997." Lee Ching paused, obviously wanting to draw her out on the subject of the imminent takeover of the Crown Colony by the People's Republic.

Ellen smiled. "I believe, as Sheldon does, that Hong Kong will prosper under the new government."

Lee continued to study her without expression. If he believed differently, he didn't say so.

About thirty minutes later they met again in the lobby of the Peninsula Hotel after Ellen had checked in. They drove just one block inland, turned on Peking road, and were in front of the Harbour City complex within minutes.

"You are right, Lee. It is an easy walk. I will see to it that I get my exercise."

Lee Ching had a key to the new premises of Waterfront, Inc. The inside was clear of any construction, and it looked very much like a spacious empty warehouse. The whole interior would have to be built from scratch. Ellen walked over to an external wall and peered through a small window offering a magnificent view of Victoria Harbour.

"This wall will have to come down, Lee. We plan to have a terraced dining room along here. Every patron will have a glorious view of the harbor."

Lee looked dubiously at the large wall. "That will

cost much money, and will take a long time," he offered.

"Yes, it will take much money. But it will be done very quickly," she replied, thinking to herself that the money would be spent much more quickly than Lee Ching would ever surmise. She glanced at her watch. "Lee, it will soon be time to meet the bank honcho you mentioned. Maybe we'd better go."

"Honcho?" Lee looked perplexed.

"I'm sorry, Lee. I meant to say president, or big mucky-muck." She laughed aloud and finally got a smile from the staid businessman.

The ferry across Victoria Harbour from Kowloon to Hong Kong's Central District was made through a humid haze across Victoria Harbour. The seemingly endless cluster of skyscrapers ahead of them vanished into the mist in both directions. The bank was a short cab ride from the Star Ferry terminal.

Laurence Greenstreet was ready and waiting. He introduced himself as Senior Vice President for Commercial Development. He was tall, thin, and spoke with a decided British accent. "Miss Lambert, I want you to know that our commitment to your project goes beyond the money involved. We want to do everything we can to ensure your success in Hong Kong. As a first step, we would like you to join us for lunch tomorrow, if possible. I'd like you to meet the important people on our staff here, so they may help you."

Greenstreet was obviously taken aback by the startling beauty of his important new client. His eyes never drifted to Lee Ching, who sat quietly nearby. At one point in the conversation, when Greenstreet needed to speak confidentially, he circled his desk and bent over next to Ellen.

"This amount has been deposited in your account for immediate use." His long finger ran along a column of figures in the open portfolio until he reached the total that read, "$3,000,000, U.S. Currency." An additional column showed that the amount equated to over twenty-one million Hong Kong dollars. "An equal amount has been guaranteed to replace this as it is used. Sheldon Blake has assured us that more is at your disposal as construction demands."

Ellen Lambert took the portfolio from Greenstreet's hand and smiled enthusiastically. "Mr. Greenstreet, I plan to proceed with the work tomorrow. And I will be pleased to join you for lunch." She extended her hand to cement the deal.

"Ah, Miss Lambert, I don't think we have ever entertained such a world-famous restauranteer. We've planned something very special. You will enjoy it."

"I want you at our grand opening, Mr. Greenstreet, as an honored guest."

With those pleasantries over, Greenstreet walked Ellen and Lee to an elevator. On the way down, she couldn't suppress a broad smile as the blinking numbers traced their way down the tall building. Six million dollars, she thought to herself. And I have the checkbook. Sheldon Blake was a real sweetie-pie. And there could be much more to come!

Halfway around the world, Hacker awoke to find himself looking into the eyes of a nurse. The kindly eyes of the graying woman shifted downward to study a piece of apparatus taped to his arm. He was in a hospital ward flanked by other patients. He had apparently been in a sedated sleep for some time. The view from a small window revealed that it was dark outside. He had no idea of either the time or the day.

The woman addressed him in a motherly tone. "Sir, I have some good news and some bad news. The good news is that your fever has come down and that messy infection in your shoulder is going to get better. The bad news is that you are going to have to stay put for a while."

Hacker reflexively grabbed at the loose white hospital robe. Then vague memories began to surface. His last thoughts were of walking down a highway, fighting dizziness. He vaguely remembered stuffing the long-barreled .22 and most of the contents of his pockets under some shrubbery along the highway. "Where am I, lady?"

"You are in Charity Hospital, right here in New Orleans. And you are going to be fine." The nurse made some notations on a chart at the foot of the bed. "Now that you are feeling better, I need your help. We have some paperwork to do. You must help me fill out these nasty old forms. But rest for now, I'll be back soon."

Hacker stared at the nurse for a few moments, then nodded. Soon, he dropped off again into a deep sleep.

41

The next day, when Coley arrived at LAX, he had two calls to make—one to Willy to bring him up-to-date, and one to Marissa Chablis.

His call to Willy ran on for some time. The news he had from New Orleans contained nothing solid. But he was certain that Ellie-Jo was indeed Ellen Lambert. The fact that Ellie-Jo, Ziggy Lemon, the stripper, and Hacker had all vanished into thin air didn't seem to bother Willy.

"Great work, Coley!" Willy was enthusiastic. "It all adds up. I think you'd better fill in Joe Martin. If we can convince him that we're not on a wild-goose chase, maybe the cops will get hot on the case."

"I will do just that, pal. I'll try to reach him today. Can we get together on the *Tashtego* in the morning?"

"You betcha. Ginny is back. We'll all hash this over together. Maybe you can talk her out of going to Hong Kong. She wants to play detective with us."

"Oh Jesus!" groaned Coley. "If you can't control your woman, how do you expect me to? Four different alimony payments every month doesn't qualify me too well. How is Ginny, anyway?"

"She's being obstinate. She's packing for Hong Kong. We're leaving the day after tomorrow."

Ginny's voice came over the phone. "I'm going, Coley, end of conversation. Anymore static from you, and you'll have to fix your own breakfast tomorrow."

The two gabbed for a while. When they finally hung up, Coley was doubtful that he would be able to change her mind about Hong Kong.

Coley ran his credit card through the slot on the phone again and dialed the number for Waterfront, Inc. Marissa Chablis answered. He could picture those beautiful lips forming the words as she spoke: "Waterfront, Inc."

"Marissa, this is Doug Johnson. Just wanted to remind you that we have a date tonight. Want me to pick you up from work?"

"Whoa there! Not so fast, Mr. Johnson. I'm all tied up tonight."

"Then untie yourself. Tonight is the only night I've got, and if I don't spend it with you, I'll probably go crazy."

There was a long pause. "I guess we can't have that, can we? Look, Mr. Johnson, I don't even know you. If you want to meet for a couple of drinks after I get off work, meet me at the bar of the Waterfront, Inc., in Redondo."

"Aha! You are playing it safe. You want to go where people know you and will protect you. I like that. You are a thinking man's woman."

Marissa laughed softly. "Something like that, I suppose. I'll see you around six, depending on when I can wrap things up around here."

Coley smiled. Sometimes his job was fun, and having cocktails with a looker like Marissa Chablis would surely be one of those times.

Coley arrived at the Redondo Beach restaurant well before six. The evening rush hadn't begun. He selected a couple of spaces at the bar that looked out over the small harbor, ordered a Chivas and water, and began to ponder the evening ahead. It would be great to have a source of information inside the company, but dangerous if the receptionist was palsy-walsy with Ellen Lambert, which was possible, but not likely. He would just play it by ear before determining how open he could be with Marissa Chablis.

He had spent the afternoon with Joe Martin, who seemed more interested in the case than he had been before. He had passed along the information that Hacker's joint in Manhattan Beach was still closed, the crude sign still in the window. Also, a check on the property revealed that the title to the building was held by Doris Hackley of Laguna Beach. That would be Hacker's sister, the one who owned the flower shop. Martin said he would check her out in his attempt to locate Hacker. Coley didn't tell him about Willy and Ginny heading for Hong Kong.

Marissa Chablis turned heads when she entered the room. The bartender gave her a big hello, and she stopped to talk to the hostess and a couple of other employees before walking toward Coley. She was a knockout, taller than Coley had remembered. Maybe the spike heels accounted for that. Her short, sleek, blond hair bobbed with life as she walked his way. The wide-set blue eyes were truly dazzling.

She offered her hand. "Mr. Johnson, am I late?"

Coley glanced at his watch. "You're four minutes late. I decided to wait." She smiled broadly. No doubt she could keep a lot of men waiting a long time.

"I want you to know, Mr. Johnson, that I am not in the habit of making dates on such short notice. This time it just seemed like the right thing to do." She shrugged and beamed another smile. "It was so nice of you to bring Mr. Hauser his lost papers. Most people wouldn't have given it a second thought. I figure you can't be all bad."

Coley felt captivated. "Well, thanks for the compliment, I think." The woman was sharp. He sensed that if he was going to spend the evening with her, he couldn't just sit there and ogle her. "You are a dynamite lady, Marissa. You should bottle and sell whatever makes you the way you are. You'd get rich."

"Thank you. I run in the morning, work hard all day, and eat lots of veggies in between. I don't think you can bottle that. I do stare at tall handsome men who stand in our foyer, but only once have I dared to ask one to call me. I'm so happy you can read lips." She touched his wrist as she spoke.

"I'll bet you're the one who taught Ellen Lambert how to take care of herself. She isn't as attractive as you, but then, who is?"

"Oh, please! Miss Lambert is in another league. But thanks for the comparison, anyway. Where do you know her from?"

"I met her in New Orleans once." Coley watched Marissa closely. If his words meant anything to her, she gave absolutely no indication of it. "Nothing close, just business."

"Why don't you tell me something about yourself, Mr. Doug Johnson. If you don't play basketball, how do you make a living?"

Coley hesitated. It was a perfectly logical question. She knew nothing about him other than the fact that he couldn't keep his eyes off *her* eyes. Coley turned slowly on the barstool and let his jacket drop loosely from his shoulders. The hilt of the nine-millimeter Glock became visible, neatly tucked under his left arm. Her wide-set blue eyes grew immense as she stared at the weapon.

"Oh my God," she murmured quietly. "My mother never told me there would be days like this." Marissa looked around nervously, making certain that she alone was aware of the gun. "Look, pal, see that corner table over there? Nice and private. We're going to go over there and have dinner, and you are going to tell me all about yourself, and it better be good."

"Hey, that's nice!" said Coley with affected gusto. She hadn't lost her cool. Then another thought crossed his mind. Maybe she was just turned on by the gun. It wouldn't be the first time.

Marissa Chablis motioned to the hostess, who quickly seated them at the corner table. They were each supplied with menus and another drink, a Chivas and water for Coley, and, appropriately, a glass of Chablis for Marissa.

"Wow! Your very own drink. I guess if there were a liquor called Johnson, I'd always have one." Coley watched the flicker of a smile as Marissa put up with what must have been a tired old joke for her.

"That's pretty good, Doug, I'm glad you got that out of your system. Now we're going to play twenty questions."

Damn, thought Coley to himself. She is smart. She's staying in control. In the soft candlelight of their table, her blue eyes were even more captivating.

"Question number one. You're a gangster?"

"Nope, ain't no gangster."

"You're a cop?"

"Nope, ain't no cop."

Marissa shrugged. "You're just a concerned citizen looking out for yourself."

"Nope."

"You're a private detective?"

"Yep."

"Are you investigating me?"

"Nope."

Marissa started to laugh. "Gee, I was hoping you were. I would look forward to that." She picked up the menu. "Okay, Doug, you passed the test. Let's order."

Now it was Coley's turn to chuckle. Marissa Chablis was something else. He could love a woman like this.

"I'll tell you what," said Coley. "You must know about everything on the menu. I love seafood. Why don't you just order for me."

"You're a brave man, Doug. I'm going to try some things we just added to the menu. If you do the same thing, we can both have a sample, and I'll be a big hero back in the office. Armand Hauser loves critiques of his menu."

"Sounds okay to me. How about Ellen Lambert? Does she tolerate criticism?"

"Actually, she's friendly to a point, but then stays pretty aloof. The prez is a very private lady. A little mysterious." Marissa looked thoughtful for a moment. "In fact, she is damn mysterious."

"Now, what could you mean by that?" Coley tried not to be too obvious with his question.

Marissa focused her eyes on the last vestige of sunset across the harbor. "I guess it's because she never talks about anything but business. Oh, you get the normal pleasantries from her, but what she does from noon Friday to Monday morning is never mentioned. She'll say she's going out of town. But if you ask her, 'Where to?' she will just say, 'I wish I didn't have to go.' Or sometimes, she just doesn't answer. No one pushes her for an answer. After all, she's the boss."

"That is strange," mused Coley.

"Every Wednesday night, late, she leaves with Sheldon Blake. He's chairman of the board. I guess technically he is her *only* boss. Once, I saw them kiss in the elevator, just as the door was closing. I was floored. It seemed so out of character for both of them."

"Aha! Maybe Mr. Blake stakes out all her spare time."

"No. He's actually around on weekends. In fact, he's likely to show up every day of the week." Marissa began to study the menu. "Why are we talking about Ellen Lambert? You, Mr. Doug Johnson, are supposed to be telling me about yourself."

"Okay. I'll tell you my life story as quick as I can. Born in Watts. Basketball player, Syracuse. Some people picked me All-American. Law school. Passed the Bar in Florida. Married four times. Became the best private eye in LA. Met Marissa Chablis. There, that pretty well covers it. Are you happy with all that?"

"Married four times! Are you serious?"

"Of course I am. I knew you would jump right on that. Nobody dwells on all the good things. Marrying got to be a habit very young before I knew what the hell I was doing."

"Tell me, Doug, are you married right now?" Marissa Chablis was actually laughing between words.

"Nope. I wouldn't be here if I was. Believe it or not, I never played around."

"Oh, so you think we're playing around?" Marissa teased.

"Of course not. We're both on a preliminary fact-finding mission. That, I think, is pretty standard behavior. If we were playing around, you would know about it."

"Doug, let's eat dinner. I'm famished."

"That's another thing. I wish you would quit calling me Doug."

"Why?" The smile vanished from Marissa's face.

"Because that ain't my name. It's as simple as that. I'll tell you my real name after we eat."

Marissa started giggling hysterically. "And what do I call you between now and then?"

"Just say, 'hey, you.' Or just start right in talking. I can't stand Doug. It makes me sound too much like a white Southern Cal quarterback."

The waiter came and Marissa ordered for both of them. Every time she looked at Coley, she started smiling again. At one point she became serious. "You told Armand Hauser you were Doug Johnson. Are you investigating him?"

"No, not exactly." Coley decided to take a plunge. "Do you know Ellen Lambert's Harley-riding boyfriend?"

"Oh, come on now! Ellen Lambert with a biker boyfriend? I'm sure she would be mortified with the whole idea. I think your investigation took a wrong turn someplace."

"Ever heard her mention a guy named Hacker?" Coley watched Marissa's eyes grow sober and reflective.

"Yes . . . Yes! Just once. A few days ago somebody called for Ellen. He was very rude and insisted that he be put through. Ellen Lambert was in a closed-door meeting. He said his name was Hacker. After a second call, I went into the meeting and handed her a note. She left the meeting immediately to talk to him. Hacker, that was his name. I forgot all about it until you brought it up."

Coley produced a small leather folder that held his

badge and his private investigator credentials. He slid it across the table to Marissa.

She read the data carefully. "Coley Doctor, so that's your name. So what about this Hacker guy?"

"I think he's a killer."

Marissa pushed her plate aside and dropped her hands into her lap. "You must be wrong. Ellen Lambert is totally dedicated to her business. I can't imagine her having anything to do with someone like that. Coley, you may be the best detective in the universe, but you're wrong about her." Marissa put her elbows on the table and sat her chin on her folded hands. "So that's why you called me. It wasn't for me, it was done as part of your misdirected investigation."

"Oh, come on now. I just leveled with you, didn't I? I couldn't very well go into this on the telephone. Think about what you just said. You say she is totally dedicated to her business. But I say that four-and-a-half-day weeks are not an example of total dedication. And that includes a late tête-à-tête with the chairman of the board every week. Marissa, I could tell you a lot more, but I don't want you to get into trouble."

Coley met her steady gaze with his own. "Believe me, I would have called you under any circumstances. I made up my mind before calling you that I would straighten out the little fibs I used with Hauser. I expected to confront Ellen Lambert that day. Remember?"

"So what do you want from me, Coley?"

"Nothing. Just be careful around that joint. The people she may be connected with are ruthless. Give me or the police a yell if you ever feel uncomfortable. There is something screwy going on there."

Marissa took a sip of wine and started to pick at her food. "Okay," she said quietly, "I'll behave."

"Oh, shucks! I didn't mean to spoil everything. I'll

tell you what. Let's strike the last ten minutes from the record, like they do in court. You can even call me Doug Johnson for the rest of your life. I promise I'll get used to it."

Marissa couldn't suppress a smile. "Okay, Coley, let's go back. I don't care much about Doug Johnson either, though. Mind if I call you Coley?"

"Thanks, Marissa. I guess I have spoiled your evening. But I'll make it up to you."

"Coley, I've never in my life been out with a private eye. They're always big and fat on television. How do you stay in shape?"

"I play a little one-on-one with a buddy now and then. Every day that I can, I run a little and shoot a few buckets on a court down by Long Beach State."

"All-American, huh? Would you play a little one-on-one and shoot a few buckets with me sometime."

"Anytime of the day or night. I'm going to pester you until you do."

"Pester me, Coley, but let's take it a little slow, okay?"

42

Ellen Lambert left the Peninsula Hotel before 7:00 A.M. Moisture hung heavy in the 80-degree air as she walked the short distance from the hotel in Kowloon to the Star Ferry, which would take her across to Hong Kong Island. She carried a large handbag containing a change of clothes, her passport, the usual cosmetic necessities, and a palm-sized video recorder to be used in moments when she preferred to look like a tourist.

Tucked away in a zippered side pocket of the bag were eighty thousand Hong Kong dollars in bills of large denomination. Late yesterday she had cashed a Waterfront, Inc., check drawn on the new account at Hong Kong Western Bank for the amount that was equal to about ten thousand U.S. dollars.

The entire trip was a trial run for similar trips to come later. The run to Macau aboard a scheduled hydrofoil would take about an hour and a half. She was

275

happy to find the swift vessel offered comparative luxury. It was clean and comfortable. She sat in one of the upholstered seats and caught up on the news in the *Tribune* and the *Strait Times*, which she had bought in the hotel. She also wanted to refresh herself with the *Baedeker's Guide to Macau* she had brought along.

Sitting next to Ellen was a portly man sporting a neatly trimmed black beard. They had exchanged glances on the boarding pier. He was the only other Caucasian aboard the hydrofoil on this trip, so the exchange of glances had seemed a normal enough thing.

The distinguished traveler opened a briefcase and scanned business papers for about ten minutes, until the hydrofoil had cleared Victoria Harbour and veered to the port to skim the northern coast of Hong Kong Island. Then he abruptly closed his briefcase and spoke. "Excuse me, I am going to go get a cup of tea. Would you care for something?"

She studied the man's face for a moment and decided that she would. "That would be nice." She reached for her handbag, but the man gently waved his hand in protest.

"Please, it's my pleasure." He got up and made his way to a concession stall toward the aft of the cabin. He returned shortly and held out a steaming cup to her. "My name is Hercules Valdez. I am in shipping. I assume from the *Baedeker's Guide* you have there that you are a tourist."

"Well, sort of," she replied. "Whenever I visit Hong Kong I love to visit Macau. Window-shopping in the gold center is always fun. And I have a few friends in Macau that I hope to find."

"Ah, the gold is always such a magnet to the tourist. That and the casinos. Best to shop for gold with the money that would be lost in the casinos. Then you have something to show for your visit."

"That is just the way I feel. I'm a very casual gambler. I don't like to lose." She smiled at the man who seemed to be studying her every spoken word. "You said you were in shipping?"

The man reached inside his jacket and produced a card. It read, "Southeast Asia Coastal Shipping Lines. Hercules Valdez, Owner." "We operate freighters from Hong Kong to Singapore and Djakarta. We do quite nicely and expect to do a lot better." The man spoke with a self-assurance that seemed to be genuine.

"I'll bet your business is exciting, Mr. Valdez. There is so much hustle and bustle around the harbor. Things seem to be popping on the Pacific rim right now. Are you a native of this part of the world?"

"For as far as I can trace back, my family have been natives of Macau. Originally, they came from Portugal. I was fortunate enough to be educated in Britain. I'll bet you are an American. You have a very charming speech pattern." Valdez smiled appreciatively as his eyes focused intently on her.

"Well, I guess that's a little bit of Texas, if you go way back." She was sorry she had responded at all to him at this point. Cultivating friends was not on her agenda for the next several weeks. She picked up the *Strait Times* and tried to look absorbed in it.

The hydrofoil had now risen to full plane and was skimming across the light chop. The hanging moisture had turned to rain that peppered against the windows. Outside, the visibility had dropped to a few hundred yards, obscuring any view of land.

Valdez leaned over to speak to her again. "I noticed you looking out the windows. There is nothing to worry about. These new hydrofoils have the very best radar, and the Macau channel is well marked."

"I am glad you said that. Now maybe I can concentrate on my reading."

A flicker of disappointment crossed his face, then he settled back in his seat, folded his hands across his lap, and closed his eyes.

They reached Macau in a driving rain. Nothing had changed at customs since her last visit with Sheldon Blake several years ago. It took her nearly thirty minutes to clear the long lines. Valdez had followed behind her.

Once outside, Ellen proceeded quickly toward a cab stand. To her surprise, Valdez continued to follow. Customs had evidently waved him through immediately. He stepped to the curb and signaled with a wave of his hand. A black Mercedes moved quickly in front of him.

"Perhaps I can drop you somewhere. I'm heading toward downtown. Come . . . Please let me do that. The rain will get you soaked quickly."

He was certainly right about the rain. Ellen climbed into the spacious rear seat to share it with Valdez. He looked at her questioningly. "So, where will it be?"

"Actually, I am meeting a friend at the Hyatt on Taipa. So just drop me anywhere downtown."

"Nonsense! It's only a mile and a quarter across the causeway. Driver, we're going to take this young lady to Taipa." He turned to her looking very concerned. "Now, young lady, I have given you my card. Please call me if I can help you in any way. Perhaps you might use my car and driver. You know it is terrible of me, but I don't believe I got your name."

"Ellen. And I do want to thank you for keeping me from getting soaked. And if I get a chance I will call you." She purposely didn't give him a last name,

278

though she realized such information could be found easily enough by a man of Valdez's apparent status.

They arrived at the hotel on Taipa in a matter of minutes. Ellen thanked Valdez profusely and breathed a sigh of relief once she was out of the limo.

A late evening hydrofoil back to Hong Kong in the foul weather was out of the question, so Ellen checked into the hotel immediately. It was almost 11:00 A.M. before she returned to the lobby, fresh and dry.

Outside, the driving rain had turned once again to heavy fog. A doorman paged the hotel-courtesy jitney, which Ellen took back across the causeway. She got out and walked to the Bank of Macau, only several blocks away.

She opened a checking account under her own name and deposited sixty thousand of the Hong Kong dollars. The rest she carried for window-shopping the gold market along Avenida de Almeida Rubeiro.

It was late afternoon by the time her walking tour brought her to the Lisboa Casino. She entered the casino, purchased ten thousand Hong Kong dollars worth of chips, and sat down at a blackjack table where she lost it all within minutes. Despite her atrocious luck, she tipped the dealer handsomely. When she rose from the table she came face-to-face with Hercules Valdez.

He shook his finger playfully. "Naughty, naughty, now look at all the gold you've thrown away."

"Hercules," she smiled. "Do they really call you Hercules?"

"Why don't you call me Cristo. My friends seem to prefer that over Hercules."

"Cristo, I must confess that blackjack is a weakness of mine. Every time I come to Macau, I must lose a few dollars."

279

"Fortunately for Macau, many visitors feel the same way."

Ellen made a decision to refuse the offer of a ride from Valdez that she felt sure was coming. "Cristo, it is urgent that I get back to my hotel. The hotel runs a little bus across the causeway. It is time for it to come back. Thanks again for the lift this morning."

Surprisingly, Valdez made no move to accommodate her. "Young lady, I do expect to hear from you. Make a little time for a new friend when you next come to Macau." With that, he kissed her hand, bowed slightly, and walked off into the casino.

She had the distinct feeling he had probably been stalking her the entire day.

The next three days were consumed by meetings with interior designers and contractors gleaned from a list Sheldon Blake had given her. One of the three days was spent with Lee Ching and a contractor at the site of the new restaurant along Canton Road.

Lee Ching had been right. The wall to be reconstructed into a tiered veranda overlooking Victoria Harbour was proving to be a major cost concern. The wooden beam construction prescribed by Sheldon Blake's blueprint wouldn't do. The building standards demanded steel, and that meant the cost factor for the veranda, which was to be a centerpiece of the restaurant, would be doubled. Lee Ching saw no hope for any compromise with the contractor. Ellen refused to give in without first contacting another builder for an estimate. All this effort would eat up valuable time.

Armand Hauser was due to arrive in one more day. Fortunately, some work could begin immediately on those portions of the plan not affected by the construction of the new wall.

During those times when Ellen found herself free of

Lee Ching and the builders, she visited different banks, carefully setting up personal accounts. In all, she established six different accounts within walking distance or a ferry trip from the Peninsula Hotel.

One by one, she met with contractors. Ellen Lambert was developing a reputation for being a ruthless negotiator. She demanded massive deferred payments until work was completed, dangling the carrot of attractive bonuses for contractors who completed work ahead of time.

Potential creditors were barraging Hong Kong Western Bank with requests for assurances of Waterfront, Inc.'s, ability to pay. Laurence Greenstreet called. A late candlelight dinner was arranged in Kowloon, ostensibly to discuss these matters. Before their evening together was over, Ellen Lambert had absolutely convinced him of her business acumen.

"You know, Miss Lambert, you are a pleasure to watch in action. I know a lot of hard-driving businessmen who would not take on some of the tough cookies that you have. You have talent that they do not suspect women to have over here. They are not used to it." While he spoke, Greenstreet gaped at the top of her low-cut cocktail dress, obviously minus any support other than the magnificent torso of Ellen Lambert.

"What a wonderful compliment! Larry, I'll drink to that." She signaled for the waiter and asked for a bottle of his best brandy.

"Do you really think we should? I want to be in shape to give those blueprints of yours a going-over tomorrow." Greenstreet's staid banker's demeanor was slipping away rapidly. He was beginning to slur his words.

"Of course we should, Larry. You men drink together and talk over business deals all the time. I know you guys." She winked teasingly and maneuvered in her chair to allow the low-cut gown to fully expose her for a few seconds. "Larry, I've got a great idea. Instead of me bringing the blueprints of Waterfront, Inc., to the bank tomorrow, let's have our drink and then go straight to my hotel. The blueprints are already laid out on a table in my suite. Please, I insist."

"That would certainly save us some valuable time tomorrow, wouldn't it?" He downed a half snifter of brandy in several quick gulps.

Ellen Lambert sensed that he was trying to steel his courage with brandy. He was obviously no Don Juan. She would have to lead him all the way. "Okay, Larry, it's time. Come on, the walk will do us good."

"My dear, dear lady. We ... we ... haven't had dessert. It's not fitting that such a lovely lady not have dessert." Now, the senior vice president of one of the Orient's largest banks was getting sloppy.

"Larry, dear, don't worry one bit about that. I have some chocolate truffles in my suite that we'll enjoy as I show you the blueprints." She stood up and he joined her, his gait surprisingly steady.

"Aha! Truffles. I love chocolate truffles." Every now and then he would pause as they walked to stare down at her gaping neckline.

"Now, Larry, you've got to stop that. You are attracting attention. I don't think people appreciate that over here, do they?"

"Then they're nuts, my dear." He took her arm and marched them toward the hotel.

"Now you be good, Larry, and I'll show you a delightful new way to eat chocolates."

Laurence Greenstreet did his best to feign sobriety as he looked through the blueprints. Several pages were actually upside down as he studied them, nodding his approval. "Magnificent, my dear, magnificent. I've never seen anything quite so impressive. My colleagues will be pleased with my report in the morning."

Ellen Lambert had kicked away her high heels and propped up her feet on the large sofa. Her knees were bent, and her silk skirt rode up her long thighs. "Oh, Larry, you are too easily impressed, I'm afraid. It's not the Taj Mahal, it's a new restaurant."

Greenstreet turned to face her, and was obviously stunned by her provocative pose. "Ellen, you look like one of those American movie stars. I—I . . . really can't find words to express the feeling I get when I look at you. Joy, I think, would describe it best."

"Joy?" Ellen smiled seductively. "You are a devil, Larry. I've never heard it described quite like that. Come over here and sit. After a busy day at your bank, it really wasn't fair of me to spring these blueprints on you tonight. Let me help you relax."

Greenstreet joined Ellen on the sofa.

"It feels so good to have you close to me, Larry. Why not show me exactly what is on your mind."

He leaned awkwardly toward her on the sofa, lavishing a kiss on each of her knees while ripping at his collar to free himself from the constricting shirt and necktie.

"Mr. Greenstreet! Do you give all your customers this kind of attention?"

"Oh, no," he murmured between kisses. "Only you." Then he looked up, deadly serious. "But we won't tell a soul, will we?"

Greenstreet left the suite a little before sunrise, thoroughly sated with the taste of chocolate and the lingering fragrance of Ellen Lambert. He decided to take the Star Ferry, thinking that perhaps he could catch a few minutes of sleep.

43

Hacker banged away on the back door of Doris Hackley's flower shop in Laguna Beach. It was 8:00 A.M. on Saturday, and Doris was busy arranging and potting items in a workroom at the rear of the shop. "I'm coming, just a moment," she called out, determined to put the finishing touches on the flower arrangement before her.

Then came another series of bangs on the door. She threw up her hands in annoyance and went to the alleyway door. There, she found herself looking at the mangled face of Hacker. "Hacker! Why didn't you let me know it was you who was knocking?"

Hacker grunted and pushed his way past her into the workroom. "Still screwing around with posies, huh, Doris? How's business?" He walked around the shop that was packed with orders tagged for customers picking them up that day.

"It's fine, Hacker. How's business at the Pair-a-Dice

Club?" She stood across a workbench from him, finding it difficult to be civil as he glared at her.

"Business is good, Doris. It's so good, I'm taking a little vacation. Gonna go to Mexico and check out a few senoritas."

"You're a liar, Hacker. The club has been shut down for a week, and everybody's been looking for you. You're on the run again, just like the old days. You're in big trouble, and really, Hacker, I don't want to hear about it this time." Hacker looked menacingly at her. They had gone through many shouting matches in the past, but never had he become physically violent with her.

"What do you mean by everybody, Doris? Who's lookin' for me?"

Doris Hackley was feeling real fear now. She couldn't recall Hacker ever looking so wild-eyed and tense. She walked to the front of the flower shop and unlocked the door, hoping early customers might enter the shop. Hacker trailed behind her.

No sooner had she unlocked the door, then he stepped in front of her and reclosed the dead bolt. He turned to face his sister. "Goddamn it, Doris, I asked you a question. I want an answer, and that's a fact."

"Okay, Hacker, you asked for it, and you aren't going to like it. Just remember, whatever mess you are in, it's your own doing. The LAPD sent a detective down here. The Reno, Nevada, police have been here twice. Two private investigators have been looking for you. They all look like they mean business." Doris gaped at Hacker, who stared icily at her as she spoke. "Just yesterday, I got a phone call from a detective in New Orleans who insisted that he had some information for you. Hacker, for God's sake, don't tell me what you've done! I don't want to know. Understand?"

"I ain't done nothin', Doris, and that's a fact."

"Oh, yes, one other thing, Hacker. Somebody from Vegas called. Seems you won a five hundred dollar bet on the Phillies. You listed my phone number but gave no address when you mailed it in. How they going to pay you off?"

"So what did you tell him?"

"I gave him the address to the Pair-a-Dice Club."

"You're a dumb bitch, Doris."

"I guess you're right. I'm sorry I opened my mouth. Jesus, Hacker, I'm no mind reader." She glanced toward the front door, praying for a customer to show up. "Why bug me now, Hacker?"

"I need my passport, Doris. Remember when a gang of us went to Mexico City about four years ago? You kept my passport in a bag with yours. I need it, and that's a fact."

Doris Hackley felt relieved. She remembered seeing his passport with hers when she was preparing for her recent honeymoon. "I know just where it is. I'll bring it in tomorrow. But you said you were going to Mexico. I don't think you need it down there."

"I may stay awhile, Doris. It's best I have it with me." Hacker looked a little calmer now.

"I'll have it here bright and early in the morning, Hacker." Doris was thinking to herself that she wished Hacker would stay away forever. She moved casually to the door, flipped the dead bolt open, and stepped out onto the sidewalk, pretending to study the window displays.

Hacker now stood in the doorway, shaking his finger at her. "Don't screw up again, Doris. I need that passport." Hacker turned on his heels and walked toward the rear of the flower shop.

Doris Hackley watched Hacker open the rear door and leave the potting room. She quickly reentered the shop and rushed to lock the alleyway door. She prayed

that tomorrow would be the last time she would see
Hacker. Right then, she decided that if the authorities
continued to pester her about him, she would just tell
them what Hacker had told her. She'd tell them that
Hacker had left for Mexico.

The next day, shortly before noon, Coley Doctor
walked though the door of the flower shop. He idly
studied the arrangements around the shop and
waited for Doris Hackley, who was waiting on a customer. She eyed him warily. Even though he was
dressed in sweats and sneakers now, she recognized
him as the investigator who had come in recently to
ask about Hacker.

"How much are the roses? The long stems?" Coley
asked when she was free.

"Forty dollars a dozen," she said, without her usual
friendly smile, wondering when he was going to bring
up Hacker's name.

"Box me up a dozen," he requested, much to her
surprise.

"Sure, you get the pick of what we have." She
walked toward the glassed-in display that held the
roses.

"I'll leave it to you to pick them out. You know more
about roses than I do. Will they be all right in the car
for two or three hours?"

Doris Hackley looked out at the damp, cool haze
that hugged the shore. "I'm sure they will be. Just tell
the lucky recipient to get them in water right away."

"By the way, have you seen your brother lately?"

Doris dropped her hands to her side, momentarily
stopping the selection of roses. "I knew you were going to ask. Really, mister, if you don't want the roses,
you don't have to buy them. I'm going to run out before the day is over, anyway."

"Oh no, I really need them. I think they're perfect for one of the really beautiful people, don't you?"

"Absolutely," Doris Hackley agreed. "As far as Hacker goes, you missed him. He was here early this morning. He wanted his passport, which was good news for me. It means he is going somewhere. I hope he stays a long time."

"Well, I'm an unlucky investigator, but a very lucky flower buyer. These are truly beautiful. Did he say where he was going?"

Doris quietly boxed the roses. Then she said, "He said Mexico. He didn't say where in Mexico. Tijuana would be Hacker's style. Frankly, I don't give a damn—just like Mr. Clark Gable said." Doris Hackley smiled warmly, then slid the box of roses toward Coley.

Coley peeled off forty dollars. "Thanks, Miss Hackley. I'll try not to bother you any more, unless it's to buy more flowers." He picked up his roses and walked out the door, turning once to wave to Doris, who watched as he walked away.

Coley arrived at the basketball court a little late and was disappointed at not seeing Marissa Chablis's car. He got out of his car, took a basketball from the trunk, and began to shoot a few baskets. He was beginning to think she had been joking about meeting him, when she pulled up in a racy red Corvette with the top down.

Marissa hopped out of the car, looking like a goddess even in sweat togs and sneakers. "Hi, big guy. I thought you might chicken out," she winked and smiled. "I got backlogged at the office today, believe it or not. I had to put together a Hong Kong mail pouch for her highness. Sheldon Blake said it couldn't wait." She walked over and kissed Coley lightly on his chin.

"You are a noble employee to give up a big part of

your Sunday. Where in the hell is Ellen Lambert staying over there, anyway?"

"At the Peninsula Hotel in Kowloon. It must be some posh joint. I'd swap the daily room rent for a week of pay." Marissa fielded the ball, which Coley had bounced off the backboard, and fired it at him, hitting him solidly in the gut.

"Hey! You're something. Where did you learn to pass like that?"

"You ain't seen nothing yet, Mr. All-American." She arched a one-hander through the basket.

The two worked out strenuously for about forty-five minutes before Coley decided to call time-out. He grinned broadly at his companion. "Okay, tell me. Where'd you play basketball?"

"Southern Cal, but darn it, they made me play with the girls."

"And you'd rather play with the boys." Coley grinned.

"Cool it, Coley!" She fired another pass solidly into his gut. "Thanks for the great workout. I'd like to do this again." Marissa mopped the stream of sweat from her brow and sat down on a bench near the edge of the court.

"Doll, you give me a better one-on-one than a lot of guys," Coley said sincerely. "I'll play you anytime you can get away from that sweatshop you work for."

Marissa nodded. "That's not very often. But Armand Hauser is leaving for Hong Kong tomorrow, and today I booked a ticket for Sheldon Blake. He leaves in about ten days. Then the pressure is really going to be off, and this little mouse is going to find time to play."

"Now that's what I like to hear." Coley walked back with her to the two parked cars. He reached inside his car and produced the florist box. "These are for you."

He paused for a moment, remembering her advice to go slow. "How about dinner tonight?"

"Only if you come to my place," was her unexpected reply. "Gee, they are beautiful!" she exclaimed, lifting the corner of the box to peek at the roses. "I've been trying to refine my cooking. Waterfront has spoiled me. We can sit and look at the roses, then dine on one of my noble experiments."

"I'm yours. When and where?"

"Oveta Terrace. It's in the hills, north of Sunset." She fished around in her handbag, produced a pencil and notepad, and scribbled down an address and phone number. "Let's make it about seven, okay? Give me a call if you get lost."

"I'll be there." When Marissa stood up, Coley put his arms around her and gave her a firm hug. She arched backward when he tried to kiss her.

"Coley!"

"I know, cool it."

"Go slow. Remember, Coley, slow is better." Marissa smiled and stepped into the open Corvette.

He watched the car speed away until it was out of sight. Exhilarated, he dribbled rapidly back onto the court, let fly with a shot far outside the three-point circle, and watched it swish through the net. Marissa Chablis was truly something else.

Willy was wrestling with luggage on the aft deck when he spotted Coley. "Hey, you're just in time. Help me lug this stuff to the car. We're off to Hong Kong in the morning."

"You and everybody else." Coley told him about Armand Hauser and Sheldon Blake. "By the way, Ellie-Jo's staying at the Peninsula."

Willy gave Coley his full attention. "You're just full of information today."

"I got it all from heaven, from an angel named Marissa Chablis. She's my mole at Waterfront, Inc."

"Very good, Coley!"

"It's good information, Willy. When you come face-to-face with Ellie-Jo, what are you going to do?"

"I'm going to confront her, and if she blinks, I am going to call the police, the American Consulate, and the number you gave me for Interpol."

"I got some bad news, Willy. Hacker is back in town. He picked up his passport from Doris down at the flower shop and flew the coop. She said he's heading for Mexico."

"Good. At least I won't have to keep looking over my shoulder in Hong Kong." The second he said it, he saw the worried look on Coley's face.

"Damnit, Willy! We don't know he's going to Mexico for sure. All we know is he's on the run with a valid passport. So keep looking over your shoulder."

"Okay, Coley. But Tijuana is more Hacker's style."

"Hey, that's just what his sister said."

They picked up the luggage and locked it in the trunk of Ginny's Porsche.

"Willy, if I get any evidence that Hacker is off for Hong Kong, I'm hopping the next plane."

"You worry too much, Coley. Get some rest."

"I'm having dinner with Marissa Chablis," Coley volunteered with a big smile. "We're eating at her place. All in the line of duty, of course."

44

Armand's plane arrived six hours late, well after midnight. Ellen Lambert met him at Kai Tak Airport with a Rolls Royce and a driver, standard hotel procedure for important guests.

"Armand, poor man, your eyes are circled with dark rings. You look like you haven't slept in days." Ellen cuddled next to him, tracing her fingers lightly over his brow.

He was staring blankly out the window. The sea of lights along Nathan Road, mostly in Chinese script, extended down many of the narrow, curving side streets. There was just too much to absorb after an eighteen-hour flight with only fitful sleep.

"Funny, it's just as I pictured it," he murmured. "I really didn't get much sleep. We left almost four hours late. Then, a couple thousand miles east of here, we had to circle a typhoon. It was a huge storm. The clouds and continual lightning in the distance was quite a show. It seemed to go on forever."

"How dreadful! Unfortunately, I have some other bad news for you, Armand. I'm afraid there's no room at the inn," she teased.

"Oh no, what happened?" Armand looked wearier than ever.

"When I found out your plane was arriving so late, I canceled your room until tomorrow. Poor Armand. You will just have to share my room tonight."

He looked at her with very little expression. He couldn't tell when she was teasing. "Is that wise, my dear?"

"Wisdom has nothing to do with it, Armand. Are you disappointed?"

"Of course not." He finally broke into a smile. "Our nights together in the past have always been spent on some sandy beach. With all that water out there, I figured you would have chosen one for us by now."

Her soft lips brushed his ear gently. "I have found one, my dear, but that will come later."

"Aha! I knew it. Is the Peninsula far?"

"We're almost there. Have you had dinner?"

Armand chuckled. "I don't know what I had. The time got all fouled up. I ate a couple of meals during the flight. They were actually quite good for airline service. But it has been some time."

"We'll just see if we can have something sent up to the suite." She kissed him again, circling the back of his neck with soft kisses. "There is a box of chocolate truffles in the room, courtesy of the hotel. Maybe you can snack on those. I must confess that I've already had my share of them. I am a naughty girl, Armand." She nudged him, pointing to a side street. "There's Peking Road. The new Waterfront, Inc., is just a few blocks away. It's an easy walk."

"Good, I know I won't be able to resist going over there tomorrow. How does it look?"

"The potential is spectacular, though the site is quite a mess right now. Don't worry about that. I'm handling all the construction plans with the contractors. Your job is to survey our potential competitors and come up with a food supply service. Also, you will want to supervise the details of the kitchen area. Study the blueprints, and make certain that the kitchen will be the finest in the world."

"Ah, that is a job I will relish; after I get some sleep, of course." Ellen was pressing close to him in the Rolls Royce. He sensed that sleep was not on her mind right now.

Armand closed his eyes and thought back to the time when he had happily tended the business in Galveston. What was happening now, halfway around the world, would have seemed impossible just a few months ago. Here was Ellen, with one of her endless legs crossed over his, tracing deft circles on his brow, and he was riding a Rolls Royce quietly through the garish glitter of Hong Kong. He shook his head in disbelief.

"What's the matter, Armand?" Ellen cooed softly.

"Look around us, dear. We're a long way from the beach at San Onofre." He turned toward her and kissed her on the lips. Despite his exhausted state, he felt the raw passion pushing everything else from his mind. He gently touched her nyloned leg.

"You are such a romantic, Armand. No wonder I missed you so much. It takes you to remind me that the whole twenty-four hours of each day cannot be allocated to business."

Once inside the suite, the lights were doused quickly. Armand moved over her in relentless, passionate pursuit of the ecstasy that was always their reward. Finally, sleep came to them both.

As the dawn broke, Armand was stirred from his deep slumber. Ellen was burrowing beneath the covers with a trail of kisses that would draw the last vestige of energy from him.

It was midmorning before he awoke again. Ellen bent over him, fully clothed in a dark silk pinstripe jacket and matching short skirt. Her hair, bound neatly in a prim bun, was adorned as usual by the string of pearls. She kissed him gently. "Darling, Lee Ching will be here in an hour to show you the new quarters. You are to meet him in the lobby. I'm going to Hong Kong Western Bank and then on to Macau. I'll see you tomorrow morning. Did you understand all that, lover?"

"I think so," he replied, pulling himself up on one elbow and rubbing his eyes. "You didn't tell me this last night, did you?"

"No, you seemed preoccupied with other things last night. Do you remember?" She stroked his hair.

"I'll never forget." Armand was now wide awake. "Is Macau safe? I've seen some perfectly grisly old motion pictures about that place."

"That's nonsense, Armand. It's perfectly wonderful. I'll take you there soon." She walked to the door, turned and blew him a kiss, then left.

In a few moments, Armand leaped from the bed, strode to the drapes, and pulled them wide. He stared across Victoria Harbour at the endless skyline of Hong Kong Island. A bundle of energy now, he showered and dressed for his meeting with Lee Ching.

On the short drive to the Waterfront location, except for when he was asked a question Lee Ching was silent. The sun blazed on this day, the usual humidity breaking to a tolerable level. "We flew around a typhoon way out beyond the Philippines. Do you get much trouble from them here in Hong Kong?"

"Oh yes, we are famous for typhoons here in Hong Kong. It is not unusual to have several during the season." Lee Ching waved his hand toward the north. "Just a few miles that way is the Yau Ma Tei typhoon shelter. Thousands of boats crowd behind a huge breakwater when a typhoon comes. We have learned by experience just what to do."

They pulled up in front of a large building, three stories high and connecting to other buildings beyond. A sign mounted on two posts advised that it was the "New Home of Waterfront, Inc., Selective Seafood Cuisine." The message was repeated in Chinese characters. A large double door was raised where a big semi-rig was unloading lumber. Lee Ching walked with Armand to the open door and went inside.

Lee handed Armand a key on a large ring. "Miss Lambert told me to give you this. This is the key to the door at the far end of the building. It is always kept locked, even when you are inside."

"Thanks. I'll make sure it stays locked when I come here by myself." Armand turned to examine the inside of the building. What he saw was extremely depressing. The building itself was little more than a shell, completely without internal walls or ceiling. There were crates and stacks of lumber everywhere. It took great imagination to visualize it as anything but a warehouse.

A crew of workmen had opened a large section of wall fronting the harbor. They were busy installing huge temporary jacks meant to hold the roof until a supporting structure was put in place that would hold the dining veranda, which would overlook the water. In one corner of the building stood a ten-foot square cubicle that held the construction office. Armand noticed blueprints spread out over a table inside. He tried the door. It was open.

"Lee, I am going to spend some time with these plans now. There's no need for you to stay." Armand looked at his expressionless driver, who seemed in no hurry to leave.

"Miss Lambert says I am at your disposal."

"I understand that, but I can walk back to the hotel when I am finished here. Why don't you go on and enjoy this beautiful day while it lasts." Armand waved toward the door.

Lee hesitated. "Very well. Call if you change your mind. I have a beeper and will be close by." He walked out of the building and climbed into the car, where he sat for a few moments before slowly driving away.

Armand leafed through the blueprints, which were duplicates of those he had looked at with Sheldon Blake. He noticed that the notations for steel supports to hold the veranda were exed out and replaced by descriptions of supporting wooden timbers. He wondered why Ellen Lambert hadn't mentioned such a significant change to him. Of course, any substantive conversation with her had been usurped by their all-night sexual marathon.

There were other changes as well, most seeming to reflect a cost-saving pattern. But it was when Armand got to the page that depicted the kitchen area that he stopped, stunned. Almost half the space allocated to the kitchen had been eliminated. Missing was the in-house bakery and an area for several broilers and ovens. Lettering on the plans indicated that it had been reassigned as management office space.

The new plans for the kitchen were absurd. In no way could such a kitchen handle the volume expected by Sheldon Blake. Armand would have to take that up with Ellen as soon as she returned from Macau. Perhaps some of the other changes could be effected, but the kitchen now proposed would just not do.

Several inside walls were originally designated to be finished in teakwood. In each case, teak was scratched out and underwritten by the designation of stained plywood.

The day passed by quickly. Armand had lunch brought to him in the construction shack, where he continued with his work throughout the afternoon. As the day drew to a close the workers began to leave the building. The last person to leave lowered the big double-freight door.

Armand continued to study the building plans, pausing only now and then to walk into the building and pace off certain measurements.

It was already dark outside when Armand heard a distinct, loud, scraping noise. He rose and stared into the warehouse, now illuminated just with several bare, hanging bulbs. He walked out into the construction area, weaving his way between piles of building materials, but found nothing. He decided that the noise had come from outside, or that some carelessly placed tool or piece of wood had fallen.

Armand opened the door, pausing to test the key that Lee Ching had given him. He exited the building and shut the door behind him.

There was a scraping noise from somewhere above his head. He jumped forward quickly as several massive cinder blocks crashed down onto the pavement beside him. Another smashed onto his shoulder in a glancing blow that narrowly missed his head.

Armand cried out in shock and pain as he clutched his arm and tried to put distance between himself and the building. By the time he reached Canton Road, he was overcome by nausea and dizziness, and he fell to the ground, unconscious.

When he woke up the next morning, he was in a hospital bed. Lee Ching stood at the foot. "Good morning, Mr. Hauser. I hope you are feeling better."

45

Ginny and Willy arrived on a Cathay Pacific flight that landed at about noontime. They took a cab from Kai Tak Airport to the Sheraton Towers in Kowloon. The hotel was located at the end of Nathan Road on Salisbury.

Looking across Nathan Road, Willy spotted the Peninsula Hotel. "That's certainly a piece of luck. Ellen Lambert is practically our neighbor, if Coley's information is correct."

The sight of the Peninsula so nearby had a sobering effect on Ginny. Though the long flight had been tiring, they had enjoyed the uninterrupted conversation time. They had talked at great length about exploring Hong Kong together. Now, the Peninsula served as a reminder to Ginny that there was unpleasant business ahead.

They unpacked quickly in their hotel. Ginny parted

the drapes in the corner suite. One wide window offered a magnificent view of the harbor; the other faced the Peninsula. "So what are you going to do, Willy? What exactly do you plan to say when you meet her?"

Willy stared for a moment at the Peninsula and scratched at the stubble on his chin. "Let's take a nap. Neither of us slept much on the plane. Later, we'll order up some lunch and talk it over. We have a big advantage. She has never seen me or you. But I saw her on the day that Coley and I staked out her apartment in Santa Monica."

"Baby, I'm all for that nap. We can play detective later. Maybe we can even do a little shopping first." Ginny, still fully clothed, stretched out across the big bed.

"Ginny, sometimes you talk just like a woman."

Ginny grinned impishly. "My God, Willy, that's Nathan Road out there. It goes on for miles and you can buy anything at any price."

"Maybe you would like to shop your fanny off, and I'll chase down Ellen Lambert. How does that sound?"

"Idiotic. If you think I'm going to let you go out and chase than man-eating bimbo alone, you've got another thing coming. Now come over here. I have something for you to do."

"What?"

"I want you to take my clothes off. The flight was just too tiring. I need help."

"There you go, talking like a woman again."

Three hours passed before Willy awoke and slipped out of bed. He showered, slipped on a robe, and went straight for the telephone to place a call to the Peninsula Hotel.

"Miss Ellen Lambert's room, please." He counted a dozen rings before the operator came back on the line.

"Miss Lambert is not answering. Do you wish to leave a message?"

"No, thank you, I'll call back later." He hung up, vaguely relieved. He had at least established that she was registered.

He turned to speak to Ginny, but she had abandoned the room for the shower. He stared at the telephone. Coley's call was almost an hour late. This wasn't like Coley at all, he thought. Maybe he got the time differential screwed up.

Ginny emerged from the dressing room, looking like a million dollars in a softly tailored dark silk suit. Willy finished dressing quickly and within minutes they were strolling across Nathan Road toward the Peninsula Hotel.

Soon they were settled into plush sofas in the elegant lobby of the old hotel. Willy pretended to be absorbed in a copy of the South China *Morning Post*, while Ginny lost herself in a tourist map.

They didn't have to wait long. Less than half an hour later, Ellen Lambert walked through the lobby right in front of them. She was dressed in a dark pinstripe jacket with a provocatively short tight skirt. A string of pearls secured the bun of auburn hair. She walked to the desk where she picked up a message from the clerk. She spent several moments reading it, then, unexpectedly, she turned and walked back out of the hotel. Outside, she ordered a taxi from the doorman, who appeared to relay her destination to the driver. She climbed into the cab and soon vanished down Salisbury Road.

Willy moved swiftly to the doorman. "That woman—

who took the last taxi—we're late and were supposed to go with her. She will be so disappointed. Do you know where she went?" Willy pulled out a twenty and held it in full view.

"She went to the hospital. Queen Elizabeth Hospital. She seemed quite upset." The doorman hailed another taxi with a flourish as Willy passed him the twenty.

"Now what?" Ginny whispered quietly once inside the cab.

"I certainly don't want to confront her in a hospital," Willy answered. He shrugged and then moved forward on the seat to communicate with the driver. "We're not going to the hospital after all." He fished around in a jacket pocket for a slip of paper with the address of the new Waterfront, Inc., location. "Take us here instead."

He handed the slip of paper to the driver.

"It very close," the man replied in halting English. He turned a corner, drove for only a couple of blocks, and stopped in front of a darkened building.

They read the sign posted in front of what appeared to be an abandoned warehouse.

The driver looked dubious. "You want here?"

Willy looked around, making a mental note of the location in relation to their own hotel. "It looks like they are closed. Please circle around and take us to the Sheraton Towers."

The driver turned to look at Willy directly. "Sheraton Tower?"

"That's right. I guess we've made a mistake," Willy said.

"That's the first one we've ever made," Ginny added with a smile and then turned to Willy. "Willy, I can't be a detective on an empty stomach."

"Let's eat at the hotel. They must have a good restaurant or two. That way I can make arrangements to receive Coley's call when it comes through." Both were very much aware that Coley's call was now three hours late.

46

Coley stared at the large round clock on the wall. It was a Western Union electric clock that had probably been in the precinct house for fifty years, and in all that time he doubted that it had ever been cleaned or even dusted. He watched the second hand sweep around the dial, comparing it to his own wristwatch. The second hand made it downhill from twelve to six in twenty-six seconds, and it took thirty-four seconds to climb back to the twelve.

He had been in the small room for over two hours, handcuffed and under guard. His phone call to Hong Kong was hours late. Willy would think something was wrong for sure—and there was.

Detective Joe Martin entered the room, trailed by a short, suave-looking fellow, fastidiously dressed in a dark suit and a perfectly knotted and painted silk tie.

"Joe! What in the hell is going on here? For Pete's sake, let's get these cuffs off."

Joe sat on the opposite side of a bare wooden table, facing Coley. He flipped through some papers clamped to a clipboard. The suave, dark little man chose to stand, rather than sit down in the only other available chair. Joe Martin still hadn't acknowledged Coley's existence.

"Will someone please tell me what's going on." He leaned as low as he could over the table, trying to catch the detective's eye.

"Do you want to call a lawyer, Coley?" Joe spoke in a low, clipped voice.

"I am a lawyer, as you well know."

"Damnit, Coley. You know what they say about people who defend themselves. You'd better get a real practicing lawyer, Coley." He motioned to the man behind him. "This is Captain Jean Bonaparte of the New Orleans Police Department."

The man nodded at Coley. "Are you prepared to answer some questions for us right now?"

Coley looked back at his old friend Joe Martin, who looked to be in deep concentration, drumming the eraser tip of his pencil on the table.

"Mr. Doctor, did you hear my question?" The New Orleans detective spoke in the low, serious tone one would expect from a doctor inquiring about somebody's chest pains.

"What do you want to know?"

"Were you in New Orleans two weekends ago, on Friday, Saturday, and Sunday?"

"Yes."

"When was the last time you saw Lazy Boy Garcia?"

"I remember a prizefighter with that name, way back when I was a kid."

"Yes, Mr. Doctor, the prizefighter." Bonaparte now sat in the empty chair and stared directly at Coley.

"I never saw him in my entire life." Coley knew he

was in trouble. This police captain from New Orleans had evidently flown all the way to Los Angeles to interrogate him.

"How about Mr. Sammy Lasker? When did you last see him?" The detective looked formidable despite his small stature.

"Sammy Lasker? I never in my life heard of anyone by that name."

Joe Martin and Jean Bonaparte exchanged glances. Coley got the distinct feeling that Martin, at least, believed him.

"Mr. Doctor," started Jean Bonaparte, "maybe you would like to tell us why you rented a storage room from the Bayou Quick Storage Company on Airline Highway in New Orleans."

"I didn't, and I never heard of such a place. You guys must be way off on the wrong track. I admit I flew to New Orleans on Friday. I stayed at the Royal Orleans for two nights. I staked out a house. I came home on Sunday. That's the whole thing. It was a miserable, nonproductive trip for my client. I will swear to God and my mother on that statement."

Bonaparte persisted. "Maybe you had somebody rent the space at Bayou Quick Storage for you. Maybe this somebody was a wiry-looking little tough guy with a busted nose all over his face and a bandaged arm."

"Absolutely not, but I am aware of a person who fits that description. That could be Hacker." Coley glanced at Joe Martin. He had already told Joe about Hacker. "Come on, guys, take these cuffs off. Let's talk about this thing. Maybe we can come up with something."

"Maybe this Hacker fellow is out of town. Maybe he is in a big wooden box tucked away in another private warehouse." Jean Bonaparte turned his wide eyes toward Coley. Bonaparte seemed to never move his head when his eyes swung from person to person. He was an economist with his neck muscles.

"Big wooden box! I saw that damn box!" Coley's thoughts flashed back to the morning in front of Flo Dupre's apartment. The big box had been maneuvered into a panel truck equipped with a hydraulic tailgate lift. At the time, he had not suspected the workman was Hacker. "Who was in the box? I was staking out this house in New Orleans where I thought a friend of Flo Dupre might show up. Up drove a panel truck. A man took the box in and brought it back out in a few minutes. If there was a body in it, there was no logical reason for me to think so at the time. I figured the guy was moving household goods of some kind."

"Mr. Sammy Lasker was found in the box that was deposited in a unit of Bayou Quick Storage. That unit had been rented by Coley Doctor the day before." Bonaparte swung his wide gaze at the old Western Union clock for a moment. "Sammy Lasker was beaten to death with a hard object, probably brass knuckles."

"That dumb bastard, Hacker. He tried to frame me. I'm the one who pushed his nose all over his face, you know." Coley slammed his cuffed hands down on the old wooden table.

"Mr. Doctor, fortunately for you, the manager of Bayou Quick Storage who rented the warehouse unit did not say he had rented it to a tall black man. In fact, he described a man similar to your Mr. Hacker." Bonaparte stood up and circled the table. "Mr. Doctor, for now I am willing to accept that you did not rent the space or even put Lasker into storage. But it is obvious from all you have said that you know some things we do not know. Detective Martin, take the cuffs off him and let's all sit and really get down to business here. If this case involves more than a hoodlum named Sammy Lasker, I think we ought to find out. Frankly, I am very distressed about Lazy Boy. He had his heroic days around New Orleans, you know."

Coley held his hands out in front of him and Joe Martin unlocked the cuffs. Coley looked at Bonaparte. "This Sammy Lasker, why should Hacker have wanted to kill him?"

"Well," began Bonaparte, "our information from the street has it that Sammy Lasker was carrying a large sum of mob money. He had a lot of enemies. That's why he hired Lazy Boy as a driver and bodyguard."

"Where's Lazy Boy?" Coley asked.

"Lazy Boy Garcia was found stuffed in the trunk of Sammy Lasker's Cadillac with a bullet through the top of his skull. The vehicle was found in the long-term parking lot at the airport. Now, why don't you tell me something I don't know, Mr. Doctor. Who were you expecting to show up at Miss Dupre's house?"

"I was expecting Ziggy Lemon, a piano player who might have some information about Ellie-Jo and Hacker."

"Mr. Doctor, I want to teach you a lesson you should have learned years ago. If you had come to the police first, we would have been able to tell you all about Ziggy Lemon. He has played one-nighters for years all around the French Quarter. As for Miss Dupre, she is an exotic dancer and dominatrix of some note." Jean Bonaparte locked his eyes on Coley's, waiting for a response.

Joe Martin spoke instead. "Captain, in California, Coley has a reputation for working well with the authorities. What happened this time, Coley?"

"I was trying to get something more solid. You know how flimsy the whole case is."

Jean Bonaparte forced a wide grin. "Well, we have

a long list of solid facts now. Sammy Lasker is dead. Lazy Boy is dead. Flo Dupre and Ziggy Lemon have flown the coop. Apparently your Mr. Hacker spent one night in Charity Hospital in New Orleans and slipped out when no one was looking. At least someone of his description did."

Coley repeated some of the story he had previously told Joe Martin. He told Bonaparte about Reno Airport, where he had seen Ziggy Lemon meet Ellen Lambert's plane.

For the first time, Jean Bonaparte smiled as if he was really amused. "Ziggy Lemon and a woman like that? Such an attraction defies explanation. Most people would suspect the little fellow is hardly a ladies' man. Ah, in our business we get surprises every day, don't we?"

Coley was pleased to hear him say "our business." Bonaparte seemed to be regarding him as an associate now, rather than an adversary.

Joe Martin left them for a moment to pick up a phone call. When he returned, he was scanning a fax message he had just been handed by an assistant.

"Gentlemen, apparently we know where Hacker can be located. A screening of passenger lists on flights to Hong Kong revealed that Clarence Hackley boarded a Northwest flight from Seattle thirty-six hours ago, destination Hong Kong. According to tax records for the Pair-a-Dice Club, Clarence Hackley is the man called Hacker."

Head immobile, Jean Bonaparte rolled his eyes, first at Coley and then at Joe Martin. "I've always wanted to go to Hong Kong." He appeared thoughtful for a moment. "Lazy Boy Garcia was held in high esteem by many of us in New Orleans. I would like to bring home this jackal Hacker."

Coley grimaced. He was thinking about Willy and Ginny, probably in Hong Kong by now. And Hacker could already be waiting. Coley had two priorities. The first was to call Willy and Ginny, the second to ticket himself on the next flight out to Hong Kong. He decided he wouldn't tell Bonaparte. An argument would serve no purpose.

47

Armand was sitting up in his hospital bed when Ellen Lambert arrived. He was so absorbed in a copy of the *Wall Street Journal* that it was some moments before he noticed her. "My dear, you are a sight for aching eyes. Did everything go well in Macau?"

"Of course." She leaned over the bed to kiss his lips. "What happened, Armand?" she asked, while inspecting the fresh bandages and arm splint.

"I'm not sure I know. While locking the door to the new location, several concrete blocks fell from the roof. Someone must have stacked them very sloppily." Armand looked soberly at Ellen. "The doctor said I have a hairline fracture of the ulna in my left arm, a concussion, and some bruised neck and shoulder muscles. Says I should be back in action quite soon, though. Lee Ching is looking into things to see just what did happen."

"Lee will find out." Ellen leaned over the bed and kissed him gently.

"Frankly, I am more disturbed by what I read in the *Journal* here than I am about my wounds. It seems that Waterfront, Inc., stock has dropped almost twenty percent since last week. This short article states that the cash reserves of the company have deteriorated unexpectedly during the last quarter. One analyst says that perhaps the company has been too aggressive with their expansion plans."

"Nonsense! I am sure Sheldon would not permit that to happen. Frankly, Armand, now is the time to invest more in the company." Ellen scanned the article herself. "I think we are in a much better position to assess things than the press. They seldom seem to get things right." She tossed the paper aside and sat on the edge of the bed, trying to comfort him.

"Ellen, if you don't mind, I would like to talk about the new building for a moment." Armand winced as he pushed himself up to a sitting position. "Someone has changed the plans for the kitchen. It will be impossible to operate out of such limited space. And the bakery, what in the devil happened to that space?"

"Don't worry, Armand. Sheldon changed a few things trying to cut costs here and there. He knows of many fine bakeries already established in Hong Kong, and in his infinite wisdom, he thought he was doing the profitable thing. Don't you fret, Armand, I have already talked to him and restored the old blueprint."

"Thank God! I thought we had big problems." He watched as she stepped away and closed the door of the hospital room.

"I am so sorry that I didn't tell you about the problem I had with Sheldon." She sat again on the edge of his bed. "Really, Armand, I had no idea you would go through all those blueprints. I can imagine that you

313

were furious." Her hands were busy now exploring beneath his skimpy hospital gown, her deft fingers trailing down his chest, feather-touching little circles until they reached his abdomen.

As much as his neck and arm ached with pain, he could not keep himself from responding to her quiet attention. Still caressing him, she bent low over the bed to open her lips to his.

After a few moments, she spoke. "Everything will be fine, Armand. Shame on you for worrying without talking to me first." She began to trail kisses down his chest.

"Ellen! This is madness. You must stop." He pulled her up to him with his healthy arm. "Nurses come in and out of this room constantly."

Ellen backed away from him and stood with her arms folded, smiling broadly. "Oh my, I didn't think men ever refused such attention. I think my Armand needs a moonlit beach to revive his courage."

"Maybe I do. Frankly, I hope I can get out of here tomorrow. I'm glad you have a beach picked out already."

"I do, but do you suppose you can handle being a one-armed lover?"

He looked at her, all the time thinking of the beach at San Onofre. "Ellen, you are a wonder. I can't wait to get out of here. I'll *demand* that it be tomorrow."

"I will stop by the office and tell them, Armand. I must go to Macau again in the morning, but I'll try to return late in the day."

Armand nodded in approval, then frowned. "Ellen, just before the concrete blocks fell off the roof, I heard something. It was like a scraping noise. To tell you the truth, I think someone pushed the concrete off the roof. I think someone may have tried to kill me."

Ellen Lambert forced a smile. "Armand! That is

preposterous. You must be suffering from jet lag. No one here even knows you, much less wants to kill you. Now try to rest, so we can get you out of here tomorrow."

Armand closed his eyes. All he could think about was the scraping sound he knew he heard before the blocks crashed to the sidewalk. There was no doubt in his mind that someone wanted him dead.

Ellen bent over the bed and brushed a light kiss on his lips. "Goodbye, lover," she whispered.

Moments later, he opened his eyes and caught a glimpse of her walking away from him down the hall. The sleek legs and the subtle movement under the tight skirt made him want to call her back. Now he was sorry that he had stifled her aggressiveness a few moments earlier. Such thoughts combined with his aches and pains would make sleep impossible. Idly, he wondered why it was necessary for her to spend so much time in Macau.

48

It was about midnight in Hong Kong when the phone rang in Willy and Ginny's quarters at the Towers. Willy heaved a sigh of relief. It was Coley Doctor calling from Los Angeles.

"Coley! Damn you! You're almost nine hours late. Ginny and I have been worried sick."

"Sorry, old pal. But I've been in the clink." Coley proceeded to bring them fully up-to-date. He told them all about the murder of Lazy Boy Garcia and Sammy Lasker and of Hacker's attempt to frame him.

"Jesus, Coley! That's at least five people we know of who were probably knocked off by Hacker. The cops should be getting in on this investigation fast."

"They're in, Willy. Lazy Boy was an old prizefighter, and happened to be a favorite of a New Orleans police captain, Jean Bonaparte. He's headed for Hong Kong."

"Why Hong Kong?"

"Because Hacker flew there thirty-six hours ago from Seattle. Bonaparte has already brought Interpol in on things. He and Joe Martin have also had their heads together." Coley paused to let it all sink in. "Willy, Hacker could turn up at any time over there. You've got to be on the lookout. He knows exactly what Mr. Monday Night Football looks like."

"The cops don't tolerate any bullshit over here, Coley. Hacker runs a crude operation. He's out of his element. There's a good chance he'll screw up."

"Just keep looking over your shoulder. Hey, I got some more news. Marissa Chablis says that Armand Hauser is in the hospital over there. He was damn near crushed by some falling construction material."

"That explains a lot, Coley. We tailed Ellen Lambert to a hospital today. We had no idea why." Willy felt himself champing at the bit to get back on the chase. "I'll get up early tomorrow and try to confront Ellen Lambert. Coley, you might as well wrap up the investigation over there. Everyone who matters is over here."

Coley hesitated. "Boss, I've already booked a flight on Cathay Pacific. I'll see you in about twenty-four hours."

"Coley! No use you sticking your neck out. We can handle it here. After all, Lefty was *my* friend."

"Like I said, boss, I'll see you in about twenty-four hours." Coley quickly hung up the receiver.

Ginny had listened in on most of the conversation, but Willy rehashed it for her benefit as he considered what to do next. "Doll, we're going to keep on doing what we're doing. Tomorrow morning we'll wait for Ellen Lambert and confront her as soon as we can get her alone. We'll have to keep our eyes peeled for Hacker. He's a short, tough-looking guy with broad shoulders. He has a busted nose that screws up his whole face. I don't think you would miss him."

"What about the police, Willy? Life's getting pretty exciting. Don't you think we ought to call them in?"

"Jean Bonaparte and the LA police have already tipped off Hong Kong authorities to pick up Hacker. Frankly, I don't think we have much to worry about from him. He'll stand out like a sore thumb on the streets of Hong Kong." Willy thought about his conversation with Coley. "I hope things get squared away before Coley gets here. He stands out from the crowd even more. He'd be an easy target for Hacker."

Despite the news that Hacker might be prowling Hong Kong, Willy and Ginny slept soundly until their 6:00 A.M. wake-up call. The contact with Coley had given them renewed confidence. They decided to walk over to the Peninsula and have breakfast, while keeping their eyes peeled for Ellen Lambert.

At breakfast, Willy scanned an early edition of the *International Tribune*. The major story told of typhoon Jasmine, now estimated to be on a collision course with the Philippines, though it was still said to be two days southeast of Manila. The small map traced a route that would put it near Hong Kong several days later.

He pushed the paper toward Ginny. "I hope we get the hell out of here before the storm hits. Typhoons are not on my list of favorite things."

Ginny nodded in agreement. "At least the *Tashtego* is safe and snug back in Long Beach." She touched his hand lightly with her own. "Willy, this is our lucky day. Look who's here."

Ellen Lambert had just entered the dining room accompanied by a tall, thin, fastidiously dressed male companion. Willy groaned as the couple was seated several tables away from then. "I wonder who the guy is."

The dignified gentleman carried a black leather briefcase. The two ordered quickly, then became engrossed in conversation. Ellen Lambert seemed to be enjoying herself. Once she reached over to stroke her companion's clean-shaven chin.

"Whoever it is, she knows him pretty well." Ginny kept her eyes on the couple. "In fact, Willy, I'll give you odds that they just crawled out of the same sack."

"Well, whoever he is, I wish he'd disappear. I would prefer to catch her alone." Willy signaled to a waiter. "I'm going to pay the check now so that we can leave immediately after they do."

It wasn't long before Ellen Lambert and her companion rose abruptly from the table and walked toward the door. Ginny and Willy trailed some fifty yards behind them as they crossed Salisbury Road and began walking toward the Star Ferry terminal.

Once aboard the Star Ferry for Central District, Ellen Lambert produced a palm-size video recorder from her large handbag and proceeded to shoot tape of the sights in the harbor. Once, she turned around in a 360-degree circle, filming the inside cabin of the large ferry in one slow sweep.

"Damnit, we've been immortalized," Willy mumbled. "But so have a couple of hundred other people. I guess it's nothing to worry about. We'll talk to her soon, anyway."

Once across Victoria Harbour, Ellen Lambert and her tall companion walked up the gangplank and strode rapidly through the terminal. Outside, they veered to the right at a brisk pace and entered a seemingly endless walkway that led along the waterfront. The crowded walkway led through a shopping complex, then a hotel lobby. At one point, the walkway broke into the open. Ellen Lambert and her companion hesitated for a moment, stood in each others arms at the railing, and kissed.

"See, I told you. They know each other pretty darn well," Ginny said.

"Can't argue with that," said Willy. Their embrace had all the body language of the morning after a night before.

The two disentangled and resumed their brisk pace until they reached a large building, identified in tall letters as the Macau Ferry Terminal. They stood at a ticket window for a few seconds. Then Ellen Lambert turned, ticket in hand, and once again kissed her companion. This time it was a kiss goodbye. She proceeded up a ramp to a boarding area, and her companion turned around and walked directly toward them.

Willy moved swiftly to catch his attention. "Sir, excuse me, but wasn't that Ellen Lambert?"

The tall man looked sharply at him, not expecting the question.

"I know her from Los Angeles. She runs a large restaurant chain. We had a little business relationship there," Willy persisted.

The man broke into a faint smile. "Yes, that was Ellen, all right. Too bad you missed her. Waterfront, Inc., is opening a new restaurant in Hong Kong."

"Really! How exciting. I am sorry I missed her."

The man was beginning to look more at ease. "Perhaps I can pass along a message. She would hate to miss an acquaintance so far from home."

"That would be very kind of you. Just tell her you met Lefty Grogan."

The man pulled some papers from his pocket and jotted down the name. Willy extended his hand. "And who are you, sir?"

"I'm Laurence Greenstreet with Hong Kong Western Bank." He handed Willy a card. "Any friend of Ellen's is a friend of ours. If I can ever be of service to you, sir, just give me a call."

"I certainly will." Willy saw the man glance at his watch and then walk swiftly back to the long walkway along the shore.

Willy returned to the ticket line to find Ginny waiting for him with two tickets in hand. "Good thinking, doll. Let's get aboard."

"Who was he?"

"A banker. See, bankers have fun, too."

The ferry was fairly crowded as they left the dock. Ellen Lambert had not taken her seat, but instead was wandering about the deck with the small video camera in hand. She looked very much like a tourist, intent on recording the passage to Macau in detail.

"Who does the banker think you are?" asked Ginny.

"I told him I was Lefty Grogan, a business acquaintance from back in the States."

"Don't you think that was stupid, Willy?" Ginny posed the question, never taking her eyes off Ellen Lambert.

"Nope. I want her to feel as insecure as possible. I'd love to eavesdrop on the bedroom conversation the next time she gets together with her banker."

Ginny clasped Willy's hand tightly as the hydrofoil pulled up on plane and began to skim across the water.

Ellen Lambert paced the decks of the ferry for most of the trip before taking her seat several rows in front of them. She removed a folio of papers from her large purse and began to study them, and she remained engrossed in them for the rest of the trip. In a little over an hour they reached Macau.

By mere chance, Willy and Ginny picked a customs

line that moved more rapidly than Ellen Lambert's
when they reached Macau. They rushed outside the
terminal where Willy shoved a U.S. twenty at a cab
driver and told him to pull ahead and park along the
curb. It had always been his experience that U.S.
twenty-dollar bills had a way of bridging any language barrier.

When Ellen Lambert emerged from the terminal, a
shiny black Mercedes pulled curbside in front of her.
A portly, broad-shouldered man with a stylish black
beard climbed out and Ellen embraced him. They
climbed into the back seat of the Mercedes, and were
still embracing when the car passed their taxi.

Willy urged the cab driver to follow them through
the heavy traffic to downtown Macau. They stopped
for a moment on the Avenida de Almeida Rubeiro
when Ellen Lambert got out and entered the Bank of
Macau. Her smiling, bearded escort lowered the window and gently blew her a kiss. The Mercedes then
moved on.

"Wow!" exclaimed Ginny. "Talk about a sailor with a
girl in every port, this gal seems to have a tycoon for
every hour of the day."

Willy slipped the cab driver another bill and told
him to hang close to them. "Okay, doll, let's hoof it
awhile and see what she's up to." They got out of the
cab and began to casually window-shop along the
gold-market stalls.

Ellen Lambert emerged from the Bank of Macau,
walked across the town square, then picked up her
pace as she walked several blocks beyond.

"No doubt about it, Willy, that gal's in shape. No
wonder she's got legs like Cindy Crawford."

Just when it looked like she was headed across a
long causeway that stretched across to an island off
the tip of Macau, she turned abruptly to the left and

entered the Hotel Lisboa's large gambling casino. They hesitated for a moment and then followed her inside.

A long hallway led past the lobby of the hotel and opened into a large gambling casino. The place was alive with afternoon action. The noise of coins bouncing into the metal trays created a din. Ellen Lambert stood at one of the crap tables located in a vast pit that extended several hundred feet across the casino. Standing beside her was the heavyset, bearded companion who had met her at the ferry. He was wearing a black Greek fisherman's cap.

Ellen Lambert was betting heavily and attracting much attention from the other players. Her bearded companion was not gambling, but he often leaned close to her to offer advice that she apparently took.

Willy bought a couple of rolls of patacas, quarter-size coins that were needed for most of the slots abutting the casino. He and Ginny positioned themselves where they could watch the action. Ellen and her companion gambled for over an hour, during which time Ellen Lambert amassed several stacks of black chips.

Finally, she and her friend stacked and carried all her chips to the cashier's window, then quickly exited the casino. Once outside the hotel, they climbed into the waiting black Mercedes.

Willy's driver was also waiting faithfully. They followed the Mercedes until it turned abruptly on Rua Pedro Jose Lobo, then stopped in front of the Restaurante Mundo Novo. Ellen and the portly companion were smiling broadly as they went inside.

Willy shoved another twenty at their driver. "Who is that man with the beard?" he asked, pointing to the couple.

The driver fingered the twenty and stuffed it into

his jacket pocket. "That is Hercules Valdez. He own many ships."

Willy had not really expected the driver to answer the question. "He is well known in Macau?"

"Yes, well known," the driver replied.

"You wait here. We'll come back later."

Their driver nodded his head several times. "Yes, yes. I wait." He was obviously pleased with the flow of twenty-dollar bills.

Willy and Ginny toured the shops in the immediate vicinity of the Mundo Novo, always casting an eye toward the waiting Mercedes. Finally, they sat at a sidewalk stall and had a cup of coffee and some unidentifiable bakery rolls that turned out to be delicious.

"What do you think, Willy? She likes banks, gambling, and rich men. But what does that tell us?"

"It tells me that I wish Coley were here with some answers. So far we've been damned lucky. Sooner or later, their driver, or one of them, will become aware of us. Whenever that happens, I think our loyal cab driver friend will disappear." Willy glanced at his watch. The sun was now casting long shadows, ominously darkening the narrow streets. "We'll give it another hour or so and then head back to Hong Kong."

In a short while, with the dusk rapidly closing in, Ellen Lambert and Hercules Valdez emerged from the restaurant and got back into the waiting Mercedes. Willy and Ginny hustled back to their taxi and followed close behind down the Avenida de Almeida Rubeiro. The street narrowed and soon emerged on the waterfront in front of the Macau Palace, a huge, ornate, floating gambling barge. It was a glitzy contrast to the dark waterfront on either side.

Willy and Ginny stared at the garish barge. Massive round columns circled by elegantly carved wooden dragons supported several upper decks. Loud music wafted from the floating baroque establishment.

Willy looked at Ginny, who was gaping at the gaudy barge and the darkness surrounding it. A brisk breeze turned up wavelets on the South China Sea that caught and reflected the lights from the casino. "Well, are you still game?"

"I wouldn't miss it for anything," Ginny replied without hesitation.

"You're a brave lady," Willy murmured, as he fished another twenty for the driver. "Wait right here," he instructed.

Inside the floating casino, Ellen and Hercules were nowhere to be seen. Willy and Ginny walked around the lower deck, feeling conspicuous. The patrons were mostly working-class Chinese, and many of them gaped at the handsome couple as they circled the casino.

Gathering their courage, they climbed an ornate staircase that led to an upper deck. There, the atmosphere changed. This lavishly decorated casino obviously catered to a more cosmopolitan and affluent clientele. Ellen Lambert and Hercules Valdez stood at a crap table crowded with a noisy group of players.

Willy pushed into an open seat at a blackjack table and began to place modest, luckless wagers. After awhile, Ellen backed away from the crap table and brushed a kiss on Hercules' cheek. To their surprise, Hercules continued to play as Ellen Lambert made her way to the stairwell leading to the first deck. Willy and Ginny moved immediately to follow her, but she had a significant head start. On the first deck she was nowhere to be seen. Now they were practically running to the doors leading outside where a narrow companionway circled the vessel.

"There she is!" Ginny pointed to Ellen Lambert, who was striding rapidly down the companionway a hundred feet away. They followed quickly until Ellen stopped, now less than fifty feet from where they stood.

Willy held Ginny in his arms at the rail, pretending to enjoy the sight of the dancing lights on the water. To their amazement, Ellen Lambert climbed over the rail and lowered herself out of sight, evidently down a ladder they could not see.

Peering over the side, they spotted a sampan nestled close to the hull of the Macau Palace. In the darkness, they watched her form disappear under the canopy stretched across the small vessel. They moved closer to the ladder.

A squat figure appeared on the stern of the small sampan and dropped to his knees to tend to a small outboard motor. They could see the motion of the man as he pulled the cord and the small outboard sputtered and came to life.

From the top of the ladder leading to the water below, they watched the small boat putt away from the Macau Palace. For an instant, the man at the tiller stood up and turned to be illuminated in the light coming from the casino.

"My God! It's Hacker!" Willy whispered hoarsely to Ginny. They both watched the tiny sampan vanish into the murky darkness now covering the South China Sea.

They stood in silence until they could no longer hear the tiny motor that powered the vessel. Willy cursed at the darkness. He had come halfway around the world looking for Hacker and Ellie-Jo. He had miraculously found them. Now he helplessly watched them slip away.

"Willy, it's so unbelievable. Are you sure it was

him?" Ginny was shaking, snuggling close to him in the darkness.

"Honey, I guess you never forget the face of a man who points a loaded gun at you like Hacker did at me on the Redondo pier." He led Ginny back along the companionway, turned the corner, and walked toward the gangplank leading away from the Macau Palace.

Hercules' Mercedes was gone. They hurried back to their taxi, still parked where they had left it on the Rua das Lurchas.

The driver was upset. "Mr. Valdez. He just leave. You are too late."

"Don't worry about it, pal. Take us to the Hong Kong ferry terminal." Willy shoved another twenty at him.

Fortunately, they made the last ferry from Hong Kong to Macau that night. During the passage, they passed what must have been a thousand sampans rafted together near Macau. As they approached Hong Kong island, there was an even larger colony of sampans and junks. Finding the one that might hold Hacker and Ellie-Jo would be like finding the proverbial needle in a haystack.

"Don't worry, Ginny. Given the resourcefulness of Ellen Lambert, she'll probably be curled up in the Peninsula before we get back to the Towers. A gal like her isn't about to make that trip in a little sampan."

"Who do you think she'll be curled up with, her banker, her shipping tycoon, or Hacker?" Ginny treated Willy to the smile she reserved especially for him.

49

Coley Doctor checked his baggage through to Hong Kong two-and-a-half hours before his Cathay Pacific flight was to depart. He walked over to a concession stand and purchased a cup of coffee, then stood at a counter to watch the hustle and bustle of the international terminal at Los Angeles International Airport.

He was impatient for the trip to begin. Thoughts that Hacker might be on the loose in Hong Kong had permitted him little rest the night before. He had kissed Marissa Chablis goodbye only a couple of hours ago. I'll be gone for a few days, he had said. Big secret deal, he had told her, I'll let you know as soon as I can. Trusting totally, she had not questioned him further. It bothered him now that he had not leveled with her about the full purpose of his trip. After all, he did not want her involved in the mess that was sure to develop at Waterfront, Inc.

The passage of a few minutes seemed to take forever. He finished his coffee and paced through the terminal. He took an elevator down to the lower level. The doors opened on a long hallway that featured a currency exchange. He proceeded to the vacant counter and exchanged five-hundred U.S. dollars for Hong Kong currency. Turning away from the counter, he looked up after stashing his wallet in his jacket and groaned.

Standing a few yards away, and watching him, were Joe Martin, Jean Bonaparte, and an old friend from out of the past, agent Mark Whitcomb of the FBI.

Whitcomb strode toward him, extending his hand. He was tall and lean, dressed in the usual blue business suit cut a little too close, allowing the nine millimeter to bulge visibly under his jacket. "Well, what do you know about that? Coley Doctor is leaving the country."

"Goddamn it, Mark! I've got a client in trouble. It's my business to protect him."

Whitcomb's thin face showed a hint of a smile. "What is it this time, Coley? You and Willy Hanson trying to bring down another international drug syndicate?"

Coley grimaced at the reference to their past exploits.

"Relax, Coley. Your business is your business, but I think we have to talk."

"Then start talking. I'm leaving in two hours." Coley shook his hand and looked at Bonaparte, whose fish eyes were darting from person to person.

Whitcomb glanced at the currency exchange clerk, then pointed down the long, empty hallway. "Let's take a little walk so we can talk privately."

They went back up the elevator, then outside the terminal, and stopped at a bench along the walkway to the next terminal. Whitcomb put his foot up on the bench and began to talk. "Coley, there's been a big development in the case you're working on. Remember Hacker's gun that slid into Redondo Bay the night you had a fight with Hacker?"

"Yep," Coley nodded.

"Your friend here, Joe, had it fished out of the bay. Ballistics tell us that the bullets fired from it match the bullet that went through the head of Henri Belanger up north on Lake Tahoe. The slug was recovered from Belanger's car."

"It figures. Ellie-Jo was up there that night too. I saw her at the airport in Reno. It was the week before Hacker went to New Orleans." Coley paused reflectively. "Now, I hope you guys agree with me that we've got a serial killer here who'll blow out anyone with five cents in their pocket."

"Your case looks good, Coley. That's why we're here to help you. The sheik claims Belanger had over a hundred thousand on him. Bonaparte here says Lasker had over a hundred and twenty-five thousand on him. The good doctor killed in Vegas had a good-sized bankroll. We've got the case all plotted out, Coley. We think you were right from the beginning, even though it's puzzling that they would fool with a small fry like Lefty Grogan."

"Well, if we hadn't got you all started with the investigation of that small fry, you guys wouldn't have got started on the case at all." Coley stood up, looking sullen. "Now, if you don't mind, I'm heading for Hong Kong."

"Of course you are, Coley. In fact, we think so much of your case, that Jean Bonaparte and I are going with you. If you'd like, you can join us over there when we meet with Interpol and the Hong Kong authorities."

"Look, Hacker is secondary to me at this point. My

objective now is to get Willy and Ginny back on a plane pointed toward the States. Nailing Hacker would be icing on the cake. Let's just make sure that we don't get so many people involved that we start stumbling all over each other."

Whitcomb stood up. "Okay. There will be plenty of time to talk up in the sky. Let's get back to the plane."

50

The night was without a moon, but it was clear and the lights of Macau clearly etched the waterfront. The tiny sampan moved southward along the peninsula, putted slowly to the port, then passed under the causeway and turned north toward a cluster of other sampans and larger junks.

Ellen Lambert sat on a half-barrel that served as a seat amidships of the small vessel. "Okay, Hacker, this is far enough. You've got what you want, so drop me off near the causeway. I can easily make my way back to the ferry terminal."

"Sorry, Ellie-Jo. I let you slip away with the loot last time. This time I've gotta make sure." Hacker was tinkering with the small sputtering outboard while trying to spot his own destination.

"Look, Hacker. Whatever loot there was is in the hands of Flo and Ziggy. Find them and you find the money. I have no idea where the bastards are."

Ellie-Jo peered into the harbor ahead of them toward a dark cluster of small coastal boats, all rafted together. Now they were well out into the harbor.

"I don't believe you, Ellie-Jo. You lie a lot, just like your fancy friends." Hacker grinned, his misshapen nose making him gargoyle-like in the dim light. His muscles bulged under a tight sweatshirt.

Ellie-Jo was frightened. Hacker was strong as an ox, and she was no match for him under these circumstances.

Hacker shut off the tiny outboard as they approached the cluster of boats ahead. A man stood on the deck of a small junk, slowly waving his arms at them. Hacker let the sampan drift until it gently nudged the side of the junk.

"Chan, baby. Is that you?" Hacker whispered coarsely into the darkness.

"Mr. Hacker, it is Chan." The man helped him lash the sampan alongside the junk.

"Okay, Ellie-Jo, up and out. Welcome to our new home."

"Hacker, do you know what you are doing?" Ellie-Jo stared dubiously at the old junk. She could feel her heart pounding as she climbed aboard. She was at the mercy of Hacker and the stranger.

Chan, looking quite aged and frail, wore a coolie hat. He opened a small hatch that led below to a cabin dimly lit by a kerosene lamp that hung in a corner. There was one long bunk covered with what looked like empty flour sacks, and a couple of half-barrels that served as chairs. A small kerosene stove sat on a table. The smell of fish permeated the air. The opulence of the Peninsula Hotel seemed a million miles away.

"Hacker, for God's sake, your money is in my bag.

Take me back to the causeway. Take me back to the causeway, or I'll scream."

"Go ahead and scream, Ellie-Jo. There ain't nobody around that cares. There are probably a few guys out there who wouldn't mind getting a little of what you got. I'd be damned quiet if I were you. And that's a fact, Ellie-Jo." Hacker went forward and closed the hatch, latching it with the flimsy hook that pushed through a loop in the bulkhead. They could hear Chan walking on the deck above them toward the bow of the old junk.

All at once the junk gave a sharp lurch forward. The sound of water washing by the hull on the outside told them they were moving. The kerosene lantern swung crazily for a moment on its short line.

"Hacker! What in the hell is happening?" She stood for a moment, rocking unsteadily as the junk picked up speed, and then fell headlong onto the bunk.

"Relax, Ellie-Jo. We're on our way to Hong Kong. That's where you want to go, isn't it? This is Chan's choo-choo train." Hacker opened the hatch again. "Come here. Take a peek."

Ellie-Jo stared out over the stern of the junk. They were connected by a line to another junk, maybe a hundred feet behind. And she could see more, perhaps a half dozen stretched out into the distance. From somewhere in front of them, she could hear the laboring of a powerful engine. Peering ahead, over the bow, she could make out a large junk that furnished the power to pull all the others across the narrow arm of the South China Sea.

Ellie-Jo remembered seeing the same sight on one of the hydrofoil trips to Macau. Valdez had explained that frequently the master of a powerful vessel would tow others to distant destinations, usually smaller junks and sampans that had no power or whose engines were in poor condition. This was done for a fee that would be shared with authorities who would overlook their passage in the night. Ellen, in fact, had filmed such a towline with her video camera one day.

"This is crazy, Hacker. We could have taken the hydrofoil."

Hacker leered at her. "Sure, you'd like that, wouldn't you? You'd like to see old Hacker nailed at customs with a bag of loot. Hey, that reminds me, it's payday. It's time to count money."

Ellie-Jo squirmed. There were enough Hong Kong notes in the bag to add up to a half million, U.S. currency. Hacker expected one million.

"Hacker, it isn't easy. I only have half the money. The rest will come next week. You still have one more job to do, you know." To her relief, Hacker remained calm.

He opened the heavy tote bag and lifted out one of several packets of Hong Kong thousand-dollar notes. Laboriously, he counted the contents until he got about halfway through the packet. He peered into the bag at the other packets.

"You lied to me again, Ellie-Jo. I'll wait, but you're going to have to pay for your lies."

"Don't be such a jackass, Hacker. Nobody ever made a half million so quick, anywhere. You'll get the rest, Hacker, just finish your job."

"Maybe I will, and maybe I won't. A half million ain't bad. Maybe I'll just fly the coop, like Flo and Ziggy did."

"Hacker, you'll blow the whole thing if you don't take care of Sheldon Blake."

"When is he getting in?"

"Noon, Thursday."

"I want my money before dark the same day."

"You got it." Ellie-Jo breathed a sigh of relief.

Maybe, just maybe, she thought, she would get back to Hong Kong alive. "Hacker, how long is it going to take us to get to Hong Kong?"

"Chan says we'll be in Aberdeen Harbour within six to eight hours." Hacker walked over and sat on the bunk next to her.

"By the way, where the hell is Chan?"

"He sleeps up on the bow. Don't worry about him, Ellie-Jo. He's an old man." Hacker ran his rough hand along Ellie-Jo's thighs. "You know, you ran out on old Hacker last time. I ain't no chump, Ellie-Jo."

"What in the hell are you talking about, Hacker. You've got a half million in your pocket. Now you can have all the women you want, two or three at a time right in Hong Kong."

Hacker forced his arms around her and pressed a savage kiss to her firmly closed lips. "That ain't the way to act, Ellie-Jo. We got six or eight hours and old Hacker is hurtin' bad. And that's a fact." The brute force in his powerful shoulders forced her back down to the bunk.

She struggled mightily for a few moments until she realized that there was no way she could stop Hacker and stay unharmed.

"Okay, okay! You've got me. Don't hurt me, Hacker. If I don't get back to Hong Kong looking like a lady, the whole deal goes down the drain. Now relax for a minute, sweetie. This is your lover, Ellie-Jo. Remember?"

Hacker eased up his grip as Ellie-Jo began to shower his face with kisses. He backed off and grinned broadly as she became the aggressor.

She forced a lewd smile and leered back at him. "How do you want it first, Hacker, French or straight?"

51

Armand Hauser sat on the small chair next to the window of his hospital room. Getting dressed had been a slow chore. The aches and pains around his neck and shoulder still persisted when he moved too quickly. The cast on his arm extended beyond his knuckles and greatly restricted the use of his hand. Nevertheless, he was determined to leave the hospital.

Where the hell is Ellen Lambert? he asked himself. She hadn't shown up last evening, and now it was well past noon. Her phone at the Peninsula kept ringing. Was it possible that she was still in Macau, and if so, what for? He felt isolated and forgotten. In fact, it had taken several attempts to summon Lee Ching, who had assured him he would always be available.

There was a tap on the door behind him. "Mr. Hauser, good morning." It was the sober-faced Lee Ching. "Ah, you look much better today. But are you sure you are ready to leave the hospital?" Lee studied him closely, his eyes coming to rest on the bulky cast.

"Lee, I'm afraid I don't have much love for hospitals. It's time for me to get back to work. It will help me forget my troubles." Ching watched dubiously as Armand gingerly rose from the chair. "By the way, have you seen Ellen Lambert today?"

Lee Ching shook his head. "I think she is busy in Macau," he said, without further explanation of what busy might mean.

"Well then, let's be off. I want to check at the Peninsula and then go directly to the building. Did they ever find out what made those blocks fall from the roof?"

"No one seems to know. It must have been an accident."

"Yes, maybe the wind blew them off, except the blocks were concrete and I don't remember any wind at all that night, do you?"

Lee Ching again shook his head, offering no further information or opinion.

They arrived at the Peninsula Hotel in a matter of minutes. Armand, remembering that he still had a key to Ellen Lambert's room, proceeded upstairs, leaving Ching in the lobby. He knocked and then opened the door. The room was empty. It was also made up, showing no signs of having been occupied lately.

He noticed the sheaf of blueprints spread across a table. Curiosity forced him to look at the page depicting the kitchen and bakery. No correcting revisions had been made.

Armand left one note for Ellen in the room and one downstairs at the desk, telling her he would be at the new construction site for a while. He left then, frustrated and on the verge of being angry.

Armand and Ching approached Waterfront, Inc.,

slowly, staring up at the roof from where the cement blocks had fallen. There were still marks on the sidewalk and a few scattered chips of shattered block.

Once inside, Armand counted four workers, all of them busy installing more of the massive jacks that would support the roof until the tiered veranda was constructed. He was overcome with pessimism as he wandered back through the building. It was even more cluttered and disorganized than before. The kitchen and bakery area were still marked off on the floor without the corrections promised. There were more stacks of cheap plywood and no sign of the high-grade teak.

More disturbing was the fact that no one at all was working except the four men on the roof jacks. It was insane to think that they could open in ten weeks. Where were all the workers Ellen had hired?

He watched the four men wrestle with the giant jacks that were the only support now to a one-hundred-foot section of the roof. The top ten feet of the building wall on the harbor side had now been cut away, fully exposing the inside to the elements. It had rained the night before, soaking the floor and piles of lumber and plywood stacked along the wall. It was true that construction was not his game, but Armand felt with little doubt that the whole project was without proper supervision. Weary from the disturbing thoughts, he asked Lee Ching to return him to the hotel.

Ellen Lambert was still not there, and there were still no messages. Armand plopped down in a big leather chair in the lobby where he could see both the reception desk and the corridor leading outside. He picked up a copy of the *International Tribune* from an adjoining table and idly started to page through it.

One article dealt with Typhoon Jasmine, now due to

bear down on the Philippines within thirty-six hours. The map inset traced the anticipated future course of the storm slightly north of Hong Kong. He thought of the roof of Waterfront, Inc., resting loosely on the makeshift jacks, the entire side of the building exposed to weather.

Where in the hell was Ellen Lambert? Unless she showed soon, he decided he would have to go to the authorities and inform the home office in California.

He looked up, hearing the familiar click of high heels on the marble floor. It was Ellen! He leaped to his feet, forgetting for a moment the pain his effort would cause. "Ellen, I've been worried sick. Are you okay?" As he spoke, he couldn't help but feel shocked at her appearance. She looked as if she had slept in her clothes. Her short silk skirt was wrinkled and her long legs without pantyhose. Her auburn hair trailed wildly down her back, and the string of pearls that usually held it was wrapped around her wrist. Most shocking of all were her eyes, sunken and circled with dark rings.

She looked down at herself. "Relax, Armand. I'm fine. My hotel reservations were messed up in Macau. I wound up gambling all night and trying to sleep on one of the ferries. If you don't mind, I'm going straight to bed. Let's plan on having breakfast in the morning."

"Ellen, we must talk. I went over to the location today, and it's a mess."

"Armand, you worry too much. Things couldn't be going better. I'll see you at breakfast, and then I'm off to see our bankers and our construction foreman."

She turned on her heels without another word. He watched as she strode over to the desk and picked up her messages, then boarded the elevator. Not once did

she look back at the wounded Armand. He walked
slowly back to the leather club chair.

In her suite now, Ellen Lambert tossed the stack of
messages on her dresser and began to peel off her
clothes. Piece by piece, she dropped everything she
had worn into a wastebasket. She smelled of fish, the
same odor that had saturated the air of the junk.
She wondered if Armand had picked up on it.

She turned on her shower and stepped in. Her body
ached and her head throbbed. Hacker hadn't left her
alone the entire night, and the bus ride from Aberdeen on the other side of Hong Kong had been pun-
ishing. Later, wrapped in a luxurious towel, she
walked back to her dresser to finger through the stack
of messages. There were several from Sheldon Blake,
and one labeled Super Urgent from their comptroller,
Kevin Billingsly. Then came two that jarred her like a
slap in the face.

Lefty Grogan had called twice! "Hacker, you bastard!" She screamed the words aloud as she kicked
the wastebasket against the wall. Hacker had missed.
The jerk who had slobbered all over her at the bar in
Tonopah, Nevada, was right here in Hong Kong.

She crumpled the messages in rage. Hacker had unfinished business. He wouldn't get the balance of his
payoff until he put an end to Lefty Grogan. She'd help
him lay a trap for the son of a bitch.

52

"And so, Chan, it seems we have some unfinished business." Hercules Valdez was staring at the old man slumped over in the chair. The frail Chan had worked on the intercoastal boats for years. No longer able to perform the rigorous duties of a working seaman, he now plied small sampans for the tourist trade in Macau and Aberdeen. Chan huddled over the cap that lay in his lap. He was afraid. The big motor cruiser owned by Valdez had powered right up to his junk now moored in Aberdeen. A man as important as Valdez would not do a thing like that without good reason.

Chan turned his crinkled, faded eyes upward to face those of the imposing Valdez. "Lady and her friend insisted that I take them to Aberdeen. I tie sampan at mooring in Macau and we get tow to Hong Kong. That is all."

"That is not quite all, is it, Chan?" Valdez persisted.

"Our agreement was that after you picked the lady up at the Macau Palace, you would transport her directly to the Hong Kong ferry terminal back on Macau. It was the lady's wish for you to do so. Why the change of plans? You caused me great unpleasantness. I waited for hours for her there."

Chan's gaze fell back to the hat in his lap. He picked it up and ran his fingers inside the headband. He pulled out a crumpled thousand-dollar Hong Kong note and handed it to Valdez without looking at him. "Man give me this for trip to Aberdeen."

Valdez took the note and fingered it thoughtfully. He reached inside his jacket pocket, withdrew his wallet, and selected a similar thousand dollar note. He handed both notes back to Chan. "Now, Chan, whenever this lady or the man who was with her offers you money, you are to tell me about it. When you do, I will match whatever they give you. Is that perfectly clear, Chan?"

Chan looked up at him with his watery eyes. "Yes, sir, I understand."

Valdez watched the old man tuck the two notes into his hatband. "Good, I am glad we understand each other. One more thing, Chan. Tell me about the man who accompanied her."

"He was strong young man. Had broken nose at one time. He and lady argue a lot." Chan hesitated, wondering if he should say more.

"And what else, Chan? You act like there is something more," Valdez persisted.

Chan again bent low to avoid Valdez's eyes. "They make love many time, all the way to Aberdeen."

Valdez scowled. "Are you sure, Chan? Did you watch them?"

"Yes, I watch sometimes through crack in deck. He made her do many things."

"That is enough, Chan. I am going to leave you now." Valdez bent low in order to speak directly into the old man's ear. "If you displease me again, I will feed you to the sharks. Is that clear, Chan?" Then Valdez turned and left the junk and boarded his boat.

Chan shuddered and huddled down in his chair, remaining there until he heard the engine of the big powerboat rev up. Then he stood to watch the wake of the cruiser until it disappeared at sea.

Chan studied the sun in the southern sky. It was already well past noon. He still had time to meet the man named Hacker as planned.

His eyes focused on the horizon to the southeast. Barely visible was a swirl of high white clouds. The feathery finger was ominous. In the harbor at Macau the fishermen had told him about a typhoon, still east of the Philippines. The wisp of high cloud in the distant sky was something he dreaded. Many times in the past he had witnessed the same phenomenon. The monster storm could be four or five days away, but it would come, as they always did when such clouds appeared. Though well hidden from the prevailing winds, the floating docks at Aberdeen would take punishment.

His eyes ran the length and breadth of the battered old junk. In his heart he knew it would take a miracle for the vessel to survive a sustained gale. Still, he would pick up some lengths of new line and do his best to secure his rickety old home.

Chan, for all his age, moved with a steady pace down the road leading away from the boat basin. He reached the causeway to the main island, crossed it, and turned to the left down Heung Yip Road, entered an alleyway, and rapped hard on a door.

"Chan, old man, you're right on time." Hacker

opened the door, and he was invited inside. The woman was nowhere to be seen.

Hacker had evidently been to the street stalls and bought new clothing. He was almost presentable in new slacks, a washed silk shirt, and a tan sunhat with a floppy brim that hid the damaged features of his face rather well. He had trimmed the new growth of beard, which gave him a different appearance. Chan didn't take his watery blue eyes off him. He thought of the woman Hacker had abused on the overnight run from Macau.

"Chan, I want to leave Hong Kong early Friday morning and return to Macau. I want you to drop me off on Taipa."

Chan shook his head slowly. "Not possible, Mr. Hacker. That four days from now." Chan lifted his arms high in the air and began swinging them around.

Hacker looked at Chan, puzzled by the response. "I have to go then, Chan. I will give you five-thousand Hong Kong dollars."

"We must wait, maybe two more days after Friday, and then maybe we go." Chan was thinking of the money. If Valdez gave him five thousand more, that would be ten thousand. For that much money he could repair the engine in his old junk. "There is typhoon coming. Big storm. Even Star Ferry will not be making trip to Macau then. We will go as soon as it is possible."

Hacker grabbed the old fisherman by his shirt. "Listen, old man. Nobody knows what the weather will be like in four days. I said we'll go Friday morning, before the sun comes up." He shook him roughly to emphasize his words, and then pulled a roll of money from his pocket. "Here, I'll give you two thousand now."

Chan shrugged. "There are signs. But I will be ready." He decided to humor the strange man who peeled off thousand-dollar bills like fish scales.

Hacker pulled a map from his back pocket, one that Ellie-Jo had given him. "What is the best way to get from here to Kowloon?"

Chan pointed out the bus route from Aberdeen, then marked the Star Ferry terminal in Central District.

"Okay, old man. I will see you before the sun rises, on your boat, Friday morning."

Chan followed Hacker outside and pointed to the nearest bus stop on Wong Chuk Hang Road. He watched until Hacker was out of sight, then began the trek back to his junk. He fingered the two banknotes in his pocket and decided to stop at one of the food stalls in Aberdeen and have a big fish dinner. He wished that Valdez would show up again. He hadn't felt so prosperous in years.

53

Ellen Lambert watched the persistent blinking of the red light on her telephone as she awoke from a deep sleep. It was 7:00 A.M. She pressed the answering playback button.

Sheldon Blake had called to tell her he would be in a day early, on the same flight. Kevin Billingsly's call warned her about a serious cash flow problem. He wanted some explanation for the four-and-a-half million that had already been used from the Hong Kong bank. He went on to say that someone was dumping Waterfront stock. It had dropped another five points during the week. He urged her to "talk to Sheldon when he gets there. He doesn't pay any attention to me."

The next taped call brought her to her feet. "I'll see you sometime today, at your convenience. Lefty Grogan is really getting pissed. He's going to blow the whistle on this whole operation unless he gets satisfaction. See you later."

Whoever this bastard was, he obviously wanted a payoff. Today, she had to get this guy set up for Hacker. Also on the agenda, she had to make another round of the banks and then meet Hercules Valdez at Happy Valley Racetrack. As much money as possible had to be laundered before Sheldon showed up. She needed to make one more trip to Macau. And then there was Armand, who was much too curious for his own good. He would have to be dealt with much sooner than she had planned.

Armand answered the phone in his room immediately. "Ellen, are you all right? You can't imagine how I've worried about you since seeing you yesterday. It must have been a horrible experience being stuck in Macau like that. Are you better rested now?"

"Armand, I feel glorious. And I'm thoroughly ashamed of myself for having treated you so poorly yesterday. I was so tired I was at my wit's end. Forgive me, Armand. I'll make it up to you, dear. Come up and join me for breakfast in my suite. We have so much to talk about."

Armand Hauser could feel his spirits soar. Once again Ellen Lambert sounded like the Ellen Lambert he knew. "Give me just a few minutes. You can go ahead and order, and I'll be there soon."

Armand hung up the phone, marveling at the effect Ellen Lambert had on him. Yesterday's pessimism had now vanished. All of the excitement about opening the new Waterfront had returned. There were problems, but with Ellen's help they would surmount them.

Armand arrived at the suite within minutes. Ellen opened the door. She stood there in a short terrycloth robe, hanging open, the belt trailing down across her hips. Her auburn hair was primly set in a loose bun bound by the string of pearls. Her eyes flashed brilliantly in the room drenched with morning sun. Armand gaped appreciatively. "Ellen, you look like a goddess."

Inside the suite, she opened the robe fully and drew him inside, snuggling against him. She took the loose terrycloth sash and tied it behind him, binding them together. Her full, open lips moved eagerly against his. "Armand, you devil, do you know how much I have missed you? I didn't order breakfast. I thought it a waste of time."

Armand found himself responding swiftly to her, and he began to burrow kisses in the hollow of her neck. "Breakfast be damned. That's what I say."

They moved to the bed, still bound together, Armand struggling to rid himself of his trousers. Then he covered her with himself and they moved together with an ecstasy that he had known only with her. Finally, their furious movements climaxed, and they lay wrapped snugly in each others' arms fully sated.

"Armand, shame on us and our weaknesses. Now we must shower again, and get our busy day started." Their lips touched lightly for a few moments and then she sprang to her feet.

"Armand, I have a special job for you today. I have discovered the most spectacular wood carving in Aberdeen. I want you to see it and make arrangements to send it to the new location."

"Tell me about the carving." Armand rolled over to face her, not able to fully adapt himself to the business of the day so quickly.

"It is a twenty-foot-long, twisting dragon, gilded in gold, red, and black lacquer. It once stretched across the dining room of an old restaurant in Aberdeen. It would be perfect above the back-bar at Waterfront."

"It sounds wonderful. Why even ask me?"

"Armand, they want twenty thousand dollars for it. You know how Sheldon feels about such expenses. I think it would be wise if you were as in love with it as I am."

"I agree to be in love with anything that pleases you. How's that?" Armand stared at her, feeling himself become aroused again.

"Please be serious. It is just a short bus ride to Aberdeen. I want you to do that for me while I get the new workers started. When you get back to the location today, you will see every one of them feverishly at work."

"Okay. You've convinced me. I admit that the lack of progress I saw yesterday left me in a blue funk, but now you've changed all that, my dear." He watched her disappear into the shower. For just a moment, his thoughts returned to the way she looked when she first entered the hotel yesterday. If he didn't know better, he would have thought she was a slut off the street.

When they were finally dressed for the day, Ellen went to the desk and jotted down an address in Aberdeen, 26a Heung Yip Road, where the ornate dragon was warehoused. "Armand, if the dragon truly pleases you, make arrangements to have it delivered. Say that we will pay cash on delivery."

Armand stuffed the address into his pocket, kissed Ellen on the lips again, and opened the door to leave.

"Goodbye, Armand. I will never forget our breakfast." She looked serious, regal.

Armand walked across Salisbury Road, took the Star Ferry to Central District, then walked to the nearby bus terminal, stopping to buy a late edition of the *International Tribune*. The sky was unusually blue for the time of year. Far to the southeast, a wheel of high clouds looked like long feathers poking over the horizon. Turning his attention to the paper, he read that Typhoon Jasmine now had a 50 percent chance of reaching Hong Kong. It was to brush the Philippines during the night, pick up strength, and then move into the South China Sea.

He got off the bus just beyond the causeway at Heung Yip Road. Walking some distance, he found 26a at the end of a short alleyway.

He knocked, then tried the door of what appeared to be an old warehouse. It was open. A narrow flight of stairs led to the second-floor landing and to another door, where he knocked again.

"Come on in," a voice encouraged in clear English.

He opened the door, which led to a short hallway and an open room. Entering the room, he gasped and froze. He was looking at a short, broad-shouldered man with a tan sunhat pulled low over his face. He sat in a chair holding a long-barreled gun equipped with a fat silencer. The gun was pointed directly at Armand.

"I'll teach you to go bangin' around my Ellie-Jo."

Then came a muffled shot that Armand never heard.

54

Less than a half mile from the old warehouse on Heung Yip Road, Chan stirred in his bunk. He had slept restlessly during the night in his old junk, now rafted up with hundreds of others in the harbor at Aberdeen. The chatter of the other boatsmen had kept him from getting much rest. The fishermen had been listening constantly to their radios. A force eight typhoon was now predicted to strike Hong Kong.

Chan scrambled to his feet and looked out into the daylight. It seemed like it must be about noon. The boat colony hummed with activity. The virtual certainty of a powerful typhoon had everyone securing their vessels with additional lines. It was time for him also to get busy.

But first he had a task to complete. He needed to go to the warehouse and advise Mr. Hacker that he absolutely would not be able to make the crossing to

Macau on Friday morning. Even if his junk survived the blow, the harbor would be awash with debris as it always was after a typhoon. No intercoastal traffic would be possible.

He dreaded facing Mr. Hacker with the news. His cruelty to the beautiful woman had angered him. He decided that Hacker was a monster. Yet he would have to be told about the certainty of the typhoon. And, of course, as frightening as the man was, there was the matter of those thousand-dollar notes that fell from his wallet like leaves in a wind.

Chan made his way to shore across the raft of junks now making preparations for the storm, stopping now and then to talk about the coming storm with friends.

Finally, he left the boat colony and made his way to Heung Yip Road. He was still surprised that Hercules Valdez had given Hacker his approval to stay in the old warehouse. He paused at the door, fishing in his pocket for a duplicate key. To his surprise, the door opened without needing one. He called out Hacker's name. There was no answer.

Steeling himself for this unpleasant task, he climbed the narrow flight of stairs. He knocked again at the closed door at the top. Again, there was no response.

Turning the knob, he swung the door open. He permitted his eyes to become accustomed to the dimly lit room, and then he gasped with horror. A man lay sprawled across the floor, just inside the door. The man was not Mr. Hacker. His head lay in a puddle of blood. There was no one else in the room.

Chan trembled and backed away from the body and out of the room. Shutting the door behind him, he stood breathing heavily and shaking with fear. In all his years of keeping an eye on the old building for

Hercules Valdez when it was not in use for freight storage, nothing bad had ever happened.

He steadied himself and made his way slowly down the steps. Once outside, he closed the door and made his way back toward the boats. Still shaking, he could think of only one thing. He would have to reach Mr. Valdez at once.

55

The offices of Waterfront, Inc., in Santa Monica were in a state of bedlam. Office personnel and newspaper reporters clustered around the reception area where Marissa Chablis was doing her best to fend off questions regarding Armand Hauser. The news was out that Hauser, a vice president, had absconded with over five million dollars in company funds in Hong Kong, and had been missing for over ten hours. The wire service story stated that Ellen Lambert had filed a complaint with the Hong Kong police following Hauser's disappearance.

At one point, Kevin Billingsly, comptroller of Waterfront, Inc., emerged from behind locked doors to announce that he had just spoken to Ellen Lambert, the CEO of that company now in Hong Kong in connection with the opening of a new restaurant, and confirmed that the information was true.

Billingsly stated that Chairman of the Board

Sheldon Blake was now in communication with the Hong Kong police and had spoken with the U.S. consulate in Hong Kong. He would have a statement to make to the press within the hour.

One reporter, Sonny Lester, who had obviously done his homework, asked, "Could this have anything to do with the wild plunge of Waterfront, Inc., stock lately?"

"Absolutely not," snapped Billingsly. "This company is a leader in its field and is absolutely solid." Reporters crowded around him, persistent with their questions. "I'm sorry, I have no more information. You will have to wait for Mr. Blake's statement."

Reporters milled around Marissa's reception desk. Under Blake's instructions to keep all lines open, she steadfastly refused access to her phones to any of the reporters. She thought of Coley Doctor, now actually on his way to Hong Kong, and wondered if he knew anything about what was going on.

Sheldon Blake suddenly appeared from the inner office and quieted the small group with his booming baritone voice. "Gentlemen, I have a short statement to make that will bring you up-to-date on the facts as I know them." Blake read from his notes that listed several items.

"First of all, Armand Hauser is certainly one of our most trusted employees. It is difficult to believe that he could do what he is supposed to have done. He has been in Hong Kong working with our company president on the construction of a flagship restaurant on Victoria Harbour. Our president, Ellen Lambert, tells me that he left her after a business breakfast on an errand to inspect and arrange for delivery of new material for the construction. He was able to get his hands on a large part of the working capital we had supplied for the Hong Kong project, and has disappeared with an excess of five million U.S. dollars. We are working now on a complete investigation of how this was accomplished, and have taken the matter to the authorities in Hong Kong." He paused momentarily to clear his throat and scan his notes.

"As a matter of record, I myself had planned to fly to Hong Kong this afternoon in connection with the Victoria Harbour project. I will make that trip as planned and hope to make another statement after arriving in Hong Kong. I would like to point out that the colony of Hong Kong, though heavily populated, is quite compact, with thorough customs facilities that keep track of all movements in and out of their borders. Authorities there tell me it is unlikely that Armand Hauser will be able to leave the colony undetected. They have hopes that he will be found even before I get there. Of course we are all hoping that there is some reasonable explanation for his disappearance and the disappearance of the funds."

As Sheldon Blake turned to leave, Sonny Lester persisted. "Sir, there is an item on the wire service out of New Orleans this morning that Ellen Lambert is wanted for questioning about possible information concerning the homicide of a prizefighter, Lazy Boy Garcia. Can you comment on that?"

Sheldon Blake scowled at the reporter. "The only possible comment I could ever have about that, is that it is absurd! If you knew Ellen Lambert, you would realize what I mean. The story does not have anything to do with our Ellen Lambert. Maybe there is another woman someplace who goes by the same name." He forced a smile that drew a few sympathetic laughs from some of those in the room. "Good day, gentlemen!" With that, Sheldon Blake returned to his private quarters.

Marissa Chablis sat wide-eyed through the whole press conference. She was stunned by the purported actions of Armand Hauser. He had always been open and cordial with her. Armand was basically a chef, and their incidental chatter had almost always centered on food preparation. Not in her most vivid imagination could she picture Armand stealing a nickel, much less millions of dollars.

When they had all left, she glanced at her watch. She was counting the hours until Coley landed in Hong Kong. She already missed him. She wondered whether all this had anything to do with his investigation. Coley had mentioned New Orleans the night they had met for dinner. He had been insistent about Ellen Lambert having been there. She thought of the nine millimeter tucked under his arm and wondered if he ever used it. She shrugged and then smiled. It had been a long time since she had worried about a guy this much.

56

Willy arose about 6:00 A.M., unable to get more quality sleep. Coley was to arrive on Cathay Pacific early in the afternoon. Willy shaved quickly, slipped on his clothes, and turned around to find Ginny staring at him with eyes wide open.

"I'm sorry, honey, I just can't rest. I'm going to buy some papers and sit in the lobby over at the Peninsula. Maybe I can find out who Ellen Lambert slept with last night."

Ginny smiled sleepily. "Just don't get any ideas about being next on her list. I think I'll pass on joining you this time. The Peninsula might call the cops if I do any lobby-sitting over there at this hour."

"It would be nice if I could confront her alone about Lefty. I haven't picked up much of anything that will help Coley when he gets here." When he turned around, Ginny had closed her eyes again.

He walked out of the Sheraton Towers and turned

right on Salisbury Road. Just as he was about to walk into the Peninsula, Ellen Lambert came out walking at a fast pace, crossed the broad street, and turned toward the Star Ferry terminal. He followed about a hundred paces behind and boarded the ferry to Central District shortly after she did. The ferry ride would take less than ten minutes. He decided to wait until they had crossed and then to confront her at an opportune time.

On the other side, she walked north at the same rapid clip. It was the same route that had led him and Ginny to the Macau ferry terminal the last time. Now she was fairly running. It was all he could do to keep up and not lose her in the crowd of early commuters.

Sure enough, she purchased a ticket for the Macau hydrofoil. Willy looked at his watch. A round-trip to Macau would take almost three hours. He decided to get aboard. It would be a great place to strike up a conversation.

The early midweek hydrofoil held only a few passengers. He was in luck again. He took a seat in the same row, leaving a space between them. Ellen's face was already buried in the South China *Morning Post*, Hong Kong's most popular English-language newspaper.

"Excuse me, miss, I'm going to get a cup of tea over there. Would you like one?"

She turned to face him with wide-set eyes, their color somewhere between hazel and green. Her sleekly groomed auburn hair complemented her warm smile. "You know, every time I ride the ferry, some man offers to buy me tea, and I always accept."

"I wonder why they do that?" Willy smiled. "How do you take it?"

"Hot, just hot."

Willy strolled to the concession counter and came back with the tea. She had folded her paper and was staring at the clouds in the southeast. The sky, lightly overcast, darkened perceptibly to the southeast. The water was mirror flat. Already the hydrofoil was flying on plane.

"Looks like the typhoon will be here sometime tomorrow," volunteered Willy.

"Are they really bad?" she asked.

"Ellen, they are terrible."

She snapped her head to face him. "How do you know my name?" All the warmth washed out of her, but she was still beautiful.

"A friend of mine described you to me once. His name was Lefty Grogan." To his surprise, she continued to look him right in the eye, staying very calm.

"And what did he tell you about me?"

"He told me you were a real knockout. And he was right. He also said that you like good cold beer on hot nights in the Nevada desert." She continued to stare at him, as if she was really trying to understand what he was talking about, and why.

"Are you the man who has been pestering me for the past few days with notes and phone calls?" She crossed her legs, now showing a good stretch of well-toned thigh.

"Yep. You're just like Lefty described, lady."

"You know, you aren't so bad yourself. You know my name. What's yours?"

"I'm Willy, Willy Hanson." He extended his hand, which she totally ignored.

"I'll tell you something, Mr. Hanson, you had better explain yourself before this trip is over, and it better be good. Because if it isn't, you are going to be in big trouble when we get to Macau." She turned on the warm smile again. "Now tell me about yourself, Mr. Willy."

She was one cool customer. If she had anything to hide, nothing in her demeanor indicated it. "Ellie-Jo, I had this good buddy, an old high school pal named Lefty Grogan. He wound up with a bullet in his head north of Tonopah, Nevada, the same night Hacker's sister got married in Tahoe."

She blinked, then it was gone. But he saw it—it was just a shadow in the middle of a long, warm smile. If he had blinked at the same time, he wouldn't have caught it. "Ellie-Jo, I'd like for you to help me put the blocks to the guy who did old Lefty in. How about that?"

"Ellie-Jo?" She laughed a little.

"Yeah, Ellie-Jo. Say, I hear you do a mean strip-tease once in a while down in New Orleans." What the hell, thought Willy, I might as well shoot the works.

"Mr. Hanson, I am a busy person. I wish I could help you. I wish I were this mysterious person named Ellie-Jo with such excitement in my life. It is either an absurd case of mistaken identity, or you have a very unusual line." She continued to smile. "I guess it beats the hell out of the usual 'Haven't I seen you someplace before?' "

Willy sipped his tea and continued staring at her.

She folded the newspaper with deliberation and twisted toward him in her seat. "Mr. Hanson. I want you to listen very carefully. Right now I am beginning to regard you as a nuisance. A nut, to be more exact. If you continue to harass me, I have connections in Macau that can make the rest of your day quite miserable. Do you understand?"

"Actually, I intend to return to Hong Kong on the next ferry anyway."

She continued to look at him, now frowning, as if really perturbed. "Did you get on this hydrofoil just to follow me?"

"I thought beautiful women were used to that. The answer is yes and no. I really thought that you might be meeting Hacker again down at the Macau Palace, and perhaps go putting around in his sampan."

"I don't have to put up with your fantasy any longer," she muttered.

Now she was really putting on a convincing act. She stuffed her newspapers into her oversized handbag, got up, and moved to an empty seat many rows back toward the rear of the hydrofoil.

Once they reached Macau, she ran ahead of most of the others in order to be one of the first in line for customs. For a moment, Willy wondered if she really might turn him in on some sort of pretense. It didn't happen, though. After all, Ellie-Jo had much more than that to think about now.

Once through customs, Willy turned around to begin the process of boarding another hydrofoil now loading for Hong Kong.

Ellen Lambert rushed to the curb in front of the terminal. Lights blinked on and off far to her right and Hercules Valdez's Mercedes sped toward her.

The chauffeur stepped out and opened the back door. Ellen climbed in and accepted a warm hug from Valdez. Rather than his usual fastidious business dress, he was wearing dark workclothes. His fisherman's hat was adorned with a scramble of gold braid. She sat silently for a few moments, breathing heavily.

"My dear, you look upset. Something is wrong?"

She turned to him, kissed him lightly on the lips and forced a smile. "Not really. Just some bothersome pest, on the hydrofoil. An American. You'd think he'd never seen a woman before."

"You should have told me before we left. I could have given him a talking to. I suspect, my dear, that you are plagued with this sort of thing often, however."

"Oh, Cristo, I suppose I am just so nervous about everything. I want to hear your plans in detail. I want to leave Hong Kong tomorrow afternoon."

Cristo Valdez shook his finger at her. "Impossible, my dear. The typhoon will be at full force then. It is coming in, you know. They are predicting only a glancing blow with the storm passing slightly to the north. Perhaps we can leave early the next morning."

"Oh, Cristo, I am anxious to go sooner." She huddled close to him.

Valdez shrugged. "Most things I can do, but I cannot change the wind. For a few hours at the height of the storm, any ships caught in the South China Sea are tossed around like balsa chips in a giant fishbowl shaken by God himself."

"What will we do, Cristo?"

"We will do what we have to do. I have made careful plans. You have nothing to fear, my dear. Tell me your schedule for the day?"

"I have to transact some business at the Bank of Macau. It is not necessary to go to the casino again. I suppose I should go back to Hong Kong as early as possible."

"Ah, very good. I think you will like the plans that I have made for us. You go about your business here in Macau. I will leave you with my car and driver."

"That is not necessary, Cristo. I know my way around here very well."

"This time, I insist. We have a schedule that is important because of the typhoon. When you finish your business, my driver will bring you to the *Chek Chau Eagle*. It is my personal yacht. We will return to Hong Kong. I have made arrangements to moor the *Chek Chau Eagle* in the Camber typhoon shelter in Kowloon. There the yacht will be well protected by the large breakwater. It is only about a mile north of the Peninsula Hotel. I plan to spend my time aboard during the storm. You will meet me there as soon as the storm subsides. Bring your friend Mr. Blake, and we are off on the grand adventure within hours after the storm passes."

"You make it sound so easy, Cristo. You will be waiting only a mile from the Peninsula. Wonderful! Tell me the rest of your plans, Cristo."

"From the shelter, we will return to Macau. Then you will board one of my finest freighters, the *Malacca Moon*. The ship has elegant separate quarters for you and your friend. We will then make the run to Djakarta. It will take about two days. From there you will take a cruise ship to Brisbane. You won't even have to go ashore. I will put you aboard with my auxiliary. Arrangements have already been made. From then on, my dear, you must make your own plans, which should not be too difficult. How does that sound?"

"What if at the last minute Sheldon Blake decides not to join me?"

"Then I suppose we would just have to make the trip without him. Would that be satisfactory?"

She answered him with a kiss that lasted until the driver stopped in front of the Bank of Macau.

As she departed his Mercedes, he rolled the window down and cautioned her. "Please act as quickly as you can. I must tie up at the typhoon shelter in Kowloon in the early afternoon."

Ellen smiled, waved, and walked quickly through the tall glass doors of the bank.

57

Willy slid his key-card into the door of his suite at the Sheraton Towers, and walked in.

Ginny sat with Coley on a sofa, facing three other men sitting in chairs. She stood up quickly to greet him. "My God, Willy, it's been almost five hours. Are you okay?"

"I'm sorry, Ginny. I had to make a quick trip to Macau. It seemed like the best thing to do. I didn't realize Coley would be here quite so soon." He walked over to greet Coley. "Howdy, pal. Welcome." He glanced at the others. "What do you know. It's Mark Whitcomb, the pride of the FBI."

"Willy, glad to see you again." Whitcomb stood and shook Willy's hand. "Ginny here was getting pretty nervous, but I assured her that bad pennies always show up." Whitcomb spoke as he almost always did— laconic, with a stab at dry humor. "I want you to meet some important people here." He quickly made the introductions. "This is Chiang Lew, inspector with the Hong Kong police, and Jean Bonaparte, New Orleans police captain. Jean is here investigating the Lazy Boy Garcia homicide. There is strong evidence from Coley here and Joe Martin of the LAPD that Mr. Clarence Hackley is a suspect. Ellen Lambert might also be a suspect."

Willy looked expectantly at Coley for an explanation.

"Willy, there have been a bunch of developments. Remember the fight we had with Hacker in Redondo when I knocked Hacker's gun into the bay? LAPD fished it out. Ballistics says a slug from that gun killed the sheik's son-in-law up in Tahoe. There is a good chance he knocked off two guys in New Orleans, the doc in Las Vegas, and also Lefty. It's all fitting together, Willy."

Whitcomb pointed to Chiang Lew. "The inspector here would like to know what you know about Armand Hauser."

Willy shrugged. "Not very much. He's here, I suppose, to help Ellen Lambert open her new restaurant."

Whitcomb shook his head. "You'd better sit down for this one, Willy. Hauser flew the coop with five million in cash belonging to Waterfront, Inc., according to Ellen Lambert."

"That's incredible!"

Whitcomb frowned. "I'm ashamed of you, Willy. I always thought you read the papers. It's all over the South China *Morning Post*."

"Jesus," groaned Willy. "When I talked to Ellen Lambert this morning on the Macau hydrofoil, she had her nose stuck in that paper. I never got to read it myself." Willy brought them up-to-date on the round-trip ride.

"It just doesn't figure at all, Willy," Coley said. "I've met Hauser. The man's a pussycat."

"You're always jumping to conclusions, Coley," Whitcomb rasped. "The man may be a pussycat, but right now he is evidently a rich pussycat. Where did you part with Ellen Lambert, Hanson?"

"At the hydrofoil terminal in Macau. She stayed. I came back on the return trip."

"Gentlemen." Chiang had been listening to everyone intently. "If Miss Lambert wants to return from Macau, she must return before midnight. Because of the typhoon, all ferry service will stop at that time." A beeper began signaling from somewhere on the person of Inspector Chiang. "Excuse me, gentlemen."

While Chiang answered his page, Whitcomb continued talking. "Our immediate concern is Clarence Hackley. The man seems to kill people at the drop of a hat, as Mr. Bonaparte here can attest to. Where do you think he is, Hanson?"

"I saw him on a sampan in Macau Harbour two nights ago. He picked up Ellen Lambert from a gambling barge. I don't think he saw me. Of course Ellen Lambert wouldn't acknowledge that this morning."

"Maybe he's still in Macau," said Whitcomb.

"We can't be sure of that. Ellen Lambert came back. Maybe he came with her," suggested Coley.

Whitcomb looked sternly at Willy. "Hanson, I want you to lay low. If you shot off your mouth to Ellen Lambert, as you say you did, you've succeeded in making yourself a target." Whitcomb shook his head.

Chiang Lew returned from an adjacent room where he had answered his page. "Please, everyone listen. I have some very grave news, some very upsetting news. I must share it with you all, but please, we must keep everything in confidence." He paused until he had everyone's attention.

"One of my contacts received a telephone tip from a fisherman in Aberdeen. For those of you who may not know, Aberdeen is a community on the southwest shore of Hong Kong island. A man, identified by the documents he carried as Armand Hauser, was found dead on the second floor of a vacant warehouse in Aberdeen. He had a single, small-caliber bullet wound in the center of his forehead."

"My God!" Coley said. "That's practically Hacker's signature."

"How about the five million bucks?" asked Willy.

"There was nothing like that found. My men opened the warehouse and found the man we presume to be Mr. Hauser, with nothing on him except the usual contents of a man's pockets. He was carrying a small amount of money in his wallet, and all of his identification."

Jean Bonaparte, who had been quiet until now, spoke up. "Whoever killed him, wanted him identified. We are now led to believe that since the stolen money wasn't with Hauser, it is now in the hands of thieves unknown."

"Good thinking, Bonaparte," observed Whitcomb. "Of course he may never have had five million dollars. The only way we even know about that is because Ellen Lambert made a complaint to the Hong Kong police."

"And Ellen Lambert is a lair. You can be sure of that," murmured Willy.

"Gentlemen, we must find Mr. Hackley. He is our top priority," said Chiang. "The fresh homicide tells us he is probably back in Hong Kong. For what purpose we do not know. But he is evidently armed and extremely dangerous. I will contact all authorities and make certain he cannot escape Hong Kong. Ellen Lambert will have to wait. Eventually we will question her. But first we must locate her, watch her day and night, and hope she leads us to Hackley before he kills again."

Chiang walked over to where Willy and Ginny were now sitting on the sofa. "I am sorry, but I must ask you to stay in the hotel while my men go after Hackley. Homicide with a firearm is a relatively rare and most serious crime in Hong Kong. Under no circumstances are the two of you to make yourselves targets. My men will locate Hackley soon. Relax and enjoy the facilities of one of our fine hotels for the next day or two. The typhoon will make the streets very dangerous, in any case."

58

Ellen Lambert arrived at the Peninsula Hotel. The passage on the *Chek Chau Eagle* had been canceled at the last moment by Hercules. He had told her that some problems had arisen in making preparations for the typhoon. He went on to assure her that he would be making the trip to the Camber typhoon shelter much later in the day, and he advised her to return via the hydrofoil. Tomorrow, immediately after the storm had passed, he would have her picked up at the Peninsula and they would resume their planned schedule.

The change in plans was upsetting, but then, so was the typhoon. Valdez had every reason to be concerned about his ships and the vast preparations for the storm that was now threatening Hong Kong with a direct hit.

Entering the Peninsula, Ellen's pulse quickened as she recognized Chiang Lew. He had taken her complaint on Armand. Smiling warmly, he confronted her in the lobby before she reached the bank of elevators.

"Miss Lambert, so sorry for the inconvenience, but I must talk to you for a few moments." He bowed slightly, then eyed her closely, trying to assess her. If she was upset, she showed no sign of it.

"Of course, Inspector. Please come up to my suite if you would like. We can talk there." She returned his warm smile and walked into the elevator. Once inside, she looked at him with genuine concern. "Have you any news about Armand Hauser?"

"Please, I will tell you in your suite." Chiang Lew volunteered nothing else until they had entered her quarters.

"Armand Hauser has been shot, Miss Lambert. A homicide. We have no one in custody as yet." The inspector watched the color drain from her face and teardrops begin to flow from her eyes.

"Oh my God!" she exclaimed. "He was a scoundrel but I would never wish anything like this on him." She put her arms around Chiang Lew and held him, trembling. "Who would do a thing like that?"

"We will find out soon, Miss Lambert." Chiang Lew held her weakly. He was studying the woman's apparently sincere reaction. If she was putting on an act about her concern, she was certainly good at it.

Ellen Lambert dabbed at her eyes with a handkerchief. "Were the funds recovered, Inspector?" Then quickly, "Oh God, that doesn't matter right now. Poor Armand!"

"We have nothing more than I have told you," replied Chiang. "The investigation in Aberdeen is continuing."

Ellen Lambert, still looking teary-eyed, started walking Chiang Lew to the door. "Thank you for coming personally to tell me about Armand. You must understand that I have suffered a great personal disappointment. Armand had always been a most loyal employee. I gave him access to several of our company bank accounts here in Hong Kong. I gave him my total trust, as did Sheldon Blake, our chairman of the board. His treachery is a bitter pill to swallow."

"I understand, Miss Lambert." Chiang bowed slightly and started to leave. "Oh yes, on another subject, Miss Lambert. The typhoon is coming, as you surely know. Perhaps before midnight, the wind will begin. It will be deceptively gentle for an hour or two. Then the gentle gusts will strengthen and become steady. In only a few hours the storm will become hurricane-force. The streets will become a hazard with the air filled with all the debris that is not carefully secured. There will be falling glass and large objects will become airborne." He paused for a moment. After all, he did not want her so frightened that it might keep her from leading them to Hacker. "So if you are outside when the breeze begins, you would do well to confine yourself to the hotel."

"Thank you for warning me, Inspector Chiang. I have no intention of confronting a typhoon. I have enough troubles already." She smiled weakly and then closed and locked her door.

Ellen Lambert's heart was pounding as she stood with her back against the door for some time. In less then twenty-four hours the typhoon would come and go. At this time tomorrow she would be racing across the South China Sea with Hercules in the *Chek Chau Eagle*. But there were still some important things to do.

The phone rang, startling her. She made a pact with herself to try to calm down. Her edginess might cause her to make a mistake.

"Hello, Ellen Lambert here," she said sweetly. It was Lee Ching calling from Kai Tak Airport. Sheldon Blake's plane had just landed, and he was in the process of clearing customs. He would be at the Peninsula in a little more than an hour.

She began to methodically review her readiness for the remaining hours she would spend in Hong Kong. A small duffle bag previously filled with construction plans and work orders had been emptied. It now contained five-hundred-thousand dollars for Hacker. The payoff would give her piece of mind until she left Hong Kong. She reasoned that if he were caught with it, it would be assumed that it was part of Armand's loot.

There was an additional two hundred thousand for her own use after she reached Brisbane. The rest of the money that she had accused Armand of taking was now spread thinly in banks from the Cayman Islands to the Bahamas, and in securities accounts with brokers scattered widely throughout the United States, Hong Kong, and Singapore. The fruits of a year's work would add up to almost six million dollars, the amount supposedly siphoned away by Armand. Most of the money had been carefully laundered with the help of Hercules, for a monstrous fee.

"Dear, sweet Cristo," she said aloud. She had developed a real affection for him. Yet there was this feeling of uneasiness every time she thought of his canceling plans to bring her back to Hong Kong in the *Chek Chau Eagle*. In the words of her drunken father, however, "Hell, you have to trust somebody."

Of course, the largest dark cloud hanging over her plans was Sheldon Blake, who still believed he was a participant in her scheme.

59

Sheldon Blake arrived at the Peninsula in forty-five minutes, checked his luggage with the bell captain, and went directly to Ellen Lambert's suite.

"Sheldon, you are a sight to behold! It seemed like you would never get here." She hugged the aging board chairman and peppered kisses all over his face. "It's going to be so exciting, Sheldon. You and I, we have actually pulled it off!"

Sheldon dropped to the sofa and heaved a heavy sigh. "Not quite yet, darling. Not quite yet. But it all looks good. Is the Valdez thing all nailed down?"

"Absolutely. You will soon hear the plans directly from him. Tomorrow, after the storm slackens, we will vanish from the earth."

"How about your million dollar man?" Blake looked dubious.

"Hacker? Come on now. You know I am always able to control him. He has what he wants and now he's gone. We'll never see him again. I know what you think about Hacker, but, in fact, he is a professional." She sat on Sheldon's lap, the tight miniskirt sliding to expose all of her.

"Whoa there! We have lots to do, I suppose. We can't get involved in that right now."

"Sheldon! You dirty old man. I never heard it called a 'that' before." She leaped to her feet. "But you're right. We are meeting with Hercules Valdez at three o'clock. He has been so helpful, Sheldon. You will have as much confidence in him as I do after you've talked to him. So let's get it over with."

"What about this typhoon? Isn't it going to screw up our plans in some way?" Sheldon was eyeing her from head to toe. When they were alone, he could never keep his mind or his hands off her.

"Supposedly it will start blowing about midnight, and be history by noon tomorrow, and then we'll be off to Djakarta. Now let's go!"

"Where are we meeting Valdez?"

"He's staying at a small inn in Mong Kok. It's only a couple of miles from here, right on Nathan Road."

"Good. Let's ring up Lee Ching."

"No. Let him get some rest. The police have been following me all around town and they have Lee spotted. They insist on protecting me since the Armand thing. Let Lee get some rest. But I have a plan. Maybe we can sneak away from all this idiotic protection. I've become very good at getting around in Hong Kong."

"Okay, you're the boss. I'm too burned out by the flight to invoke my authority."

The two left the Peninsula Hotel and started walking rapidly up Nathan Road. The normally crowded retail street was even more congested than usual with people rushing home in anticipation of the storm. If anyone was following Ellen and Sheldon Blake, they couldn't tell.

All at once Ellen grabbed Sheldon by the arm and pulled him into a crowded flight of stairs that led down to the Tsim Sha Tsui subway station. She had already purchased fare cards earlier in the week. Slipping the cards through the slot in the turnstiles, they merged quickly into the crowd of hundreds of commuters. Within a minute or so they were racing north under Nathan Road toward Mong Kok station.

Pressed together in the crowded underground car, Sheldon whispered into her ear, "I'm impressed, my love. I hope you know where we are going."

She winked at him, but she winked without smiling.

Mong Kok station came quickly. Exiting at street level, Ellen hesitated, waiting for a pedestrian light to change on Argyle Road. She glanced over her shoulder and heaved a sigh of relief. Apparently, no one had managed to follow them.

They walked a couple of short blocks and paused in front of a building identified as The Rose Garden Inn.

"This is it," announced Ellen.

Sheldon Blake stared at the rather plain-looking structure. "Doesn't look like much. Are you sure?"

"You'll love it, Sheldon. It's really something special." Without hesitating, she opened a door and walked down a short hallway, leading the skeptical Sheldon Blake by the hand. She knocked once, winked at Sheldon again, and the door opened in to a dimly lit room. Once inside, she stepped aside quickly to her left. Hacker emerged from behind the opened door and crashed the butt of his automatic against the back of Sheldon's head.

Sheldon Blake slumped to the floor, groaning, but not completely out.

"Beat it, Ellie-Jo!" snarled Hacker. "This ain't gonna be pretty. This old bastard has been hittin' on my girl too long."

She left the room, closed the door behind her, and ran down the hall. Outside again, she retraced their steps to the Mong Kok underground station. Within minutes she was back at the Peninsula Hotel. Say what you want about Hacker, she thought to herself, he was an artist who really earned his pay. She was going to miss him.

Entering the Peninsula, she almost walked into Inspector Chiang Lew who was standing in the lobby. He looked at her intently, as if surprised to see her. "Good afternoon, Miss Lambert. Did your associate arrive on time?"

"Oh yes, he's out there buying a camera or something. Sheldon's a shopper." She shrugged and strode right past the inspector and into the elevator.

Upstairs, Ellen Lambert sat on the bed for a few moments. She looked at her wristwatch again, wishing the time would pass more swiftly. She was still twenty hours away from leaving Hong Kong. And there was one more task ahead of her.

She walked to her closet and carried a large traveling bag to her bed. She opened it and withdrew a small duffle bag, taking one last peek inside to look at Hacker's other half million. She wondered if Hacker would ever get it back to the States, and she toyed with the idea of keeping it. Then she thought of Sheldon Blake, groaning on the floor, facing his last few seconds on earth.

Ellen walked over to her telephone and called Lee Ching. She decided she would stuff Hacker's share in the wastebasket down at Waterfront, Inc.'s, aborted construction site. Just like she had promised Hacker, she would put it under the makeshift wooden desk in the construction shack.

Before leaving the room, she checked for messages. There was nothing from Hercules Valdez. The least that pompous bastard could do would be to call, she thought to herself. He was the only human being in the world who mattered right now.

60

Coley Doctor and Jean Bonaparte sat in the small van driven by a policeman assigned to them by Chiang Lew. From their vantage point they could see all of the Waterfront, Inc., site, including the door on the south wall. The stakeout seemed logical, but neither of them expected anything to happen there too soon. They were simply waiting until the predicted storm drove them to cover.

The small van was not built for anyone who was six foot six. Coley twisted around constantly, trying to get comfortable. "What you guys need is a big Ford Bronco or a Chevy Blazer," Coley complained to the driver. The man grinned at him. Though he wore the patch of red on his shoulder that indicated he spoke English, Coley decided his understanding was limited. At least he smiled. It could be worse.

Coley fished around in his jacket pocket and produced a packet of several pieces of mail that had been forwarded air freight from LA. He had pounced on a letter from Marissa Chablis, and had stuffed the remainder into his jacket. The letter from Marissa had mentioned the Hauser disappearance and Sheldon Blake's early departure. The rest was delightfully personal. She had been shooting baskets at her gym and claimed to have developed a new little twist that would drive him crazy. Coley let his imagination run wild. "Hell, anything she does drives me crazy."

"What was that?" Bonaparte twisted his eyes toward him. "I think you're talking to yourself, Coley."

"Jean, you ever been in love?"

"I am always in love," he sighed heavily. "Of course, it is always with Mrs. Bonaparte."

"Hey, that's neat!" Coley exclaimed as he flipped through the small packet of mail. "It's amazing how fast this stuff got here. It must have been on the same plane we were on."

"Much faster than a letter from Baton Rouge to New Orleans," sighed Bonaparte.

"Well, I'll be damned," exclaimed Coley. "Remember the peachy dominatrix Flo, the stripper? She's in the Virgin Islands with Ziggy Lemon."

Now Bonaparte was so interested that he actually turned his head toward Coley. "How do you know that?"

"Just call it professional police work, Bonaparte," chided Coley. "I got a letter from Winnie LaFrance, Ziggy's old neighbor in New Orleans. Ziggy sent her a postcard from Charlotte Amalie. He always sends her postcards when he goes out of town. Winnie thinks I owe Ziggy some money."

"Interesting," murmured Bonaparte. "I always wanted to go to the Virgin Islands."

"What are you going to do about Ziggy Lemon?"

Bonaparte paused, deep in thought. "I'm just going to let him play the piano wherever he wants to."

All of a sudden, their driver interrupted their small talk, waving his hand toward Waterfront, Inc. Ellen Lambert was getting out of a liveried Mercedes carrying a large tote bag. She walked rapidly to the door, opened it, and went inside. The driver sat in the car with the engine running.

"Well, what do you suppose that's all about? That building has been locked up for days according to Chiang," Bonaparte wondered.

Ellen Lambert came running from the building. She hadn't been inside more than a minute. Now she was carrying what looked like a roll of blueprints, in addition to the tote bag that was dangling loosely from her wrist.

Coley told the driver to follow her when the Mercedes started moving. Within minutes she emerged from the car when it stopped in the driveway of the Peninsula Hotel. She went inside carrying the roll of blueprints and the bag.

"Okay, the other guys will pick her up in there. Let's take a look-see back at the building," Coley suggested. "Tell Chiang what we are doing by radio," he said, enunciating each word for the driver, who nodded his understanding.

Soon back at Waterfront, Inc., just a few blocks from the hotel, Coley tried the door. Amazingly enough, it swung open. The larger room appeared empty. The sound of wind billowed the long tarps hanging from the ceiling.

"Okay, let's give it a quick look," whispered Coley. The three of them fanned out through the building, walking between piles of lumber and other building material. The entire western wall of the building was cut away down to within four or five feet of the ground. That certainly explained the unlocked door. It would serve no purpose.

Suddenly, there was a big snap from flapping canvas hanging from the roof and partially covering the opening. Outside, they could see ripples fanning out over the harbor.

"Typhoon coming now," advised the policeman. "Maybe three, four hours."

The three of them covered every space between the stacks of building material. There was a small office squared off in the center, totally empty except for a few papers and scattered blueprints.

"Okay, let's go," said Coley. "We'll give it a bit longer outside, until the wind picks up, and then we'll go back to the hotel." They were soon seated back in the van.

"I guess she just wanted the blueprints. Maybe she wants to show them to Mr. Blake," mused Bonaparte.

Coley was thinking about the looks of the interior of the building itself. "Did you guys notice what a junk heap that place was? A lot of that lumber wasn't fit for anything. In fact, I didn't see any construction in progress that amounted to a damn." Something else bothered Coley. He pictured Ellen Lambert walking from her car to the door of the building. She walked rapidly, the heavy tote purse hanging from her hand. Coming out, she carried the long roll of blueprints under one arm. She still had the tote bag. But something was different.

The policeman nodded his head. "That place is a real mess. Hey, look over there."

North of them, on a breakwater stretching out into the harbor, some men were hoisting big red triangular flags. "That's Camber typhoon shelter. Triangle, means force eight typhoon is coming in," advised the policeman.

They sat silently for another twenty minutes or so before Coley made up his mind to drive back to check with the others. A fine rain peppered against the windshield all the way back to the hotel.

61

Agent Whitcomb was standing behind Chiang Lew
in a small room in the Aberdeen police office. Chiang
Lew was questioning Chan. "So, you are up to your
old tricks, Chan. You admit that you smuggled Ellen
Lambert and a man called Hacker into Hong Kong.
You brought them in on a junk tow from Macau."

"I thought it okay. Valdez say they miss last ferry
and it would be okay." The old man was shaking.

"Chan, you lie. You know it is not okay. Mr. Hacker
has now killed someone in Aberdeen. You brought him
here, Chan. You let him stay in Valdez's warehouse.
What happened to the woman on that day?"

"She take bus to Central District from Aberdeen."

"Chan, I'm having you taken back to Kowloon. We'll
hold you there until we catch Hacker."

"Please, I must stay with boat when typhoon
comes."

"Not a chance, Chan. That frail old boat will not

survive. You will be better off with me." Chiang Lew glanced at Whitcomb. "Do you have any questions for Chan?"

"No. He's clinched it for me. Ellen Lambert is obviously here with Hacker. I think Armand Hauser was their patsy. If you don't mind, I would like to get back to Kowloon before the storm. We've got to find Hacker."

"I'll go with you," said Chiang. He called in one of the policemen from outside the room. "I want Chan to be taken to Kowloon at once and locked up. I want him available for immediate questioning if it becomes necessary. He is not to be permitted communication with anyone outside his cell."

Chiang had Whitcomb and himself driven to Central District, where they caught the Star Ferry for the ten-minute trip to Kowloon. By this time the water in Victoria Harbour was black. Crested whitecaps were driving up the harbor as the swelling tide surged in. Chiang looked at the sky and at the flags standing stiffly from their staffs along the shore. "Maybe another hour and a half before all hell breaks loose. Ever seen one of these things?"

"I was in Miami once when a hurricane came in. I guess this is about the same thing."

"We have so many in this area that we keep things pretty well under control. But some unexpected damage always occurs." Both watched as the ferry captain maneuvered with difficulty into the slip in Kowloon. "I would suspect the Star Ferry will shut down very shortly."

Darkness was coming on. The driving rain pelted them in the face as they hiked the two blocks back to the Sheraton Towers. They called Willy's room. Willy and Ginny were there with Coley Doctor. Bonaparte had split, deciding to lobby-sit in the Peninsula. He would be a face Ellen Lambert would never recognize.

"Mind if we come right up?" Whitcomb asked.

"By all means, we're getting stir-crazy here," Willy replied.

The two entered the suite, their clothes drenched by the driving rain. Ginny brought a handful of towels from the bathroom. Whitcomb spoke first. "Chan confessed to bringing Ellen Lambert and Hacker back from Macau by junk tow."

"Isn't that illegal? What about customs and all?" asked Coley.

"Certainly it's illegal!" Chiang was pacing as he talked. "But unfortunately it is done, occasionally. The locals try to make a little extra money once in a while with their old boats." Chiang's beeper was signaling as he talked. "Just a minute, please."

The rain was now drumming on the window. The buildings across Salisbury Road were no longer visible. Willy started pacing the floor. He felt like a prisoner. His compassion for Lefty Grogan had drawn in an unbelievable number of people.

"I want that man called Hacker. I want him now! If necessary, we will have to go out into the storm and find him." Chiang was shouting into the telephone. Finally, he hung up and immediately donned the drenched jacket he had hung over the back of a chair.

"Mr. Whitcomb, I am going to the Peninsula to question Ellen Lambert. I would like you to accompany me." Chiang looked somberly at the others in the room. "You might as well know. Sheldon Blake was found beaten to death in a small hotel in Mong Kok. A guest in an adjoining room heard the commotion and called the police. It happened less than two hours ago."

"Where's Mong Kok?" asked Willy.

"It's a business community about fifteen minutes from here on Nathan Road. The strategy of waiting until Ellen Lambert leads us to Hacker is not working." Chiang strode to the door.

"Look, if you are going to question Ellen Lambert I'm all for it, but I'd like to join you." Coley started to slip on his jacket.

"Coley, I want you here with Willy. There is every reason to believe that he is now number one on Hacker's list. We'll see you in a few minutes. Chiang has stationed a policeman on this floor to keep an eye on things." Whitcomb gave them all a good old college thumbs-up and followed Chiang from the room.

The wind was now howling eerily as it swept around the building. Torrential rain was beating against the windows with a force that sounded as if it might blow out the glass pane at any moment. The typhoon was without a doubt coming ashore.

62

Now only Coley, Willy, and Ginny were left in the suite to ride out the storm. Willy was pacing. Coley was staring off into space, picturing Ellen Lambert as she walked back to her car in front of Waterfront, Inc.

"I'm going to call room service for some food," suggested Ginny. "I think we've all forgotten to eat today."

Coley groaned. "I think I'd choke before I could swallow anything."

"Order up a bunch of finger food, Ginny. We're bound to get hungry sooner or later." Willy leaned over the back of the sofa and kissed her forehead.

Everyone jumped at the same instant when there was a knock at the door. Willy looked through the peephole. It was Jean Bonaparte.

"Jean, welcome to the party!" Willy offered. "You must know all about hurricane parties down in New

Orleans. We need a pitcher of Bourbon Street Saze-racs."

"Under different circumstances that would be very nice. Mr. Chiang suggested that I join you folks. The lobbies here and at the Peninsula look like an armed camp. Never have four people been so well protected." Neck held steady, Bonaparte rolled his eyes at each of them.

"Did you see anything of Ellen Lambert over there?" Willy asked.

"She is not answering her telephone, or her door. Agent Whitcomb is urging Mr. Chiang to break down her door. Maybe they have by now." Bonaparte sat on the end of the sofa and dipped his fingers in a bowl holding a few remaining peanuts.

"Aha! There's a man who wants to eat," cried Ginny. "I'm going to order up that food."

"I've got it," declared Coley, staring into space. "Jean, you were there. Do you remember when Ellen Lambert walked from the Mercedes to the door of Waterfront, Inc.? She was carrying that big handbag. It looked heavy. She held it low. She was walking fast, but the bag was not swinging much at all. She was holding it by the straps with her fingers."

"Of course I remember," agreed Bonaparte.

Coley continued. "And when she came out with the blueprints tucked under one arm, the bag was hanging very loosely over her wrist. It was skinny, like nothing much was in it."

It was now Bonaparte who was staring into space, trying to recall. "I remember that it did look the way you describe it. But it might have been the angle . . . or who knows what."

Willy was listening carefully. "So what you are saying, Coley, is that she took something heavy and bulky into the building and didn't bring it back out with her. She brought out only the long blueprints, and a bag that appeared lighter."

"I think Coley is right," said Bonaparte, after more thought. "But what would it mean? Perhaps nothing much."

"Maybe it was food for someone. Or maybe she was hiding something. Maybe it was something she didn't want anyone to find in her room." Coley shrugged. "Maybe we're all just tired."

"I know what it means," said Willy. "It means we have to give that warehouse a closer search."

"In the morning, when the storm is over," added Ginny.

"No, by God, we've got to do it right now," insisted Willy, standing up again. "Hell, the storm won't hit its peak for a couple of hours yet."

Bonaparte rolled his eyes toward the window where the wind was pounding water at the glass harder than ever. "It may well be nothing, but it's all we've got," he agreed.

"Willy, this is crazy. The hell with Hacker. The weather might kill you! Look outside!"

"Relax, Ginny. We'll all be back in thirty minutes."

She responded woodenly to his kiss. "I don't like this, Willy."

"Do you have Chiang's beeper code?" he asked, knowing she did. "Get hold of Chiang or Whitcomb and tell them what we are doing. If I know them, they'll have an army over there in minutes."

The three of them breezed past the guard at the door and got on the elevator. Once inside, Coley reached into his jacket and handed Willy a beat-up old .38.

"Where'd you get that, Coley?"

"Chiang released it to me, in case of emergency. I guess this is an emergency."

Downstairs, two policemen followed them to the taxi line. Willy shoved a hundred dollar bill at the first driver and told him the address, only ten blocks away. One of the policemen muscled his way into the taxi.

"What are you doing, pal?" Willy asked.

"I must detain this vehicle or go wherever you go. Sorry, those are my orders."

"Suit yourself! Let's go driver." As they pulled away, Willy saw the policeman motioning for others to follow.

Coley started laughing. "Jesus, Willy, Chiang and Whitcomb are going to blow a gasket."

There were only several other cars on the road. Water was standing between the curbs and sharp gusts of wind whipped at the taxi. Papers and awnings were flying through the air.

They arrived at the building site in about two minutes. A dim bulb still burned over the doorway; the door itself had evidently blown open. The policeman pulled a flashlight from the clip on his belt.

"Driver, do you have another flashlight?" Willy asked. He pointed to the glove compartment. "Now we have two, in case the lights go out, which they probably will."

Willy pushed with all his might, fighting to open the car door against the prevailing wind. Once outside, they all had to fight the gale to get to the door of the building.

"It is already force eight," mumbled the policeman.

Inside, it was terrifying. The wind had ripped away the huge canvas tarps that had covered the opening, and they were flapping around, covering much of the floor area. A light switch they found didn't offer much help. A dim bulb flickered at each end of the two-hundred-foot-long building.

Occasionally, a tidal surge would pound against and over the low, cutaway wall, pushing inches of water across the floor. There was a tremendous pounding noise from overhead.

They all spotted the source at once. One of the temporary jacks supporting the roof had slipped, and with each pounding gale, the jack slipped further sideways across the floor. A large section of roof began to tear away. And then the giant metal jack crashed to the floor, followed by about a quarter of the roof itself.

"Out, out!" Coley yelled, spotting another section about to give way. The four of them made it outside and stood bracing each other against the wind.

"Ahhhhh!" An eerie howl emanated from somewhere inside.

"Did you hear that?" Willy yelled to Bonaparte, who was standing right next to him. Just as he nodded yes, they all heard the tortured screaming again.

"Someone is in there," Coley yelled and pointed inside.

Willy grabbed the flashlight from the hands of the policeman and started back inside. Coley followed.

"Let's work our way back against the wall," Coley screamed. "I don't think the wall will give way, but the rest of the roof might."

They were now parallel to the construction cubicle near the center of the building. The fallen jack had crashed across one corner of the ten-foot-square office.

"Ahhhh ... ahhhh." The eerie screams were now closer, coming from somewhere around the office. The winds were howling even louder now, and a large section of the roof suddenly ripped loose. Fortunately, it cleared itself off the top of the landward wall. The rain poured into the building in torrents now.

Willy was now crawling steadily over the fallen debris, working his way toward the construction shack.

Coley was closing in from the other wall. Finally, Willy reached the open door of the cubicle and crawled in. Pointing the flashlight ahead of him, he first saw a bloody leg pinned under a timber crushed by the collapsed jack. He worked his way over until he was chest-to-chest with the fallen man. He shined the light between them—it was Hacker!

Hacker glared at Willy, teeth clenched in pain. Willy shined the light on his own face. "You recognize me, Hacker? I've followed you all the way from Tonopah."

Hacker breathed heavily, struggling to free his leg. "Sure, you're Mr. Monday Night Football. I saw you and your chick in Macau." He was gasping, trying to keep from passing out. "Look in the wastebasket there. I'll split it with ya. Okay?" Then his eyes closed.

"Oh no, pal, you ain't dying on me now." Willy turned toward Coley who was now crawling into the shack under the fallen roof. "Coley, I found Hacker. The son of a bitch is about to die. Help me get him out of here."

"Sit tight, Willy. We got help. There's a bunch of people coming." Light from handheld searchlights began to fill the demolished flagship of Waterfront, Inc.

Soon they were all outside. The howling winds were rapidly accelerating to typhoon force. Willy sat on the ground in a pool of water, watching the police struggle in the wind with the stretcher that held Hacker. They got him inside a van, the swirling lights went on, and they took him off into the night.

Willy turned to his right, surprised to find FBI Agent Whitcomb kneeling in the mud beside him. He shouted into Willy's ear. "Got to hand it to you, pal. You found that son of a bitch. Ten thousand miles from home, on strange turf, you found that son of a bitch."

63

It was about ten o'clock the next morning when Ginny and Willy were startled from their deep sleep by a dazzling shaft of sunlight through their window.

Willy energetically sprung to a sitting position on the edge of their bed and then groaned. He surveyed the multitude of cuts and bruises accumulated during his search of the collapsing building. "I slept like a rock. I guess I'll live."

Ginny stroked his head gently. "This time you'll live, Willy. I hope there isn't a next time."

She became quiet. He knew that he hadn't heard the last from her about his mad rush out into the storm the evening before. Their life together had been fated with one harrowing adventure after another. He could tell that she didn't want any more.

"Honey, in a couple of days we'll be back on the *Tashtego*. Maybe we'll take that cruise down through the canal like we've always talked about."

"Sure, Willy, but first, let's take some time to get to know each other again."

The phone rang. It was Coley. "Morning, boss! Bonaparte, Whitcomb, and I are down here in the lobby bar sipping tea. We need your company."

"Give us a few minutes, Coley." When he hung up, Ginny was already in the shower.

He walked to the window. Victoria Harbour was agleam with sunlight. The flying triangles had been taken down. The water was still black, with a steady white chop, but the Star Ferry was already plying her route to Hong Kong island.

By the time they joined the others in the lobby, Chiang had joined the group at a circle of lounge chairs in a cozy corner.

Willy looked at Whitcomb. "What's up with Ellie-Jo? I guess we can call her Ellie-Jo now."

"She's never really admitted to that, but it doesn't matter anymore," said Coley.

"She's in her room, and she has notified the hotel that she is leaving soon," Chiang stated. "We have decided to wait her out. It will be fascinating to see who tries to pick her up. We have a force that will move in on any vehicle that tries to move her from the hotel. There is no other problem since Hacker is no longer on the scene."

Willy looked at Whitcomb. "What about Hacker? Will you try for extradition?"

Whitcomb and Chiang exchanged glances. It was Chiang who spoke. "We have very strong evidence here in Hong Kong. He cannot escape spending the rest of his life in a Hong Kong prison, at best."

"Mr. Chiang, the people of New Orleans would like to prosecute him very much." Bonaparte was emphatic. "But I suppose they would settle for the news that he is forever secured in your prison."

Whitcomb spoke up after hearing the others. "Obviously that is all for the judges and the politicians to decide."

"What about Ellie-Jo?" asked Ginny.

"The charges against her are more complex, but easily provable. It will be many years before she leaves Hong Kong. Regrettably, she has gotten one very highly placed bank official here in trouble for money laundering. The charges against him, and her as his accomplice, are irrefutable."

Willy had a question for Chiang that had been on his mind for a long time. "Who is this Hercules Valdez whom Ginny and I saw escorting her around in Macau?"

"He owns a sizable shipping company that does business throughout Southeast Asia. Supposedly, he has much influence with the gambling moguls in Macau. His penchant for beautiful women is well known." Chiang paused, deep in thought. "Strange that you bring Mr. Valdez up at this time. He had reserved a mooring at the typhoon center for the *Chek Chau Eagle*, his personal yacht. I am told that this reservation was canceled late last evening."

A policeman entered the lobby and walked over to Chiang, interrupting their conversation. He whispered something to Chiang, who turned and confronted them again. "It is time to go back to her hotel. She has ordered that her baggage be taken to the limousine area. She will be checking out soon."

By the time Willy, Ginny, and Coley arrived at her hotel, she was sitting alone on a bench in the limousine waiting area. She sat, waiting for almost an hour, before standing and stretching and then sitting down again.

She glanced repeatedly up and down the driveway.

Now, in her heart, she began to realize that Hercules Valdez would never appear. Still she sat.

Coley walked across the lobby where Chiang and Whitcomb were waiting, just inside the door. "Mind if I say a few words to her?"

"What the hell for, Coley?" Whitcomb asked.

"I just want to ask her one more time about Lefty Grogan."

Chiang looked at Whitcomb and shrugged. "Go ahead, Coley. But please, do not mention Hacker, or anyone else."

Coley walked over and sat near her on the bench where she was waiting. "You've got yourself in a real mess, Ellie-Jo."

She turned and stared at him with her large hazel-green eyes sparkling in the sun. "Ellie-Jo?"

"Yeah, you should have stopped and paid attention back in New Orleans. You would have saved yourself a peck of trouble."

She continued her emotionless stare. "What's your name?"

"My name is Coley Doctor. I'm working on the Lefty Grogan case for some people back in Nevada."

She turned her head forward again, without comment. After what seemed like forever to Coley, she set her handbag on the bench and lifted both her hands to the back of her head. Slowly and deliberately she began untwining the string of pearls that held the mane of auburn hair in a prim bun. Finally, the hair tumbled to her waist.

She carefully coiled the pearls in the palm of her hand, then extended her hand to Coley and placed the pearls in his.

He held them for a second and shook his head.

"Coley, would you keep them safe for me? They were my momma's. Please?"

A spate of tears gushed from both eyes as she stood erect. She walked several steps to the doorman and asked for a cab to the airport.

The doorman glanced at Chiang, who nodded his head. Ellie-Jo was immediately surrounded by a ring of policemen. Inspector Chiang then walked among them and led her by the hand to his waiting car.

OTHER NOVELS BY
RALPH ARNOTE
YOU MAY HAVE MISSED

☐ *Fatal Secrets*   53451-4 $4.99
                                                  $5.99 Canada

☐ *False Promises*   55043-9 $5.99
                                                  $6.99 Canada

☐ *Fallen Idols*   51612-5 $4.99
                                                  $5.99 Canada

---

Call toll-free 1-800-288-2131 to use your major credit card, buy them at your local bookstore,
or clip and mail this page to order by mail.

Publishers Book and Audio Mailing Service
P.O. Box 120159, Staten Island, NY 10312-0004

Please send me the book(s) I have checked above. I am enclosing $ _____
(Please add $1.50 for the first book, and $.50 for each additional book to cover postage and
handling. Send check or money order only — no CODs.)

Name_____
Address _____
City _____State / Zip_____

Please allow six weeks for delivery. Prices subject to change without notice.

🛠 THE BEST OF FORGE 🛠

THE BEST OF FORGE

☐ 55052-8   LITERARY REFLECTIONS $5.99
            James Michener   Canada $6.99

☐ 52046-7   A MEMBER OF THE FAMILY $5.99
            Nick Vasile   Canada $6.99

☐ 52288-5   WINNER TAKE ALL $5.99
            Sean Flannery   Canada $6.99

☐ 58193-8   PATH OF THE SUN $4.99
            Al Dempsey   Canada $5.99

☐ 51380-0   WHEN SHE WAS BAD $5.99
            Ron Faust   Canada $6.99

☐ 52145-5   ZERO COUPON $5.99
            Paul Erdman   Canada $6.99

Buy them at your local bookstore or use this handy coupon:
Clip and mail this page with your order.

Publishers Book and Audio Mailing Service
P.O. Box 120159, Staten Island, NY 10312-0004

Please send me the book(s) I have checked above. I am enclosing $_____$
(Please add $1.50 for the first book, and $.50 for each additional book to cover
postage and handling. Send check or money order only— no CODs.)

Name_____

Address_____

City_____State / Zip_____

Please allow six weeks for delivery. Prices subject to change without notice.